Acknowledgements

Warmest thanks and hats off to:

My New York editor Linda McFall, whose smart suggestions greatly improved this book.

The MIRA team in the U.K., especially Catherine Burke; and the MIRA teams around the world.

My brilliant agent Broo Doherty of Wade & Doherty, who had to work hard with this one—I really appreciate it, Broo.

Margot Weale and Sophie Ransom (Midas PR) and Grainne Killeen (Killeen PR) for top-notch media work.

Crime writer Michael Jecks for sterling input on weapons—any remaining oversights are my responsibility alone.

My siblings Claire and Alan and their families— for love, hospitality and…guitar advice.

Ali Karim, number ONE fan.

And, last, but most of all— love and only love to Roula and Maggie.

THE
PAUL JOHNSTON
SOUL
COLLECTOR

MIRA®

*First published in Great Britain 2008
by Harlequin Mills & Boon Limited, Eton House,
18-24 Paradise Road, Richmond, Surrey TW9 1SR*

THE SOUL COLLECTOR © Paul Johnston 2008

ISBN: 978 0 7783 0236 0

58-0908

*Printed and bound in Spain
by Litografia Rosés S.A., Barcelona*

In memoriam
Stephanos Kassopoulos
(1921–2007)

And welcome to
Alexander Johnston (9/1/2008)

"I do haunt you still."
—John Webster

"I cut mine arm, and with my proper blood
Assure the soul to be great Lucifer's.
Chief lord and regent of perpetual night."
—Christopher Marlowe

Prologue

The black cat rubbed its flank against Mary Malone's fleshy arm. They were on the window seat on the third floor of the house in Ifield Road, Fulham, West London.

'Yes, Noir,' the writer said, looking down at the tombstones in Brompton Cemetery. 'It's a nasty night. But you don't have to go out.'

The cat gave her a supercilious glance, then jumped down and headed for the stairs.

'Stubborn creature!' Mary turned back to the view from the high window. It had been a cold February with frost crimping the grass. In the last few days, the temperature had risen slightly and the evenings had been misty. It seemed to the writer that the patches of visible air above the graves were like exhalations of the restless sleepers in the frigid earth. Then again, she'd always had a vivid imagination.

Mary went back to her desk. She had written half of her latest Doctor Kasabus mystery. The series was set in eighteenth-century Paris and her hero was a freethinking medical man who had a secret life as an investigator specialising in cases of a religious nature—priests who sanctioned murder, heiresses locked up in nunneries, bishops who abused boys. Rather to her surprise, she had gained a large readership on both sides of the Atlantic. Not that she ever met her fans. At five feet one, fifteen stone and with a face best suited to radio, she kept herself to herself. The memory of school—saliva-spattered girls' faces eagerly poking fun at the class 'hippo'—still made her weep on bad days.

Mary Malone (real name, Shirley Higginbottom) leaned back in her specially constructed office chair and looked at the lines of script. She could feel one of her periodic bouts of melancholy coming on. What did she have to show for twenty years of slavery at the typewriter and computer? Twenty-five books, good sales, some decent reviews, every day a host of e-mails from her fans—most complimentary, but some from people who didn't hide their desperation to know what she looked like. She had never allowed an author photo to be published and she never appeared at bookshop readings or crime-writing conventions. Her face and body were hers alone.

'Piss and shit!' she said, trying to repel bitterness. So she couldn't have what every other person had—a man, children, a normal family life, friends who made much of her at parties. Instead she spent her evenings looking at the websites of beautiful, blonde, female and handsome, young, male crime novelists. Her books did better than most of theirs, but she was in self-imposed exile, a fifty-one-year-old hermit, a repulsive gargoyle.

Mary heaved herself to her feet and went down to her sitting room on the ground floor. Negotiating the stairs was her only exercise, not that it seemed to make any difference to her weight.

'That's enough self-pity,' she said, pouring herself a

gin and tonic that was heavy on the former. She headed for the sofa, picking up a copy of the latest *Clues* on her way.

The sudden, ear-splitting yowl from the back of the house made her drop both glass and magazine.

'Damn!' Mary took a few deep breaths, and then lumbered to the door with the cat-flap that led to her garden. 'Noir!' she called. 'What are you doing? Come in this minute, Noir!' She turned on the light.

And felt her stomach somersault.

Her beloved Noir's head had come through the flap onto the carpet, but it was detached from the body.

Mary Malone let out a long moan. 'No,' she gasped. 'No…' Despite her revulsion, she kept moving towards the cat's bloody head. She was a few steps from the door when she realised that the handle was depressed. She stared into the darkness beyond the glass, her heart thundering. She didn't think of turning and running—she knew she couldn't move fast enough. She made out only a vague shape.

Then the door was pushed open violently and a figure dressed from head to toe in black entered. In the right hand was a knife streaked with blood and in the left was Noir's body. It was tossed towards her.

Mary couldn't speak, couldn't make any sound at all.

The figure came up to her, holding the blade horizontal to her throat. Then a face appeared beneath a hood, but it wasn't human. The mask was white, the eye-holes ringed with red. There was a goatee beard on the chin and the lips were turned up in a mocking smile. Worst of all, the surface was covered in discoloured warts and lumps. Medieval depictions of people suffering from the Black Death flashed through Mary Malone's mind.

At last, she found her voice. 'What is this?' she gasped. 'Who are you?'

The intruder nodded slowly. 'I think you know, Mary.' The voice was steady. There was a pause. 'You're face to face with the devil.'

There was a loud thud as the fainting novelist hit the floor.

1

I was putting the finishing touches to my weekly column in the *Daily Independent*—'Matt Wells on Crime'—when I heard the key turn in the lock.

'Hi,' I called. 'It's a filthy night, Detective Chief Inspector.'

Karen Oaten hung up her coat and sat on a chair to pull off her knee-high black boots.

'Oh, no,' I said, as I went to greet her. 'I was looking forward to you dominating me in those.'

She raised her blonde head and gave me an intimidating look. 'Don't push your luck, Matt. I have not had a good day.'

I leaned over and kissed her, feeling cold cheeks and only slightly warmer lips. 'What's up? You been pounding the streets?'

She got up and pushed me away gently. 'No, I couldn't find a bloody parking space anywhere near these poxy rich people's flats.'

'Oh, shit.' I'd moved into the Chelsea Harbour block about a year back, after my book *The Death List* had been a global success. Although I was a novelist at heart, the book was non-fiction and detailed my battle with the vicious killer who called himself the White Devil and had put all my other efforts in the shade. The fact that Karen featured in it, but didn't get a penny of royalties, needled her when she was feeling down. Not that her career prospects had exactly been damaged.

She went over to the drinks table, her long legs striking even without footwear.

I caught up with her. 'What would you like, darling?'

She looked at me curiously. After years of living on her own, she was still surprised when I did things for her when she came to my place three or four times a week. She hadn't given up her own house. We'd been together a couple of years, but she still needed her independence.

'Oh, I don't know.' Her stern features relaxed. 'A gin and tonic would be great.' She went to the nearest of the four black leather sofas I'd bought to fill the enormous living area. 'What have you been up to today, Matt?'

'My column,' I replied, handing her a glass and sitting down beside her. I picked up the stereo remote and got Peter Bruntnell's latest CD playing.

She took a long sip of her drink. 'I thought you were meant to be starting the novel.'

I gave a wry smile. 'I did. Pages of deathless prose, done and dusted.'

She jammed her elbow into my ribs. 'Smart-ass. What's it about?'

I put my arm around her and took a slug of malt whisky. 'The usual stuff—killers, stunningly beautiful cops, violent death…'

She didn't push me off. If she'd wanted, she could have floored me in under a second. She'd been a seriously good athlete as a student and she'd recently got her Judo black belt. Then again, so had I.

'Oh, nothing much,' she said with a yawn. 'The usual run-of-the-mill Violent Crimes Co-ordination Team fare. A drugs gang killing in East London, an unidentified torso in the river and the Assistant Commissioner all over me for the quarterly report.'

'Lucky him,' I said, and got another, harder nudge for my pains. 'Can I have the inside story on the gangland killing for next week's column?' Since we'd met during the White Devil case and subsequently started dating, Karen had used me as an unofficial conduit between the Metropolitan Police and the public. Several times I'd been given information that had elicited information from readers, leading to arrests.

'Depends,' she said, emptying her glass.

'On what?'

'On how nice you are to me.'

'How about a steak, a good Claret, crème brûlée and a massage?'

'You're on.'

I went to the kitchen at the far end of the living area. 'You can talk to me while I slave over the stove.'

Karen sat at the bar that separated the kitchen from the eating area. She shook her head. 'I shouldn't be telling you this.'

'That's what you always say. Come on, Karen. Your boss knows you talk to me about cases.'

'About cases that he approves. He hasn't cleared the latest killing.'

I laid the steaks on a board and started to pound them. 'He will.'

She shrugged. 'Maybe. But how many of the *Daily Independent*'s readers are going to send you e-mails identifying a gangland hit man?'

'Several members of the opposition gangs?' I suggested.

'Oh, yeah, like that will stand up in court.'

I turned to the stove. 'All right, it doesn't bother me. I've got plenty of other contacts in the Met.'

Karen laughed. 'Plenty of other contacts who want to take you down the cells and kick the shit out of you.'

It was true that my diligence in publicising Karen's cases had made me some enemies at New Scotland Yard. I laughed. 'I seem to remember *you* wanted to arrest me once.'

She screwed up her face at me. 'No, I didn't. That was Taff.'

'How is that Welsh sheep abuser?'

'I'll let him know you called him that.'

Karen's sidekick, Detective Inspector John Turner, wasn't my biggest fan. Then again, he didn't like anyone except his wife and kids—and Karen.

I tossed a green salad and served the steaks. We both liked them rare.

'Let's not talk about work right now,' Karen said.

'Okay,' I said, pouring her a glass of seriously expensive wine. 'What do you want to talk about?'

'Mmm, this is good. I don't know…is everyone all right?'

'I thought we weren't discussing work.' I sniffed the wine's bouquet and took a sip. 'God, it's actually worth what I paid for it.'

'Just checking,' she said, eyes on her plate.

What she wanted to know was whether my family and friends were in one piece. The White Devil's partner, my former lover Sara Robbins, had escaped and threatened revenge in the most chilling fashion, although I hadn't heard anything from her for over two years. I was still scared shitless of Sara. She'd pretended to be a normal person when we were together, while she'd been busy graduating to stone killer level. That included pounding one victim's head open with a hammer, biting off another's nipples and gassing several others, including children, fortunately not fatally. She'd also put several bullets into my best friend. Who could blame me for setting up a daily reporting system with my ex-wife, my mother and those of my friends who'd been involved in the hunt for the White Devil?

'Everyone's okay,' I reassured her.

'Including Caroline and Lucy?'

My ex-wife had custody of my eleven-year-old daughter. They'd moved to Wimbledon. I saw Lucy every weekend, but I still missed having her nearby.

'Including Lucy and her mother.'

Karen stretched out a hand. 'I know how difficult it is for you, Matt.'

I squeezed her hand. 'It isn't long till the Easter holidays.'

'Have you decided what you're going to do in your week?'

'Lucy wants to go to Euro Disney. I'm trying to get Caroline to do that.'

'Good luck.' Karen and my ex-wife couldn't be left alone unsupervised. 'What are you going to fob Lucy off with?'

'I thought we could walk in the Peak District.'

Karen laughed. 'Yeah, that ought to do it.'

'At least it'll get her away from the big city,' I said defensively. 'My little angel has become worryingly streetwise.'

Thinking of Lucy always made me anxious. The divorce hadn't been easy for her. I regretted that, but back then I couldn't handle Caroline's scorn for my lack of success as a writer any longer. I managed to cheer up by the end of the meal, mainly because I'd succeeded in not torching the dessert to a blackened crisp like the last time.

'Well, Chief Inspector,' I said, as I put the last of the cutlery in the dishwasher. 'I believe I owe you a massage.'

Karen gave me a foxy look. 'Neck or full body?'

'Whatever Madame desires,' I said, in a ridiculous French accent.

'Madame desires the latter,' she said, opening the buttons of her blouse.

'*Très bien,*' I said, feeling my blood quicken as I wiped the table and then followed her to the master bedroom. There was a trail of discarded clothing on the parquet floor.

Karen was lying naked and facedown on my bed, her head turned to the side but her features obscured by the blonde hair she had loosened from its chignon. I managed to get my clothes off before I reached the bed. I straddled her and put my hands on her shoulders. She giggled and squirmed when she felt me between her buttocks. I started to work my fingers across her impressively muscular upper body, all the time moving my lower torso up and down. Things were getting very interesting.

And then her mobile phone rang.

'What are we doing here, guv?' DI John Turner was waiting for DCI Oaten on the steps of number 41 Ifield Road. There was a uniformed policeman below him and a crime scene investigator in a dark blue coverall on his way into the house.

'Ask the Assistant Commissioner, Taff,' she said. This time she hadn't cared about finding a space. She'd double-parked her silver BMW 318i next to the CSI's white van.

'He seems to think this is up our alley.' She stamped her booted feet in the cold and had a flash of Matt's face when she was taking them off. She smiled and then let out a groan. 'Shit.'

The inspector followed her gaze down to the high-heeled boots. 'They'll look good with a pair of overshoes on.' He grinned, but not for long. Oaten, known only behind her back as Wild Oats, had a notorious temper.

A middle-aged man in a white coverall appeared at the door. 'Any sign of the very important VCCT?' He made no effort to keep the scorn from his voice. Most other detectives saw the elite Violent Crimes Co-ordination Team as a gang of interfering glory-snatchers.

'DCI Oaten and DI Turner of the same,' Karen said icily, taking out her warrant card. 'And you are?'

'DI Luke Neville, Homicide Division West,' he replied, his cocky manner suddenly missing in action. He chewed his unusually large lower lip as Oaten and Turner got into protective gear. 'Bit of a weird one, this.'

Oaten glanced up at him. 'Who called it in?'

'Next-door neighbour,' Neville replied, angling his head to his right. 'He was ranting about loud music coming from number 41. Said the lady was always quiet as a mouse. He'd hammered on the door, but got no reply.'

'What kind of music?' Turner asked.

Neville was looking pleased with himself again. 'Well, that's one of the weird things.' He paused for effect, then started speaking rapidly when Oaten's eyes bored into his. 'We found a CD with only one song repeated ten times on it.'

Oaten went up the steps. 'And the song was…?'

'An old Rolling Stones one, actually.' Neville gave a

weak smile. '"Sympathy for the Devil." The volume was turned up full.'

Oaten raised an eyebrow. Matt had got tickets when the band had played Twickenham a couple of years back. That song had been the standout number, Mick Jagger high above the stage in a red top hat and tail coat.

'I was always more of a Beatles man, myself,' Turner muttered.

They followed DI Neville inside. The house was impeccably clean and tidy, shelves full of books on every wall. At the far end of the long sitting room, a familiar figure was standing over the short but bulky female corpse lying facedown on the floor. The dead woman wore a calf-length blue skirt, and pink slippers with pom-poms were lying at irregular angles to her feet, about a metre away.

'DCI Oaten, what a pleasure.'

'Good evening, Doctor Redrose,' Karen said, her tone formal. She didn't much like the potbellied, red-cheeked pathologist, even though he was good at his job. 'What have you got here?' She bent over the remains of the obese woman. The thick legs were bare and marked by the purple cobwebs of varicose veins. There was a patch of blood on the grey carpet at the left side of her head.

'What I've got,' said the medic, 'is something less than pleasant.' He looked up at his assistant, who was standing by. 'All right, the police photographer's finished and we've taken our shots. Let's turn her over.'

The woman was moved onto her back, the two men grunting with the effort. The victim's face was a mess of blood and ripped skin.

Taff Turner swallowed hard, trying to prevent his weak stomach from erupting.

'And also rather unusual,' Redrose said, his normally languid tone replaced by one that suggested a fascination bordering on the unhealthy. 'Severe lacerations and heavy blows to the face.' He extended an arm. 'And the left ear has been removed.'

'Jesus,' Turner said, averting his eyes from the sight.

Oaten looked at the carpet around the body and the nearest wall. There was no blood spatter. 'I take it the injuries were inflicted after death.'

Redrose nodded. 'I've examined the skull. There's a serious depressed fracture, probably from a fall.' He shook his head and then smiled. 'But that wasn't what killed her.'

Oaten was irritated by the pathologist's ability to take pleasure from his work, but she didn't show it. That would only have encouraged him. She looked back at the dead woman. It was impossible to tell if any other trauma had been inflicted. Apart from the face and head there was no blood, and her clothing didn't appear to have been disturbed.

'Let me help you, Chief Inspector,' Redrose said. He turned the victim's head to the right and put his forefinger close to an area of the neck. 'You see the ligature mark?'

Oaten nodded. The dull red line was narrow. 'Any sign of what was used?'

'Not in the immediate vicinity, ma'am,' a uniformed officer said.

The pathologist laughed. 'Careful, laddie. The chief inspector's one of those female officers who prefers to be called "guv".'

Oaten gave Redrose a tight smile. 'So she was strangled.'

'Correct. The marks suggest by something pretty narrow, like a shoelace. I'll see if there are any fibres later.'

'And the time of death, Doctor?' Oaten asked.

The pathologist looked affronted. 'Surely you realise it's too early to say.'

She raised her eyes to the ceiling. 'Would you care to hazard a guess?'

'Oh, very well,' Redrose said, with a brief smile. 'Given the body temperature, I'd say no more than two hours ago.'

Oaten looked at her watch. It was nearly ten.

DI Neville appeared at her side. 'The neighbour called about the noise at 8.43 p.m. So that gives us a pretty tight window of eight to around eight-thirty. I've just been talking to the guy next door. He isn't sure, but he reckons that the music started about a quarter of an hour before he made the call.'

'Did he see anyone leave the house?' Turner asked, his notebook and pen out.

Neville shook his head.

Karen Oaten stood up and took in the room. The back door was ajar and on the carpet near it were some small bloodstains. 'What happened there?'

Neville stepped up. 'The CSIs have already taken them away.'

'Them?'

'The severed head and body of a black cat,' the detective inspector said. 'There's more blood on the paving stones out back. It looks like it was slaughtered there.' The bottom lip went between his teeth again.

'Do we know if it was the victim's?' Oaten asked.

Neville nodded. 'The neighbour confirmed she had one like that. It, or rather he, was called Noir.'

Black, thought Oaten. The victim must have liked black humour. Or was she into old crime movies? She turned to Neville. 'Do we know who she was?'

'No formal identification yet. The neighbour declined, but we'll work on him once she's been cleaned up in the mortuary. There are bank and credit cards in a purse in the hall. The name's Shirley Higginbottom. There's a name-plate on the front door-frame that says S. Higginbottom, so there isn't much doubt that was her.'

'Any cash?' Turner asked.

Neville looked at his notebook. 'Sixty-four pounds and eight pence. And there are two laptops, a plasma TV and a load of jewellery upstairs.'

Oaten was looking at the body again. 'Well, clearly we're not looking for a burglar who was interrupted—'

'Inspector?'

They all turned to the back door. A fresh-faced young man in a crumpled suit and white overshoes stood there, looking at Oaten and Turner in confusion.

'DC Lineham,' Neville said unenthusiastically. 'Two weeks on the job and thinks he knows it all,' he said to Oaten, not bothering to lower his voice. 'What is it then? You can talk in front of our colleagues from the Violent Crimes Co-ordination Team.'

'I thought I recognised DCI Oaten from the TV,' Lineham said, stepping forward.

'Not inside!' yelled Neville. 'You need a coverall and a change of overshoes, idiot.'

The young constable's cheeks reddened. 'Sorry, guv,' he said. He was well-spoken, probably a graduate on the fast-track scheme. 'Perhaps you'd like to come out here then.'

'What have you found?' Neville said wearily. 'Don't tell me there's another headless moggy in the garden.'

'No, sir. It's a bit more…em, sinister than that.'

Oaten and Turner exchanged glances and went to the back door. They took off their bootees. Steps led down to a garden that was lit by lamps set into the side of a paved path. A CSI was on his knees on the grass next to one of the stone slabs, examining it close up.

As they got closer, Karen Oaten's heart began to sink. This was the last thing she needed.

The investigator looked up at them. 'White chalk, drawn with a steady hand, I'd say. It's a—'

'Pentacle,' Oaten and Turner said in unison. They'd worked more than one case involving the paraphernalia of Satanism.

'What's that writing in the middle?' Neville asked, peering forward from the closest stepping plates that had been put down to protect any footprints.

'It's Latin,' put in DC Lineham eagerly. '"FECIT DIABOLUS".' He looked round the blank faces excitedly.

'Meaning?' Oaten prompted.

'Meaning "The devil did it".'

Inspector Neville groaned and slapped his forehead. 'This and the bloody Stones track. We've only gone and got ourselves a sodding Satanist murder.'

Oaten looked at John Turner, then they both concentrated on the pentacle.

'Black cat cut up like that,' Turner said, 'and the victim's ear removed…' He broke off. 'I presume it hasn't been found in or near the house.'

'You presume right,' Neville said, squatting down by the pentacle. 'What is this shit? Why can't people just kill each other and leave it at that? The press are going to have a field day.'

'Well, you'd better not encourage them, Inspector,' Oaten said firmly. 'At this point, we don't know if the pentacle has any connection to the killing. The victim herself might have had an interest in devil worship.'

'Excuse me, Chief Inspector,' Lineham said. He looked like a boy bursting for the toilet. 'Don't you think—'

'Don't interrupt me when I'm thinking,' Oaten ordered.

DC Lineham stared at the pentacle, looking aggrieved.

'Is there something I'm missing here?' Inspector Neville said suspiciously. Then he made the connection. 'Oh, Jesus. You're the ones who investigated that other devil case, the one with the heavy-duty killings.'

'That was the *White* Devil,' Taff Turner said. 'And he's dead.' He glanced at his boss. They both knew that wasn't the whole story.

Neville was looking at Oaten. 'Are you taking over the case then, ma'am?'

Oaten was sure that he was deliberately using the traditional mode of address for female superiors, despite Redrose's warning to the other officer. To her, it was sexist, old-fashioned and demeaning. Not only that, it made her feel like the Queen. None of those things were acceptable, but she decided against correcting Neville. He would imagine he'd put one over her. 'Not yet, Inspector. Please make sure that I receive a copy of the full case file and daily updates. And give me your contact numbers.'

They exchanged cards, and then she and Turner headed for the door.

'Aren't you going to attend the post-mortem, Chief Inspector?' Redrose called after her. 'You never know, I might find a message tucked away somewhere…personal.'

Karen Oaten looked over her shoulder. 'No,' she said.

'Ghoul,' she continued more quietly to Taff. 'He loves seeing us squirm in the morgue.'

'I hope you aren't going to send me,' Turner said dolefully.

She smiled grimly. 'No, that wide boy Neville can have the pleasure.' On the pavement, she stripped off her cover-all and overshoes.

'So you don't think the devil angle should concern us?' the Welshman asked. 'Could it be—'

'Don't say it,' Oaten interrupted. She shrugged. 'Whoever's responsible, it's not exactly a run-of-the-mill murder.'

'It certainly isn't as straightforward as a drugs gang killing, not that we've got a handle on the scumbag who did that.' He paused. 'Even if we don't mention you-know-who, some smart-arse in the press is bound to.'

Oaten gave him a fierce look. 'Let's just hope this isn't the first of a series, then,' she said, heading for her car.

Turner watched her drive off. His stomach was still queasy from the sight of the dead woman's face, as well as from the fact that all his instincts and experience were telling him this wouldn't be a one-off.

2

The atmosphere in the crypt off the main cavern was thick, the air filled with the smoke from guttering black candles, dozens of them. The walls of the confined chamber were festooned with animal skulls, the jaws and teeth of wolves and bears dark with dried blood. There were also the skins of lions and antelopes, medieval swords, axes with notched blades, and the battered helms of long-dead knights. In the middle of the flagstones on the floor, a pentacle had been drawn in yellow chalk. Arcane symbols and letters in a strange script adorned each point of the star-shape.

A figure in a plain grey tunic was kneeling inside the pentacle, holding a curved knife in the left hand.

'Come to me, sweet Mephistopheles,' the supplicant intoned. 'I am in need of your subtle services.'

There was silence, broken only by the hiss of candle wicks as the flames consumed the wax.

The supplicant raised both hands again. 'Come to me.' The voice was tenser. 'Do not desert me in my hour of need.'

A wooden panel slid open in front of the kneeling figure. The person who came out was initially obscured by the smoky air. Then the supplicant saw that the devil's representative was wearing the usual monk's black robe and cowl.

'Have you forgotten what you must pay?' The voice was soft, but it had a steely edge.

'I have not, sweet Mephistopheles.' The knife cut into the lower right arm and sliced open the skin beneath five similar scars, one of which was still livid. Blood welled up instantly.

The masked figure leaned forward and held out a tarnished silver goblet decorated with precious stones to collect the liquid tribute.

'Very good, Faustus.' The monkish apparition stepped back. 'Tell me how the evening went.' A finger was raised. 'And omit nothing.'

The supplicant nodded avidly and started to speak. Then a demonic shriek rang out and cut the flow of words off immediately.

I woke up the second that Karen came into the flat—my experiences with the White Devil had made me a permanent light sleeper. She took her boots off on the sofa opposite the bed, but this time there was no question of me making a leading comment. It was after two and she looked like she'd sucked a bag of lemons.

'What happened?' I ventured, going over to embrace her. She resisted for a few moments, and then crushed her body against mine.

'Oh, some sick bastard strangled a woman, beat her face to a pulp and cut off her ear.'

She sighed and I thought I heard a sob. I held her tighter and buried my face in her hair. 'It's all right, my sweet,' I said, feeling for her. Although she was a tough woman cop on the outside, deep down she was a mass of conflicting emotions. That was why I loved her. She was complicated and hard to fathom, hard-edged but also caring. I sometimes wondered what she saw in me.

'Matt, I'm worried,' she said, her voice faint.

I felt a quiver of apprehension. 'Don't be,' I said. 'I'll look after you, Kar.' I only used the diminutive of her name when I was being more tender than either of us was usually comfortable with.

She turned her head so her lips met mine. 'What would I do without you?' she murmured.

'Why would you be without me?' I asked, feeling even more apprehensive.

Karen pushed herself away far enough so she could focus on my eyes. 'Because there are things we can't do together.' She dropped her gaze.

'What's happened? Who was the murder victim?'

'Shirley something…' She rubbed her head. 'Higginbottom. I've left it with Homicide West, at least for the time being.'

The name stirred something deep in my memory. I tried to excavate it, but failed.

Karen looked up at me and I saw she was about to come out with something bad. She tightened her grip on my midriff. 'Look, it probably isn't significant…'

'Just tell me,' I said, taking a deep breath.

She nodded. 'There was a pentacle drawn on flagstones in the garden. And there were Latin words inside it.'

'What were they?'

'You know Latin?' Karen asked.

'I did it for a few years at school.'

Karen sat back. 'Okay. Let's see if that's enough. "FECIT DIABOLUS".'

'I can get that, all right. "The devil did it."' I looked at her, feeling a sudden chill. 'Did what? The murder?'

She shrugged. 'I suppose so. It would hardly be the first Satanist killing in Greater London, would it?'

I shook my head. 'I don't like it, Karen. It makes me think of the White Devil and his sister.' I felt a surge of panic. 'Jesus, is Sara back?'

'Don't jump to conclusions, Matt,' Karen said. She got up and went into the ensuite bathroom. 'There was nothing connecting the murder to you or any of your friends and relatives.'

That didn't make me feel much better. The White Devil had taunted me with quotations from revenge tragedy previously. Maybe this was Sara's adaptation of that, and she was using Latin to muddy the waters. She was cunning and vicious enough to play that kind of game.

Karen came back into the bedroom and looked at me. 'Get hold of yourself, Matt.'

'Tell me exactly what you found, will you?' I said, suddenly noticing that I was pacing up and down. 'Please, Karen.' I sat down next to her on the bed.

After instructing me not to mention anything about the murder in my column, she did.

'Are you sure there was no message on the body?' I asked, when she'd finished.

'Redrose said there wasn't. You know how keen he is to check that kind of thing. We'll know for certain when he does the post-mortem tomorrow.'

I got up and went over to the laptop I kept in the bedroom. I logged on and checked my e-mails. There was nothing from Sara—no taunts, no threats, no disposable e-mail addresses.

'Okay?' Karen said, giving me a reassuring smile.

'Not really,' I said.

Karen shook her head. 'For God's sake, Matt! Has it ever occurred to you that, in writing *The Death List,* you gave every psycho lunatic in London, no, in the whole country, if not the whole world—'

'The global sales *were* good, weren't they?' I said.

She ignored that '—an open invitation to pretend they were Sara. You went into such detail about the White Devil's methods that you're probably responsible for dozens of murders.' She turned away and murmured, 'Goodnight.'

Karen, used to seeing dead bodies at all times of day and night, despite her initial disquiet, fell asleep not long afterwards. Eventually I dropped off, but not before I'd got out of bed to check the alarm system. I was vaguely aware of Karen rising at some ridiculously early hour and kissing me on the cheek. Then I dropped off again. At least I wasn't disturbed by nightmares.

When I finally surfaced it was after nine. I would normally have done half an hour on my exercise bike, but today I wanted to be sure that everyone was all right. I ran my eye down the morning e-mails. All my family and friends had confirmed they were okay. I thought about raising the level of alert after the murder last night, but decided against it. Karen was right—a single mention of the devil in Latin wasn't worth getting too worked up about.

I sat back in my £2000 desk chair and considered the name that Karen had mentioned. Shirley Higginbottom. There was something familiar about it. I looked at the row of reference books on the nearest shelf. *Who's Who? Who's*

Who in the Arts? The Rugby League Year Book? None of
them seemed likely, though there was probably no shortage
of league players called Higginbottom. Further along the
shelf there was a small yellow booklet. It was the annual
directory of members of the Crime Writers' Society. Something clicked. I grabbed the booklet and found the pages
with names beginning in *H*. No Higginbottoms. Then I remembered the section that matched authors' real names
with their nom de plumes. I was in that—Matt Stone =
Matt Wells. Back when I'd started writing novels, I thought
Stone would give me a harder edge in the market. That had
been one of my many delusions.

Then I hit pay dirt. There it was: Mary Malone = Shirley
Higginbottom. Jesus—Mary Malone. She was a major
best-seller. She was also notorious for staying out of the
limelight. She'd been invited several times as guest of
honour to crime-writing festivals and had always declined.
There wasn't even a publicity photograph of her in circulation, leading to nasty speculation that she was a fearsome
hag—or, perhaps, a man. She'd sent her editor to collect
her two Historical Crime Novel of the Year awards.

I picked up the phone and called Karen.

'This isn't a good time, Matt,' she said in a low voice.

'Yes, it is. What would you say if I told you that your
murder victim last night was a best-selling crime novelist?'

'What?'

'I was expecting at least one expletive.'

'Tough. So she had a nom de plume?'

'Yup. Mary Malone. She wrote about eighteenth-
century Paris and she was a global best-seller.'

'Interesting. Look, I'm in a case conference now. I'll
pass that on to the team that's working the murder.'

'Sure you don't want to take it over? I could be useful to you. Insider knowledge of the victim's milieu, personal experience of—'

'You just want to make sure crazy Sara's not involved, don't you, Matt? Talk to you later.' The connection was cut.

'Bollocks!' I shouted into the phone. A few seconds later it rang. 'It's all right, darling,' I said. 'I forgive you.'

'Very kind of you, Matt. What did I do?'

I recognised the overcooked Cockney tones of Josh Hinkley, author of a popular series of gangster capers. He'd treated me like shit when my career was in the doldrums, but since my success he imagined he was my best friend.

'Sorry, Josh. I thought you were someone else.'

'Not the delightful DCI Oaten, by any chance?'

My relationship with Karen was common knowledge in crime-writing circles. Some authors would have paid good money to go out with a senior police officer, and Hinkley was definitely one of them.

'What are you after, Josh?'

'Oh, nothing. I was just wondering if you knew one of our colleagues was brutally murdered last night.'

'Of course I knew,' I said hastily, surprised that he'd found out so quickly. He didn't waste any time telling me how.

'Journo on the *Express,* who I drink with, rang me up an hour ago. One of the cops told him they found a Crime Writers' Society membership card in the name of Mary Malone when they went through her desk. Wondered if I knew her.'

'And what did you tell him?' I asked, wishing I could have told him I'd already tipped Karen off.

I heard Hinkley draw hard on a cigarette. 'Well, what

could I say? I never met her, did I? None of us ever met her. I did check the membership directory, though. Confirmed that Shirley whatever was her real name.'

'And no doubt *your* name will get mentioned in tomorrow's paper,' I said snidely.

'Of course, old cock.' He laughed. 'I don't need a column in the *Daily Indie* to show how smart I am. You can pass the pseudonym on to your girlfriend with my compliments.'

'You're too late, Josh,' I said, terminating the call. Sometimes he could be a gigantic dickhead. Then it occurred to me that Karen obviously wasn't being kept up to speed by Homicide West. Someone was going to get their ears burned. I considered calling her again, but decided against it. She would only have told me to get on with my own work. But the crime writer's murder was very much in my domain. Could the killer be making a point to me? That was exactly the kind of thing I'd been expecting Sara to do for the last two years.

I went over to the window that ran all along the south wall of my flat. Spring still seemed as far away as Acapulco, the Thames running grey and chill. On sunny days the view was great, but in winter London looked like a dead zone from the fourth floor. At my old place in Herne Hill, I hadn't had a view beyond the neighbours' overgrown Leylandii. I didn't miss it—the place in Chelsea had cost me a large part of my earnings from *The Death List,* but it already had happy memories. This was where Karen and I had begun to spend time together as a couple—the start of a new life for me. The problem was, I hadn't been able to write fiction since I'd moved in. It wasn't that I needed the money. The newspaper column covered most of my living expenses, and I'd been a journalist before I was a novelist. But something was missing. It was as if my involvement with a real serial killer had stolen my ability to write fiction. I'd lied to Karen and I didn't feel good about that. I hadn't written two thousand words of a novel. I had barely written one word.

I went to my workspace, an enormous, antique partners' desk in the corner of the living area. There were three computers on it, although I only used one. That was the problem when you made a lot of money unexpectedly— you bought a load of unnecessary gear.

I booted up and logged on to my e-mail programme. Among the new messages was one from my editor, Jeanie Young-Burke. I hadn't accepted an advance for the new novel, so there wasn't a deadline. But she was still pressing me about how I was getting on. There was also one from Christian Fels, my agent. Although he was nearing retirement, he still had the instincts of a great white shark when it came to making deals. He'd had several offers from publishers for another non-fiction crime book. The problem was, I didn't have any material.

Could the murder with the white-chalk pentacle be exactly what I needed?

'What's this about the victim being a best-selling crime novelist, Inspector?' Karen Oaten demanded, the phone pressed tight to her ear.

'How did you—' Luke Neville audibly gulped. 'I was just about to ring you, ma'am…I mean, guv.'

'I'm sure you were,' Oaten said, frowning at John Turner. 'Have you seen the preliminary CSI and postmortem reports?'

'They're just in.'

'E-mail me everything you've got. The next time you hold out on me, you'll be talking to the AC. Am I clear?'

'Yes, guv.'

Oaten slammed the phone down. 'Wanker.'

'Neville the Lip?' Turner asked.

'Yes. I've half a mind to take the case from Homicide West just to teach him a lesson.'

'We've got plenty on our hands as it is,' Turner said, in a long-suffering voice.

'I know that, Taff. But the AC's got the hots for the Ifield Road murder and I reckon he'll be even more excited when he finds out the victim was a big-name writer.'

Turner put a heap of files on her desk. 'I'll leave these ongoing case reports with you then,' he said, with a tight smile.

Oaten stood up quickly. 'Oh, no you don't. We're going through them together.' She raised a finger. 'I've got a better idea. Get Pavlou and Browning in here.'

Turner returned with the detectives a minute later.

'Guv,' they both said tentatively.

'Don't worry, I've got something delightful for you.' Oaten grinned. 'See this pile of case files?'

They both nodded. Detective Sergeant Paul Pavlou, of Greek Cypriot parents, in his mid-thirties and with a permanent shadow of beard on his face, looked unenthusiastic. Detective Sergeant Amelia Browning was a newcomer to the team, a short woman in her late twenties with bobbed brown hair.

'Split them up between you and go through them. I want you to make lists of all the leads that haven't been followed up and rank them according to potential effectiveness.'

'Em, isn't that your job, guv?' Pavlou said, his eyes down.

'We're a team, aren't we, Paul?' Oaten riposted. 'I'm giving you the chance to show your mettle. We'll be needing another inspector soon.'

The detectives left with the files, Pavlou now with a spring in his step.

'Paul's got what it takes,' Turner said. 'Far too early to say about Browning.'

Oaten nodded. 'How are the rest of them treating her?'

The Welshman shrugged. 'Okay. They took her down the pub last Friday and tried to get her pissed. Apparently she was the last person standing—and she was drinking some brain-damaging real ale.'

Oaten laughed. 'I thought there was more to her than meets the eye when I interviewed her. Right, let's see if Neville's sent the reports over.' She opened up the internal mail programme on her computer. 'Looks like he's jumped to attention. They're here.' She clicked on the attachments and printed out two copies.

They both read for several minutes.

'Okay,' Oaten said. 'Redrose's post-mortem. He was right about strangulation by ligature being the cause of death. He found traces of what he expects tests will show is leather—so, maybe a decent-quality shoelace.'

'Or a cord from a pendant.'

Oaten nodded. 'Could be. The fracture on the side of the skull was probably caused when her head hit the floor.' She looked up. 'So, if the victim was lucky, she was unconscious when she was throttled. The face was pounded by a blunt object, dimensions approximately three by two centimetres, consistent with the haft of a knife or similar. The blade—sharp and with smooth edge—was used to slash her face and to sever the left ear. No fingerprints found on the body. Same serrated blade probably did for the cat. The time-of-death window is between eight and eight-thirty.'

'Listen to this, guv,' Turner said, his eyes further down the page. '"Likelihood that victim's finger and toenails were cut by her assailant. Several are uneven, with minor cuts in the surrounding skin. No clippings found at locus."' The inspector stopped abruptly and let out a groan. 'God, I hate murders done by crazies.'

Oaten continued reading. '"Also, a section of pubic hair approximately four by four centimetres has been cut recently, some hairs remaining in situ. Ends suggest single blade rather than scissors, so reasonable assumption that killer removed hairs. Victim's underwear has been repositioned with some care. So far, CSIs report no cut hairs found in house. A lock of hair was also cut from above the forehead with a similar blade, again no traces found in proximity of body."'

'Trophies?' Turner asked.

'I'd have thought the ear was enough of a trophy.' Oaten rubbed her chin. 'Remember those Satanists that we caught a year ago? They took hair and nails, and used them in their so-called spells.'

'They were vile people,' the Welshman said with a shiver.

'There's also the pentacle in the garden to suggest this is some kind of ritual murder.' Karen Oaten raised a hand. 'Hang on, Taff. We're not finished yet. Redrose is nothing if not thorough. "The prone position of the body is worthy of note—i.e. it was turned over by the murderer after the pubic hair was removed. Examination of the rectal area shows damage compatible with sexual abuse. However, no semen or condom lubricant have been detected. A possible conclusion is that the butt of the knife used to disfigure the victim was inserted into the anus. Underwear was repositioned with care.'"

'Christ,' Turner said, his face pale. 'What the hell kind of animal uses a knife-butt to sodomise a dead woman?'

Oaten caught his gaze. 'Maybe we should be thankful it wasn't the kind of animal that would have used the other end of the knife.'

The inspector gave his boss an appalled look.

'We have to keep our emotions in check, Taff.' Oaten moved to the next report. 'The CSIs say "Muddy footprints, size nine footwear with heavy tread, probably workman's boots, to be confirmed, leading from back door to area around body, mud matching that in victim's garden. Impressions from same footwear on other side of wall inside Brompton Cemetery, in direction of house, but impossible to follow far on asphalt road. Footprints lead from body to front door. Also decreasing amounts of mud on steps and pavement to right of house. Impossible to follow beyond twenty-seven point two-four metres."' Oaten looked up. 'That's interesting. He got in the back door, but went out the front, bold as you like.'

'"No other footprints apart from victim's near the back door, those at least twenty-four hours old",' Turner continued. '"But there were traces of black wool fibres around the body, as yet unidentified. No fingerprints apart from victim's on any surfaces. The CD had been burned on a computer, 'Sympathy for the Devil' copied ten times. The CD player in sitting-room was activated by the machine's timer, which had been set for 20.30."'

'Presumably giving himself time to get away.' She

shuffled through the papers. 'Someone must have seen him. Even if he got over the wall of the cemetery unseen, there are plenty of houses whose occupants could have seen him in the street.'

Turner was examining DI Neville's report. 'No witnesses found as yet, locals still being questioned by uniforms. At least they've identified the body. In the absence of any relatives in her address book, the neighbour agreed to do it. That must have been a hard job, given the state her face was in. Additional confirmation by dental records is also under way.'

Oaten leaned back in her chair. 'So what have we got? A cool customer, who managed to get in the back door—a standard Yale lock, with minimal signs of damage, so he knew what he was doing. He was also lucky as the victim must have forgotten to bolt the door. He was calm enough to draw the pentacle and write the Latin words with a steady hand. The pattern of footprints suggests that Mary Malone hadn't been in the garden for at least a day and the chalk was recently applied. So, a cold-blooded killer, who waited for the victim. I'd guess the cat was mutilated to terrify her. The killer was determined enough and had sufficient strength to tighten the ligature, though the victim was probably unconscious from the fall. Then he took the ear, hair and nail clippings, and—get this for weird—put her underwear back carefully after he'd abused her from behind. Having achieved all that, he left the Stones song playing so loud that it was bound to attract attention. Why would he take the risk?'

'Because he's a bastard who's showing off, daring us to catch him if we can.'

'Possibly,' Oaten said, frowning. 'It's not exactly the

kind of behaviour you'd expect from a Satanist. They're usually drug-crazed kids or sad, middle-aged men.' She pointed at him. 'We've both been saying "he", but there's no reason, apart maybe from the shoe size, to rule out a female killer.'

The phone on the desk rang. Oaten identified herself and listened. 'All right, thanks for that,' she said, before she put it down again. Her expression was sombre.

'What is it, guv?' Turner asked.

She paused before answering. 'That was DI Neville. They've found a witness, a fifteen-year-old boy on the top floor of a house two doors down on the other side of the road.'

'Great,' the Welshman said. 'What did he see?'

Oaten looked away. 'He saw a person of average height leaving number 41 just before eight-thirty—he wasn't sure of the time as he'd been playing poker online and was taking a break. He was a bit surprised as he'd never seen anyone go in or out of the victim's house—she got her groceries delivered.' She paused. 'He was also surprised because the figure was wearing a long black cloak and a black top hat.'

'Shit,' Turner said, in a low voice.

His boss stared at him. 'What's the matter, Taff? Don't tell me you think it was Old Nick himself?'

The inspector shook his head. 'No, guv. It's a human being dressing up as the Devil, and that makes it even worse.'

Karen Oaten tossed the reports onto her desk. 'What about the Latin devil reference then, Taff?'

'Did you mention it to Matt Wells?' the inspector countered.

'He was somewhat concerned.'

'I'm not surprised. But anyone who read his book could have been inspired to do that kind of thing.'

Oaten gave a tight smile. 'I did point that out to him.'

'So you don't think it's her? The White Devil's sister.'

'Sara Robbins? It could be, but we haven't got sufficient data to suppose so. Matt hadn't received any message from her by last night.'

'How about today?' John Turner's face hardened. 'Anyway, would he tell you if he had?'

Karen Oaten met his eyes and then looked away. She wasn't at all sure that Matt would come clean. That and the nature of Mary Malone/Shirley Higginbottom's murder gave her a very ominous feeling.

3

I spent the rest of the day trying to occupy myself with my column. When that did nothing but make me wonder if my arch-enemy, Sara, was responsible for Mary Malone's death, I tried writing an album review. Unfortunately, the CD I was to listen to was by the Willard Grant Conspiracy—good stuff, but mainly murder ballads sung by a deep, lugubrious voice that could have emanated from Hades itself. I didn't manage to write more than the first line. It was obvious that I needed help, so I called my mates. Five minutes later, I'd arranged to meet them later on in a pub near London Bridge. We called it the Zoo, because the clientele was a weird mixture of City whiz kids wearing expensive suits, stallholders from the Borough Market in grubby white coats and bewildered tourists. I didn't need to twist the others' arms too much, but the short notice made them curious. Two years back, the White Devil had set up an intricate surveillance system, so we were always succinct when speaking on the phone. Despite the fact that no one apart from us knew what or where the Zoo was, I still couldn't finish the album review.

A chill wind was blasting up the Thames from the North Sea when I came out of London Bridge Station. The lights of the City blazed out across the river. Apparently the people who ran the financial sector were unaware of global warming—or maybe they just didn't give a toss. I'd kept an eye out when I was travelling and had stepped off a couple of trains before they left, like the Fernando Rey character in *The French Connection*. I didn't think anyone was tailing me. To make sure, I took a roundabout way to the pub, before slipping in as a double-decker bus passed and obscured me from the other side of the road.

Andy Jackson had already occupied the table we always took at the rear. The Zoo's lights were as low as ever, which was another reason we liked it.

'Yo, writer man,' the blonde-haired American said, draining his glass and extending it towards me.

'Yo, chef person,' I replied, heading for the bar. I returned with a pint of Australian lager for him and one of Directors for me. 'I don't know how you can drink that wallaby-urine, Slash.' His nickname came from the way he used to cut through the opposition defensive line on the rugby pitch—nothing to do with the big-haired Guns N' Roses guitarist.

'Yeah, like that bitter wasn't sprayed out by a hog.' He grinned at me. Andy was tall and muscle-bound, the kind of guy everyone wanted on their team. He'd grown up in a town he called the asshole of New Jersey and had almost made it to the NFL, but his knee was suspect and he was let go. That turned him against his native country, so he crossed the Atlantic, trained as a chef, and now held down a job in a Mexican restaurant near the British Museum.

I took a long drink. 'No one on your tail?' I asked in a low voice.

He shook his head. 'You gonna come clean about what's going on, Matt?'

'When the others show.' I caught his eye. 'So what's new on the female front?' Andy was a serious skirt-chaser.

'Same two things there always were,' he said, with a grin. 'Judy. Brunette, long legs, big…things on the front, and sent straight from paradise.'

'Bragging again, Slash?' I looked round and saw the stocky figure of Dave Cummings, a pint in his hand. He always got his own—it was some strange ritual he'd learned in the Parachute Regiment or the SAS. He was the hard man of the group, but he was putty in the hands of his kids. 'Hello, lad.' He put an arm round my waist. Dave had always treated me like a kid brother, even though he was only three years older. Compared with what he'd seen of the world and its wars, my life was pretty sheltered.

'Hello, Psycho,' I said, pulling a stool out for him. His hair was cut close to his scalp. 'How's the demolition business?'

'Falling,' he said with a laugh. It was a long-running gag. 'Hey, Slash, what's the best way to cook lobster?'

'Are they talking about food again?' Roger van Zandt had appeared at my side. The other two nodded at him and continued talking. Curly-haired and slight, Roger had been famous for the tackles he put in on much beefier men.

'Hi, Rog,' I said, getting up and going over to the bar. 'How's it going?'

'Quiet,' he said, picking up the pint I'd bought him. 'I've been reduced to writing programmes for an advertising company, would you believe?' Rog ran his own computer consultancy.

'That bad, eh? Before you know it, you'll be giving hacking lessons to teenagers.'

'Shh,' he said, raising his hand. 'I'm already doing that.'

'The hell you are,' came Pete Satterthwaite's voice.

'Bonehead!' I said, signalling for another pint. 'What kept you?'

'A very naughty young man,' he said, with a lascivious grin. Pete was gay and proud of it. He was also a self-made millionaire, who now spent his time moving his invest-ments around and watching them grow. 'Sorry. Did I miss something juicy?' His Lancashire accent was still audible beneath the layers of boardroom English he'd acquired.

'They're talking about cooking,' Rog said, inclining his head towards Andy and Dave.

'Ooh, lovely,' Pete said, running his hand over his natu-rally bald scalp. 'I should have brought my apron.'

We all sat down.

'What's the verdict then, Slash?' I asked.

'Thermidor, got to be,' the American said. 'The dwarf here wants to make bisque. What a waste!'

I leaned forward. 'Okay, guys, huddle,' I said, my voice low. The sounds of 'Woman' by Free came from the front of the bar—the Zoo had one of the best jukeboxes in London, which was another reason we liked it.

'What's up, Wellsy?' Dave said. 'You sounded a bit…I dunno…jumpy on the phone.'

The others agreed. So much for me trying to play it cool.

'Yeah, well, there's a reason for that.'

'It's her, isn't it?' Pete said. 'The ex-girlfriend from hell, literally.' I could have lived without that characterisation of Sara, but it was true. What she'd done with the White Devil and the way she'd deceived me had turned the love I'd once felt for her into dread, something far more disabling than hate.

'Has she shown up?' Andy asked.

I shook my head. 'No,' I said. 'At least, not definitely.' I told them about the murder of Mary Malone.

'I heard about that on the radio this morning,' Rog said. 'They didn't mention anything about a pentacle or words in Latin.'

'The cops are keeping some things back from the press,' I said.

'Is Karen working it?' Pete asked.

'No,' I said. 'Not yet, anyway. But she was called over to check it out last night.'

Dave drained his glass and wiped his mouth with the back of his hand. 'So that's why you got us all over here.'

I shrugged. 'I thought you should know about it.'

'Aye, you were right.' Dave got up and collected the glasses—he bought rounds, but he never allowed anyone else to buy him a drink. 'Back in a moment.' He went to the bar, limping slightly. He'd been wounded in the legs at the climax of the White Devil case and had never got full movement back, despite wearing two physiotherapists out.

'"The devil did it",' Andy said. 'Could that mean the White Devil?'

Bonehead raised a finger. 'There you have it, my learned friend. Is it her pretending to be her dead brother, or just a common and garden murderer?' He turned to me. 'Wouldn't your ex have written "White Devil" in Latin? What's "white" in that language anyway?'

I racked my memory. '"Albus", I think.'

'As in Dumbledore?' Rog said. He had a touching attachment to the works of J. K. Rowling.

When Dave came back, we talked a bit about counter-surveillance—Rog had supplied us each with an electronic bug detector—and about checking if we were being followed. We'd spent time with Dave, as a group and in-

dividually, learning how to operate firearms and how to
fight with a knife. The other three had done the same
courses in boxing, Judo and Karate as I had—Andy was
by far the most proficient, as well as being a heavyweight.
But Dave was our main man. He'd learned dozens of ways
to kill, maim and render unconscious when he was in the
Army. We weren't going to be taken by surprise this time.

'You're sure there was no message for you?' Rog asked.
'If Sara comes back for revenge, the likelihood is that
she'll copy what her brother did, isn't it?'

I looked at him. 'Maybe. But Sara's smart and she had
a much better education than the Devil. It's quite possible
she'll come up with her own ways to make my life a misery.'

Dave kicked my shin lightly under the table. 'Don't
worry, lad. I'll look after you.'

'Aw, sweet,' Andy said, and they all laughed.

'Sod off,' I said, and the evening reverted to type—men's
talk, plenty of guffawing and more beer than was a good
idea.

It was fun. I even managed to forget about Sara for a
couple of minutes.

It was after ten-thirty when Nedim Zinar closed up the
general store in Dalston, East London. He didn't work
there, but his cousin Muhammed had asked him to check
the security a year back and it turned into a regular thing.
Nedim found that the man who worked evenings had been
taking a percentage from the till in addition to his salary.
At least he wasn't a relation, which meant that Nedim
could beat the crap out of him and throw him into one of
the nearby Clapton Ponds to bring him round.

It wasn't Nedim's fault that the asshole had drowned.

Nothing came of it. Everyone in the Kurdish community knew that Nedim was an enforcer for the King. Although the man himself had been in prison for the last three years, he still controlled his interests, both legal and illicit, by phone and coded message. Everyone in important positions was a family member. There were legitimate businesses—a freight and haulage company, travel agencies, a car dealership, estate agents and a food importing company that supplied delicatessens all over Britain. But the King also bought and distributed drugs, mainly heroin and Ecstasy, trafficked people and porn, ran brothels, financed robberies and ran protection rackets. His operations were all over East and North London. The police knew about them, but were content with a few token arrests each month. They knew that the streets would be much more dangerous if the King and the other gangs didn't keep their people in line.

Nedim checked the last lock and stood looking at the shop for a few moments. It wasn't his, but as he could walk in and pick up anything he wanted free of charge, it felt like it was. Occasionally he got a call from Muhammed— some kids who had run off without paying, or alcoholics who had stuffed bottles of cider in their stinking coats; even young mothers who had slipped tins of food under their babies. Muhammed caught them himself most of the time and if he didn't, he had a good idea who they were. All Nedim had to do was go round and talk, or knock, some sense into them. Even the junkies didn't try it again after that.

The big man—Lambros was six feet one and over sixteen stone—checked his watch. He would have time for a quick beer before he went to work the door at the nightclub the King's brother ran in Islington. He crossed Lower Clapton Road, holding his hand up to stop the traffic—he wasn't one to waste his energy walking to the lights fifty metres away. A couple of black guys in a four-by-four yelled at him, but they shut up when he made the sign of the letter *K* in the air. Only the hardest members of the Turkish gang known as the Shadows would take objection to that, and Lambros wasn't scared of them. He had a Beretta 92 in his breast pocket and people knew he would use it.

It took Nedim five minutes to reach his people-carrier. That was the only problem with Muhammed's shop—there was no parking in the immediate vicinity, and even the King's lawyers couldn't do much about the police cameras that registered infringements. The other boys in the operation had laughed when they heard he was getting a 'mummy's car', but they shut up when they saw it—the black paint and custom-built stereo system almost made it cool. It wasn't as if Nedim had any choice. He was often told to move people around in groups—tarts, illegal immigrants, men tooled up for action. Besides, he had four kids.

At least there was a narrow lane that most people never noticed a few minutes' walk away. Nedim parked the wagon there every evening and it had never even been touched—he would have known. As he walked round the corner, he pressed the button on the key. There was a chirp and lights flashed on the vehicle.

Nedim was trying to decide whether to play traditional Kurdish music or his recent discovery, Bruce Springsteen, and he didn't notice the figure crouching behind the car. He went to the rear door and walked into a long blade that went into his belly to the hilt. The breath went out of him and he looked down at the hand holding the instrument of his death. It was sheathed in black leather. He tried to scream as the blade was wrenched upwards, but he no longer had control over his voice. He dropped to his knees, dimly aware of the crack they made on the cobblestones. By then, the pain from his abdomen had made his eyes blur with tears. He felt shame, but not for long. The blade was biting, tearing into his very being. He toppled sideways, his shoulder hitting the car. Then the knife was pulled out in a rapid movement.

Nedim Zinar clutched the gaping wound, feeling the slick coils of his gut spill through his fingers. Then the horror came to a climax when he saw his killer's face.

It was that of a scarred and deformed devil.

I went home without making too many detours. People stared at me when I did my on-off performance with three trains, but I made like I was drunker than I really was. No one paid much attention—behaviour like that is pretty standard in London after the pubs shut. I took more care when I came out of Fulham Broadway Station, stopping in doorways and doubling back down a couple of alley-ways. There was no sign of anyone following me.

As I headed towards the river, my mobile rang.

'Where are you, Matt?' Karen asked. She sounded wiped out.

'Homeward bound. You?'

'My place. Sorry. I've got early meetings tomorrow.'

'Fair enough. Any news?' A stretch limo full of scream-ing young women passed and I had to shout over them. 'I mean, on the Mary Malone case.'

'Homicide West isn't much further on. I don't suppose you've had any messages from you-know-who?'

'I might have had on the land line. I'll ring after I've checked.'

'Okay.' She paused, as if there was something she wanted to say. 'Goodnight' was all she managed.

''Night,' I replied. I should have told her I loved her, and that I was going to jump in a cab and come to her house in Shepherd's Bush. I wanted to nestle up to her so we could both drop into a deep, uninterrupted sleep, rather than go back to an empty flat where a ghost from the past might be waiting to haunt me all over again. But I'd missed my chance and I was sure that she knew it as well as I did.

I shook my head and tried to get a grip. Given the security system in my so-called 'ultra-exclusive' block, Sara would have done well even to have got past the armoured glass main door. It was over twenty-four hours since Mary Malone's killing and there had been no sign of her. Some scumbag Satanists had got their kicks out of murdering a defenceless woman. Then I asked myself if I really believed that. The answer wasn't encouraging. She was coming for me—even if not now, it would happen at some point in the future.

I found myself walking more quickly, eager to get home to see if Sara was hiding in the wardrobe or even lying on my bed, bold as love. Then it occurred to me that she might not be alone. She was rich enough to hire a small army of mercenaries and hit men. I considered calling Dave. He'd have come without hesitating and he wouldn't have blamed me if the flat was clean.

'Come off it,' I told myself. 'It's been two years. Why would she come back now?'

I slowed my pace as the glass building rose up ahead of me. It wasn't completely bathed in light, but it was close. I realised that my block and its inhabitants were just as wasteful as the pinstriped specimens in the City. In some cases, they were one and the same, although a lot of the owners were self-employed. I was probably the poorest of those. Still, I'd have to raise the issue at the next building meeting. There were far too many lights in the common areas.

Then I saw something that made me stop walking. My stomach somersaulted and my heart started to hammer. My flat was on the front and the left sides of the block, on the fourth floor. From where I was, I could see up to the left-hand rooms of my place—the kitchen and guest room. Lights had just come on in both. Jesus.

I stepped into the shadows, my eyes locked on the glass running the full height of the rooms. There were Venetian blinds and curtains in both. The former had been closed when I left. Someone had opened them before turning on the lights, which suggested it wasn't a burglar, even if one had got past the doors and alarms. It was hardly likely to be Sara or anyone else who had an interest in my demise. They'd made their presence pretty obvious. I thought of ringing Dave again. As I did, I saw a shape move across the kitchen.

Suddenly I was filled with anger. Some bastard had got into my home and was strolling around, poking his nose in my things. To hell with that. I moved forward at a trot that was soon close to a full-on sprint. I slowed as I approached the building because the perimeter camera would pick me up—as it would have my visitor—and the security firm would send a man over if it looked like the place was under assault. I punched my code into the main door and headed for the stairs. I'd only been in the lift once, and that was when I moved in—I wouldn't let the removals guys carry my precious stereo system. I glanced at my watch. My record for the four flights was 19.4 seconds. I did them in 20.2 and jogged lightly down the wide hallway.

At my door, I felt my anger weaken, but not enough to stop me sliding my key silently into the lock. I got my breathing under control, then took out my mobile and found Dave's number in the memory. If anything adverse happened, I only had to press the button and he'd be connected. He would see my number on his phone's screen and get going. The five of us had set that system up after the White Devil's death and we'd tested it several times.

I was ready. I only wished I had taken some kind of weapon with me. From now on I'd be making sure I was always armed. Three—two—one…I turned the key and pushed the door open, then ran into the living area, shouting, 'Who the fuck are you?'

'Daddy?' My daughter's voice was fearful.

When I caught a glimpse of myself in the star-shaped mirror that my editor had given me when *The Death List* reached number one, I understood why. My eyes were wide, my hair was all over the place and I looked like a chest-heaving Viking in full berserk mode.

'Em, hello, Lucy,' I said, exhaling and looking around.

'What happened?' she asked. 'You frightened me.'

I squatted down and opened my arms, as I'd done since she started walking.

After a pause, she ran into my embrace. Eleven wasn't so old after all. I breathed in the scent of her hair and felt the warmth of her against my chest.

'What are you doing here?' I felt like a complete jackass. The only person apart from Karen who had a key, and knew the entry and alarm codes, was my ex-wife,

Caroline. I heard the toilet next to the kitchen flush. Any second now, she would be loose.

'I...I was lonely,' Lucy said, clutching me. 'I wanted to see you, Daddy.'

'But I'll be seeing you tomorrow,' I said.

The door opened and Caroline walked out, shaking her hands. 'Oh, there you are,' she said to me, as if I didn't belong in my own home. 'The towel in there needs changing.'

I stood up and bit back on the sarcastic response. No fighting in front of Lucy was the rule, though it had been broken far too often. 'Nice to see you, Caroline,' I said. 'Just out of interest, what are you doing here?'

'Didn't Lucy tell you?' she said, walking past us. 'She wanted to see you. For once, I gave in to her demands. It is a Friday evening, after all, and we were at a concert at the Festival Hall.' She moved her head round in a theatrical way. 'What on earth do you do with all this space?'

'Play cricket in it,' I said, provoking a snigger from my daughter, who had a wicked sense of humour. Unlike her mother. 'Did you forget the arrangement?'

Caroline was a hotshot economist with a Japanese bank in the City. She didn't forget anything, apart from the fact that she once loved me. 'I called you, Matt. Several times. You didn't answer.'

'I was on the Tube,' I said. 'It didn't occur to you to leave a message?'

'Oh, for goodness' sake, what difference does it make?' she demanded, tossing her black hair. She was still quite a looker but, according to Lucy, she didn't have a 'boyfriend', at least not one she brought home. Maybe she took them to a hotel during her lunch break and ate them.

'Absolutely none at all,' I said, aware that any mention

of Sara or the White Devil, in any language, would cause a meltdown. I smiled at my daughter. 'Well, now you're here, do you fancy a fizzy drink?'

Lucy nodded and ran to the fridge.

'Bloody hell, Caro,' I said, under my breath. 'Make sure you do leave a message the next time. What would you have done if Karen had walked in? She quite often gets here before me.'

'That's hardly my problem,' she said, looking away.

It was then that I realised I'd called her by the diminutive I'd used when we were in love. It must have been six or seven years since I'd last come out with it. I felt about as uncomfortable as a man can with his ex-wife. God knows how Karen would have reacted to this accidental intimacy. I wasn't going to tell her, but Caroline might find a way.

When Lucy came back with her glass, I took her over to the small desk where she kept her things. For weeks we'd been playing an interminable board game involving Sherlock Holmes and a group of anarchists kitted out with round bombs and lit fuses. Unfortunately, they'd never managed to reduce the game to small pieces.

After half an hour, Lucy started to yawn. I grabbed the opportunity.

'Come on, Luce. How about the zoo tomorrow?'

'Oh yes, Daddy,' she said, clapping her hands. Fortunately she didn't demand more time with the anarchy game.

Caroline was curled up on one of the long leather sofas. I looked down at her and saw the face I'd awoken next to countless times. When she was at rest, her skin was as smooth and her forehead as unfurrowed as they'd ever been. Obviously working in international finance was good for you. I wished I'd aged as well. I'd just turned forty-one and the grey hairs had established themselves for good, and not just on my head.

Then Caroline woke up and immediately frowned at me, as if I'd been molesting her with Lucy in the room.

'Come on, darling,' she said, sitting up. 'It's time we went back to our hovel.'

Lucy mouthed the last word at me after her mother walked past her.

I raised my shoulders. Caroline had bought a four-bedroom house that had been refurbished to almost regal standards by its previous owner, an award-winning architect, so I had no idea what she was complaining about. Well, I did. She thought money earned from frivolous activities like writing had less value than that gained from real work like banking. There was a time, when my early novels were flying and she was struggling to get back into her career after Lucy was born, that she'd been glad enough for literary money. That was another thing that had been erased from her memory.

I kissed Lucy, and called goodnight to Caroline down the hall. Then, after waiting in vain for an answer, I closed the door and went for my computer.

Maybe I had mail.

I was also spoiling for a fight.

4

The woman moved with catlike poise across the carpet of the room, the cold steel of the silver pistol against her cheek. She stood in front of the mirror and looked at her face. For a few moments, it was a stranger who stared back at her. Then she remembered what she'd become and smiled. She was no longer Sara Robbins. She had changed her name, her appearance, her very nature.

The hotel near Victoria Station was cheap, most of its residents being tourists from the U.S. and Australia on budget holidays. They only stayed a few days before moving on to other cities on the modern Grand Tour—Edinburgh, Paris, Berlin—spectral cities filled with memories of slaughter, medieval and modern. But she was here for the duration, had already been in residence for two weeks, preparing, checking, and carrying out the most subtle of surveillance. She'd learned the trade from masters, men who slipped unseen through streets and across squares, their weapons never more than a finger's length away.

Soon she would strike the first blow in the city so large that she could disappear at will into its backstreets and lanes, its underground tunnels and its spacious, forested parks. They would not find her, unless she made the most egregious of errors. That would not happen. Her brother had trained her well. He'd also left a directory of former CIA and Special Forces operatives, and they had completed her education in the arts of deception and death. The White Devil, her brother and lover, would have been so proud.

And yet, she didn't miss him, at least not in the sense that he was absent. Rather, she felt his presence in everything that she did. He was with her, though not as some spook at her shoulder. He was inside her—he had penetrated every cell and organ of her body, his mind was in hers.

She had felt that from the beginning, when he'd made himself known to her before his great scheme was put into action. And after his passing, she had felt it even more, the possession—not that his soul possessed her, but rather that their twin souls possessed each other. There was never any inequality. The White Devil had treated her as his partner from the start, his partner and his shared destiny. That destiny still awaited them, but her brother could now only experience it through her eyes and ears, her mouth and nose, her touch, while the man responsible for his death was still alive. That fact filled her veins with burning fire and drove her every action. She would destroy Matt Wells, but first she would turn him into a quivering wreck.

Standing at the window and looking through the gap between the dirty grey curtains, the woman took in the people on the street below. It was raining and they were walking quickly, even those with umbrellas. The early morning cloud cover and muted lights blurred everything, making the lines between cars and people indistinct. It was a semi-liquid landscape, one poisoned by exhaust gases and the fumes from boilers and pumps. A man-made hell…

…and suddenly she was back in the jungle of Colombia, a hell of nature's creation, her throat burning and the rotting vegetation making her stomach heave. She made sure her guide didn't notice that. They were under a kilometre from the target and soon all her concentration would have to be on the job. This would be her first major kill and she felt her brother inside her, urging her forward. He had made a file on the target, checked all the data personally. It was six months since he'd been executed in London. She had spent four of them being trained by different experts— unarmed combat, the use of weapons, covert procedures, advanced computing skills and the mechanics of international finance. Let loose on the world, she had already killed a pusher in Atlanta, a pair of crackheads in Jacksonville and a scumbag who had tried to rape her in the washroom of a bar in Miami. Those murders had been of her own choosing, as the White Devil had suggested in order to build her confidence. But only by hitting major players would she prove her real worth.

Pedro 'El Loco' Camargo called himself a guerrilla leader, but the reality was that he ran the area's cocaine production, treated the workers as slaves and took any girl he wanted to his bed. His private army, the so-called Golden Liberation Fighters, lorded over the villages and shot anyone who showed disobedience or disrespect. The organisation was rotten from head to toe. And she was here to remove that head.

El Loco, led astray by the typical dictator's delusion that his people loved him, allowed them to pay court every Saturday. The men and women who had aired their grievances at the first such reception were found soon afterwards with their throats cut and their faces unrecognisable.

Since then, the GLF had been forcing workers to present themselves and laud their leader.

'Remember, there will be fighters all around,' said her guide, Esteban, when they reached the tree line. He was a former sidekick of El Loco, but had been bought off by Sara's brother before his death. 'But they will be drunk and drugged up. My people are ready. As soon as you strike, they will deal with the whores' sons.'

The woman wondered, not for the first time, why Esteban's supporters had not taken the apparently simple step themselves. But she dismissed the thought, content to do her brother's will, even if the Colombian was temporarily taking advantage of her. She unslung her pack and took out tattered peasant woman's clothes. She caught Esteban's eye as she was undoing her trousers. He turned away quickly when he saw the look on her face.

After that, it was easy. She had to stand in line with the sweating, broken people, her head bent and her steps as unsteady as theirs. The long, black wig she was wearing, along with the dirt she had rubbed on to her face, arms and legs, made her inconspicuous. As she got closer to El Loco, she glanced left and right. Heavily armed men were leaning against the walls of what used to be the village school, their eyes bloodshot and vacant. They saw her, but they didn't see what she was. That meant they'd enjoyed running their hands all over her in a fruitless search for weapons.

Now she was inside—more men with Kalashnikovs and American weapons, the smell of fear and destitution more noisome. The man in front of her launched into a lengthy tribute to his master. After five minutes, Camargo, a tall, bearded man who had run to fat, nodded and the talkative man was hustled away by two GLF men. It was her turn.

She kept her head low as she stepped up to the metal chair that had been placed on the platform. She didn't know much Spanish, but she understood that El Loco was asking what she wanted to say. It was then that she looked up and gave him a smile that suggested everything she might give him. El Loco beckoned to her and she stepped on to the platform, leaned close and, in the split-second it took to pull the inch-long blade from the wooden cross round her neck, realised that her heart rate hadn't increased at all. If anything, it had slowed. The training routines had become second nature.

Camargo was grinning at her, his lips wet. Then his eyelids jerked wide apart as she buried the razor-sharp blade into his neck two centimetres above and to the left of his Adam's apple. As she moved quickly behind the chair, she grabbed the greasy hair beneath the wide-peaked officer's cap, pulled his head back and ripped the blade to the right. As she ducked down, she saw a fine spray of crimson fill the air above the next man in the line.

Immediately there was an explosion of automatic weapon fire and a welter of screaming. She stayed down, her arms over her head, but she had no fear. After a time, the firing moved outside and there was less noise from the people in the building. As she looked out from beneath Camargo's chair, she saw why. The place was full of bodies, both of GLF men and of the innocent.

The woman heard Esteban's voice. He was telling her that it was over. She snaked an arm round El Loco's body and removed a silver-plated semi-automatic pistol from his belt. She racked the slide and held the weapon in a two-handed grip as she slowly stood up. Esteban lowered his own pistol when he saw the way she was looking at him.

'Okay,' he said, with a slack smile. 'It is okay, devil-woman.'

She gave him a tight smile and then fired two shots into Pedro Camargo's groin.

The few remaining villagers in the school cheered. As she walked out, they clapped their hands. The woman ignored them. The only approbation she needed was from the soul that had merged with her own.

…she blinked and was back in London, the damp in the streets much colder than those of Colombia. But she had never forgotten that big killing, when she had first felt the attraction of silver-coloured weapons. She owned several now. It was also then that she had turned herself into the Soul Collector, on behalf of the precious soul inside her very being.

There were several to be gathered in England, and soon Matt Wells's time on the earth would be over. But there was a world of pain for him to endure first.

I woke up to the sound of the telephone. The display told me it was nine-thirty.

'Yeah?' I mumbled.

'Hello, dear. Late night?'

'Hello, Fran. What's up?' Fran was my adoptive mother and had encouraged me to call her by her first name since I went to senior school. The White Devil and his sister had also been adopted, and that was one reason that he had chosen me as his fall-guy. But he had forced his mother into a sexual relationship, while I had only the standard feelings of a dutiful son for Fran.

'Why does anything have to be up for me to call my son and heir?'

'Um, right. Full of the joys of spring, are we?' I swung my legs out of bed and reached for my robe. I had a flash of my ex-wife's face and remembered her visit from the night before. That made me groan.

'What is it, dear?'

'Nothing,' I said quickly. I could have told her about the fright Caroline had given me, but she would just have started on a rant about how she'd never been right for me and that I'd got married far too young. I usually pointed out that she wouldn't have had a granddaughter if I'd stayed single, which invariably tested her saintlike patience.

'You aren't very talkative this morning,' my mother observed.

'No,' I said, turning on the laptop and logging on to the e-mail programme. I had a burning need to see if I'd received any messages from the woman who had threatened vengeance upon me after the White Devil's death.

'I wanted to talk to you about Mary Malone.'

Having seen that there were no messages from unknown senders, I was checking my family's and friends' confirmations.

'Did you hear me, Matt?'

"Mm." Everyone was okay. 'Sorry, you were saying about Mary Malone.'

'Yes, dear,' Fran said, with a long-suffering sigh. 'You really can be infuriating sometimes. I suppose you're checking that everyone's all right.'

'Yup,' I said, irritated that she could read me so easily.

'I presume they are,' she continued. 'So, Mary Malone.'

'I never met her, Mother. None of us in the crime fiction world did. She was a loner. What's *your* interest?'

'You've forgotten that I'm a member of the Crime Writers' Society too.'

'What's that got to do with anything?' I asked testily.

'Well, if there's going to be a rash of crime novelists being killed, I'd like to know in advance.'

I rubbed the sleep from my eyes. 'Who said anything about a rash?'

'Oh, you know how the papers like to gossip. Has Karen taken the case on?'

'Speaking of gossip,' I said.

'Don't take that tone, Matt. I'm serious.'

'Mother, you wrote three thrillers for teenagers back in the seventies. I hardly think you'll be on the top of the hit list. There may not even be a hit list. It's *gossip*. And only one person has died. How's that a *rash?*'

'Come on,' she scoffed. 'That Rolling Stones song playing and the killer parading in a cape and top hat—don't tell me that isn't suggestive of an organised individual with an agenda.'

'Well, I bow to your superior knowledge,' I said, heading for the kitchen and a litre of orange juice to rehydrate my failing system.

'Has it even occurred to you that I might be frightened?' she asked, with a partially suppressed sob.

That stopped me in my tracks. 'Christ, I'm sorry, Mother. Do you want me to come over?'

'No, it's all right, dear. I know you have Lucy today.'

Shit. I'd forgotten about my daughter. I changed direction and went towards the shower.

'Surely it must have crossed your mind that…that Sara was behind the murder?'

'Em, yes, it did, Mother. But there hasn't been any

message or other form of contact, and everybody on my list has reported in on the last two mornings.'

'You still haven't told me if Karen's working the case.'

'Sorry. No, she isn't. She was called in to take a look, but the local detectives are still in charge, as far as I know.'

'All right, dear. Let me know if you hear anything I should know.'

'Okay, will do. I've got to dash now. 'Bye.'

''Bye,' she repeated, her voice weak.

I twitched my head and chucked the phone on to one of the sofas. Fran lived on her own and was a successful children's author. I hadn't heard her so concerned since the White Devil case. The bastard kidnapped her and kept her tied up for days. Mary Malone's death must have stirred up bad memories for her. She wasn't the only one.

Remembering that Lucy, let alone her mother, expected me at ten, I rushed my shave, leaving cuts that stung like hell when I had a shower. As I came out, I heard the phone ring. This time it was the special line that I used only for my mates. I dripped water over the carpet as I ran to my desk.

'Hello,' I said, panting.

'Morning, lad.' It was Dave Cummings. I registered immediately that there was something odd about his voice. 'Nice weather if you're a penguin.' The hairs rose on the back of my neck. We'd set up a series of code words in the event that Sara, or anyone else, put the squeeze on us. Between Dave and me, anything to do with nice weather meant that the speaker was in immediate physical danger.

'Yeah,' I said, trying to keep my tone even. 'What's—'

The call was terminated.

'Shit!' I yelled. After all this time, was the nightmare really starting again? I called Andy, Rog and Pete and told them what had happened. They knew what to do. Then I ran to the bedroom and changed clothes—black cargo pants with numerous pockets, a black denim jacket and boots. I called Caroline and told her something had come up. She understood from my tone that it was serious. I told her to follow plan C, which meant that she should take Lucy, drive up to my mother's house in Muswell Hill, collect her and head for the M25; she was then to drive round the motorway in a clockwise direction until she heard from me again. Caroline knew the drill and she also knew that the line might be tapped. She still managed to make it sound like it was all my fault—which, in a way, of course, it was, but I didn't have time to think about that now. I should have called Karen too, but my friends and I needed a free hand at this stage. The police would only get in the way and maybe put Dave in worse jeopardy.

I parted the hanging clothes in the walk-in wardrobe and pulled up the carpet. The floorboards looked normal, but by pressing the top right corner I released a catch that opened a foot-square panel. From the hole beneath, I removed a nine-millimetre Glock 19 and silencer, two nine-round clips, a set of knuckle-dusters and a sheathed Glock 78 field knife. I also removed my walkie-talkie and headset from the charger in the hole. Karen would have had a fit if she'd found my gear.

Dave Cummings had spent the last two years teaching me and the others how to behave like soldiers. Now I had to prove that I'd been a good pupil.

'Hello, Karen.'

'Guv.' Oaten shook the hand extended by Detective Superintendent Ron Paskin of Homicide Division East. He was her ex-boss. They were both in white coveralls and overshoes. 'I'm surprised to see you down here.'

'Mm.' Paskin was a grizzled bull of a man, who had a reputation for being hard but fair, both with criminals and his subordinates. 'I'll get merry hell from the wife. Normally we spend Saturday mornings at the supermarket.' He lifted the barrier tape and led her down the lane from the black people-carrier. A tent had been erected over it and the surrounding area. CSIs were coming and going, two of their vans on the pavement to the rear.

'As you know, there's been some shit going down among the various Turkish gangs, particularly the Shadows,' the superintendent said, his voice low. 'But this fellow is a Kurd, a pretty small-time member of the King's family.'

Oaten chewed her lip, then remembered Inspector Neville's habit of doing that and stopped. 'Do you think the Turks and Kurds are building toward an all-out war?'

Paskin took a deep breath. 'If they are, it'll be the first we've heard of it,' he said, expelling the air from his barrel chest. 'You know how it is on the streets. The small guys play tough, but the bosses are happy enough with the status quo. They all know that they can't have everything and they prefer to get what they can with a reasonable degree of security.'

'How about the Albanians?' Oaten suggested. 'They've been growing their operations recently.'

'Possible,' the superintendent admitted. 'They're the kind to gut a man, too. But we haven't had a whisper from our snouts. You?'

She shook her head. 'Not about this area. They've really got a grip on Soho now, much to the disgust of the Chinese, and they've been making inroads into Bayswater and the knocking-shops around Paddington. But out here, no.'

'Still,' Paskin said, 'it could be a splinter group from any number of nationalities. If anyone can wrest the heroin trade from the Turks and Kurds, they'll own the city—the whole of southeast England, in fact.'

Oaten nodded. 'So what happened here?' She saw John Turner, in a white coverall, come out of the tent. He didn't look a well man.

'As I said, the victim was gutted with a long-bladed knife, which was taken from the scene, probably by the killer—though you never know what kids will pick up around here. His name's Nedim Zinar. He was a big man, over six feet, and the doc thinks a smaller guy did for him. The wound suggests that the initial thrust was between the groin and the navel.'

'Delightful. Did you know him?'

The superintendent nodded. 'He was a friendly type for an enforcer—had a gang of kids. Mind you, though he'd been in the game for at least fifteen years, he wasn't much more than standard muscle. If you wanted to make an example, he wouldn't be your man. Then again, he was an easy target. From what I've heard, he parked his car here every night and supervised the locking up of a shop down Lower Clapton Road.'

'Did he have a record?'

'Only minor stuff when he was younger—a bit of thieving. I seem to remember he broke a guy's jaw outside one of the King's clubs, but he got off on self-defence.'

Oaten glanced at the tent. 'I suppose I'd better have a look,' she said, without much enthusiasm.

'Suit yourself,' said Paskin. 'Oh, there's one thing that you won't find.'

'What's that?'

'Tough guys like him carry a weapon. The CSIs found three full clips of nine-millimetre Parabellum rounds in a stash-box under one of the rear seats.'

'Shit. That means one more handgun on the streets of London.'

'Correct, Karen.' Ron Paskin smiled at her. 'Still, you high-fliers in the VCCT must be used to that kind of thing.'

Karen Oaten knew her former boss was only teasing, unlike most of the other divisional officers she came across. 'Oh, we get all sorts of weapons. Including knives.'

'Does that mean you're going to take over this case?'

'It almost sounds like you want me to.'

'Well, we're as snowed under as ever.'

'Ditto. I don't see any reason for us to come in yet, but we'll keep an eye on your reports. What about that Turk who was killed the other day? Could this be a revenge hit?'

The superintendent's brow furrowed. 'Maybe. Again, I doubt they'd have gone for someone as minor as Zinar.'

The chief inspector nodded. 'You know that if I can conclusively tie this murder to another one inside or outside your division, I'll have to take it.'

Paskin nodded. 'No problem.' He inclined his head towards John Turner. 'How's Taff doing?'

'Good. He's been my right-hand man ever since we were transferred.'

'His face looks like a three-day-old piece of cod. He obviously still has that aversion to dead people.'

Oaten watched her subordinate as he spoke to one of the local detectives, taking notes studiously. 'I sometimes wish I hadn't got so inured to the results of violence. I think Taff's more of a normal human being than I am.'

Paskin nudged her. 'Steady on, girl. You've got as far as

you have because you can shut off your emotions. I don't see Taff ever running things like you do.' He took another deep breath, and then expelled it forcefully. 'Christ, this lane stinks. Hell of a place to die.'

'Hell of a way to die, too,' Oaten added.

'Could have been worse,' the superintendent said, lighting a cheroot. 'He could have had his head chopped off, like that victim in your first big case with the VCCT. The White Devil was really something, wasn't he?'

Karen Oaten nodded. 'He certainly was. East End boy, as well.'

Paskin grinned, showing teeth stained by countless cigars. 'We have a long tradition of master criminals here. What was the name of that writer-fellow the killer targeted?'

'Matt Wells.' Karen wasn't sure if Paskin knew of their relationship. He might have heard on the grapevine, but it wasn't in his nature to pay attention to innuendo.

'There was a sister too, wasn't there?'

She nodded.

'If she's anything like that callous bastard, let's hope she doesn't resurface.'

'Here's hoping indeed.' The chief inspector stuck out her hand. 'Good to see you again, guv. Take care. You mustn't have long to go till retirement.'

'Three months,' he said with a smile.

'What are you going to do?'

'We've got a cottage in Brittany. I can't understand a word the locals say, but the food's a sight better than what the wife comes up with these days. Nothing but bloody salad…'

Karen waved her arm as she headed for Taff. She wasn't looking forward to examining the body. She'd been on edge all morning and her stomach was still upset. Chewing antacid tablets had only made her feel more queasy.

If she was lucky, the villains of London would give her the weekend off. But she wasn't counting on that.

The acrid smoke that rose from the altar made the supplicant's eyes sting and his throat burn, before it was carried away on the air current above the subterranean river. The walls were covered with frescoes depicting demons and the landscape of hell.

'Does the offering please you, Mephistopheles?'

'It is not I who must be satisfied, Faustus,' the cowled figure with the white mask said, watching the flames die down. 'There is another who receives the hair and nails of our victims with relish.'

'And…and the ear?'

Mephistopheles laughed. 'I have added it to our collection, fear not.'

The supplicant stood up slowly, licking his lips nervously. The masked figure seemed to be alone, so Faustus allowed himself to relax.

Then, with a high-pitched snarl, the beast came bounding across the cave floor, his jaws wide apart and the yellowed incisors bared.

Faustus forced himself to stand firm. At least the mandrill called Beelzebub did what his master told him. There was a human animal, thankfully not present tonight, who had begun to find their activities insufficiently visceral. Faustus swallowed hard and steeled himself. He could kill as well as anyone else and the Lord Beneath the Earth knew that.

5

I parked my black Saab 9-3 sport saloon at the designated rendezvous two streets away from Dave's house in North Dulwich. Roger van Zandt and Peter Satterthwaite were waiting for me in the latter's Grand Cherokee. A minute later, Andy Jackson arrived on his new 600 c.c. Hornet. We all got into the Cherokee to prepare.

'Any idea where Ginny and the kids are?' I asked.

'Yeah,' Andy said. 'Dave said they were going to visit her aunt today. He was going to spend the morning cooking lobster.'

'So he was on his own in the house,' Rog said. 'The place is like a fortress. How could anyone get in?'

Pete glanced in the rear-view mirror. 'Maybe the entry we're going to use isn't as hidden as Dave thought.'

As I was the one who was going to be using that entry first, Bonehead's comment didn't make me feel great.

Rog turned round. 'Did you call him back, Wellsy?'

'Several times, and on his mobile. The messaging service cut in both times. I wasn't going to identify myself.'

'What do you mean?' Andy demanded. 'Whoever's got him will know he called you.'

I shook my head. 'Cool it, guys. We talked about this

when we set the reporting system up. He called me, which suggests he was free at that time. Maybe he saw trouble coming.'

'What, up the garden path?' Pete said. 'If he was on his own, he wouldn't have used the code.'

'He might have,' I replied, 'If he suspected his line was being tapped or his mobile frequency scanned. Anyway, that's what we're here to find out. Let's get geared up.'

We each made sure our phones were switched to vibrate and checked our weapons—we all had the same pistols, knives and knuckle dusters. In the quiet time after the White Devil's death, Dave had encountered some piss-taking because of his insistence that we carry such heavy-duty weapons when the alert codes were used. Now I could see he'd been right. There could have been a squad of hard men hired by Sara in his spacious house.

'What about silencers?' Pete asked.

'The book says put 'em on,' Andy replied. He was referring to the operations manual Dave had given each of us.

'The problem is, the Glock doesn't fit in a pocket when it's that long,' Rog said. He shrugged and screwed his silencer on when he saw the way Andy was looking at him. Slash had spent a couple of deeply unhappy years in the Marine Corps, but at least he'd learned to accept orders—when he agreed with them.

'You're taking the rifle, aren't you, Boney?' I said.

He nodded. Dave had obtained a Walther WA2000 sniper's rifle with Schmidt and Bender telescopic sights from the same dodgy East London arms dealer who had supplied our pistols and silencers. Pete was the best shot apart from Dave, so he got the big gun, which was actually shorter than an ordinary rifle and fitted into a tennis player's bag.

'Okay,' I said, 'we'll play this by the book, as Slash said.' I opened the copy that Pete handed me; I'd forgotten my own in the rush to leave home. 'Rog, you're on the front, behind the inner hedge and by the garages.'

Dave's house was detached and surrounded by tall trees and thick bushes. I once asked him how he could afford it on an Army pension, even one augmented by First Gulf War and SAS service. He laughed and told me that his wife had inherited a shed-load of money from a spinster aunt.

'Pete, you cut down the path that runs along the far end of his garden.' I pointed on the map Dave had drawn.

'I remember,' Bonehead said. 'Dave showed me. The neighbours can't see me and I can cover all the rear windows.'

'Right,' I said. 'If there's a lot of people inside and we get desperate, we'll try to get to the back of the house.'

'Yeah,' said Andy. 'Just make sure you don't drill us.' He pointed to his blonde hair. 'This is me.'

Rog finished with his Glock, and turned to Andy and me. 'Are you both going in? The book leaves that optional.'

I looked at the American. 'What do you think?'

He shrugged. 'I'll hoist you in and we'll take it from there. You all got your walkie-talkies?'

Dave had insisted that we each buy an identical good-quality walkie-talkie. We were each responsible for ensuring the batteries were permanently charged, and I was glad to see that they'd all fulfilled that requirement. The units fitted to our belts and we each had a mini headset with an earpiece and a microphone that lay across one cheek like a duelling scar.

'We'll test 'em after we've split up,' Andy said.

'Uh, what do we do if someone spots us?' Rog asked. He would be in the most obvious position.

'Say you're a telecom engineer checking radiation levels,' I said. 'That should get them moving on.'

'You're joking,' he said, his brow lined. 'Aren't you?'

Pete raised a finger. 'Remember what Dave always says. When the book doesn't tell you what to do…'

'Improvise,' we all chorused. The number of times Dave had been mocked about that was huge.

'What if you two both go in and we don't hear from you?' Boney asked.

'If we don't come out after half an hour, you call the cops,' I said. 'You've both got Karen's number, haven't you?'

They nodded.

'Why don't we call them now?' Rog asked.

'Because Dave used the alert code for us,' I said. 'And we know from our White Devil experiences that we're the only people who can look after each other.' I saw their expressions change when I mentioned the monster's name.

'Come on,' Andy said, adjusting his microphone. 'We were trained by the best. We can handle this.' He glanced at each of us. 'Let's go and get the man.'

Trust Slash to look keen. The rest of us tried to match him, with varying degrees of success.

'Watches, guys,' I said. 'I've got 10.42. Check?'

'Check,' the others replied, after some tweaking.

'Right, communications check in ten minutes,' I said. 'Go, Pete.'

He had the furthest to walk and set off at a rapid pace, the bag with its lethal contents on his right shoulder. We gave him five minutes.

'Rog, go,' I said.

After two minutes, Andy and I moved off. There was

no point in splitting up. If anyone asked what we were doing, I'd say we were friends of Dave's from the Army. At least we looked the part.

'Breathing steady,' I whispered, under my breath. 'Concentration. Be aware of what's happening around you. Control the adrenaline rush.' That was easier said than done. Andy looked relaxed enough. I pulled a balaclava down my forehead, covering the headset straps.

No one was out on the pavements. We turned rapidly onto the path that ran down the right side of Dave's house. There were no cars in the drive and the garage doors were shut.

'In position?' I said quietly into my mike.

'Confirmed,' came Roger's voice, then Pete's.

'Take this as the comms check,' Andy said. 'Confirmed.'

'Any sign of Dave from where you are?' I asked.

'Negative,' said Rog. 'Curtains on the front are all open, except in the sitting room. No movement.'

'All the curtains at the rear of the house are open,' Bonehead said. 'No sign of anyone.'

I looked at Andy. 'Why are the sitting-room curtains closed?'

He raised his shoulders. 'Let's go and find out.' He squeezed my arm. 'Steady, my man.'

I checked my Glock one last time and slipped it back under my belt. The silencer jutted out and I hoped the automatic's trigger safety was as reliable as the manufacturers claimed.

Then I gave Andy a nervous smile. 'Okay,' I said, taking a deep breath. 'Here we go.'

I reached up towards the small window.

* * *

Karen Oaten drove to New Scotland Yard. There were only a few members of her team working the weekend shift. She sat down to clear the backlog of administration work, but found herself thinking about the latest spate of killings. One of the problems she had running a unit that pulled together violent crime from all over the city was keeping in check the tendency to link everything together. It was perfectly possible that the shooting of the Turk and the knife attack on the Kurd were unconnected, just as the overwhelming likelihood was that the murder of the crime writer had nothing to do with those in East London. But still, she found herself trying to make at least some connection between the deaths. That was the curse of the VCCT.

It didn't help that there was very little to go on with the shooting of the Turk. Mehmet Saka, a twenty-three-year-old, was suspected of being a heroin deliveryman. He'd been gunned down in broad daylight outside a betting shop in Stepney, taking five bullets in his chest. Witnesses had been hard to find, and no one had noted the number of the car that carried the shooter. There were even varying reports of its colour and make, ranging from a black Audi 6 to a dark-green Citröen Xsara. The bottom line was that people developed very selective memories when it came to identifying gang members. They were swift to exact harsh retribution and there was no point in pulling in known gang members, as the gangs' versions of *omerta* were just as tight as the original. Homicide East hadn't even been able to tempt the Turks themselves to talk, which was hardly surprising if they'd been responsible for the subsequent murder of Nedim Zinar. Then again, maybe the Kurd had just slighted someone. That was one of the few characteristics shared by Turks, Kurds, Greek Cypriots, Albanians and Jamaican Yardies, as well as the long-standing local East End gangs—losing face was totally unacceptable.

Oaten moved on to the latest update from the Mary Malone murder. No other witnesses to a figure in a black cape and top hat had been found. DI Neville surmised that the killer either had a car parked further down the street or had managed to change clothes somewhere nearby after the attack.

The chief inspector's mobile rang. It was her boss, the Assistant Commissioner.

'I'm in the office, sir.'

'Admirable, Chief Inspector,' he said drily. 'I'm expected to play golf with the commander of the Flying Squad, would you believe?' The Assistant Commissioner resented every minute he had to spend away from his desk. 'Update me, please.'

She gave him a run-down of the Saka and Zinar murders.

'And your recommendation?' the AC asked.

'To leave them with Homicide East. I'll make sure we see the daily case-file updates. If there's any link, I'll take them over.'

'Very well. Now, what about the crime novelist?'

She told him where Homicide West had reached.

'That doesn't sound very impressive,' he said. 'Don't you think we should intervene?'

'Do you mean because of the potential connection to the White Devil case?'

'I mean exactly that.'

Karen thought about it. If she took over the case, the spotlight would inevitably fall on Matt. He was already worried that Sara might be back, even though there was no direct evidence. Then again, she hadn't heard from him today.

'Tell me honestly, Karen,' he said. 'Do you think it's the start of a series?'

She pursed her lips. How the hell was she supposed to know that? 'It could be, sir,' she replied, hedging her bets.

'How do you want to play it? The newspapers are having a field day. It would calm things down if they knew the VCCT was on it. We might scare the killer into backing off.'

Oaten raised her eyes to the ceiling. The AC had been in the alternative reality inhabited by senior ranks for far too long. 'I doubt it, sir. How about we leave it with Homicide West for the time being? If there's another murder, we'll take over.'

Her boss considered that for a long time. 'You're not losing your appetite for messy cases, are you, DCI Oaten?'

Karen felt her cheeks redden. 'Certainly not, sir. You have no reason to suppose that.'

The AC was taken aback by her tone. 'No, of course not. I apologise. Very well, do it your way. Let's hope it's a one-off.' He cut the connection.

'Tosser!' Oaten yelled.

John Turner put his head round her door. 'Not me, I hope, guv?'

She glared at him. 'Why? Have you got something to be guilty about?'

The Welshman shrugged. He knew better than to cross swords with his boss when she was in a temper. 'I just had Neville the Lip on the phone. He couldn't get through to you.'

'Because I was talking to the idiot on the golf course,' Oaten said, shaking her head until curiosity got the better of her. 'Have they got something?'

'It isn't good news. Still nobody else in Ifield Road who saw the figure in the cape and top hat.'

'Oh, great.'

'That's not all. The rubbish was collected early this morning.'

'What, Neville didn't seal the street?'

'Apparently not well enough.'

'For pity's sake.'

'So the killer could have dumped the fancy costume in any of the bins on the street and walked off into the night. There's no sign of anyone dressed like that on the recordings at Fulham Broadway station. Homicide West is following up the owners of cars that showed on the local traffic-control cameras, but so far they all have cast-iron alibis.'

Karen Oaten leaned back in her chair. 'What interests me is why the killer chose a novelist as the victim, Taff. Is Neville doing any work on that?'

'They've been checking her e-mails for signs of a stalker or the like. Nothing so far.' The Welshman caught his superior's eye. 'You should be getting background on her from your…from Matt Wells.' He failed to keep his disapproval of Oaten's partner from his voice.

She gave him a sour look. 'I'm working on that. What are you doing here, anyway? You should be at home with your kids.'

'I'm on my way, unless you've got anything for me.'

Karen Oaten shook her head. 'Have a good one.'

'You too, guv.'

As soon as Turner had left her office, she called Matt. She got the messaging service on his land line and mobile. She was about to call the ex-directory number that only she and his close circle had when she remembered that he was to have had Lucy today.

Karen settled back to the heap of files, and hoped that there were no more murders—at least until after the weekend.

I felt around for the security lock that Dave had fitted to the outside of the window for exactly this eventuality. The hole was concealed by a blob of putty the same shade of pale grey as the paint on the frame. Only Rog, Andy, Pete and I had extra keys. When I finally located and cleared it, I inserted the key and turned it until the window was loose. Then I pushed it inwards, slowly and silently. I turned and nodded to Andy. He cupped his hands and, after I'd put one foot in them, lifted me smoothly upwards. Moving carefully, I put my hands through the open window and dragged my stomach over the ledge with Andy's help. For a moment I went into a partial dive, but I stopped the fall when my hands hit the floor. I stayed in that position until the muscles in my arms began to burn, listening. I heard nothing. I walked forward on my palms before bringing my legs in and letting my feet slide gradually to the floor. I was in. Then I felt a vibration in my pocket. I pulled my phone out and saw that it was Karen's office number. I knew she'd call at some stage to arrange the evening, but this was hardly the best moment. I let it ring out.

I moved forward and stood at the pantry door for a full two minutes. I still couldn't hear anything. That wasn't good news. Either Dave had been taken away, or he was the bait in a trap. I stopped myself from thinking about the other possibilities.

'Okay,' I said to Andy.

He heaved himself up with ease and was soon standing beside me.

'There's no noise,' I whispered.

He nodded, and then took the silenced Glock from his belt. I followed suit.

'Go for it,' Andy said, his eyes narrowed.

I opened the door slowly—it was always deliberately left an inch ajar by Dave and his family so we could get in without making undue noise. I looked around. There was no one in the kitchen. Holding the automatic in two hands, I walked very slowly down the carpeted hall. On my left was the dining room. Looking cautiously round the door frame, I quickly established that no one was inside. On my right was the sitting room. The door was a couple of inches open. Through the gap I could see no occupants, but most of the room was out of sight.

My heart began to pound and I took several deep breaths again. I turned to Andy. He pointed to his chest, meaning did I want him to go first? I shook my head. That was my job. I was the one who'd brought Dave into danger and I owed it to him to get him out of trouble now. I steeled myself and pushed the door hard and swung around it into the room, Glock raised.

I felt my mouth open as I took in the scene. I sank to my knees, unable to speak or scream and blinded by tears.

6

The Soul Collector took off all her clothes—what an inspiration the disguise had been—and stood naked in the cheap hotel room. There was a mirror near the bathroom door and she studied herself in it. Some mornings she still didn't recognise what she saw, but this wasn't one of them. She glanced at the watch she had removed from her coat pocket. It was coming up to eleven o'clock. Matt and his idiot friends would be at the house in Dulwich. She wondered how he would take the work of art she had left him. Badly, she was sure of that. He had always been weak, for all his claims to understand the criminal mind. That book—he would regret what he'd written about her brother and her, as would all the people he loved. Not that the ex-SAS man had shown her the pain he was undoubtedly feeling. Eventually, after he'd finally agreed to make the call to alert Matt and even managed not to sound like a man in terrible agony, she put an end to it. She admired him for that, if nothing else.

Eyes still fixed on her perfect body, the unsupported breasts firm and the lines of her face even more striking than they had been, she took off the black leather outer gloves and put them in an opaque rubbish bag. Her hands were still covered with latex, the pale grey flecked with blood that hadn't washed away in the target's sink. She stripped them off and put them in a different bag. Then she stepped gracefully on to the uneven bathroom tiles and into the battered shower cabinet. The hot water cleansed her, but the cold she stood under for much longer was what she really enjoyed. It made her skin tingle and her nipples harden. She always felt like this after "a mission"—that was what the men who'd trained her had called killings. She knew they used the euphemism to distance themselves from what they did to their fellow human beings. She had no such scruples. She killed because she was good at it and because it brought her closer to her dead brother—the brother who had also been her lover. She put her fingers between her legs, then took them away. There would be time for that later. Now she wanted to glory in what she had achieved, doused in the cold that was her natural medium.

She was thinking about other SAS men. The ex-soldier she'd just worked on had known the three who'd despatched her brother. Two years ago, she had stopped as she was fleeing from the wood-yard in East London, long enough to hear one of them ask her victim of today what he was doing there. That had been all she'd needed. Matt Wells hadn't said much about the three killers in his book, but he mentioned they had Special Forces experience and that they had pursued the White Devil because he'd killed a former comrade: Jimmy Tanner. She had heard that name before—Tanner was the drunk who'd trained her brother how to kill along with numerous other skills. He had also been one of the White Devil's earlier victims. She had salted away those pieces of information, but after she'd moved her brother's deposits into new accounts, finished her training and despatched her early targets in Latin America and the U.S., she was ready to act.

The woman had slipped into Britain by ferry from Belgium a month ago. She had a new look, identity and passport, but she'd waited for a busy and rainy day to ensure she didn't stick out from the crowd. Although every immigration officer in the country would have a photo and description of Sara Robbins in their laptops, she hadn't been recognised under her new name and guise. That gave her confidence for the murders ahead; no point in wasting time calling them *missions*.

She'd passed a hundred pounds to a publican in Brighton and was given contact numbers. A homely woman with two squealing kids had provided her with a driving licence that would stand computer scrutiny. A man with rat's-tail hair had sold her a brand-new Heckler and Koch U.S.P., a silencer and a hundred nine-millimetre cartridges; he even threw in a Spyderco C36 military knife with a black blade for free. Then she'd paid cash for a common-as-dirt white van she'd seen in a dealer's yard in Southampton. Her adoptive father had been a farmer and he had taught her about the workings of cars and tractors— she could tell in five minutes that the van was adequate. She'd taped over the rear windows and put a mattress and sleeping bag in the back with her bike, a red metallic XL650V Transalp.

Dave Cummings had been easy. She'd been sure Matt and his friends would have alarms on their houses. They would also have set up alert codes to be used if any of them were under threat. From the van, she had studied the movements of the burly demolition expert and his family. She'd considered murdering them all and leaving pieces of the children about the house, but decided against that—not from any qualms of conscience, but because she didn't want to risk the neighbours hearing the screams. Instead, when the wife and kids left, she'd struck.

All she needed to do now was snare the three men who had executed her brother. Her plan was already under way.

I felt Andy's hand on my shoulder.

'Oh, sweet Jesus,' he said, then his grip tightened. 'I'm going to check the rest of the house. The bastard who did this might still be here.'

I knew he was right. I wanted to go with him—maybe, when we came back, the atrocity wouldn't be here any longer, maybe I'd imagined it, I'd always had a vivid imagination….

I dug my fingernails into my palms and forced myself to look up. Dave was wearing only jeans and shoes. They were soaked in blood, as was the sofa he lay sprawled across. His arms were outstretched and his legs wide apart. Something terrible had happened to his legs. There were bullet wounds across both thighs and in the kneecaps. But worst of all was his head. It had been broken open, his features unrecognisable beneath a carpet of blood and soft tissue. Dave was no longer there. What he had been—his spirit, his big-hearted soul—had disappeared. I fell forward like a worshipper before the shrine of some ancient, blood-addicted god, my chest racked by sobs and my face soaked with tears.

'Matt?' I heard Pete say, in my earpiece. 'Are you in? There's someone moving around on the first floor.'

'This is Andy. Get in here, both of you. The house is clear.'

The American came thundering down the stairs, then unlocked the front and back doors. I felt his hand on my shoulder again.

'Come on, Wellsy,' he said, 'let's get you out of here.'

'No!' I screamed. 'I can't leave him! I'm not leaving him on his own.'

'Fucking hell,' Rog said, retching. He ran out, a hand to his mouth.

'What the…' Pete was standing next to us, his mouth slack. 'What animal did this?'

'You…you know who did it,' I said, staring up at them through the blur of tears. 'It was… It must have been Sa…Sa…' I couldn't complete the name of the woman I had once loved. But even if she had been the one who'd pulled the trigger, I knew I was the true author of Dave's death. If I had refused to get involved with the White Devil, this would never have happened. I felt the weight of that knowledge bear down on me. The sight of my friend's ruined body added years to my life in a few seconds.

Pete and Andy pulled me to my feet and walked me out of the room. I wiped my eyes with the back of my arm and saw Rog leaning over the kitchen sink, a string of vomit hanging from his lower lip.

'Call…call Karen,' I said, as they sat me at the breakfast table.

Andy dug in his pocket for his phone.

'No,' I said, batting his arm away. 'Me. You have to go, all of you. I'm…I'm responsible.'

'Screw that,' Pete said. 'We haven't done anything wrong.'

Andy lifted up his automatic and pointed at the case that held the sniper's rifle. 'Um, I think you're wrong there, Boney.' He stuck his empty hand out at me. 'Come on, Matt. Hand 'em over. Glock, knife, walkie-talkie, everything you've got.'

I complied, too numb to protest. He was right. There was no point in me putting Karen in a difficult position by being in possession of an illegal firearm.

'Car key as well,' Andy said. 'I'll drive the Saab round here for you, okay?'

Pete gripped my wrist. 'You don't have to stay here on your own, Matt,' he said. 'You can come with us. Karen will understand.'

I shook my head. 'No, Boney. I have to do this.' I swallowed a sob. 'For Dave.'

'You two go,' Pete said, tossing keys to the Cherokee to Rog. 'I'll meet you at the end of the road.'

Andy nodded at me, and then pushed Rog gently to the back door. 'Lock this after us,' he said to Pete.

I pushed my chair back and stood up.

'What are you doing?' Boney asked. 'Don't—'

I swerved past him, my breathing ragged. There were two things I had to do before Dave was taken beyond my reach. I forced myself to look at the remains of the bravest man I'd ever known. I was looking for a message—the White Devil had inserted messages inside many of his victims' bodies. His mouth was partially open. I kneeled down and mumbled an apology to him, though I knew he would have understood. I was still wearing a glove. Trying to ignore the torn tissue and splintered bone, I moved his jaws further apart and peered inside, blinking away my tears. There was nothing. I couldn't find any pieces of paper inside his blood-drenched trousers. I had to move him to each side to get to the back pockets. His blood transferred to my jacket, and I swore to myself that I'd never wash it again. I took off his shoes, but again didn't find a thing. It was beyond me to put them back on the feet that had carried him past despairing opposition players so often on the rugby pitch.

Rocking back on my heels, I took in the mutilated face and legs. The White Devil had been despatched by pistol shots to the head, and I was certain Dave's wounds were a deliberate imitation of that. She had also shot him in the legs back then—those wounds had been repeated. Perhaps those were the only messages I was going to get this time. They were enough.

I stood up and bent over the body. Then I took off my glove and closed Dave's eyes beneath the partially congealed slick of blood. I didn't care that my fingerprints would be on the eyelids. There were some duties that friends had to discharge, whatever the circumstances. I leaned close and spoke to my friend for the last time.

'We'll get her, Dave, I promise you that. And we'll look after Ginny and the…and Tom and Annie.' His son was the same age as Lucy, his daughter two years older. The horror that they would have to face made me blink hard. Then I opened my eyes again and inhaled the coppery smell of fresh blood.

'No matter how far she goes, I'll be on her tail,' I said, standing up straight.

There was only one more thing to say—the catchphrase that everyone who played for South London Bisons used when a game seemed to be lost.

'No mercy, no surrender.'

Pete arrived at my side. He repeated the words, and then

turned me round, gently but insistently. In the hall, I took out my phone and called Karen.

'Dave's been murdered,' I said, the words singeing my mouth. I gave her the address. After I'd hung up, I turned to Pete. 'You'd better get moving.'

He pushed me back towards the kitchen. 'Let him be now,' he said. 'Don't go back in there.'

I nodded my agreement. I had no appetite to see Sara's handiwork again. Besides, I wanted to check the rest of the house. It was possible she'd left a message somewhere else and I didn't want the police to find it first. After about ten minutes I heard sirens. But by that time I'd only managed to ascertain one thing: there was no sign of a break-in.

Had Dave willingly admitted his killer?

'Where are we going, Mummy?' Lucy asked from the back seat.

Caroline Zerb looked in the rear-view mirror. 'Never mind,' she said, her voice sharp. She had been watching for cars on her tail ever since they'd left the house in Wimbledon.

'It's a magical mystery tour,' Fran said, turning her head and smiling at her granddaughter. She had been a primary schoolteacher before her children's books had taken off, and her skills with children were far superior to Caroline's.

Lucy raised an eyebrow sceptically. 'How long are we going to go round and round the motorway?'

'Until I decide otherwise,' her mother said, accelerating up the fast lane, then cutting inside and slowing down in front of a lorry. Matt had given her a book about surveillance techniques and she had practised how to make life difficult for a tail. The initial shock she'd felt when her ex-husband sounded the alarm had worn off and now she was anxious about the meetings she'd been forced to cancel.

Her phone rang and she pressed the button on her hands-free kit. 'It's me,' Matt said. 'Listen carefully, I haven't much time. This is a full alert.'

'What's happened?'

'Just listen! Are you on the M25?'

'Yes.'

'Get off at the next exit and find a pay phone. Your mobile frequency may be being scanned. Follow instruction two, repeat, two. I'll be in touch. Give…give my love to Lucy and Fran.'

'Matt?' Caroline swallowed an expletive when the connection was broken.

'Is he all right?' Fran asked, her face drawn.

'I think so. He was in a hurry. He sent his love to you both.'

The two women exchanged glances. They both knew that something bad had happened. There had been a number of false alarms, but they'd never yet had to use the suitcases they had permanently ready.

Caroline indicated left and drove up the Sevenoaks exit. Matt would explode when he discovered they were in her car. The standing instruction if she picked up Fran was for them to take the older woman's considerably less noticeable Renault Clio. Caroline couldn't do without her Mazda RX-8, though. It was fast, it could outpace almost any tail. Because Matt's emergency plans were so compartmentalised, it was quite possible that he'd never find out about the car. Everything worked on a need-to-know basis—and he didn't need to know about the black Mazda.

Eighteen months ago, she'd memorised the five instructions on the list that had then been destroyed. The second required her to call a number and ask if there were any messages for Zeppelin Delta. She'd be given the address of the safe house. Matt had told her that further instructions were taped beneath the top drawer of the chest in the largest bedroom. Although he'd bought the safe house with a small part of his ill-gotten gains from *The Death List,* he'd done so via a solicitor who'd been instructed never to give the owner details of the property or its address—the story was that the terms of the divorce settlement required that confidentiality. Caroline sometimes thought it was a ridiculous overreaction to the White Devil case; then she would remember her abduction at the hands of the madman and his sister, who was still on the loose and had threatened revenge on Matt and his circle. And she would remember that Fran and Lucy had also been taken by the bastards. She glanced in the mirror. Any inconvenience was immaterial as long as her daughter was kept safe.

Fran turned to her granddaughter when Caroline got out at the service station. 'This is exciting, isn't it, dear?'

Lucy shrugged. She was on the cusp of adolescence and nothing her elders said was satisfactory. 'I don't see why Mummy had to take my phone away.'

'You have to trust her,' her grandmother said. She had turned her own mobile off. That didn't bother her, as she despised the things. She was more concerned at the disruption to her latest book. *The Flight of the Bumbling Bee* was at the crucial second draft stage. At least she'd remem-

bered to bring a disk with the text on it. Presumably there
would be a computer in the safe house. The standing instruction was that laptops were not to be brought, in case
bugs had been fitted. Fran didn't see how that could happen
as she never took her laptop away from home, and Matt
had made sure that her home was equipped with armoured
windows and doors, enough locks and chains to keep a
prison governor happy and an alarm system that must have
cost him a fortune. She hadn't been happy when he told
her that an expert could still get in and out, and leave no
trace.

'Gran?' Lucy said, her eyes fixed on the door of the
service station. 'Who's Mummy talking to?'

Fran's stomach clenched when she saw that Caroline
was deep in conversation with a woman whose back was
turned to the car.

Ignoring Matt's strict instructions, Fran opened the door
and swung her feet out. Lucy wasn't staying on her own.
She wrestled with the rear-opening door and clambered out
after her grandmother.

7

Karen sat down next to me at the kitchen table after she'd taken a preliminary look. We were both in coveralls and overshoes. All my clothes had been taken away for examination.

'This is awful, Matt,' she said, touching my arm. My hands were in clear plastic bags prior to fingerprints being taken. 'Tell me what happened.'

I had decided to come clean with her about the others' presence—detectives knocking on doors would probably get descriptions of several men in black combats and woollen hats, and I didn't want any potential sighting of the killer to be compromised. So I told her about Dave's call using the alert code and the way we got in.

She shook her head as I talked, her eyes lowered. When I'd finished, she looked me in the eye. 'I understand you've just lost a close friend, but Christ, what were you thinking of, Matt? Why didn't you call me as soon as you heard from Dave? We'd have arrived here quicker and that might have saved his life.'

I glanced away. 'I don't think so. Sara was playing with us. She'd have got away whatever, and sirens would just have given her more warning.'

Karen's eyes flared. 'We don't always use sirens. Didn't it occur to you that you might have been walking into a trap?'

'There were four of us,' I said, though I wasn't going to tell her that Pete had been out the back with his sniper's rifle and Rog had been waiting with his Glock for anyone who left by the front door.

'Coming through the pantry window meant you could have been picked off by a primary school bully,' she said, dropping her gaze again. 'What were you armed with?'

I kept my mouth shut.

'The others took your weapon, didn't they? Where are they?'

'I've no idea,' I said, and that was the truth. The plan we'd agreed on stipulated that we would split up if there was an attack on any of us.

It looked like she believed me, but I was sure there would be cars despatched to their houses to check. They wouldn't be there—we each had our own list of randomly selected hotels and bed-and-breakfast places that none of the others had seen.

There was a tap on the door. The potbellied form of Doctor Redrose approached. 'Mr Wells, I understand the deceased was a friend. My condolences.' He turned to Karen. 'I've finished. Cause of death was obviously the four close-range shots to the head. CSIs have dug out what looks like a nine-millimetre bullet from the sofa. There were single shots to each knee and two shots to each thigh.'

His small eyes moved from Karen to me and then back again. 'There's no message in any obvious place. We'll see what the post-mortem shows. As for time of death, the body temperature suggests between two and three hours ago.' He waddled away.

Karen was studying me. 'You got here at ten-fifty, you said. He was killed not long before that.'

I nodded. 'I told you, she's playing with us.'

'Why are you so sure it's Sara?'

I shrugged. 'I'll bet you'll find no traces of the killer. That smacks of Sara's organisational skills. But it's also obvious from the modus operandi, Karen. She shot Dave in the legs just before her brother was killed. He was finished in execution style by shots to the head, as the SAS men did with the White Devil.'

'And as you described in your book that's been read by millions of people.' She blinked at me. 'Why no message?'

'There might still be one,' I said, swallowing a surge of vomit. 'Inside him.'

She looked away.

There was another knock, and Taff Turner came in. Karen nodded to him to sit down. He'd already offered me his sympathy, but I knew he was unhappy about how I'd found the body.

'There isn't much to go on, guv,' he said. 'The techies are looking for prints, but they'll need to take all the family's to exclude them.' He looked down at the pair of black leather gloves in front of me. 'I'd put money on the fact that the killer was wearing gloves.' He shook his head at me. That was the nearest I was going to get to an admission that he knew I wasn't a formal suspect. 'The driveway is asphalt, so we can forget getting any shoe imprints from there.'

'Anything you find in the garden will have to be compared with Matt's miniature army's boots,' Karen said. 'The four of them were here.'

A weary sigh passed Taff's lips. 'Wonderful,' he said.

'Anything else we need to know?' He gave me a questioning look.

'How the killer got in,' I said, still bothered by that. 'The alarm was off and there's no sign of a break-in.' I held Taff's gaze. 'Is there?'

'No,' he said.

'So Dave must have opened the door to her,' Karen said, glancing at her subordinate. 'Assuming it's Sara Robbins.'

'Yes,' I said, 'but there are two heavy-duty chains on the door. Dave knew to check through the spy-hole. He must have taken the chains off.'

'Disguise?' the Welshman suggested.

Karen nodded. 'Make sure the local detectives are aware of that possibility when they're taking statements from the neighbours.'

'No one so far has reported hearing any shots,' Turner added. 'The killer must have used a silencer.'

'Interesting,' Karen said. 'That suggests it was a pro.'

'Sara was trained by the White Devil,' I said. 'You don't get much more professional than that. For all we know, she's been honing her skills over the last two years.'

Turner got up and left. At the door, he looked round. 'Are we going to take over this case?' he asked his boss.

Karen ran her tongue across her lips, an action that I would normally have found provocative in another context. 'I'll have to discuss that with the AC.' Her eyes were on me. 'I think it's time you checked your e-mail, Matt. Bring my laptop in from the car, will you, Taff?'

I wasn't comfortable with Karen seeing any communication from Sara as I needed to have freedom of action, but there wasn't much I could do. She had a wi-fi card and she also knew my two main e-mail addresses. I logged on to them with a display of reluctance that turned out to be irrelevant. There was no message from Sara, in any form or guise.

'What now?' I asked.

'Give me your mobile,' she said. 'Please, Mr Wells.'

She wasn't joking. I was an ordinary member of the public to her now. Again, I didn't have much choice.

'What's the password?' she asked. 'And don't even think of saying no, if you want to stay out of the cells.'

'2LZ7,' I said.

Karen hit the keys and scrolled up and down. 'What are "GreenBoy" and "Seven Emperor"?'

'Alarm codes—to my agent and editor.'

'They'll have gone into hiding, will they? Along with Lucy and Fran, and your ex-wife?'

I nodded. Christian Fels, my agent, had been a target of the White Devil, and had sold *The Death List* to my editor, Jeanie Young-Burke. Given that the book didn't exactly paint flattering portraits of Sara and her brother, I was pretty sure she would go after them if she could.

'You can't do this, Matt,' Karen said, tossing the phone to me across the table. 'You can't take the law into your own hands.'

'I didn't know going into hiding was illegal,' I countered, my voice weak. I felt terrible and I needed to get out of Dave's house.

'It is if you've left the scene of a crime.'

'Christian and Jeanie haven't done that.' I sat up. 'Can I go now?'

She shook her head. 'You're staying with me. For a

start, you need to be fingerprinted. Then I want a full statement.'

I shrugged. I was safer with her, but I wouldn't be able to find Sara. Even if the VCCT started looking for her, I didn't have any confidence they'd be able to track her down. I was the only person who could attract Dave's murderer, my former lover. What she felt for me now was the polar opposite of love, not that I was surprised.

Then Taff Turner came in and said that Dave's wife and kids had arrived. I'd spoken to Ginny on her mobile and told her to come home as quickly as she could. Now I had to tell her what had happened to Dave. Karen would have done it, but it was up to me. That was what Dave would have wanted.

Contrary to the agreed procedure, the Cherokee and the Hornet rendezvoused at the burnt-out remains of the Cutty Sark in Greenwich. Andy Jackson got off his bike and got into the front seat of Pete's vehicle, then looked over his shoulder. Roger van Zandt was bent double in the back seat of the Grand Cherokee, his head between his knees.

'Deep breaths, Dodger,' the American said. 'Remember that try you scored against the Lambeth Lions? You went past four players and touched down under the posts. Remember what it felt to go over the line.' He glanced at the driver. 'You remember that try, don't you, Boney? Must have been the season before we retired.'

'No. It was the year after I was voted off the committee.'

'Jeez, I'm trying to distract him,' Andy said, in a loud whisper.

Rog mumbled something.

'What?' Andy said.

'It was…it was Dave who passed the ball to me.'

Pete groaned. 'Look, Rog, we're all shocked, but we've got to be strong now. We're targets of that madwoman and we've got to get her before she picks us off.'

'Yeah, that's really gonna help, Boney,' the American said under his breath. He glanced at the dirty grey river. Sometimes he wondered why he'd settled in the U.K., not that the part of New Jersey he'd grown up in was any better. He had run with a street gang when he was a teenager and if he hadn't had a dedicated football coach at high school, by now he'd either have been a low-level dope dealer or dead. His parents had kicked him out when he was fourteen, and they didn't want to know what became of him, even when he almost made the NFL. His suspect knee had let him down, though it had been good enough for eleven seasons of amateur rugby league. His folks hadn't believed human beings could change or that everyone had some innate goodness in them. They worked in a meat-packing plant, until they'd both got cancer and died within a few months of each other. Andy had left the States to find a new life, having finished basic training as a chef and able to work anywhere. The fact that he'd met a stunning English-woman in Central Park had made the move easy, even though she'd ditched him a month later.

Andy scratched the light-coloured stubble on his chin. His mom and dad had been wrong about people. The world wasn't full of assholes. Matt and the others were stand-up guys—even Rog, whose curly hair and slim build made him look like a typical computer nerd, despite having put in some of the most bone-shuddering tackles Andy had ever seen. As for Dave, he'd been a hero and he had the medals to prove it, even if he wasn't allowed to talk about his old SAS operations. But Sara Robbins—it didn't matter if she'd killed him herself or paid some other fucker to pull the trigger, she was the exception that proved the rule. Poison ran in her veins like it had when she'd killed with her brother, and her mind was still a hive of hate and perversion.

'All right,' Rog said. 'I'll do what I have to do.' He glared at Andy. 'But after we've finished, I'm going to mourn Dave any way I like. Is that okay by you, Slash?'

'Sure,' Andy said, with a loose grin. 'We'll have a wake. Dave would have gone for that.' His expression hardened. 'In the meantime, are you both clear about what you've got to do?'

Rog and Pete nodded. They'd practised the drill. No one told the others what they were up to in case they were caught. Everything each of them discovered about Sara or any other adversary would be uploaded daily to a special site that Rog had set up.

Andy opened his rucksack. He unscrewed the silencers from his and Matt's pistols, and ejected the magazines.

'Okay, my men. I hope we see each other soon.' He punched Rog lightly on the shoulder, then squeezed Pete's thigh. 'Maybe some of us thought Matt was overdoing it on the planning side, but we all knew that Sara would be back eventually. Let's get the bitch. For Dave.'

'For Dave,' the others repeated.

'Don't forget to take the SIM cards from your cell phones and drop them down a storm drain,' Andy added. He got out and went over to his bike.

Rog watched him go. 'What do you think Matt's got him doing?'

Pete started the engine and drove away from the heritage site. 'We're not supposed to think about that, but it's pretty obvious.'

'Is it?'

'Anyway, it doesn't matter what he's *meant* to be doing. He'll be watching Matt's back.'

Rog nodded. 'Yeah, that makes sense.'

Pete nodded. 'Fuck!' he said, spittle flecking the inside of the windshield. 'I can't believe it! Dave, of all people. She knows what she's doing. He's the one we would depend on most in a situation like this.'

'I suppose Matt will have to pick up the slack.'

'Matt will have enough trouble staying alive, Dodger. It's up to us to track the murdering cow down.'

Rog nodded. He had hacked into enough sites over the last two years to have an idea of what Sara was doing with the large amounts of money and the investments left her by the White Devil, even if she was always at least a week ahead of him. He'd passed that information regularly to Pete, who had used his contacts in the business world to find out more—at one time, he'd even invested in the same company as Sara. She had bailed out a few months later, presumably by chance, since Boney had used a false identity. The fact was, they weren't so far from Sara, but they had deliberately held back to avoid spooking her. Now she'd made the first real move, the game had changed.

Rog stared out into the rain and felt a wave of loneliness break over him. He shivered at the prospect of spending every night in a different hotel, all of them chosen for their cash-only policies and laxity about registration details. But he would manage because he'd be spending every waking hour on the laptop with Internet access that he would buy later on from one of the shops in Tottenham Court Road. He had no doubt that Pete would be doing something similar, though he couldn't believe he'd be roughing it. There were luxury hotels that were just as prepared to guarantee anonymity, if you could pay for it.

Pete stopped the Cherokee near Deptford Station and pushed his seat back as far as it would go. He opened his door and got out, bending over a raised area normally covered by the seat. He pulled up the rubber mat.

'Is that a safe?' Rog asked, pointing to the LCD display.

'Correct. Look away, Dodger.'

Pete punched in numbers and there was a dull click. 'Thought you might need some spending money,' he said, handing over a wedge of fifty-pound notes.

'Bloody hell, Boney,' Rog said, counting the notes. 'There's five grand here.'

'Yeah, well, I'll be expecting you to account for it.'

'Sure.'

'Pillock. Of course I won't. Just be careful you don't run short.'

'I'm all right. I've got accounts at different banks and there are funds in each one.'

'I don't need to know that, Rog,' Pete said. 'But remember—Sara might be monitoring our finances. She has the funds to obtain that information. So keep bank card use to a minimum.'

Soon afterwards, Pete was on his own. At least Rog seemed gradually to be coping better, he thought. The poor sod had grown up in a soft, bourgeois family and had never done anything he didn't want to. Whereas Pete had dragged himself up from a broken home in a drug-ridden estate in Lancashire. He'd been mocked because he was smart, beaten up because he was gay and spat on when he'd started to make money. His mother had died from bad heroin and he hadn't been back home since he was eighteen, already halfway to setting up his computer maintenance company. That turned into a full-blown computer manufacturing operation by the time he was twenty-three and it had floated on the Stock Exchange on his twenty-eighth birthday. Selling his shares when he was thirty-five netted him a hundred and twenty million pounds, most of which was now invested in blue-chip companies and funds all over the world. The five grand he'd given Rog meant nothing to him.

But getting even with whoever had killed Dave did. Pete wasn't convinced that Matt's ex-squeeze had done the murder herself. The woman could easily have bought herself a hit man with the White Devil's millions. There were forty-two of those the last time Pete had done an informed estimate, the bitch having obviously obtained good investment advice. Now it was time to see if some of his contacts could screw with Sara Robbins's wealth. Not that she went by that name any more. She had numerous identities, only some of which he and Rog knew.

He left the Grand Cherokee in a leafy street in Bromley, having emptied the safe. With any luck, the Jeep would still be there when he came to pick it up, after Sara Robbins had been dealt with. If she came out on top, Pete would have no need of his car or his fortune—he'd have gone to the same place as Dave.

He hoisted the bag containing the sniper's rifle and

the rest of his gear over his shoulder and set off towards
the station. No one saw him in the rain that had turned
into a heavy downpour. That was just as well. When
Peter Satterthwaite was determined to achieve something, his face took on the look of a particularly savage
avenging angel.

After I'd had my fingerprints taken and dictated a statement, I was told that one of Karen's team had driven my
Saab to the car park beneath New Scotland Yard.

'You don't have to leave, Matt,' Karen said quietly. 'If it
was Sara Robbins who killed Dave, you'll be in real danger.'

We were in her office, the door ajar. She went over
and closed it.

I was slumped in a chair, my head down, trying to get
the sight of Dave from my mind. But when I succeeded,
all I saw was Ginny. She had slapped my face and told me
I should never have written my book—all it had done was
drive the White Devil's sister even more crazy. And I saw
Tom, trying manfully not to cry because his dad wouldn't
have liked that, and Annie, who looked at me as if I was a
war criminal. Which, in a way, I was.

'I wonder where she'll strike next.' She shook me
lightly. 'Rog, Pete and Andy aren't at home and they aren't
answering their phones. They need to give us statements
about this morning to corroborate your story.' She brought
her face down to the level of mine. 'Where are they, Matt?
They're in danger.'

'I don't know,' I said. I could see she didn't believe that.
'Honestly. They…they have things to do.'

'You've got a plan, haven't you? For God's sake, Matt,
you have to let me in on it. I can't protect you otherwise.'

I shrugged. 'I told you, I don't know where they are.'

She stood up and walked behind her desk. 'Bullshit. You must have ways of contacting them.'

I wasn't answering that. I got to my feet. 'Can I go now?'

Karen blinked, her expression softening. 'Please, Matt. I…I love you. Why can't you accept my help?'

I raised as much of a smile as I could. 'I love you too, but you have to let me protect my people.'

'Like you protected Dave?' she said sharply, her hand flying to her mouth. 'I'm sorry, Matt.'

I turned and headed for the door. I'd always suspected that Sara would come between Karen and me when she returned, but I hadn't thought it would happen so quickly.

8

Josh Hinkley, wearing a thousand-pound leather jacket and shoes with real silver buckles, was slouched in an armchair in a coffee shop on Charlotte Street, discarded newspapers all around him. He looked up when another double espresso was placed in front of him.

'Oh, there you are, mate.' He looked at his gold Rolex. 'Just the twenty-seven minutes late.'

'Hello, Josh, good to see you too.' Jeremy Andrewes shoved a heap of books off the armchair next to him and sat down.

'Oi, those are review copies.'

The other man shrugged. 'Which you cast an idle eye over and then flog to the shops on Charring Cross Road, even though you don't need the money.'

'Bloody journalists,' Hinkley said. 'Think you know it all.'

Andrewes ignored that and ate a piece of chocolate cake.

Josh Hinkley threw the espresso back in one. 'Aaa-ha! That hit the spot.' He winked. 'But not like the marching powder I just snorted in the bog.'

Andrewes concentrated on his cake. Josh Hinkley liked to play at being 'the bad boy of British crime writing', a moniker many reckoned he'd come up with himself. He certainly cultivated the image assiduously. He'd been arrested a couple of times for possession of cannabis, before the Met's user-friendly policy came in. That didn't impress Jeremy Andrewes, the crime correspondent of the *Daily Independent*. He had little time for crime novelists—apart from now.

'So what's this meet in aid of?' Hinkley said, running a hand through his grey hair. His face was pocked by old acne scars and his belly hung over his designer jeans. Strangely, his appearance didn't put off the surprisingly young female fans of his books. Then again, he was rolling in money.

'Another double es, darling!' the novelist shouted to the dark-skinned girl at the counter. 'Slag,' he muttered, when she gave him a haughty look. 'Not long out of the jungle.'

'Steady on, Josh,' the journalist said, catching the other man's eye. 'Civilised people don't talk like that any more.' Andrewes was an old Etonian, whose great-grandfather had made a fortune exploiting workers all over the world. That should have made the journo uncomfortable, particularly as he worked for a left-wing paper, but it didn't.

'Excuse me for breathing,' Hinkley said defiantly.

Andrewes finished his cake. It was a good one, almost as good as the cook produced at the family house in Hampshire. He wasn't looking forward to asking a favour of Hinkley, but he knew it would be worth it. The novelist was a serious gossip-hound. What the man *didn't* know about his fellow crime writers could be written on the back of one of his lurid novels.

'I have a problem.' Andrewes took a sip of his latte and tried to formulate a request that didn't make him sound too much like a supplicant before an oracle. 'Well, as a matter of fact, two.' He smiled, hoping the insincerity wasn't too obvious. 'I need some background on a couple of crime writers. And you're the man in the know.'

Hinkley didn't look impressed. He may have written novels with minimal literary merit, but he was smart. Most best-selling authors were, in the journalist's limited experience.

'I get it,' the novelist said. 'I fill the column you're paid to write. I don't think so.' He stood up and waved a twenty-pound note at the barista. 'Over 'ere, beautiful! I'll make it worth your while.'

Jeremy Andrewes tried to hide his face behind his hand. People all around were staring at Hinkley. To her credit, the girl stayed at the bar, forcing him to go and pick up his coffee.

'Bloody cow,' he said, on his return. 'There goes her tip.'

'Oh, you were going to leave one?' the journalist said snidely. Josh Hinkley was a notorious skinflint.

'Now, now,' Josh said, raising a finger. 'I might be prepared to reconsider, if you make it worth my while.' He grinned, displaying expensive bridgework. 'Then again, your paper doesn't like backhanders, does it?'

Jeremy Andrewes nodded. He had a small group of people he paid for information, but he wasn't going to add the millionaire novelist to that list.

'How about your name appearing a few times in the paper?'

'Fuck you, Jerry,' Josh said loudly, provoking an outraged gasp from the elderly woman at the next table. He stood up and bowed extravagantly. 'I do beg your pardon, madam.'

'Bugger off,' the woman responded, in a cut-glass accent. The journalist almost choked on his coffee.

Josh Hinkley collapsed into his armchair like he'd been shot, his cheeks on fire.

Andrewes saw his opportunity. 'All right, I'll share the byline with you.' He watched as Josh nodded his agreement. It was amazing how badly a best-selling author still wanted to see his name in print. Maybe that emotional need was how he still got into the top ten, year in, year out.

'Who are you so interested in, then?' Hinkley asked, leaning closer.

'The first one is Mary Malone.'

'There's a surprise. What are you hearing from the Peelers?'

'I get the distinct impression they haven't got much to go on.'

The novelist grunted. 'I heard some talk of Satanism.'

Andrewes nodded. 'They've asked us to keep quiet about that, but it won't be long before the tabloids go public. I don't suppose Mary Malone was into devil worship?'

Josh Hinkley laughed. 'Dunno, mate. I never met the woman. She was secretive with a capital *S*—no publicity photos, no public appearances. There were rumours that she was as ugly as sin.' He beckoned the journalist closer. 'I reckon she fancied herself and her smart-arse historical novels—thought the rest of us were talentless hacks.' He laughed. 'Oops, sorry.'

Jeremy Andrewes generally found laughing difficult, so he didn't respond in kind. The White Devil case, when Sara Robbins, one of his colleagues on the paper, had turned out to be the killer's sister and partner, had put paid to his never well-developed sense of humour. Besides, he came from aristocratic stock. 'Those who rule have to maintain their dignity', his grandfather repeatedly told him when he was a boy.

'What's the feeling in the Crime Writers' Society about Mary Malone's murder?'

Hinkley laughed. 'They're all crapping themselves, aren't they? Wondering who's going to be next.'

The journalist looked up from his notebook. 'Why? The police aren't treating this as the first in a series. The VCCT hasn't even taken over the case.'

'Maybe someone objects to writers who use the same investigator over and over again.'

Andrewes gave a tight smile. 'You do too, Josh. Aren't you scared?'

'Give me a break,' Hinkley scoffed. 'Mary Malone must have wound someone up. Maybe she got in over her head playing poker on the Internet and the heavies were sent round.'

The journalist didn't bother noting down that far-fetched idea. Anyway, the police would be looking at her computer. 'Had anyone you know actually met her?'

'She didn't hang out with anyone from the Society, as far as I'm aware. She just sat at home and wrote her books.'

'Well, that was enlightening.' Andrewes turned a page. 'Right, what can you tell me about Matt Wells, aka Matt Stone?'

That got the crime writer's attention. 'I know what his pen name is, Jerry. Why are you interested in him?'

The journalist leaned forward. 'You remember that book he wrote about the White Devil?'

''Course I do. It sold well in over fifty countries, I seem to remember the bastard boasting on the radio.'

'The killer's partner, Wells's ex-lover, got away at the end,' the journalist said.

Hinkley nodded. 'So?'

'One of Matt Wells's friends was murdered this morning.' He flicked back in his notebook. 'David Cummings. Apparently he used to be in the Parachute Regiment and the SAS.'

'Christ, yeah, I met him at the launch of Matt's book. He told me to fuck off when I asked him how many Irishmen he'd topped.'

'Very diplomatic of you.' Andrewes knew he'd hooked his man and was less inclined to brown-nose. 'They're not saying it publicly, but I heard a whisper that the killer may have been Sara Robbins.'

'Your ex-colleague and Matt's ex–other half?' Josh Hinkley grinned. 'Juicy, Jerry, I'll give you that. You should have clocked her, shouldn't you? And now Matt's shagging the head of the VCCT. You do know that, don't you?'

The journalist nodded. 'DCI Oaten must be close to having a conflict of interest. I know that her people hauled Wells in. Apparently he found the body at the victim's home.'

'Is that right?' Hinkley scratched his stubble. 'What do you want from me?'

'Wells won't ever talk to me. He has his column in the paper and he keeps all his material for that.'

'Oh, Jerry,' the novelist said, laughing and slapping him on the knee. 'Do I detect the smell of overripe jealousy? You don't approve of a mere crime writer being given the chance to air his views about your area of expertise every week, do you?'

Jeremy Andrewes looked away. 'Yes, well, the question is, can you give me any stuff I could use about him?'

Hinkley tapped his nose. 'I can, my friend. Matt and I have been mates since we were both on the short list for best first novel. The bastard won. We've been pissed together at plenty of events and conventions. I can dig you some dirt on him. In fact, I can do better than that. I'll go round and offer him a shoulder to cry on.' His lips formed into a twisted smile. 'You never know, he might just confide in me.'

The journalist felt a wave of relief that he wasn't one of Josh Hinkley's friends. He listened carefully as the author ran through a series of drunken antics and misbehaviour in hotels, most of which seemed to have been inspired by Hinkley. But he got some insight into Wells's character, admittedly before the White Devil case, and it was worth keeping Josh sweet in case he actually managed to get close to the other crime writer.

If Sara Robbins really was back on the scene, it would be a hell of a story.

It was raining heavily when I left New Scotland Yard in the Saab. My mobile had been returned but not my clothes, so I was still wearing a white plastic coverall and overshoes. While I was stopped at a red light, I turned the phone on. There was an envelope on the display. The message consisted of only one word—'Manassas'. It wasn't only the name of a fine Stephen Stills album. Andy was the sender and it meant that he was waiting at the Mansfield Arms in Pimlico. He'd have stashed his bike. I replied with 'SS' a couple of minutes before I got there. He was standing on the pavement with his bag.

'Head down,' I said, as he got in and threw his bag on to the back seat. 'Karen might have someone watching my place.'

'Sara or some sidekick might be doing the same,' he said, peering at what I was wearing. 'Did they give you a hard time?'

'No major sweat.'

'Why are we going to your place, anyway? I thought we'd be heading for a hotel or a safe house.'

'We've just compromised the plan by hooking up, Slash. Anyway, I'm buggered if I'm going to run from Sara after what she did to Dave. Someone has to make a stand.'

'Way to go, Matt!'

I grunted. 'Say that when you find me in a pool of—' I broke off and bit my lip.

'Hey, man, remember what Dave used to say at half-time. *Deep breaths or I'll have your nuts.*'

I couldn't do anything but laugh. Christ, we were going to miss Psycho.

I looked in the mirror and pulled away. Because of Andy's height, his head was only just below the bottom of the side window. I handed him my phone. 'Delete your message and the one I sent you,' I said. 'Karen might check if I've received anything. Manassas would definitely make her suspicious.'

'Doesn't she like Stills?' he asked, squinting up and giving me a grin that faded fast. 'What was it like with Ginny and the kids?'

'Desperate.'

'But you handled it okay, yeah?'

'I don't think so. Ginny…Ginny told me I was responsible for what happened to Dave.'

'Aw, shit, man.'

'But at least she understood the danger. Dave had got her to memorise the number of the solicitor who has the package with false passports for them all and a credit card for her. By now she should have dumped her car, hired a different model and got out of London.'

I stopped at the barrier at the side of my apartment block and tapped in my access code, then parked in my space in the underground car park and turned off the engine. 'Look, Slash, it'll be better if you disappear as per the plan. I never expected Dave to be hit first. Sara's even more dangerous than we thought. I don't want to put you in her sights too.'

'Kiss my ass,' the American said. 'You need protection and you know it. Besides, what else am I going to do? I can't track the bitch down on a computer. All I can do is watch your back. And I prefer to be obvious when I do that, not tagging along behind like some half-assed spy.'

I knew he'd react like that, but it was still good to hear the words. Andy was the best man to watch over me. Apart from Dave. I bowed my head as the blood-drenched and disfigured body flashed before me again.

Andy sat up slowly and looked around the well-lit concrete chamber. 'This place's like a car dealer's for rich people with no taste.'

Despite how I was feeling, I laughed. My fellow residents did have some seriously shitty cars—there was a pink MG, a Bentley with leopard-skin seat covers and a Range Rover sporting the logo of a porn film production company. These were people who had no shame about how they made their money or how environmentally damaging their cars were. Then again, they didn't write books that led to their friends' deaths.

'We'll take the stairs,' Andy said, hoisting his bag from the back seat. He took out a Glock and handed it to me with a magazine. 'Forget the silencer. If Sara tries anything, I don't care who hears what we do to her.' He slapped in a mag, racked the slide and held the weapon beneath his jacket. I did the same. 'I'll go first,' he said.

I locked the car and followed him. Fortunately there was no one around. I didn't want Andy's presence to be registered. There were security cameras at the top of the car park ramp, in the block's entrance hall and in the elevators, so we were all right. Presumably the company that installed them assumed burglars would be too lazy to use the stairs.

I looked through the round window in the fire door on the ground floor. There was no one in the hall. If Karen had someone watching me, it wasn't from there. Maybe there would be a cop in the hall on my floor. I tapped Andy's back as we reached the fire door there. I saw no one.

I turned the keys and opened my door. The alarm immediately started beeping. I punched in the code number to stop it. By the time I'd done that, Andy was already checking the spare room. He knew there were no sensors in the bedrooms. I watched as he ran across the expanse of the living area and went into the master bedroom at the far side. Theoretically, a skilled intruder could have worked the locks and overridden the alarm electronically, then hidden in a bedroom after turning it on again.

'Clear,' he said, appearing at the door and lowering his automatic.

I headed to my desk. I needed to find out if Lucy and Fran were all right. I booted up my second computer. Rog had protected it with a series of firewalls that would puzzle the world's best hacker. Then I logged on to a mail provider where I kept an account that I only used once every quarter, just enough to keep it in operation.

There should have been a message from Caroline saying that they had made it to the safe house.

There wasn't.

The young men were hanging around outside the Kurdish youth club on Green Lanes in north-east London, happy that the rain had finally let off. Dressed in the latest sports gear and trainers, the three looked good and they knew it. They weren't welcome inside because the organisers knew they worked for the King. That didn't stop them talking to the boys who went in to play table-tennis and pool, or selling them small quantities of grass and hashish when they came out. Nedim Zinar's murder had put them on their toes, but business went on as usual.

'Hey, Faik, look,' said one of them, in Kurdish. He pointed to a white BMW 6 series coupé across the road. 'Is that who I think it is?'

His friend peered over. 'I think so.'

They watched as the front window came down and an arm was waved at them.

'Yes, it's Aro Izady,' Faik said. He watched as the driver waved, and then pointed only at him. 'Looks like he's got a job for me. See you around.'

Faik Jabar ran across the road, provoking a loud blast from a lorry that almost clipped his heels.

'What's up?' he asked the moustachioed man in the driver's seat. The passenger was a bearded man he hadn't seen before.

'Get in,' Izady said, in English. His voice was hoarse, as if he'd been shouting.

Faik paused momentarily before obeying. You did what the King's family said, without question, but he had the feeling that something wasn't quite right. After he had closed the rear door, the man with the moustache pulled out and drove towards Manor House Station.

'Where are we going?' Faik asked.

'Speak English,' Izady ordered.

Faik repeated the question in the language he'd learned at school, from which he'd been expelled for dope-dealing when he was fourteen. It wasn't the first time a King's lieutenant had brought a stranger along. The guy was probably a buyer who wanted to see how reliable the Kurdish operation was.

'It isn't far,' the passenger said. 'You know where it is, don't you, Aro?'

The driver nodded.

Faik looked at the stranger's thick brown hair that reached his shoulders. There was definitely something going on. Aro Izady wasn't one of the King's street commanders. He was a money counter, who gave the impression that he despised the young men who did the dirty jobs. But the story went that he'd killed one of the Turkish competition, a Shadow, with a snooker cue when doubts were cast on his sister's virginity.

Izady made a left turn and pulled up outside a dark house. It looked derelict, the windows boarded up and a steel bar padlocked across the front door.

'Out,' Izady said over his shoulder.

The young man obeyed. When they were on the pavement, Faik felt for the cutthroat razor he always carried in his back pocket. He didn't like this. Maybe it was a dope pickup, but he'd never been to the place before. He kept his eyes on the passenger. His upper body was bulky beneath a black leather jacket. Faik couldn't tell what age he was, what with the beard covering the lower half of his face.

Izady pointed down a flight of rubbish-strewn steps. 'Basement,' he said.

Faik went first, stepping over old pizza boxes and newspapers, with the stranger close behind. Izady followed, his head tilted slightly backwards, as if he was trying to hear what the bearded man was saying. But no words were spoken.

Izady pushed Faik aside and put a key in the door—this one was not barred.

'After you,' the stranger said, his arms extended wide.

The two Kurds paused, and then complied. The basement hallway was rank with damp and decay, as well as something more pungent. When the four of them were inside, the stranger pulled the door shut and turned on a light.

Faik gasped. The front room was piled high with boxes containing plasma TVs, computers and stereo systems. There was also a green metal trunk on the floor.

'I take it the drugs are in there,' the bearded man said, his hands in his pockets.

Izady looked at him and nodded slowly.

'Let's have a look then,' the stranger said, with a tight smile.

Faik was watching the man carefully. There was something wrong about him, all the Kurd's instincts told him that, but he couldn't identify what it was. Could he be an undercover cop? If so, he was taking a hell of a risk coming down here with them. Something else bothered Faik. Why hadn't he been told the man's name and crew? He seemed to be native English. Was the local mob playing games with the King's operation?

'Tell him where we are,' the bearded man said to Izady.

The King's cousin ran his hand across his damp forehead. 'This is a Shadow store.'

Faik stared at Izady. Their lives were forfeit if the Turks discovered their presence.

'What?' Faik said. 'Where are the guards?'

'They were told to take the evening off,' Izady said, his head down.

'Yes,' the bearded man said. 'You see, Aro Izady doesn't only work for the King. He's also a Shadow.'

'No!' Faik said. 'That's impossible!'

The stranger was now standing behind Izady. 'Tell him,' he said.

'It's…it's true,' Izady said, his eyes not meeting those of his fellow Kurd.

'But the Shadows hate us,' said Faik. 'They'd never have a Kurd in their organisation.'

'Aro is the exception,' the bearded man said. 'And, in case you're wondering, he isn't playing them off against each other. He's loyal only to the Turks.'

Faik stepped forward and forced Izady's chin up so he couldn't avoid the young man's gaze. 'Is he speaking the truth?'

'Ye…yes,' he said.

Faik had the cutthroat out and open before the man with the moustache could move, but he failed to slash the traitor's throat. There was a spitting sound and the blade spun away. Faik watched as blood welled from the palm of his right hand.

'Impressive,' the bearded man said. 'But this is my show.'

Izady froze as the muzzle of the silenced pistol touched the side of his head. His eyes bulged, then he started to babble in English. There was a cracking sound, then a spray of blood and brain launched from the other side of his head. He dropped to the floor like an unstrung puppet.

'Wh…why?' Faik said, clutching his wounded hand.

The bearded man smiled. 'I like you. You've got a pretty face. Pity.' He turned his weapon on the young Kurd.

'No!' Faik screamed.

The man stood in front of Faik, then raised the hand that wasn't holding the gun and tugged his beard and hair.

Faik's eyes opened wide. 'No,' he said in horror. 'No!'

Then the shooter smashed the butt of his weapon against the side of the Kurd's head and darkness overtook his world.

9

'Sara couldn't have found Lucy and the others, Matt,' Andy said. 'It's impossible. *You* don't know where they are. How could she?'

I looked at the curtains that I'd drawn across the wide expanse of the windows. If anyone was watching from across the river, he or she wouldn't even be able to see that the lights were on.

'There are plenty of things Sara could have done,' I said, turning away from the screen on my desk. 'She or a sidekick could have followed Caroline and Lucy from Wimbledon, or got on their tail when they picked up my mother. She could have put bugs on both cars. It wouldn't surprise me if she got a bug into Caroline's handbag.'

Andy shook his head. 'You'll drive yourself crazy thinking that way. They've probably just had computer problems.'

'She could have sent me a text. Even Lucy could do that.'

The American raised an eyebrow. 'You're losing your cool, man. You told Caroline to take Lucy's mobile away, to turn it and her own off.'

He was right, though I had the feeling Caroline would be reluctant to turn her phone off. I took some deep breaths and tried to get my head in order. I'd just about succeeded when the doorbell from the main entrance rang.

Andy grabbed his weapon. 'You expecting anybody?'

I shook my head. 'Karen's got keys, but she told me she wouldn't be coming tonight.' I went over to the entry-phone. It had a screen that showed who had rung the bell, as long as they stayed within camera range.

'Shit,' I said.

'Trouble?' Andy asked.

'No, just an asshole.'

'Don't pick up then.'

'Then he'll come back.' I looked at the face that was mugging at the camera. It was conceivable that Josh Hinkley had heard something useful. He had contacts with criminals, who got him to buy numerous rounds of drinks and generally took the piss.

'Bit late, isn't it, Josh?' I said, after signalling to Andy to stay back.

'It's not even eleven. Come on, Matt, let me in.' He held up a bottle of Highland Park. That immediately made me suspicious. He wanted something. I needed to find out what. It wasn't beyond the realms of possibility that Sara had got to him, either directly or indirectly.

I pressed the button, then went over to my computer. 'You'd better go into my bedroom, Andy. I don't want Josh Hinkley to know anyone's here. He's got a mouth that motors all over London. Leave the door ajar so you can hear what's going on.'

He departed with his weapon, his jacket and his bag. I switched off my computer and made sure my Glock was out of sight. When the interior bell rang, I went to the spy-hole and checked he was on his own. Then I opened the door with the two chains still on, to make a hundred per cent sure.

'Hey, Matt,' Josh said. 'Sorry about your fr—'

I shut the door in his face, realising that he would have heard about Dave's murder. It had been on the TV and radio news, though Karen had managed to keep my name out of the bulletins—that wouldn't last much longer.

After I'd unhitched the chains, I let Hinkley in.

'As I was saying, sorry about your friend.' He handed me the bottle of whisky and walked into the living area. 'This is one hell of a pad, Matt.' He turned to me and grinned. 'Got a football?'

I cracked the seal and pulled the cork. He got a large measure, I took a small one. 'Look, Josh, this is a bad time for me.'

'I know,' he said, his expression serious. 'That's why I came. Bit of moral support. You on your own?' He looked towards the bedroom door.

I nodded and led him to one of the leather sofas. 'Well, it's good of you, Josh,' I said, not buying what he'd said for a moment. 'I think what I most need now is to get some sleep.'

'Fair enough. I'll wet my whistle and then I'll be off.' He took a slug of the neat whisky. 'Ah, that does the business!' He looked round at me as he put his glass down on the mahogany coffee table with a thud. 'Oops, sorry.' He tried to look sombre again, but it was a state that he found difficult. His default mode was cynicism spliced with crudity. 'We go back a long way, don't we? Being a crime writer, I thought I might be able to…um, like I said, offer support with a bit of empathy in it.'

I eyed him sceptically. 'How many of your close friends have you seen with their heads blown apart, Josh?'

His cheeks reddened. 'Well, when you put it like that…'

'I'm not putting it like anything,' I said, the anger that had been building up all day finally erupting. 'That's the reality. Some fucking bastard shot my friend to death from close range. It was a horror show. Don't tell me you've ever seen anything like it.'

Josh had his hands out, like a zookeeper trying to calm down a rabid bear. 'Whoa, Matt, steady on. I'm your mate, remember?'

'Yeah,' I said, 'some mate. When *The Death List* went to number one, you wrote an article saying that true-crime books were written by voyeurs who didn't have enough imagination to produce decent novels.'

He grinned slackly. 'Well, you did knock me off the top spot.'

I wasn't finished. 'You're the mate who told my agent I'd been bad-mouthing him, and my editor that I'd said she was a randy witch.'

Hinkley was busy putting some distance between us, his arse sliding squeakily over the leather. He wasn't grinning now.

'So exactly what kind of support do you think you're qualified to offer, you poxy shithead?' I sat back, my heart pounding. Then the anger slowly dissipated. I could see out of the corner of my eye that Josh was watching me intently.

'Don't worry,' he said quietly. 'I know what it's like, all right. My old ma died last year.'

Christ, now I'd given him some leverage. 'Sorry,' I said, looking at him. 'I hadn't heard.'

'It's okay. She was over ninety. You're still unprepared for it, though.' He took another pull of whisky. 'All I was trying to say was that crime writers know something about death and killing.'

'Correction—*imaginary* death and killing. They're not the same as what I saw this morning.'

He shrugged. 'So…how come you were down at your mate's house? I mean, your finding him seems a bit…well, a bit of a coincidence.'

I tried to keep my breathing regular. The scumbag had just given himself away. I moved closer and poured him another drink. 'Coincidence?' I said, handing him the glass. 'How do you mean?'

There was a flash of concern in his eyes. 'Well, people are saying your ex-squeeze, excuse the expression, is in the frame for the killing.'

'You mean Sara?' I said, stringing him along. I wanted to see how much he knew.

'Er, yeah. I don't suppose she tipped you the wink? Gave you a call?'

'What, along the lines of "Morning, Matt. I've just executed your friend Dave Cummings in his front room"?'

There was apprehension in his eyes again. 'Yeah, that sort of thing.'

I stood up and leaned over him. 'Who have you been talking to, Josh?'

'What do you mean?'

'The Met's press release didn't mention that I discovered the body.' I grabbed the lapel of his leather jacket and pulled him up. 'So who told you?'

He hung unevenly, trying to find his footing. I drew his face close to mine.

'Who have you been talking to, you piece of crap?'

'Andrewes,' he muttered.

'Jeremy Andrewes! I might have known.' I dropped him back on the sofa. 'Let me guess. You told him you'd pump me for information.'

He nodded, his gaze away from mine.

'What was he going to give you in return? A weekend at the family mansion?'

He scowled at me. 'A shared byline.'

'Jesus, you're pathetic,' I said, turning away.

'Maybe, but at least I don't write books that get my friends murdered.'

I stayed with my back to him. Tears had flooded my eyes, but I wasn't going to let him see them. 'Just go, Josh,' I said, managing to keep my voice level. 'You can take your whisky with you.'

'Fuck you, Matt,' he said, as he moved away. 'I might be a loud-mouthed bastard, but I'm a harmless one. I hope you can live with yourself.'

The door slammed behind him.

Andy loped across the room. 'Want me to kick his ass?'

'Forget it,' I said, walking to my desk. 'Now I know that the crime correspondent of my own paper doesn't care who he uses to hang me out to dry.'

'This Hinkley guy, there's no chance Sara could have got to him? Maybe he dropped a bug in here.'

I looked at him over my shoulder. 'I doubt it. He isn't reliable enough. But he could easily have bugged me for that ponce Jeremy Andrewes, or even for his own reasons. I'll do a sweep with the scanning unit later.'

'I'll do it now. Where do you keep it?'

I directed him to the broom cupboard, then booted up my computer. I was desperate for a message from

Caroline. If I didn't get one, the guilt I was feeling about Dave would be augmented by helpless trepidation about Lucy and my mother.

Could Sara have got to them already?

The Soul Collector was in a fallow field in Warwickshire. About fifty metres away, beyond a low hedge and a wide lawn, stood a detached house. There were lights on both upstairs and downstairs. So far, through her Zeiss binoculars, Sara Robbins had made out a boy of fifteen, a girl of eleven and an over-made-up woman of thirty-eight. She knew their ages from the research she'd done on the family. Direct observation told her that the man of the house was not present. But she knew that already. She had instructed a lawyer to hire him and his colleagues.

The woman stretched her legs on the groundsheet. She was wearing green combat fatigues, hiking boots and a black Gore-Tex cape. By her side lay her Spyderco knife and her silenced H and K pistol. It would be easy to go into the house and slaughter its occupants; the temptation tugged at her. She resisted, knowing that would only drive the husband and his comrades underground. Wolfe, Rommel and Geronimo, they'd called themselves in the SAS. They'd been discharged from the elite regiment and the Army when the finger had been pointed at them for the shooting of her brother. She smiled. She had the worm Matt to thank for that. He had mentioned Special Forces in his book and, although there was no concrete evidence, the hard men in charge apparently had little difficulty in working out the likely perpetrators. A deal was done and they were paid off without publicity. They had even been helped to set up their own private security company.

And now Wolfe, the former sergeant whose house she was watching, had taken Rommel and Geronimo off to Aberdeen to carry out surveillance on an oil company executive they'd been told was suspected of industrial espionage.

The question was, when it came to it, which of these three potential victims would she take? The boy was well-built—he'd probably been put on a fitness programme by his father—but she could neutralise him easily enough. The wife was heavy; she must have been at least twelve stone. She could handle that too, but why take the trouble? The girl, Amanda Mary, was the one. Slim, almost fragile-looking, she was still at the pre-teen shy-as-a-mouse stage. Amanda Mary would be easy and her father would no doubt do anything to save his precious little girl.

An owl hooted from a nearby tree. The woman looked across, and then up at the cloudless, star-sprinkled sky. There were familiar spirits all around her, creatures that lived only to hunt in the dark. During her training and on the tasks she'd set herself on the other side of the Atlantic, she had become part of the community of the night. She felt most at ease when she was out of doors, when ordinary people slept. The Soul Collector had learned how to make use of the forces of darkness.

Karen Oaten got out of her car in the street near Manor House Station in East London. CSI vans and police cars, marked and unmarked, were all around.

'Right, Amelia, let's go.' She led the petite young woman with the bobbed brown hair to one of the white vans.

''Evening, guv,' said a bespectacled technician she knew from her time in Homicide East. 'You'll be wanting a suit.'

'Two, please, Vince. This is my new sergeant, Amelia Browning.'

The man smiled. 'Hello, Amelia. First time at one of these?'

Browning shook her head vigorously. 'Good heavens, no. I was in Homicide South before I got into the VCCT.'

'I hear it's nasty, south of the river,' Vince said, handing them sealed plastic bags containing white coveralls, over-shoes and caps. 'Never been over there, myself.'

Karen laughed, while her subordinate tried to work out if she was being teased. 'You might want to beef up your vocabulary, Amelia.'

'Guv?'

'"Good heavens"? We're not in an Agatha Christie novel.'

Browning nodded. 'Got you, guv.'

When they'd finished covering up, Karen ducked under the tape and headed for the basement stairway, her much shorter sergeant close behind. A techie was photograph-ing the garbage on the steps and they had to wait.

'Footprints?' Browning asked.

'Among other things.' Oaten walked on when the steps were clear.

Ron Paskin was standing in the hall. 'Ah, there you are, Karen.'

'Guv.' She introduced Amelia again. 'We're getting seriously stretched,' she explained. 'DS Browning only joined us a week ago.'

'In at the deep end, then,' the superintendent said, with a smile that didn't stay long on his lips. 'We got an anony-mous call. One dead male Kurd inside,' he said. 'Shot once in the head at close range with a nine-millimetre pistol. There was a cartridge case on the floor, by the door. Funny thing is, there was also another one. They've taken samples of the blood.' Paskin pointed to the spray on the floor and on some of the many cardboard boxes in the room ahead. 'And they're collating footprints. It looks like there were three people in here and two of them left.'

'One having been shot by the other?' Oaten said, her brow furrowed.

'Maybe the shooter's accomplice got in the way,' Amelia Browning suggested.

Paskin led them into the front room. A body lay face-down in a slick of dried blood. He inclined his head towards a smaller patch of blood. 'We reckon that may be the other victim's, the one who's gone AWOL.'

The two women nodded. DS Browning was taking notes keenly.

'So there may be a witness to the murder,' Oaten said.

'If he's still alive,' Paskin said.

'Or she,' Amelia put in.

The superintendent gave her a long-suffering look. 'This is a Shadow store,' he said. 'You know who the Shadows are?'

The young woman nodded. 'Yes, sir. Long-established East End Turkish gang with interests in—'

'All right, Sergeant,' Oaten said, 'you've made your point.'

Paskin smiled. 'Good to come across people who read the files. Anyway, the Shadows don't use women. As far as they're concerned, women stay at home and look after their children.'

Spots of red appeared on Amelia Browning's cheeks. 'Maybe the killer wasn't a Shadow.'

'Or a man,' Oaten added. She frowned at her subordinate. 'Let's stick to the evidence, shall we?'

Paskin nodded. 'Whether the second victim ever shows is another matter. He was hit fairly badly, judging by the amount of blood, so he'll need medical treatment. Of course, the King's men have got their own doctors.' He looked over at Browning. 'Have you read the King's files too, Sergeant?'

'She's done her homework.' Oaten looked at her ex-boss. 'What have the Kurds got to do with this?'

'He was one of them.' The superintendent held out a photograph of a moustachioed man. 'He's Aro Izady, a cousin of the King. The question is, what was he doing here? He was an accountant and he didn't have a record. He wasn't the kind of man you'd expect to find in a storage depot owned by the opposition. There was a rumour a few years back that he killed a Shadow with a snooker cue, but there was no evidence. Actually, there was no body.'

Oaten was studying her ex-boss. 'Could that be why he's been killed now? But why in a Shadow store?'

'They are rather pointing the finger at themselves,' the superintendent said. 'Maybe they assumed no one would phone the shooting in.'

'Where were the Shadow guards?' Oaten said, looking at the piles of boxes containing electrical equipment that had doubtless been stolen. 'They wouldn't have left without a fight. Unless they were called off.'

'So far we haven't found anyone who heard shots,' Paskin added. 'Some of the locals won't talk to us on principle, but they're not all like that.'

Oaten's gaze rested on the green metal trunk, the bottom of which had been spattered with blood. 'Has anyone looked inside that?' she asked, pointing.

The superintendent nodded. 'It's empty. Or rather, almost empty. There are traces of cocaine all over the inside.'

'Meaning that maybe the shooter may have taken the stash with him,' Oaten said.

'Or her,' Paskin said with a grin.

Amelia Browning didn't appear to have heard him. 'Maybe the guards were lured out and disposed of. The shooter may not have been alone.'

Karen Oaten bit her lip. 'I still don't understand why a Kurd would be murdered here.' She looked up at the letter *S* that had been spray-painted on the wall. 'And no one in their right mind would steal drugs from a Shadow store.'

Browning raised her hand. 'Maybe Izady was a turncoat and the King found out. Killing him here would be a good way to get back at the Turks.'

'Imaginative,' said Paskin. 'But you haven't got a shred of evidence.'

The sergeant went back to scribbling in her notepad.

The women headed up the steps to the pavement. Paskin followed them, pausing to catch his breath.

'This is getting out of hand,' Oaten said. 'A Turk, a Kurd and now another Kurd. Soon we'll have a full-scale gang war on our hands.'

Paskin's expression was blank. 'It's a possibility.'

'Still nothing on the grapevine about another gang moving in?' Oaten asked.

Paskin shook his head. 'That's the strange part of all this. No one's saying anything about Albanians or Russians. And this is too neat for the Jamaicans. It can't be internal, because both Turks and Kurds are being hit.'

Karen Oaten took off her protective cap and smoothed her hair down. 'You know, there was another shooting with what we presume was a silenced pistol this morning. South of the river.'

'I heard. Potential connection to the White Devil.'

The chief inspector nodded. 'Maybe the same person's screwing with the gangs up here. Some serious money's been spent to get the information these hits would have needed.'

Paskin looked away. 'Sounds like a job for the VCCT then, Karen. Are you going to take these cases away from us?'

She sniffed. 'As if I have the personnel. Taff Turner's running the Dulwich murder. Obviously I can't have any direct involvement…'

'I know about your conflict of interest,' the superintendent said gently.

'And DS Pavlou's trying to kick some life into Homicide West over the woman author who was murdered. That's another dead end so far, though at least she wasn't shot.'

Paskin touched her arm. 'Are you taking over my cases or not?'

Oaten shook her head. 'Not for the time being.' She smiled weakly. 'They're in good hands. We still have no direct evidence connecting the three gang murders. The AC has insisted we take the Dulwich murder because of the press interest in the White Devil connection.' She rubbed her forehead. 'If there are any more murders, my job's going to be harder than a Middle East negotiator's.'

'You'll manage,' the superintendent said. 'And the weather's so much nicer in London.'

Karen Oaten snorted and watched Ron Paskin walk away, the coverall making him look like an overweight polar bear. She didn't remember him making that kind of quip when she worked for him. Maybe he kept them for jackasses parachuted in from New Scotland Yard.

She certainly felt that someone was committed to ridiculing her in public. If she didn't get a break soon, the AC would put her head on the revolving sign outside the Met.

'Mummy!' Lucy screamed.

Caroline came down the stairs in a tumble. 'What is it?' she asked, eyes wide as she looked around the hall of the detached house.

'You gave me the wrong password. That's why we haven't got e-mail. I've been trying other combinations and finally I got in.'

Her mother glared at her. 'You screamed as if you'd been…as if you'd seen a ghost because of that? I almost had a heart attack.' Something similar had happened when Lucy had run up shouting at the motorway services, when Caroline had been talking to a woman who had asked her about her shoes. The child had her father's tendency to overreact.

'It's your fault,' Lucy said. 'Daddy will be so worried, not hearing from us. I'm going to send him a message now.'

'Don't stay online any longer than you have to,' Caroline ordered. She was sure she'd typed in the right password. She'd been required to learn it by heart after being handed a sealed envelope by a solicitor over a year ago. He had then taken the envelope and its contents back, and run them through a shredder. She normally had an excellent memory for numerical and alphabetic codes, but she had so many to remember and today had been very tense. She would have killed for a gin and tonic, but whoever had stocked the cupboards had not included alcohol. Maybe Matt was behind that.

'Daddy's sent a reply,' Lucy called from the front room. 'He's angry that you took your car.'

'You told him?' Caroline said in disbelief. 'Get off that chair.' She pulled it from beneath her daughter and peered at the screen.

...you might have compromised the operation and put all three of you in danger. Caroline, this is not a game. If you've watched the news, you'll understand that. Please follow every other instruction to the letter. And do *not* stay online for more than a few minutes at a time. M.

Caroline leaned forward and typed a reply.

Time's up. Logging off NOW. C.

That would teach him to order them about, she thought triumphantly. But what did he mean about the news?

'Lucy,' she said, 'it's well past your bedtime. Upstairs now, young lady.'

'Oh, Mu—' The child broke off when she saw the look on her mother's face. ''Night,' she said, kissing Caroline on the cheek. ''Night, Gran.'

'What, dear?' Fran said, raising her eyes from the book she was reading. 'Oh, goodnight. Sleep tight.' She watched as Caroline turned on the television and moved from channel to channel. Only BBC24 was showing a news bulletin. It was from there that they learned of Dave Cummings's murder.

'Oh my God,' Caroline said, her hand to her mouth. 'Poor Dave. How awful for Ginny and the children.'

Caroline and Fran looked at each other and clasped hands, something they'd never done before. It made them feel better, but not much.

10

I thought about calling Karen before I turned in, but decided against it—she needed distance from me if she was to do her job properly. As I lay on the big bed that we'd shared only two nights earlier, I thought about our relationship. I loved her and she said she loved me. But what sort of love was it when both people's work was the most important thing in their lives? I also had Lucy, Fran and my mates, while Karen, whose parents had died when she was a student, was a loner, with no friends outside the police and, from what she'd said, not many inside—she certainly didn't meet up with people after work. I was all right as my needs were fulfilled, but it was difficult to tell what she wanted from the relationship as she'd built a protective shield around herself. Sometimes I wondered if a steak, a decent red wine and a massage followed by energetic sex were all she required. When I caught a wistful look or she embraced me more passionately than usual, I realised that she really did love me. I was more open about what I felt for her, but I was also sceptical about the ultimate power of that emotion. The divorce from Caroline and Sara's comprehensive betrayal had caused that, though I knew I was at fault for much that went wrong in my marriage. I also should have paid more attention to Sara. Every day I've blamed myself for failing to perceive her true character.

I didn't think I'd sleep, especially not with Andy stretched out on a row of cushions on the floor in my bedroom—he'd insisted on staying close—but I dropped fairly quickly into an exhausted slumber. Soon I was jolted awake by a vision of Dave. He was covered in blood and he started to speak. I heard the words, but couldn't make sense of them—only that he was frightened, and kept looking over my shoulder. I turned to see Sara, her eyes red and her mouth twisted into a demonic smile…

'Matt!'

I came back to the real world, to find Andy shaking my arm.

'You too, huh?' he said, blinking. His hair was all over the place. 'Dave… Christ, it was so real…'

So we sat side-by-side on the bed and talked about our friend, recalling his exploits on the rugby field, his bravery at the climax of the White Devil case and many nights of epic mayhem in the pubs of South London. I don't know if that made me feel any better, but it did send me eventually into a dreamless sleep. Dave's ghost, it seemed, had receded. I hoped he had crossed the bar and passed into the fields of Elysium, avoiding rebirth into this hard and bitter world.

Andy had also gone when I woke up, but it didn't take long to find him. The smell of bacon from the kitchen was enticing.

'Hungry?' he said. 'I've got scrambled eggs with red and green peppers, devilled kidneys, French toast, sausages, mushrooms and black pudding.'

'Bloody hell, Slash,' I said, taking in the array on plates. 'There's enough food for an army here.'

'We weren't up to eating yesterday, remember?'

My stomach was making clear that it needed filling, but I had to check my e-mails first. People I hadn't told about Dave's death were asking what had happened. I kept my replies short and told everyone to leave home for a few days if they could. Caroline had sent a brief e-mail saying the three of them had passed the night without problems, and demanding to know why I hadn't told her about Dave's death. I didn't reply. She'd never liked any of my friends and sharing my grief would have felt like disloyalty to Dave. I knew that was immature and that I'd get past it— but not yet. I opened the ghost website Rog had set up. Both he and Pete had checked in. They were okay and had started their separate searches for Sara via her financial dealings.

By the time I got to the table, Andy had started eating, but he had scrupulously left half of the food on each platter.

'Everything okay?' he asked, his mouth full.

I nodded. 'Apart from catching Sara.'

'Eat!' he ordered. 'It'll set you up for battle.'

I did as I was told. It was one of the best meals I'd ever had. I was putting the plates in the dishwasher when the phone rang. It was Karen.

'Good, you're at home,' she said, after greeting me. She sounded all in.

I glanced at Andy. 'Em, yeah, but I'll be going out soon.'

'Do you want to see me or not?' she asked testily.

'Of course I do,' I replied.

'Said with a *huge* amount of sincerity. I'll be round in a quarter of an hour. Don't worry, I won't be staying long.'

'Oh, shit,' I said, after she'd terminated the call. 'Karen's coming in fifteen, Slash. You'd better find somewhere to lie low. If she finds you here, she'll take you back to the Yard and squeeze a statement out of you.'

He got up from the table slowly. 'She won't look in the spare bedroom, will she?'

'She's a detective, big man. She might look anywhere. The walk-in wardrobe there is full of old coats and the like. You could lurk behind them.'

Andy grinned. 'I like a good lurk.' He continued clearing plates and stacking them in the dishwasher.

I went back to the computer. There were a few other people I needed to alert—crime writers who lived beyond the South East and who weren't obvious targets, and a few distant relations in the North. I logged back on to my e-mail programme. That turned out to be a very bad idea, though at least I didn't lose any time. There were two new messages that caught my eye. The first was from Josh Hinkley. He said that he understood I was in shock and that he didn't expect an apology for the way I'd spoken to him last night. Asshole squared. The other should have made me suspicious earlier than it did. The sender was *who's-next?* At first I thought it was to do with the Who—I subscribed to the band's newsletter. I should have been so lucky. After I read the first couple of lines I bellowed out Andy's name.

Hail, Matt Wells, aka Matt Stone, purveyor of crime fiction and non-fiction to the world. Except there haven't been too many novels lately, have there? Doesn't matter. I can help you on the ideas front. Who am I? That's for you to find out. I read your column in the *Daily Independent* and I know how well-endowed you are, so to speak, as regards knowledge of crime. That's why I've chosen you. I've also read *The Death List*—what a great book! But would you have been able to corner the White Devil without the help of your friend Dave Cummings? Oh, by the way, my condolences on his death. Very sad, deeply distressing, tragically pre-mature—all the meaningless bullshit people come out with when the 'd' word gets uncomfortably close to their pathetic lives.

'Who is this fucking shithead?' Andy shouted over my shoulder.

'Cool it,' I said. 'Let's see where this goes.'

Anyway, time moves ever onwards and, as you'll see, time is very important. I'm delighted to be in a position to issue a challenge—in fact, a series of challenges. As the title of this message says, the question I'll be asking you is "Who's Next?" I know from the archive of concert reviews on your website that you're a big fan of the Who. Sorry to disappoint you, but this has nothing to do with those aged rockers, or rather, Mods. No, this challenge concerns the other side of your writing life, crime fiction.

First, let me tell you various things that haven't come out in the media. I'm sure you know the details already since you spend so much time with the delectable DCI Oaten, but they'll establish my credentials, so to speak. The murder of Mary Malone: I took hairs from her head and pubic area; I drew a pentacle in white chalk in the garden to the rear of her house—within it, I wrote the words FECIT DIABOLUS. Is that enough? I hope you liked the reference to the Devil and that you approve of my choice of music. I know you love the Stones...

'Jesus,' I said, my stomach now revolting against breakfast. 'Unless someone in Karen's team is playing a seriously bad joke, this is Mary Malone's killer.'

Andy was staring at the screen. 'It gets worse, man.'

I scrolled down and read on.

So, da-daaah!—here's the challenge. All you have to do is solve the puzzle I've set for you by midnight tomorrow, Monday. I'll contact you by e-mail (obviously not using this address or provider—I learned that from the White Devil...) and ask for your answer. The rules are simple and I promise I'll observe them. If you e-mail me straight back with the correct answer, I won't kill my next target. If you don't, it's 'Goodnight, sweet lady' or 'prince'—no, I'm not going to ask you to identify that; anyone who read English at university, as you did, will spot that I'm riffing on lines from *Hamlet*. How can you trust me? Well, you haven't got much choice, have you? I already promised to play by the rules, Matt. That's all I can say.

Here it is—puzzle number one:

The sun set by the westernmost dunes of Alexander's womankind.

By the way, Matt, this is for *you* to work out. I know you'll ask your mother and your friends to help, there's nothing I can do to stop that. But if I discover that you've told Karen Oaten or anyone else in authority about the challenge, I swear I'll kill all the names on my list, including your family and everyone else you care for without giving you a second chance. Clear?

Till 23.59 tonight—I'll give you a minute to reply then. And remember, I've killed already. Not just Mary Malone, but her black cat as well. Off with its head! That wasn't reported either, was it?

You could call me Flaminio, but I prefer D.F.

'What is this shit?' Andy said, glancing at me. 'Have you got any idea what's going on here, Matt?'

I blinked and tried to concentrate. 'I know that Flaminio is the chief villain and white devil—meaning liar and hypocrite—in Webster's play of that name.'

Andy's brow furrowed as he tried to keep up. 'The White Devil? So Sara's behind this.'

I raised my shoulders. 'Maybe. But she's been busy already, assuming she killed Dave too.'

'Doesn't seem too likely that you've got another mad person on your ass.'

'Thanks for pointing that out, Slash.'

'What's D.F.?'

'Search me. Direction finder?'

'Yeah, we could use one of those.'

'Defender of the Faith? That means the Queen, in case you were wondering. No, it's probably not her.'

Andy looked at me dubiously. 'What about this half-assed challenge? You think whoever wrote this is really going to kill someone just because you can't work out their identity?'

I raised a hand. 'Hold on. We have to assume the writer is serious. Jesus, that clue could lead to Lucy or one of our friends. But you're messing up the motivation. The next target won't be killed because of anything I do. The killer's working to another plan—there's mention of a list. We'll have to work out who's on it from the message—I mean both how it's written and what it contains. And—if I blow it—by the modus operandi.'

'Yeah, well I think I'll leave solving the riddle to you,' the American said. 'I haven't done that kind of stuff since high school, and I screwed up in English literature big-time.'

I was looking at the line in red. 'The sun set by the westernmost—'

Then I heard keys turn in the locks. I'd forgotten about Karen.

'Into the wardrobe in the guest room,' I hissed to Andy, as the door opened and the chains rattled. Fortunately he'd already stashed the bag containing his weapons and other gear. I clicked off my e-mail and went quickly to the door.

Roger van Zandt opened the curtain of his room a couple of centimetres. The pavements in the back streets around Paddington Station were dotted with the rubbish left by representatives of the local subcultures—tarts, junkies, down-and-outs and the people who preyed on them. Rog didn't view himself as a prude, but this area made him wish that some morally superior politician of the kind he never voted for would launch a cleanup campaign.

He went back to the small desk that he'd been working at until sleep claimed him as dawn was breaking. His laptop sat there, a silver machine that had taken him all over the world from the grimy room. He had bought a cutting-edge processor, and the wireless card meant that he was completely mobile. Later he'd be slipping away from this dump and checking into another hotel. But before then he had to post what he'd found on the impregnable ghost site.

Rog sat down on the rickety chair and started to work on the document. What he had done was follow the money trail from the White Devil's accounts. He and Pete had originally found them two years back when they were on the trail of Matt's persecutor. After the madman's death, Matt had decided not to pursue the money. He didn't know that Rog and Pete had kept tabs on Sara's funds. Dave's murder meant that they had to track Sara down fast via her money, and Rog was glad they had only a small number of transactions to catch up on. It had taken him no more than a few minutes to realise that someone who really knew what they were doing had done their utmost to obscure the trail. Sara had obviously hired a top-notch techie before she went after Dave.

Not that Rog had been stymied. It had taken some time, but he now had a list of bank accounts, ranging from Switzerland to Macau, via the Cayman Islands and Bolivia. He knew where Sara had invested part of the forty-two million dollars she'd acquired—in U.S. and German government stocks, but also in a range of public companies. Pete would be able to work on that side. Last, but definitely not least, Rog had discovered several properties that Sara had bought. Four of those were in the U.K., three in the south-east of England.

The interesting thing about the U.K. properties was the name of the owner—Angela Oliver-Merilee. Rog had run identity checks and had found two women with that name. One was a ninety-two-year-old resident of a nursing home in Yorkshire, the other the seven-year-old daughter of a classics teacher living in Manchester. Rog was sure the name had been chosen for a reason. Matt would probably have some thoughts on that.

Rog finished the text and sent it to the ghost site, then logged off and shut down his machine.

A few minutes later he was in the shower, water spraying all over the yellowing tiles from a faulty head. Having devoted himself to nailing Sara for so many hours, now Rog couldn't get Dave out of his mind. Tears ran down his face and were immediately washed down the drain by the jets of lukewarm water.

He stumbled from the shower, dripping water over the floor. Pausing only to dry his hands, Rog logged on to the ghost site again and sent a message to his friends:

I can't do this on my own, guys. What are we doing hiding from the bitch? Dave would have wanted us to stand up and fight her in the open. Matt, at least let me and Pete work together. We'll look after each other. Please. I'm fucking dying in this dump.

Then Rog cut the connection to the Internet and buried his head in his hands.

'Matt?' Karen called.

'Coming,' I said, trying to remember what I'd done with my Glock. Had I left it anywhere obvious?

'Morning, Karen,' I said, sliding the chains off and admitting her. I kissed her on the mouth and then ran to my bedroom. 'I left the tap running,' I shouted. The pistol was lying in full view on my bedside table. I quickly buried it in a drawer full of old South London Bisons shirts. I didn't think she'd look there.

When I came out, she was dangerously near my computer. Fortunately she didn't have the nerve to touch the keyboard and mouse in front of me, though I suspected she might have had a look if I'd stayed away much longer. She'd be expecting the family and friends who'd gone to ground to be keeping in touch by e-mail. If she saw the message with the clue, she'd be duty bound to investigate it. That could be very costly, if the writer was as ruthless as he or she threatened.

Karen turned to me after she'd shrugged off her coat. 'Did you get any sleep?' she said, opening her arms.

Feeling a complete bastard for doubting her feelings, I fell into her embrace. 'Some,' I said, after a while. 'You?'

'Under an hour.' She sniffed the air. 'You've had a rugby player's breakfast.'

I nodded, hoping she wouldn't open the dishwasher and see the second plate. 'What happened?'

'I was called out.'

My heart missed a beat. 'What was it?'

'A dead Kurd at Manor House.'

I breathed out in relief. 'Another gang killing?'

'Looks that way. God, I need a large dose of coffee.'

I went over to the kitchen, leading her away from the computer. As I was spooning coffee into the filter machine, I asked her about the investigation into Dave's death.

'Taff's handling it,' she said, sitting on one of the stools at the kitchen island. 'It would be fair to say the VCCT is stretched to breaking point.'

'You've taken the case over?'

She shrugged. 'Didn't have any choice,' she replied. 'The AC's running scared because your friends in the press are drooling at the prospect of another White Devil.'

She frowned. 'Thanks to your book, they know all about Dave, not to mention Sara.'

I felt the sting of her words. 'Has Taff got anything?' I asked, after I poured her a mug of the black stuff.

'Not much. The neighbours only saw you and your friends. No one saw a woman, or anyone else in the vicinity of Dave's house yesterday morning.'

'Are you sure? It was a Saturday morning. Most people would have been around.'

'The whole street's been questioned. Most of them were off shopping or taking the kids to ballet, football, whatever.'

'What about the houses at the back? Maybe she got in that way.'

'Those people have been asked, too. They only saw your friend Pete. What exactly was he doing back there?'

I tried not to be evasive. If someone had noticed the bag he was carrying, Karen would nail me. 'He was covering the back in case an intruder bolted. He took a tennis racket with him, would you believe?'

She held my gaze. 'I wouldn't, but you're not going to admit to anything else. I don't suppose you've received a message from Sara.'

I was able to answer that truthfully, at least as regards the names used by the sender. 'No.'

'I'm wondering if there's some connection with the murders in East London. I don't suppose Dave ever had a run-in with any of the bad men there.'

'Not that I'm aware of. I don't remember him ever working in that area.'

She sipped from her mug. 'Maybe someone's taking out ex–Special Forces people.'

'Like an Irish paramilitary group?' I hadn't thought of that. It wasn't completely beyond the realms of possibility. 'And they copied the modus operandi from my book?'

She shrugged, avoiding my eyes. 'The military intelligence people are following that up with Special Branch. Christ, what am I doing telling you this? Don't you dare put it in your column.'

'Oddly enough, my column is the last thing I'm thinking about right now.'

Karen stood up. 'I've got to go.'

'Hang on,' I said, opening a cupboard and finding a plastic travel cup for her coffee. I stalled before giving her it. 'Anything new on the Mary Malone murder?'

'It's still with Homicide West. Why? Do you think it's connected?'

'With Dave's death? Anything's possible in that mad woman's universe.'

Karen leaned forward and took the cup from me. 'Why though?' she said, pouring coffee from her mug. 'To put the shits up you?'

'Yes, before killing me.' I looked at her, only now aware of the dark rings round her eyes. 'Nice thought. You should sleep.'

She gave a hollow laugh. 'If that was an attempt to get me into bed, you need to work on your technique.' She put the lid on the cup and moved round the island. 'I'll call you later,' she said, kissing me on the mouth.

'Okay,' I said, watching her go. I went over to the door and put the chains back on. I felt bad about pumping her for information while concealing the message I'd received, but my experience with the White Devil had showed that involving the authorities wasn't a viable option.

I went into the spare room and knocked on the wardrobe. Andy opened the door, his silenced Glock raised. 'Christ,' I gasped. 'It's only me. Karen's gone.'

He looked past me. 'You can't be too careful, man.'

I knew he was right, but the problem was I had just over fifteen hours to figure out the clue I'd been sent. Right now, I hadn't the faintest idea whose name was concealed behind 'The sun set behind the westernmost dunes of Alexander's womankind'. The only Alexander I knew was a critic who'd been killed by the White Devil. Was Sara really hiding behind the revenger's name Flaminio? And what the hell did D.F. mean?

Faik Jabar was cushioned in something like cotton wool, his limbs and body softly supported. His sight had become so acute, he could make out the mountains of the Kurdish homeland he had never visited. The snow on the peaks was bathed in a golden light, and in the villages below the people were waving to him, calling for him to come down, saying that his place was with them, that he was their brother—

He screamed as he suddenly plummeted earthwards and crashed on to the stony ground. Opening his eyes, he did not recognise where he was. His right hand hurt like the bite of a rabid beast. He tried to move, but couldn't. Looking down the iron bedstead, he saw that his wrists and legs had been strapped to the frame. The mattress he was lying on smelled of sweat and urine.

'Hello?' he called out, first in English, then in Kurdish. He heard sounds behind the faded door. A key turned in the lock.

'So the brave soldier is awake,' said a man in Kurdish. He had a thick moustache and was wearing a well-cut suit. 'A pity about your friend.'

The scene in the basement flashed before him, the traitor Aro Izady lying in a mess of his own blood. Faik tried to scream again, but his voice had disappeared. Then he saw the face of the killer, the man with the beard. What was it about him? Something weird… What was it? The image came back to him—the beard had come away, revealing part of the face beneath. It had not been a man's. It was the face of a demon from—

Faik felt a powerful slap on his cheek.

'You will listen when I speak to you, Kurdish shit!'

Faik blinked away the involuntary tears that had filled his eyes. He made out a different man, this one younger, maybe in his early thirties. He was wearing a brown leather jacket and his face was covered in heavy stubble.

'Now do you hear me?' the man said. He was speaking English, but with a strong accent that Faik immediately recognised. His captor was a Turk.

'Yes,' Faik replied. 'I hear you.' He gasped as his wounded hand was squeezed hard.

'Oh, you're beginning to remember things, are you?' the Turk said, his voice mocking. 'The doctor here is one of your people, but he is happy to take our money. He cleaned the wound and stitched it. You were lucky. The tendons are in good shape. With rest, full movement will be restored.' He gave a laugh that turned into a grunt. 'If you live that long.'

'Who are you?' Faik demanded, grimacing as the pain struck again.

'Hurts like hell, doesn't it?' the Turk said. 'Particularly since we haven't given you any painkillers.'

Faik struggled to look impassive. It took him some time. He was aware that the Turk continued talking, asking him what he had been doing in the basement, what had happened to Aro Izady, but most of all, asking who had shot Izady and him.

Faik clenched every muscle he could when the butt of a pistol came down hard on his injured hand. He closed his eyes and saw only red, a similar red to the blood that had fountained from Aro Izady's head.

'Who fired the shots?' the Turk yelled. 'Tell me his name.'

Faik opened his eyes and saw the gun over his shoulder. 'No name,' he said with a gasp. 'Izady brought him in his car.'

His captor paused. 'What happened to Aro?'

Faik wondered who the man was, to be on first-name terms with Izady.

'Answer!' the Turk said, his mouth close to Faik's head.

'Izady was a traitor. He was working for you. You are a Shadow, are you not?'

There was silence, then the man's mouth came close again.

'Describe the man who shot you.'

'He…he had dark hair and…and a beard.' Faik broke off, trying to put his thoughts into words. 'Medium height, well built, black clothes.'

'What language did he speak?'

'English. He wasn't one of us.' Faik paused. 'Or you.'

'What else?' the Turk demanded. 'You're hiding something. Watch my hand!'

Faik saw the point of the pistol rest against the bandage on his hand.

'Unless you want two holes instead of one, you'd better come clean, you blue-eyed fuck!'

'I…I don't know…how to say…'

The Turk turned his head. 'Doctor!' he shouted.

The man in the suit reappeared, looking uneasy.

'Tell him in your own language,' the Turk ordered Faik.

The young man gabbled to the other Kurdish. The doctor seemed puzzled and spoke again. Faik repeated what he had said.

'It seems that the beard was false,' the doctor said to the Turk. 'Part of it came off.' He broke off.

'And?' the Turk said, going over to the man in the suit. 'What did he see?'

'He…he says he saw a terrible face, like a devil's…'

'What?' The Turk looked at the bound young man. 'What the fuck are you talking about?'

'It was a devil face,' Faik said. 'Out of shape, swollen, scarred. I saw black and red wounds, lumps… It was horrible.'

The Turk stared at Faik and then brought the pistol down on his wounded hand again. 'Bullshit! You know who it was, don't you?'

Faik Jabar was in agony. He shook his head. 'It's true,' he said. 'That's what I saw.'

'Let me try another question,' the Turk said. 'Do you know who I am?'

The young man shook his head. He didn't want to know. If he could identify his captor, his life would be worth nothing.

The Turk grinned. 'I am known as the Wolfman.'

Faik groaned and shut his eyes. The Wolfman was the savage who did the Shadows' dirtiest work. But the face he'd seen beneath the false beard was much more frightening than that of the unshaven Turk.

'Again the hair and nails of an unbeliever burn to the greater glory of the Lord Beneath the Earth!'

The masked man in the cowl and robe lowered his arms. He looked around the cavern. The mandrill Beelzebub was squatting by the sluggish stream, splashing his paws in it. There were no fish in the shallow water. Perhaps he was trying to catch his reflection. One might have thought the fangs would scare him, but the beast was made of sterner stuff.

As was the naked supplicant at the altar. Mephistopheles had seen some wonderfully sinister devotees in the years he had directed the order, but there had never been one such as this. His faith in his Master had been restored, as, soon, would be the family fortunes.

Beelzebub screamed and came charging over the stone floor. When the supplicant turned, the mandrill stopped immediately and lowered his head. He had always respected the stronger, more vicious creature whose face was uglier than his own.

11

'Shit,' I said, leaning back from my desk.

Andy was quickly behind me.

'Don't worry, it isn't another puzzle,' I said. 'It's Rog.'

The American read our friend's plea, then looked at me. 'He's right, Matt. We're sticking together. So should Rog and Pete.'

I thought about it. My instinct for safety told me it was a bad idea, but there was no question that Dave would have wanted us to get in Sara's face. 'All right,' I said, leaning towards the keyboard. 'I'll tell them to set up base at Pete's place. Even Sara will have a job getting past his alarm system.'

Andy nodded. 'And maybe we'll catch her trying.'

I wasn't convinced by that, but it was worth a shot. Besides, Dave had taught us how to look after ourselves and each other. Not that it had done him any good. I also sent Rog the puzzle and asked him to run it through any deciphering programmes he had access to.

An hour later, Andy and I were going through the sheets I'd printed off. Rog wasn't convinced that the line about the sun setting on the westernmost dunes of Alexander's womankind was algorithmic or mathematical in form, but he'd tried anyway. He knew a lot about ciphers from the programmes he wrote all the time. I'd also asked Pete to think about it. He had the kind of mind that picked up unusual information and noticed things that most people didn't. Again, I wasn't very hopeful. I had the feeling the line was more like a crossword clue. The problem was, I'd always been crap at cryptic crosswords.

Before I got down to serious consideration of the clue, I looked at the material Pete had sent to the website. He'd been talking to his friends in the City and was following up several of Rog's leads. Background material was attached, but there wasn't enough to act on yet.

'What now?' Andy asked, papers on the floor around him. He looked substantially out of his depth.

'We have to work out a strategy, Slash. I'm going to see if I can make any sense out of that bloody riddle. There's a deadline on it, literally.'

'Ha,' the American said. 'What do you want me to do?'

I'd been thinking about that, and about the woman who was the owner of the four British properties bought with Sara's funds.

'Angela Oliver-Merilee,' I said. 'Mean anything to you?'

Andy ran a hand through his blonde thatch. 'Should it?'

'Oh yes. What was the White Devil's real name?'

That made him think. 'Shit, man, I can't remember. Lonnie something?'

'Close. Leslie Dunn. Except, he was adopted, remember? When I was writing *The Death List,* I got a copy of the adoption papers.' I held up the file that I'd taken from my safe earlier on.

'Spit it out, smart-ass,' Andy said impatiently.

'Well, his birth mother's name was Doris Merilee.'

He stared at me. 'All right. But I still don't see where you're going with this.'

I opened the file and pointed to a section of the poor-quality copy. 'He wasn't christened, but his birth mother had given him a name. She called him—'

'Oliver,' he completed. 'Jeez. What does that mean?'

I shrugged. 'That depends. Sara's still hurting about her twin brother's death and she's been planning carefully. The first of those properties, the farmhouse in Kent, was bought six months ago. The last, the cottage in the Scottish borders, was bought only a month back. But that's not all.' I pulled another sheet from the file. 'Doris Merilee gave Sara a name too.'

Andy's eyes widened. 'Angela.'

I nodded. 'On the button.'

'I still don't understand where this leads us.'

I wrote an address on a slip of paper and handed it to him.

'47 Northumberland Crescent, Sydenham,' he read.

'That's where the birth mother lives.'

Andy stood up slowly. 'Christ, she's still alive?'

'According to the phone directory. She married three years after she gave the twins up for adoption. Her name's now Doris Carlton-Jones.'

'Okay. Shall I bring her in?'

I laughed. 'No, Slash. You aren't a cop, remember? I'm going to give you my camera. You need to hire a van. Park it near the house and use it for cover while you carry out surveillance. Take photos of her if she comes out.' I gave him a serious look. 'Take your gun with you. It's possible that Sara's re-established contact with her and is down there. She might even turn up for a visit.'

'Jeez, that would solve a lot of problems.'

I raised my hand, aware that what I was about to say was a waste of breath. 'Don't try to grab Sara if she shows. Call me and I'll get Karen involved.'

He looked at me dubiously and then nodded. 'Okay.'

'Call in every hour on the hour, on the secure line.' Rog had done what he could to make the land line I used only for my friends secure. There was still a risk, but it was small and I preferred to know that Andy was okay.

He nodded. 'What about the other two properties Sara bought?'

'There's a house in Oxford and a flat in Hackney.'

'Hackney, East London? That's a bit down-market for her, isn't it?'

I thought about that. 'It isn't clear what she's doing with the properties. Maybe they're just investments. Or potential safe houses.'

'Not any more. We have to check them out.'

'We do. But I have to solve this bloody clue first, remember?'

'Shouldn't I take a look at the places in and around London rather than watch on the mother?'

I shook my head. 'When we go in, we go in together, okay?'

He was reluctant, but he accepted that.

'Stay sharp,' I said, when he'd got himself ready.

He slapped me on the shoulder. 'Ditto. Good hunting with that puzzle shit.'

I undid the chains and replaced them when he'd gone out. Then I went back to my desk and concentrated on the puzzle. I'd done some research on cryptography for one of my novels set in the seventeenth century. People back then were keen on codes because of the political and religious turmoil. The problem was, there were a hell of a lot of different methods—substitution codes based on arithmetical figures, such as shifting every letter forward by three; transposition ciphers, where the order of letters is changed; anagrams, where rearranged letters make a different word; acrostics, where the first or last letters form different words—and that was just the start. I tried all those basic ideas with the 'sun sets' line and got nowhere. The problem with both substitution and transposition is that, without the key, you can waste huge amounts of time crunching the numerous possibilities. That was where computer software came in, and Roger could use it—but time he spent on the clue was time not spent tracking down Sara. He was better employed doing the latter, not least because there was a good chance she was the one who had sent the message and he might kill two birds with one well-aimed stone.

I got up from my desk, its surface covered in crumpled pieces of paper, and walked up and down the living area. My mind was all over the place, and the fact that someone's life hung in the balance didn't do a lot for the state of my nerves. I thought about turning the message over to Karen. Would the sender ever find out? This was different from the White Devil case—then, my flat had been bugged and cameras had been secretly installed. Andy had been over my apartment with the locating device and got nothing except the alarm system. So was it safe to tell Karen? No chance. Even if she was prepared to keep quiet about the fact that Mary Malone's killer had contacted me, the nature of police work meant that someone would spot their involvement, even if they didn't use sirens or send in the Armed Response Unit. Besides, the VCCT had a history of leaking to the press. As I'd seen with Jeremy Andrewes's use of Josh Hinkley, those hounds were already on my trail. No, I had to keep Karen out of this loop as well.

So what now? The first time I'd read the line, I'd thought of a crossword clue. That was bad news, as I struggled to get through the so-called quick crosswords in the papers. Cryptic ones I avoided like the Black Death. I had a stockbroker friend who used to do three cryptic puzzles as he was being driven into the City every morning—and he still had time left to scan the financial pages and close a few deals. I told him that just proved he had the cold, calculating mind of a money-making machine; he told me that any writer worth his place on the earth should be able to do a cryptic crossword in under ten minutes. We'd stopped being friends.

'The sun set by the westernmost dunes of Alexander's womankind.' What was going on there? I went over to the shelves where I kept books that had defeated me, but weren't so bad that they went to the local charity shops— among them were the later poems of Ezra Pound, *Finnegan's Wake*—was the line a quote from it?—and the novels of Dorothy L. Sayers. There was also a guide to solving cryptic crosswords. I'd bought it second-hand when I was trying to emulate my former friend. I took the tattered book back to my desk and ran through the clue forms it suggested. I tried inserting a comma, and then commas plural, to change the sense. No joy. I looked into the question of anagrams again, though I couldn't see any of the usual words suggesting that reordering was necessary—there was no 'mix up', 'shuffled' or the like. Then I looked into word exchange—'orb' instead of 'sun', 'group' instead of 'set', 'desert' instead of 'dunes', and so on. Nothing flashed up. Were there words hidden in other words? I saw 'stern' in 'westernmost', but I didn't know anyone of that name. I saw 'lex' in 'Alexander's'—that was Latin for 'law', which seemed relevant if the next target was a crime writer, though it could also apply to a judge or a policeman. A shiver ran up my spine. Was that a reference to Karen? The word 'womankind' certainly suggested that the victim would be a female. Again, I felt guilty about keeping the clue from her. If her life was in danger and I allowed the killer to catch her unawares, how would I feel? Shit. This was almost as bad as the contortions the White Devil put me through. Which was, no doubt, the point.

I sat back in my chair and looked up at the ceiling. Maybe I was being too clever. Maybe the clue was more basic than I'd thought. How many Alexanders could I think of? Alexander worked as a male first name, and as a surname. 'Womankind' suggested a female. Did I know any Ms Blank Alexanders? I couldn't think of any. I had a look at the Crime Writers' Society directory. There were a couple of guys called Alex, including one whose surname was Black and whom I vaguely knew. He lived in Edinburgh. I thought of the cottage in the Scottish Borders that Sara owned. It was too close for comfort. I sent Alex Black an e-mail via a single-use account, suggesting he go to ground until further notice. The other Alex lived in Egypt. I reckoned he was safe enough there. As for women, there were none with the surname of Alexander. I checked the nom de plume section—no Alexanders there, either.

'Bollocks!' I yelled, throwing the directory over my shoulder. I went back to the crossword book. Abbreviations? I didn't see any. Words with two or more meanings? That was more suggestive. Apart from the definite article, all the words had multiple meanings, especially if you considered the symbolic undertones. 'Sun' implied light; enlightenment; the central point around which everything else revolves—did the target have a large ego?—and riches, which could imply a best-seller. 'Set' could mean group, but also something that hardens, as in jam. But on a basic level, the sun sets in the west. Was that the point? It seemed unlikely, given that 'westernmost' was already in the sentence. 'Sand' could be the stuff on the beach— was this a reference to some beach in the far west? But it could also refer to time, as in the sands of… Even a seemingly innocent word like 'by' could mean several things— a book written *by* an author seemed suggestive, but how did that fit with the dunes? Neither of the guys in the directory called Alex had written books whose titles or settings had anything to do with beaches or the west. 'By' could also mean 'close to'—again, I'd already drawn a blank with proximity to beaches.

I stretched out and grabbed the *Oxford Classical Dictionary,* one of my favourite books. But this time it left only a bitter taste in my mouth. There was a lengthy section on Alexander the Great, as well as entries for several other kings of that name. I discovered that the Greek name originally meant 'he who wards off men'— a good name for a warrior, but not much help to me now. 'Alexander's womankind'? What women was Alexander involved with? His mother Olympias was reputed to be a witch—could that be significant? Maybe it was a link to the pentacle. Alexander married Roxanna. I knew no one of that name. Besides, the Macedonian general was better

known for his relationships with men. Was there some
subtext about homosexuality in the message? Anyway,
what did Alexander's women have to do with 'westernmost
dunes'? The north of Greece wasn't sandy, at least in the
inland parts where Alexander and his mother came from.
There was plenty of desert in central Asia where Roxanna
originated, but so what?

Then I remembered. I knew another Alexander. One of
the White Devil's victims was a slimeball of a critic who
had slammed my books out of spite—his name was Alexander Drys. I felt the hairs on the back of my neck stand
on end. It would be very much in character for Sara to be
taunting me by referring to the critic. And the fact was that
Alexander Drys had been a notorious womaniser, as I'd
discovered when I was writing *The Death List*. Men in his
club had told me that he was forever boasting of the whores
he'd screwed. He wasn't the kind of man who would have
attracted many women into a long-term relationship, so he
took pride in paying for sex. I'd even tracked down one of
the women he'd used. She was a Bulgarian called Katya,
an English-language student who'd been kidnapped and
forced into a brothel in Soho by a vicious Albanian gang.
Now I thought of it, Albania was to the west of Alexander
the Great's Macedon. Was that what the clue was hinting
at? Could Katya be the target?

After scribbling a note for Andy and leaving it, as we'd
agreed, in my copy of *Rugby League—Sport of Heroes,* I
slipped my pistol into the pocket of my leather jacket. I put
the silencer and a set of knuckle-dusters into the other
pockets. If I was going to walk into the belly of the
Albanian beast, I would need all the weapons I could pack.

I thought about my field knife, but decided against it. If I couldn't use my Glock in time, I'd be finished.

As I walked out of my apartment, I thought about texting Andy. I knew the number of his new mobile. Running down the stairs, I decided against it. We needed to spread our resources. If I didn't show, he'd know where to look for me, though I'd told him in the note to concentrate on nailing Sara. The problem was, he'd never been much good at following instructions he didn't like. Improvisation was the American's major virtue, but it was also his Achilles' heel.

Even though the radio in the white van, playing Son Volt's latest album, was turned down low enough so that passersby couldn't hear it, Andy Jackson felt very uncomfortable. He had tried to fit his tall frame across the front seats, but that had resulted in serious muscle pain and cramping. Now he was crouching behind the seats, in the empty cargo space. The problem was that he would struggle to get into the driving-seat to follow Doris Carlton-Jones if she got into the Japanese hatchback in her driveway and turned right. She might get away before he could execute the necessary three-point turn.

Andy fingered the pistol in his belt. If he should see Sara, he would save Matt and everyone else a lot of trouble by drilling her full of holes. He didn't give a shit if he was arrested for murder. As far as he was concerned, he'd be doing a public service. Besides, he was pretty sure that Sara would be armed and he'd be able to claim he fired in self-defence. But first he had to find her, and he wasn't going to do that by sitting in a back street in Sydenham.

He was about to clamber over the seats when he saw the front door of number 47 open. He dropped back into cover and watched as a well-preserved, grey-haired woman wearing a dark blue trouser-suit came out. She headed for her car.

'Shit,' Andy said under his breath. 'Turn left, lady. Turn left!'

He waited until the car was moving before getting into the front. As he did so, he saw the left indicator come on.

'Way to go!' he said, turning the key in the ignition. Then he waited till he saw the red hatchback indicate right at the end of the road. He eased the van into gear and drove off in restrained pursuit.

Andy Jackson reckoned Matt would have been pleasantly surprised.

I took the Tube to Leicester Square and came out to a blustery squall. Even though it was Sunday, there were plenty of people around, not all of them foreign, judging by the swearing in various English accents as umbrellas were blown inside out and clothes were drenched. I was wearing a leather cowboy hat with a wide brim that I'd bought in Texas. It had the additional advantage of shielding my face from the CCTV cameras. I didn't want to compromise Karen by showing up on video, should things get nasty at Katya's place of work.

The rain drummed on my hat and I could feel the brim being weighed down. It only took me a few minutes to find the place I'd chosen from my list of businesses controlled by the Albanian mob. Six months ago, I'd written about gangs that had moved into London in recent years.

The joint was a walk-up, the entrance-door open. The

battered sign said !Sexy Susie's Sauna etSEXera! I wondered if the Albanians had come up with that. At the top of the stairs my way was blocked by an unshaven gorilla in a black T-shirt that was stretched to the limit by his biceps.

'Hat off,' he grunted, as I reached the top step.

'Okay,' I said, depositing a wave of rainwater from my hat over his trousers and shoes. I smiled. 'Oops.'

The gorilla thought about belting me and decided against it. First, they'd take my money, then he could kick my arse.

I put my hand into my pocket and came out with a fifty-pound note.

'Not for you,' I said, whipping it away from the wet muscle-man.

'Thank you, sir,' said a middle-aged woman, who had appeared from the rear of the premises.

'Are you Sexy Susie?' I asked.

She snorted, ran a test pen over the note and then put it through a narrow slit in the door to her left. Anyone who tried to rob the place would not only have to deal with the gorilla, but break down the armoured door and face the heavily armed gang member behind it. I didn't think there would have been many successful attempts.

'Would you care to see what we have to offer, sir?' the woman said. The lines on her face were visible even beneath the thick layer of make-up, and her voice, despite the customer-friendly vocabulary and syntax, was as warm as an ice floe. She pointed to the plasma screen behind her. It was split into eight squares, three of which were blank— danger, men at work. The other five showed women wearing very little and sitting in contorted poses. I looked closer. None of them was Katya.

'No good,' I said. 'I want Katya.'

Sexy Susie glanced at the muscle behind me. 'Katya?' she said. 'I don't think we have a Katya.' Her tone dripped fake bonhomie. 'How about Lena?' she said, pointing to one of the squares.

'Is she over sixteen?' I asked.

The madam lost patience. 'Muzzie,' she said, 'this gentleman's just leaving.'

Two large hands came down on my shoulders and turned me round. I could see his belly was slack. Dave had taught us exactly what to do with guys like him. I drew my right hand back quickly and drove it into the upper part of his abdomen, just below the sternum. He went down like a sack of lead weights. Unfortunately for him, the stairs were right behind. He slid down them on his backside, his head hitting the street door with a satisfying thud.

I turned back to Susie. 'Katya,' I said. 'Now.'

'She isn't here,' she said, stepping back as I advanced on her. 'I swear it.'

'Where is she, then?' I asked, hearing a rattle at the door to my right. I pulled out my Glock and pointed it at the woman's face. 'Stay in there unless you want her brains on the wallpaper!' The rattling stopped.

'I dunno,' the madam said, her voice quivering.

I moved closer, the muzzle of my pistol almost touching her forehead. 'You know, all right,' I said, smiling. 'I'm counting to three. Not out loud. And I've started.'

The woman glared at me, her eyes damp. 'Put it away, mister,' she said desperately.

'Talk first.'

'I... Oh, for fuck's sake. Katya's with one of the bosses.

Jesus, you don't know what you've walked into. They'll cut your pathetic cock off and stuff it in your mouth.'

'What's his name?' I said, holding the Glock steady.

'Shkrelli,' she replied. She was trembling now.

'Which one?'

'Safet.'

The Shkrelli clan kept a low profile, but it was one of the Albanian mob's most powerful operators.

'Have you got a number for him?' I asked.

'You're out of your fucking mind,' the woman said, shaking her head.

'I know,' I said, smiling again. There was nothing like a smile to convince criminals you were serious—it was an unwritten rule for major hard men. I wasn't one of those, but I could play the part for a while.

She took a pencil with a chewed end from the pocket of her over-tight jeans and wrote on the back of a betting slip. 'You'd better not use that,' she said, as she handed it to me.

I nodded. 'Thanks for the advice. Do you want me to hit you?'

She understood what I meant. 'Nah, they heard it all anyway. They'll be the ones doing the hitting.'

'You can walk out of here with me,' I said, lowering the Glock.

She thought about that, then shook her head. 'No point,' she said. 'You're going to be dead soon.'

I laughed, which surprised her. I was thinking how disappointed Sara would be if I was taken out by the Albanian mob before she got to me.

'Go, you idiot,' she said, a smile flickering on her lips. 'And don't come back.' The rattling on the door started up again.

I shrugged. 'Thanks,' I said, then turned on my heel and ran down the stairs.

The gorilla was just coming round as I reached the street door. He made a half-hearted attempt to grab my legs, but stopped when I knocked his head against the wall.

'Don't,' I said, pointing the pistol at his face.

He cowered, even when I'd put the Glock back in my jacket. Then I put my cowboy hat back on and stepped confidently on to the street like a well-satisfied customer.

As I turned the corner, I realised that my heart was in overdrive and my throat was as dry as a Balkan mountain in high summer.

12

Karen Oaten went out of New Scotland Yard and headed for the café where she often bought lunch—although she wasn't often there on a Sunday. She was served by Dino, one of the owner's swarthy sons. They all had a good line in risqué patter, but Dino was the master.

'It is good in the beautiful signora's life, everything?' he asked, as he put together Oaten's tuna sandwich. The brothers had been to school in West London, but Dino liked to play the cute Italian boy only recently arrived from the old country.

'Wonderful,' she said, surprised by the bitterness in her voice. Even though her desk was piled high with murder files, Karen wasn't usually daunted by her job. She'd been through worse times—the White Devil's reign of terror, for example.

'I can help the signora in many ways,' Dino said, raising an eyebrow at her. 'Especially in bedroom.' He handed over a plate with her sandwich and an Americano.

'I'm sure,' Karen said, ignoring the innuendo. She paid and headed for a table in the corner. As she ate, she thought about why she was bitter. It didn't take much effort to pinpoint the reason. Dino, by chance rather than design, had identified the problem. She needed help, but it wasn't the kind you could get from anyone else—she needed self-help. It was hardly the first time in her life that she'd been troubled by affairs of the heart. Where did that old-fashioned phrase come from? She didn't read Regency romances or the like. But in the past, such problems had been easily sorted. A sweet-tongued, two-timing barrister had been sent reeling back to his chambers by a well-directed kick to his groin; a chief inspector from Vice whose demands got ever more disturbing was reined in after Karen called his wife; and a VCCT sergeant with ideas substantially above his station was back in uniform, policing football matches. None of those techniques would work with Matt, though.

Karen looked at the people at the counter. A few of them would be police officers in plain clothes or civilian support staff, but most were ordinary members of the public. She wondered what it would be like to work in a nine-to-five job, with nothing more to worry about each day than which TV channel to watch and what to cook for dinner. She never had time to watch television, except occasionally the late news, and Matt always cooked when they were together, even at her place. She was a disaster in the kitchen and survived on frozen meals and tins when she was alone. So what was her problem? She had a man who cared for her, and a job that she treasured, even if it sometimes got to her.

'Is okay?' Dino was standing over the small table, arms akimbo.

Karen knew he wasn't only asking about the food. 'Leave me alone.' She got no pleasure seeing the young man's head jerk back as if he had been slapped, but she really did need to think things through. Matt loved her, she knew that. And she loved him. That would be enough for most people, but they were different. Weird, in fact. She knew what her problem was—the job made her cold and dispassionate, or rather she had always been that way and working murder cases had made her more so. But Matt, he was a collection of different people in a single body—admittedly a very attractive one, especially since he'd been hitting the gym. He was a father, though she hadn't had kids so she couldn't fully fathom that side of him. He was a lover, true to his word and tender as any man she'd known. But he was also a writer, following in his adoptive mother's footsteps—and writers, particularly those in the crime genre, were skilled liars, experts at concealing motive and ruthless at achieving their ends. That was the problem with Matt. It had been that way during the White Devil investigation, when he hadn't been able to trust her. Something similar was happening now. He had found one of his best friends dead and suddenly he was putting into operation a carefully organised plan that she was sure she knew only a small part of. Where were the other guys? Andy Jackson, Roger van Zandt and Peter Satterthwaite were up to something—some of them probably trying to pick up Sara Robbins's trail via her financial transactions, as they had done with the White Devil. She had sent officers to the three homes, but none of them had been there. Matt was keeping things from her, she knew that. If she wanted, she could take him into protective custody—forcibly if necessary. That would put a terrible strain on their relationship, but would it be worse than Matt carrying out a private war against the woman who'd betrayed him? What if that war led to innocent victims?

'Guv?'

Karen looked up. 'Oh, hi, Taff.'

'Can I join you?'

'*May* I join you,' she said. 'I had a pedantic old English teacher. Obviously you're physically capable of joining me. You want to know if I'll give you permission to join me, which requires "may".'

'I'll take that as a "yes", shall I?' the Welshman asked, pulling up a chair. He was carrying one plate piled high with toast and another with three fried eggs.

'Going for the premature heart attack?' the chief inspector said, finishing her wholemeal sandwich.

'I haven't eaten since six this morning.'

'I think you owe me an explanation. Where have you been? I've left you several messages.'

John Turner avoided her eyes as he bit into a double layer of toast. 'The AC,' he mumbled.

'What?' Karen said loudly, making heads turn. 'Has he had you doing things behind my back?'

The inspector wiped egg yolk from his mouth. 'He thinks you're overwhelmed.'

'Fuck that!' she said, provoking stares. 'He should have come to me first.' She glared at her subordinate. 'And you should have told me what was going on as soon as you left him.'

Turner held her gaze. 'He told me not to. He knows how loyal I am to you.' He raised his shoulders. 'So I thought about it and came to find you. But he is the senior officer and—'

Oaten leaned over the table. 'Don't worry, I'll be speaking to the senior officer shortly. In the meantime, you'd better tell me what's been going on. I'm still in charge of the team, remember?'

The Welshman gave her a weary look. 'I was about to fill you in, guv.'

That stopped the next cannonade before it was fired. 'Fair enough, Taff,' the chief inspector said, smiling. 'Let's have it, then.'

'He called me before I woke up,' Turner said, pushing away his plates. 'Told me to go straight to his office. He was waiting for me there. He made me run through all the outstanding case files with him.'

'That must have achieved a lot.'

'Mm. I did my best to make him see that you were doing all you could. It's the idea that the White Devil's sister might be back that's got to him. Or rather, it's got to the politicians and the Commissioner, and the AC's nuts are in a vice as a consequence.'

'I wish they were,' Oaten said. 'I'd give the handle a couple of full turns, clockwise.'

The Welshman laughed. 'Me too.'

'So why did he let you go?'

'Because there wasn't anything else I could tell him. The Mary Malone case is dead in the water. Homicide West have got no suspects and the top brass are wondering if there's a connection between that case and the murder of Matt Wells's friend, Dave Cummings.'

'They think *she's* back,' Karen said. 'Which means everything that happens in the city is down to her. Don't tell me they're trying to pin Homicide East's gang murders on Sara too?'

Turner shook his head. 'I gather old Ron's happy he's still got the cases. They still haven't found the witness who was shot, I heard.'

'I doubt they will,' his superior said. 'He's either made it to his own people or the Shadows have caught up with him.'

'In which case, bits of him will already be setting in concrete.'

She nodded. 'What about Dave Cummings? The last time I looked, you were heading up that case.'

The inspector's cheeks reddened. 'I still am, guv. We found an old woman who thought she heard a motorbike making a racket. A powerful machine, she reckoned.'

'What time?'

'She isn't sure. Mid to late morning, so within the pathologist's parameters for the time of death.'

'Sara might have a bike. Though I remember Matt telling me not long ago that his friend Andrew Jackson has got a new one.'

Turner frowned as he took that in, then made a note. 'I've got Morry Simmons and a team of uniforms checking CCTV and traffic-camera footage in the area. Maybe we can get an identification.'

'What, through her helmet? She'll probably have dumped the bike by now.' Karen Oaten shook her head and looked away.

After a long silence, the inspector tried to bring her back. 'What is it, guv?' he asked gently.

The words made his superior glance back. 'Oh, not a lot,' she said ironically. 'Matt's keeping things from me. And I've just decided to bring him in.'

The Welshman nodded. 'Good idea. If we have him, maybe Sara will do something stupid.'

'Or maybe she'll just kill people at random till we let him go again.' The chief inspector got up. 'I'm going to talk to the AC, then find Matt.' As she walked past the counter, she raised her hand at Dino. He responded with a bitter smile.

John Turner stirred another spoonful of sugar into his tea. He was trying to make up his mind about who he'd rather not be—the AC or Matt Wells. Not that he cared. In his opinion, both needed a long and loud reading of the riot act.

'Hello, Safet,' I said, from a public phone in Piccadilly. I'd checked that no one had followed me from the sex club.

'Who's this?'

The Albanian had an American accent. I remembered he'd spent five years running his clan's operation in Baltimore.

'Matt Wells,' I said, deepening my voice for effect. I needn't have bothered. He hung up.

I called the number again. 'Don't do that, Safet. This is the Matt Wells who writes a crime column in the *Daily Independent.*'

There was silence, and then the gang boss spoke again. 'What do you want?' I made out the sound of a keyboard in rapid use. 'You have an eleven-year-old daughter named Lucy, living at 32 Oxborne Gardens, Wimbledon. And a mother, Frances Wells, address—'

'All right,' I said, my palms damp. 'You've made your point.'

'Would you care to make yours?'

There was a hard edge beneath the veneer of politeness. Although I hadn't met the Albanian, I'd heard stories about his urbanity—he collected seventeenth-century Dutch art and owned a chain of hyper-trendy restaurants.

He was also said to attend the executions of rival villains and to participate in the torture that preceded them.

The only way to get anywhere with professionals like Safet Shkrelli was to go on the offensive. They respected that, though they'd still happily slit your throat at the first opportunity. 'I just came from your place in Lexington Street,' I said.

'Ah, that was you,' he said. 'Mustafa wants to kill you.'

'Mustafa being the slob who took a dive?'

'Correct. Holding a gun on a woman isn't very brave, Matt Wells. Is there any reason why I shouldn't tell Mustafa where your daughter lives?'

Even though Lucy and Fran were hidden away with Caroline, the threat still made my hands shake. Then I thought of Dave as I'd last seen him. That stiffened my spine.

'Try this one, Safet. Your girlfriend Katya could be the target of a seriously dangerous killer.'

The Albanian gave a dry laugh. 'My girlfriend? I am happily married, Matt Wells. And who is this killer?'

I laughed back. 'You remember the White Devil?'

There was a pause. 'He is dead.'

'But his sister isn't.'

'Why would this woman want to kill my…want to kill a girl called Katya who maybe works for me? I noticed that you used the words "could be".'

I had to take a calculated risk. 'I haven't the faintest idea why Katya could be the target. Perhaps because I spoke to her when I was writing those columns about the Albanian crime wave.'

'You spoke to her? And she answered your questions?'

'I paid her for her time and, as you well know, she gave

me nothing more than background information. I made sure that I didn't connect your clan to any known crimes.' That was true, though only because Katya had been too terrified to say much and I'd found a braver, or more headstrong, girl who gave me the names and descriptions of men working for a rival clan.

'Very kind of you, I'm sure,' Shkrelli said.

'I wouldn't hesitate to mention your name if anything happened to Katya.'

'And how would you know?' The question was barked out, all traces of politeness gone. Then he laughed softly. 'Don't worry. Katya will not be treated badly. But tell me this, Matt Wells. How will your killer get past the security system I have installed in my house, never mind the men who are much better than Mustafa?'

'No security system is a hundred per cent reliable, and guards can be bribed.'

'True, but my men are family. They are willing to die for me.'

'Men can be bribed,' I repeated.

'And men can be killed, Matt Wells. You are at a public telephone in the underpass beneath Piccadilly Circus.'

Christ. I looked around, but saw no one watching me.

He laughed again. 'Don't worry. I have more important things to worry about than a newspaper columnist.'

'Even one who has close connections with the police?'

'If you have close connections with them, why aren't they calling me? You haven't told them. How is it you come to have information about this killer?'

I'd had enough of the smooth-talking gangster. 'Make sure Katya isn't harmed,' I said. 'This isn't a joke. I can damage your operation, Safet.'

'And I can dispose of you and everyone you care for in a matter of hours. Do not threaten me.'

I cut the connection. The Albanian sounded worryingly like the person who'd sent me the message. Or maybe *he* was the target. I wondered if there were any Albanians called Alexander. Then I got moving as quickly as I could. The last thing I needed right now was a Shkrelli clan hit man on my tail.

Faik Jabar woke up in agony, his eyes jerking open. He looked around the seedy room, then tried to sit up, forgetting that he was tied down. That brought another wave of pain, this time from his thighs. The memory of the Wolfman working on the flesh with a screwdriver made him retch. The Turk was still trying to get him to identify the shooter whose false beard had slipped. He wouldn't accept that Faik didn't know the man. At first Faik had been glad of that, because he was sure that as soon as he gave a name, he would be killed. But now, with the torture seemingly endless, he wished he could be done with his life.

He must have cried out, because the door opened and the middle-aged Shadow who was on guard duty came across.

'Shut up, scum.' The man picked up a length of stained cloth from the floor. 'Or would you like me to put the gag back on?'

Faik looked away as his entire body started to shake uncontrollably.

'What's the matter?' the Shadow said. 'Does the little boy want his mummy?'

Faik felt the man's rancid breath on his face as he leaned closer.

'Fuck,' the Turk said, in a low voice. 'You aren't faking, are you?' He walked to the door and pulled out his mobile.

Faik drifted away, the pain still gnawing at him and a high-pitched wail almost deafening him. He was back in the basement, watching the traitor Izady fall to the floor as though he'd been poleaxed. The wail Faik heard came from his own mouth, as he took the bullet in his hand and then the blow to his head. The face, the devil's face beneath the beard, was all he saw before he was sent into the dark abyss.

When he woke the next time, it was to the sound of whispered words in Kurdish. The doctor's mouth was close to his ear, telling him that he'd be all right, and that he'd cut his bonds.

Faik opened his eyes and blinked. He wasn't dreaming.

The doctor stepped back and shook his head at the Shadow. 'He's very weak. Another session with the Wolfman will kill him.'

'So?' the Turk said, with a twisted smile.

The doctor put his left hand into his pocket. 'Look at these wounds,' he said, pointing to Faik's thighs. He waited for the Shadow to approach.

'What about them?'

'They are the work of a pig.'

The Turk's eyes widened and he turned towards the doctor. 'What did you—'

The needle of the syringe punctured his chest near the heart. The doctor pushed the plunger down and stepped back. The Shadow stumbled forward, one hand scrabbling at the syringe and the other stretched out. Then he collapsed to the floor.

'What…?' Faik said.

'I've been waiting to do that for years,' the doctor said,

lifting the young man up by the shoulders. 'Don't worry, he'll wake up soon.'

'But…but the Shadows will hunt you down.'

'Swing your legs round.' The doctor smiled at Faik. 'That's it. They can try, but I think the King's men will protect me if I deliver you to them.' He shrugged. 'Besides, the last hold the Turks had over me was my father in Istanbul. He died yesterday.'

Faik was breathing deeply, trying to summon the strength to stand up. 'I'm…I'm sorry.'

'Don't be. He was old and he wanted to join my mother. Now, let's get you walking. I don't think I can carry you.'

The young man managed to stand, his injured thighs making him wince. 'Where…where are we?'

'At a Shadow safe house in Hackney. My car's outside. Where shall I take you?'

'My father's house, off Green Lanes.'

They moved to the door, the doctor's arm round Faik's back. The room was on the first floor. The young man almost fainted as they went down the stairs, but his saviour kept talking to him, encouraging him and praising his bravery. Then they were at the front door.

'Is there…anyone outside?' Faik asked, gasping for breath.

The doctor smiled. 'I hope not. There isn't usually. The lads across the road play at being hard men, but we'll be in the car before they do anything.' He put his hand on the lock. 'Ready? Here we go.'

He opened the door quickly and helped Faik out. The sun wasn't very bright, but it made the young man blink. They got down the steps to the pavement and moved towards a green Opel Astra. The doctor opened the front passenger door and helped Faik in.

'Doctor!' came a shout.

Faik turned and saw the Wolfman running down the street towards the Citröen. 'Get in,' he said, in Kurdish. 'Get in!'

The doctor remained standing. 'No, I'm not going to let this animal hurt you any more.' He fumbled in his pocket.

'Hands where I can see them!' the Wolfman said. He was pointing a silver pistol at the doctor, who reluctantly complied.

Faik lowered his head, vaguely aware that a veiled figure in a *burqa* and *chador* was approaching the car. He was desperate, he wanted to get out of the car to face the Wolfman and finish things, but he couldn't, he was too exhausted, too feeble to help the doctor—

The three rapid spits and the slap of bullets hitting flesh at close range made him look up. He had heard that sound before. He looked round and saw the Wolfman lying prone on the pavement with his arms flung out. Blood was emerging from holes in his shirt.

'Don't follow me,' came a voice that Faik recognised.

He saw the figure in the black robe and headdress bend to scoop up the Wolfman's pistol. 'Get in the car, Doctor,' he said. The young men on the other side of the road were beginning to gather, staring at them. The killer had already disappeared round the street corner.

The doctor opened the driver's door and got in quickly. He started the engine and pulled out. Faik turned his head and saw a cluster of people around the dead Shadow.

'Who was that?' the doctor said breathlessly.

'Don't ask me,' Faik said, twitching his head. He wasn't going to admit that he recognised the killer's voice—not to the doctor and not to any of the King's men. He had no idea why his life had been spared in the basement and then saved on the street, but he had a nasty feeling that he'd have to repay the debt.

In the meantime, he just wanted to eat and sleep. Then he saw again the face of the man who had killed Izady and the Wolfman—an inhuman, devilish face.

Faik Jabal suddenly realised that he was nothing more than a pawn in a world full of pain and betrayal. He let out a sob for his lost innocence, and then another as the doctor, who had risked his life for him, gently squeezed his arm.

The Soul Collector was in the back of her van, holding a torch over the notes she'd made. Over the previous twelve hours, she had staked out the homes of the SAS men known as Rommel and Geronimo. Although the men were no longer in the regiment, they still lived close to its base at Hereford—Rommel in the town itself and his comrade in a village ten minutes' drive to the east. Geronimo didn't have kids, so she would have to take his wife. She seemed to be the lazy type, who rose late and sat around the house drinking numerous cups of coffee. Like many middle-aged women who were losing their looks, she seemed to be locked in a world of her own—in the six hours the Collector watched her, she never once spoke on the telephone. As for Rommel, he had two girls under five and a boy who was in the second year of primary school. His wife looked exhausted and incapable of putting up much of a struggle.

The woman turned a page and studied the timeline she

had constructed. She was sure that the ex-SAS men would have set up a reporting system with their families—they would be aware of potential reprisals by Irish paramilitaries and foreign agents. That meant she had to snatch her targets as quickly as possible. Rommel's and Geronimo's people didn't present a problem as they were close together. But she then had to get to Wolfe's house in Warwickshire, a drive of at least an hour, before the alarm was raised. With the men far away, she was sure that would be long enough.

Sara turned off the torch and smiled as she stretched out on the sleeping bag. Her knee banged against the steel box that contained her gear.

She had everything she needed to kill, maim and incapacitate. Which of the three she used would depend on the circumstances. She was prepared for anything.

13

I was about five minutes' walk from my flat when I realised that Karen would be going crazy. I'd changed the SIM card in my phone and only Andy knew the new number. I stopped at a public phone and called her office number. I got her secretary, so I hung up and tried her mobile.

'Matt!' she said. 'Where the bloody hell have you been?'

'Pardon?' I asked, playing the innocent.

'Don't mess me around. I've been ringing you for hours.' She paused. 'Where are you?'

Something about the way she asked the question made me suspicious. 'Em, around and about. Hang on, I'll call you back.' I broke the connection, retrieved my phone card from the machine and walked back towards Fulham Broadway Station. I had the distinct feeling that Karen's interest in my location wasn't casual. There was a good chance she'd been told to bring me in—technically, to protect me, but really to make sure I couldn't take unilateral action against Sara. One thing I wasn't going to be doing was calling her back. Not only could she put a trace on the phone—I wasn't going make that mistake again after Safet Shkrelli—but she might manage to talk me into seeing things her way. I couldn't risk that, and I wasn't going to leave Andy and the others to face Sara. I was her main target, and I didn't intend to leave them in the lurch. The only way we would catch her was by me taking her on. Karen would never be able to allow that, even if she understood it.

I sent Andy a text message—we'd agreed to keep calls to a minimum. He said he'd followed Doris Carlton-Jones to a bridge club in Beckenham. I told him to stay on her. It was just possible that Sara would have arranged to meet her birth mother. Then I had a thought. Maybe she was also keeping an eye on Doris Carlton-Jones. She knew what Andy looked like. I texted him again, telling him to keep out of sight as much as possible, and not to go back to my flat.

On the bus into the centre, I thought about what I was doing. Dropping out of sight would piss Karen off and it might anger Sara too. There was no right way to act. I thought about leaving the country and making it clear to Sara that I'd done so. Would that stop whatever devious plan she was working to? I knew it wouldn't. She was implacable and relentless, and I was sure she'd spent the last two years honing the skills that the White Devil had introduced her to.

I hit several cash machines, using different accounts each time, and then went to a computer shop that I hadn't used before on Tottenham Court Road. I emerged with a laptop and a wi-fi card. Then I headed for the first hotel on the list I'd memorised. It was a cheap place in Blooms-bury, with clanking water pipes and dingy rooms, but the clerk was happy to be paid in cash and didn't ask for iden-tification. I signed in as Mr R. Thompson and gave an address in Leeds. Both were real, as I'd checked the local telephone directory—it wasn't a good idea to make things up, given the heightened security situation in London.

I locked the door and set up the laptop on a rickety table. I'd got the techies in the shop to initiate the system, so I was ready to roll. I logged on and checked my e-mails. There was nothing unexpected. I went to Rog's ghost site to see how he and Pete were getting on. They were making progress, but it was slow.

I got back to thinking about the cryptic clue I'd been sent. There were under six hours to go. I was suddenly plagued by doubts about Katya being the target. Why would Sara go for a woman I'd only met briefly? Also, she could hardly have come up with a more difficult target, given how seriously a gangster like Safet Shkrelli would take security. Then again, I told myself, it would be just like Sara to choose an unlikely victim, and just like her to take on almost impossible odds. I hoped Shkrelli had paid heed to my warning. I'd liked Katya. She hadn't lost her human warmth, despite the horrors she'd been through. Maybe that was why the gangster had chosen her. But was it really her name in the puzzle?

I looked at it again. 'The sun set by the westernmost dunes of Alexander's womankind.' The sun. Apollo? Oddly enough, I didn't know anyone of that name. Who else was associated with the sun? Louis XIVth of France had been known as the Sun King. Again, I didn't know anyone called Louis, first or second name. I logged on to one of the search engines and came up with a list of sun-gods— Sol, Ra, Shamash, Inti, Surya Deva. I couldn't link any of them to a recognisable person, unless I was expected to warn every person named Sol or Solomon of imminent death. Then there were all the newspapers with 'sun' in their titles. I didn't see how they might fit in to the rest of the clue. I thought about the dunes again. The westernmost dunes. In the U.K., that would mean Cornwall—there were plenty of beaches there, as well as a burgeoning surfing scene. Cornwall. I didn't know anyone by that name. Shit, this was getting me nowhere.

Then I remembered the name and initials the sender had used to sign off. Flaminio. That was an obvious link to John Webster's play *The White Devil*. I'd initially assumed that meant Sara had written the message. But Flaminio was a male name. She would surely have used the name of Vittoria, the main female 'white devil' in the play. As for D.F., I couldn't make any link between those letters and Webster's play. I began to have the feeling that I was playing a game with rules I only vaguely knew. Then I ran D.F. through a search engine and came up with the protagonist of a play by another writer born in the 16th century—Christopher Marlowe's vainglorious but ultimately tragic Doctor Faustus. Why would Sara—or anyone else—cast themselves as the man who made a pact with the devil and ended up in hell?

I had a bad feeling about this. It looked like Sara might not have written the message. Was I being pursued by a male who had, in some way, done a deal with the devil? Everyone made compromises, everyone did things they didn't want to for some temporary gain. Then I remembered what Karen had said about the book I'd written: *The Death List* was in effect a pact with the devil and, by writing it, I'd lost part of my humanity. Maybe Sara, or someone else, was hinting at that.

I got up and smacked my hands together. It was just after eight. I had four hours to come up with a name. Katya was still a possibility, but I wasn't convinced about her anymore, despite the connection with Alexander Drys.

I went back to the computer and started from scratch. The sun. Could the message be a series of opposites or pairs? 'The moon rose far from the least eastern grains of—'— whose? Alexander the Great's father Philip? His chief enemy Darius? His soul-mate Hephaistion? I let that go. And mankind instead of womankind? So the target was a male? Going back to the beginning, I didn't know anyone called Moon, apart from the long-dead drummer of the Who. 'The moon rose…' Rose was a common enough name. I'd once done a radio programme with a chicklit author called Rose Jones. I found her e-mail address on the Internet and sent her a message suggesting she keep a low profile. After I'd done that, I realised that she didn't fulfil the new criterion of being male. If that was right…

And so I went on, driving myself up the wall with abstruse ideas and unlikely solutions, as the clock steadily ticked towards twelve midnight.

Karen Oaten stopped in front of the police barrier tape in the street in Hackney. The uniformed officer with a clipboard recognised her and lifted the cordon so she could drive in. The area that had been shut off was lit up by bright lights powered by a generator.

'Here we go again, Amelia,' the chief inspector said.

'Yes, guv.' Detective Sergeant Browning got out of the car quickly, enthusiasm all over her face.

Oaten smiled, remembering when she'd been like that. She accepted a bag of protective gear from a CSI and began to pull the contents on.

'This is getting ridiculous,' said Detective Superintendent Ron Paskin, still looking vast in his white coverall.

'Certainly is,' Karen replied. 'What happened this time?'

'No one's talking, at least not yet. This is Shadow territory. The man on the pavement over there is a Shadow too.'

'Jesus. This is going to turn really nasty.'

Paskin nodded. 'Hello, DS Browning,' he said. 'Would you like a transfer to Homicide East?'

'No chance, Superintendent.'

'There's plenty of action here.'

The sergeant smiled. 'Even more at the VCCT.' She went over to the body.

'Only if you actually take these cases,' the policeman said to his former subordinate.

'Are you asking me to?' Oaten asked.

Ron Paskin shrugged. 'Not yet. Though I reckon this killing is connected with the other ones in this area.'

'Any evidence of that?'

'The cartridge cases are similar to those found in the basement. Ballistics will prove that one way or the other.' He pointed towards an open door. 'And there's blood on a bed and on the floor upstairs. There are ropes up there, too—they've been cut. Someone who was tied down got cut loose.'

'So what happened?'

'Hard to tell. According to the pathologist, the victim was shot three times in the chest at close range, at between five and six o'clock this evening.'

Oaten looked around the houses. 'And no one saw or heard anything?'

'Oh, they saw and heard, all right. They're just not telling us. Don't worry, we'll find out. I've got Turkish-speaking officers. They're going round now.'

A man in his thirties with rings round his eyes came up. 'You're not going to believe this, guv.'

'DCI Oaten, meet DI Ozal. He's one of the Turkish-speakers I was telling you about.' Paskin looked at his subordinate. 'Go on, then. It isn't every day you get the chance to show how smart you are to the senior investigating officer of the VCCT.'

Ozal gave Karen a wary glance. 'No, guv. Well, I managed to get a couple of the lads to talk. They won't give formal statements, but I'll work on them.'

'What happened, then?' Paskin asked impatiently.

'Like I say, guv, you're not going to believe this. The guy on the ground's the Wolfman.'

The superintendent whistled through his tobacco-stained teeth. 'So that's what he looks like.' He turned to Oaten. 'You remember him?'

She nodded. 'The Wolfman was in the frame for a string of killings and near-fatal assaults on behalf of the Shadows. We never managed to lay a finger on him when I was here.'

'That's not all, guv,' Ozal said, his face flushed with excitement. 'He was shot by someone wearing the *burqa* and *chador*. That means the Wolfman was killed by a woman—and she used a silenced weapon.'

Karen Oaten raised a hand. 'Hold on, Inspector. How do you know it was a woman?'

Ozal looked like he'd been asked if the earth went round the sun. 'No man would wear those garments, Chief Inspector.'

Oaten looked at him. 'Maybe not in your community. But that wouldn't stop a non-Muslim.'

'Who said anything about non-Muslims?' Paskin put in. 'The killer could have been a Kurdish woman with a relative who was a victim of the Wolfman. Anyway, what else did they see?'

'A couple of men came out of that house.' Ozal pointed to the open door. 'One of them, in his twenties, was only wearing a T-shirt and boxer shorts, and there was blood all over his legs. He had a bandage on one hand too. The other was older, with a moustache. He was supporting the first one. Neither appeared to be armed. The Wolfman came running along the road, shouting, after the younger guy got into a green car, probably an Astra. When he got close, the woman…the *person* in the *burqa* and *chador* passed close by. No shots were heard, but the Turk hit the deck. Then the man with the moustache got into the car and they drove off.'

'Did anyone get the registration number?' the superintendent asked.

Ozal shook his head.

Oaten and Paskin exchanged looks.

'The young man had a wounded hand,' the chief inspector said. 'Maybe he was the survivor from the basement.'

'A Kurd, then, like the dead man?' Paskin said. 'Since he had blood on his legs, the Wolfman had probably been working on him.'

Karen Oaten rubbed her forehead. 'When you've got the paperwork done and the tests from the blood on the bed are in, let me know. If they match that found in the basement, I'll talk to the AC. Obviously we'd have to take this murder and the previous one. I'll see if you can keep handling the groundwork.'

Her former boss nodded. 'Fair enough.'

'Let's just hope there aren't any more killings,' Oaten said.

Paskin grunted. 'That'll be a squadron of pigs I can hear flying over.'

DI Ozal, a devout Muslim, looked at him in disgust.

Andy Jackson was getting seriously pissed off with hiding behind the seats in the van. He liked action, not skulking. More than once, he'd had to stop himself going over to the bridge club and dragging Doris Carlton-Jones out. He reminded himself that people in the U.K. found most Americans to be extremely polite. Most Americans hadn't grown up in the back streets of New Jersey's most underprivileged city.

It got dark, and still Sara's birth mother was playing cards. Andy wondered if money was involved. Maybe she'd be there all night trying to win back her stake. And now it was getting cold in the van. He considered turning on the engine so he could let the heating blast out. No, that would make it obvious that there was someone inside. He stuck his hands into his armpits to warm them up. It was either there or his groin.

He wasn't even able to look forward to a night in Matt's well-heated luxury apartment, as the text message had told him to hit the first hotel on his personal list. Matt was obviously busy and Andy didn't want to disturb him. He'd be working on that puzzle. Andy still wasn't sure how seriously to take it. Sure, if Sara had owned up to sending it, they'd know to watch out. But why would she hide behind those other names? And why was she giving Matt a clue in the first place? That wasn't her style, as she'd shown with Dave. The only heads-up they'd been given was the call to Matt. That didn't give them any time to stop her. So why all this bullshit now?

A triangle of orange light appeared on the grass in front of the bridge club. Andy leaned forward and watched as people came out. He caught sight of Doris Carlton-Jones. He pulled himself over the seat backs and got behind the wheel. The woman was walking towards her car, which was parked further up the street. Andy started the van's engine and checked his wing mirrors. He'd been doing that regularly since Matt's warning that Sara—or some sidekick—might also have been watching Mrs Carlton-Jones. Anything was possible, but he wasn't convinced about that. Sara was too smart to hang around her mother.

The elderly woman drove to the end of the road, turned right and headed back towards Sydenham. Andy kept a couple of cars behind her and had no difficulty keeping in touch, even when a heavy drizzle started. The street lamps were blurred, but the Japanese car had bright red tail lights. While they were waiting for the traffic lights to change, Andy checked his wing mirrors again. They were covered in raindrops and he had to open the window and wipe the one on the driver's side with his sleeve. That was when the motorbike came past. At first he didn't pay it much attention. The rider was in dark-coloured leathers, bent low over the handlebars. Having passed the vehicles behind Doris Carlton-Jones's car, the biker then stopped behind her. That got Andy's attention. There were another three cars between her and the traffic lights, and the motorbike had plenty of space to get past and take pole position. But the rider spurned that opportunity and stayed behind the Japanese car.

The lights changed and the line of vehicles began to move. The road ahead was single-lane and there was no chance of overtaking—unless you were on a bike. But the rider stayed behind Doris Carlton-Jones. Andy drove closer to the car in front, provoking violent hand movements from the driver. He hit the van's brakes when he saw the Baby on Board sticker on the rear window.

The line of traffic went past Crystal Palace, and still the bike sat on Mrs Carlton-Jones's tail, though not close enough to bother her. Andy considered texting Matt, or even calling him, but there wasn't much he could do from wherever he was.

Then it struck Andy. Maybe Sara's birth mother was the target. He had no idea how that would fit the clue, but that didn't matter now. He had to make sure nothing happened to the woman. She wasn't responsible for how her daughter had turned out, let alone for the White Devil. But Sara could easily have resented the fact that the birth mother had given her and her twin brother away when they were still babies. Was that a reason to kill her? In Sara's perverted world, it probably was.

Doris Carlton-Jones turned off the main road and headed for her street. None of the other drivers hit their right indicator, not even the motorbike. Then, at the last moment, the rider accelerated and took a sharp right turn. The driver of the car behind hit his horn and gesticulated wildly. Andy took the corner and found himself close to the motorbike, seeing that it was metallic red. He reckoned it was a Transalp. The rider was bound to have spotted him. He dropped back, but kept his eyes on the bike. It stayed behind the Japanese car, despite the fact that it could easily have overtaken it on the quiet back street.

That made Andy even more certain that something bad was about to happen.

Mrs Carlton-Jones indicated left and turned into Northumberland Crescent. A few seconds later she was manoeuvring into her narrow driveway. Andy slowed before making the turn and turned off his headlights. The street lamps were bright enough, so he could see but he could also be seen by the motorbike rider, who had followed Mrs Carlton-Jones as far as the pavement outside her house. Andy stopped the van a few yards into Northumberland Crescent, but kept the engine running. The drizzle was heavier now and he was having difficulty seeing. The rider had got off the bike and was walking towards the house. Doris Carlton-Jones was locking her car and seemed unaware of the rider's presence. She moved away from the car and headed for her front door, then saw the figure in leather, helmet still on, and stopped. It looked to Andy like she was speaking to the rider—probably asking what he or she wanted. Then the person in leathers raised a hand.

'Shit!' Andy yelled, stamping the accelerator pedal. The van lurched forward and he drove it at the bike. As he was closing, the rider turned quickly and dropped the object he or she was holding, taking something else from the pocket in the leather jacket.

The windscreen was instantly covered in a web of cracks. Andy hit the brake and smashed his elbow through the glass, noticing a small hole in the middle just before he made contact. The glass gave way and rain dashed over him. The van had come to a halt a few metres in front of the bike. Andy felt a bullet whip past his left ear, but didn't hear a shot. The slug ricocheted around the metal sides of the van's cargo space. He saw the muzzle of a silenced pistol aiming straight at him and ducked as low as he could. Again, a bullet whistled past, this time over his head. Then there came the sound of the motorbike being started. Andy put his shoulder to the door and dropped to the road. There was a roar as the rider revved hard. Andy rolled forward, only to see and hear the bike rocket down the curved street. In a couple of seconds it had disappeared into the rainy night.

'What on earth…' Doris Carlton-Jones stood stock-still, staring down the street. It was only when Andy got to his feet that she moved her head. 'Are you all right?' She moved towards him.

'Yes,' he said, trying to lose his American accent. 'You?'

'I'm fine,' she said, but she looked traumatised. 'He…he shot at you.'

Andy nodded, his mind in overdrive as he constructed a plan that would win her trust. 'I've been following that motorbike.' He looked down at the road. There was nothing there except four cartridge cases. He took out a paper tissue and picked them up. Whatever it was that had originally been in the rider's hand was no longer there. 'The name's Andrew Ja…Jansen. I'm with the police.' He told himself to get a grip. Giving his real name would have been seriously dumb.

Doris Carlton-Jones had put up an umbrella. She beckoned him under it. 'You're with the police?'

He nodded. 'Undercover major crime unit. We've been carrying out surveillance on a gang of diamond thieves.'

She stared at him. 'But what… Why was he here?'

Andy looked at her. 'I was hoping you could tell me that. First of all, you say the rider was a 'he'. Are you sure of that?'

'I need to go inside,' the elderly woman said, moving

to the front door. 'No,' she said, as they got there. 'No, I'm not sure about that. He, I mean the rider, raised the visor, but all I saw was the eyes. Now I'm thinking about it, I couldn't say if it was a man or a woman.' She stared at him. 'You say you've been following the motorbike. Don't you know who was on it?'

Andy realised that he had to be careful—Mrs Carlton-Jones was obviously not senile. 'I'm afraid not,' he said, in his best South London accent. 'I saw the rider make a pickup from another suspect, helmet on the whole time.'

Doris Carlton-Jones put her key in the lock. She opened the door and then stopped. 'I'm sorry, I can't let you in,' she said, then moved swiftly forward and closed the door after her. There was a rattle as the chain came on.

Andy swore under his breath. 'Please, madam, I need to ask you some questions.'

'And I need to see your warrant card,' came the surprisingly level voice behind the door.

'I'm working undercover,' he said. 'We don't carry identification, for obvious reasons.' He'd taken out his mobile and was texting Matt at speed—the other guys laughed at how quickly he could work the keys, saying he was a teenager in disguise. After he'd sent the message, he put the phone back in his pocket. 'If you like, I can give you the number of the officer in charge of the investigation.'

The door opened a few inches, the chain visible.

'Very well,' the elderly woman said, her tone business-like.

Andy gave her Matt's mobile number, hoping he'd had time to read the message. The woman left the door open on the chain and went to the telephone in the hall.

'Oh, hello,' Andy heard her say. 'My name's Doris Carlton-Jones. One of your officers has just been shot at outside my house.' She paused and listened. 'Yes, his name is Andrew Jansen. Oh, he is.' She looked at Andy, her gaze still unwavering. 'I see. Very well, hold on.' She brought the cordless phone over to the door and passed it through the gap. 'He wants to talk to you.'

Andy took the phone. 'Yes, guv,' he said. He'd seen enough British cop shows to have picked up the jargon.

'Jesus Christ, Slash!' Matt said. 'What the fuck are you up to?'

'I know, guv,' Andy replied, his eyes on Doris Carlton-Jones. She was watching intently. 'I tailed the motorbike from Beckenham. The rider seemed to be following the lady's car. When I approached, four shots were fired from a silenced pistol. I'm afraid I couldn't pursue. I wanted to make sure the lady was unharmed.'

'Was it Sara?' Matt asked breathlessly.

'Unclear, guv. The witness isn't sure about gender, let alone identity. Em, please advise course of action.'

'Shit, I don't know. I can't come down there. She knows what I look like. I doorstepped her when I was researching *The Death List,* not that she would speak to me. Is the van mobile?'

'Yes, guv.'

'All right, get out of there. Tell her that because it's an undercover operation, we won't be making it a scene of crime. Did anyone else hear the shots?'

'Doubt it. No one's come out.'

'You are a tosser, calling me DCI Oates.'

'Right, guv. See you later.' Andy handed the phone back.

'Thank you, Sergeant,' Doris Carlton-Jones said. Then

she closed the door, took off the chain and opened up again. 'Why don't you come inside now? You're getting soaked.'

Andy looked back at the van. Its rear was sticking out into the road, but not too excessively. He decided it was worth cultivating Sara's birth mother.

'Thank you, madam, just for a minute.'

'I'll make some tea,' the woman said. 'Go into the sitting room.'

Andy did as he was told. The house was spotlessly clean. The long sitting room was filled with what seemed to him to be good-quality antique furniture, and the sofas had tasteful burgundy covers. He looked around for family photographs, wondering if there might be any sign of Sara and her brother as babies. But there was only a series of shots of Mrs Carlton-Jones with a man, who had less and less hair as he got older.

'Your husband?' he asked, as she bustled in with a tray.

'Yes, that's Neville. He passed on four years ago.'

'I'm sorry.'

Mrs Carlton-Jones seemed momentarily to have lost the tight grip she kept on herself. 'It was cancer,' she said, shaking her head. 'He only lasted three months after the diagnosis.'

Andy sensed that nothing he could say would comfort her.

'Anyway, how do you take your tea?' the elderly woman said, twitching her head.

'Em, two sugars, please.' Andy never drank tea, but he didn't want to spoil the mood. Who had ever heard of an English policeman who didn't like tea?

After they were both settled with cups and saucers,

Mrs Carlton-Jones turned to him. 'So, Sergeant Jansen, what happens now?'

'Well,' he said, gathering his thoughts, 'because this is an undercover investigation, there won't be the usual fuss with the street being closed off and everyone in the vicinity being questioned.'

Doris Carlton-Jones raised an eyebrow. 'Won't you even be taking a statement from me?'

'Later,' Andy said. 'When the investigation has run its course. Was there anything else you wanted to tell me?'

She shook her head. 'No. The first thing I was aware of was your van careering towards us, after I asked the rider what he wanted.'

'And he—or she—didn't speak to you at all?'

'No. At least not that I could hear above the sound of your engine.'

'I thought you were in danger. What was it that the rider was holding out?'

'I don't know. A small package. I think it was wrapped, like a birthday present.'

Andy scratched his head. 'And is it your birthday?'

'No, it isn't.' She looked at him calmly, waiting for the next question.

The American took a surreptitious deep breath. 'What about children?' he asked.

Mrs Carlton-Jones's eyes opened wide. 'Children? What do they have to do with what happened outside?'

Good question, Andy thought. 'No, I mean, is there anyone you'd like to come over? Do you have children?'

'Oh, I see.' She looked him straight in the eye. 'No, I don't.'

Andy held her gaze. Now he knew she was a liar.

* * *

The man in the mask and cowl walked away from the smoking altar. He heard the footsteps of the naked supplicant behind, as well as the cackling of Beelzebub.

'Where is Faustus tonight?' the supplicant asked.

'Busy,' Mephistopheles said, his tone brooking no further questions.

He slid open the door to the outer chamber. 'Your offerings are always welcome, Asmodeus. But this one was somewhat lightweight.'

The supplicant started to dress, and then looked round at the leader of the order. 'I am sowing the seeds of destruction, my lord. Soon, great riches will fall into my hands.'

'Into our hands,' Mephistopheles corrected. 'We are all depending on you.' He took off his mask. 'I am depending on you.'

Asmodeus took in the flawed face. 'I will not let you down.'

'Good,' the leader said, shrugging off his cowl and robes. 'I wouldn't like to think that you were only killing for pleasure.'

The supplicant remained silent.

'All that we do is toward the greater glory of our master Satan,' Mephistopheles said. 'Do not forget that.' He took the head of a cockerel from his pocket and tossed it to the mandrill.

The two humans watched as the creature's jaws crunched together, then they smiled.

14

Andy's performance in Sydenham put me right off my stride with the clue. At least, that was what I told myself. The truth was, I hadn't got any further with it. Slash's suggestion in the message he texted that Doris Carlton-Jones might be the victim was smart, but I found it hard to believe. Sara might have had issues with her birth mother, but I didn't think she'd murder her. Then again, what did I know? I'd spent over a year sharing a bed with her, and it had never occurred to me until the end that she was working with the White Devil.

Looking at the puzzle again, I couldn't see any direct link to Doris Carlton-Jones, but I didn't have enough information to be sure about that. Maybe the sun setting, the westernmost dunes and Alexander's womankind would mean something to her. I considered getting Andy to ask her, but decided against it. I texted him, saying that he should stay in the vicinity till further notice, just in case she was the target.

I looked at my watch. Under two hours to go. The floor of the hotel room was covered in crumpled paper. I was still trying out ideas, but as the deadline approached, they were getting more and more abstruse. I logged on to the Internet and went to the site Rog had set up. Neither he nor Pete had come up with anything coherent regarding the clue. Rog had managed to run it through all sorts of encryption software and got nothing but gobbledygook. I was sure it was the kind of puzzle that needed a human rather than a digital brain.

I found myself tantalised by some of the words. 'Set'—there was something lurking in the back of my mind about that. What else could it mean? As a noun, a number or group of people or things; a complete series; a team of horses; a receiving apparatus, like a wireless set; the movements in a dance. Where did that get me? As a verb, to cause to sit; to place; to sink, like the sun—as in the clue; to prescribe; to adjust; to come into a rigid state. Great—that was also going nowhere. I had the feeling this was a puzzle that didn't abide by the unwritten rules of crossword clues. Maybe there wasn't even a logical answer.

It was nearly eleven o'clock. I thought seriously about calling Karen. But what good would that do now? The police were unlikely to come up with a convincing answer when Rog, Pete and I, plus numerous computer programmes, hadn't. If I'd given it to Karen in the morning, she could have got a warrant to find who had set up the *who'snext* e-mail address—but that would have been pointless too, because the writer wouldn't have given a real name and address. Then I remembered the message. Flaminio or Doctor Faustus, whether Sara or not, had told me not to involve the cops, but that I was expected to show the clue to my mother. How did the writer know that Fran was a cryptic crossword addict? Sara did, because she'd seen my mother doing the *Guardian* crossword and had asked why she didn't do the one in the *Daily Independent,* where Sara used to work. Fran had told her that the setter there had an infantile sense of humour. Shit! 'Setter'—that derived from 'set'. Was that what was going on? Sara had *set* the clue and hinted in the message that Fran would spot the answer?

There was under three quarters of an hour to go. Was this a deliberate move on Sara's part to get me to contact my mother? Could she have some sort of surveillance on me or my mother that would be activated by an e-mail or telephone call? I didn't see how. I'd changed phone and laptop, and Fran would have put a new SIM card in by now. But I was still reluctant. I'd managed to get my mother and Lucy, plus Caroline, out of the killer's sights. I didn't want to do anything to put them back in them.

In the end, the steady ticking of the second hand on my watch got to me. I sent an e-mail to Caroline. Nearly half-past eleven. Would they still be awake? My heart started pounding and I paced around the room until the person in the room beneath thumped on his ceiling.

There was a chime from my computer. Caroline had answered.

I've woken your mother. She's looking at the clue. We'll reply by 11.55. C.

I breathed a sigh of relief. One of the good things about Caroline was her crisis management. She'd got used to panics at the bank and reacted well to pressure. Unless it was from me—somehow she'd never managed to reproduce her cool office manner at home.

Then another thought struck me. Katya. I didn't know her surname. If she really was the target, Sara might easily disqualify my answer if I didn't give the full name—the

White Devil had done that kind of thing. I called Safet Shkrelli.

The phone was answered with a grunted monosyllable that presumably meant something in Albanian. I explained what I wanted.

'Ask her yourself,' Shkrelli said. There was a rustling noise, then Katya came on the line.

'Are you in a safe place?' I asked.

'Yes, I think so. We are at—'

'Don't tell me!' I said, the words coming out in a rush. 'There may be surveillance. What's your full name?'

She paused, as if reluctant to give up the last remnant of her self. I was pretty sure that Safet Shkrelli had never bothered to ask her name.

'Katerina Petrova Georgieva.'

'Thank you,' I said. 'Take care. And remember, I can get you out of there.'

There was a bitter male laugh. 'You, Matt Wells? You're the one who has put her life in danger. Fuck you.' The connection was cut.

I sat down on the lumpy bed and dropped the phone. Was that really what I had done? Had Sara—or whoever Flaminio/Doctor Faustus was—chosen Katya because of the one meeting I'd had with her? Now, as the minute hand neared twelve, it seemed desperately unlikely. I looked again at the clue, but the words blurred into a meaningless jumble of letters. At least the whole sentence wasn't an anagram—Rog's digital tools had checked that.

Five minutes till my mother came back with her thoughts, nine till I had to answer… The full significance of what was happening hit me. Someone's life hung on what I sent. If Sara had set the clue, she'd found a perfect way to get revenge for the White Devil's death. In effect, I was being turned into a murderer.

The woman woke in the late evening, without a clue where she was.

'Come on, girl,' she said, her Texan accent at odds with the whimsical decor of Wilde's. It claimed to be the city's premier hotel for the discerning gay traveller but, as far as she was concerned, lime-green net curtains and pink-and-white-striped wallpaper were several steps too far down the road to Reading Gaol.

'Yeah, that's it,' she remembered. 'I'm in London—according to the incomparable William Cobbett, the Great fuckin' Wen.'

She got up and went into the bathroom. A large, old-fashioned bath took up most of the room. For someone who was over six feet, that didn't leave much room for other functions, even if she had kept her weight below the 140 pound mark. As she straddled the toilet, she recalled what had happened earlier in the day. Her publishers had taken her out to lunch, during which her editor had made it very clear that they wanted to sign her up for at least another four books.

'Talk to Lenny,' she'd said. Her agent would know how to squeeze every last drop of money out of them. When her editor, a youngish guy with an earring, went off to the john, she'd spoken to her publicist.

'Lavinia, honey, you gotta get me outta this hotel. Yeah, I know it's supposed to be the coolest place in town, but it is definitely not my kind of cool.' She listened as her publicist reminded her about the interview she was scheduled to give at Wilde's the next morning.

'Oh, well, all right, but just tonight. I'd rather stay in a motel than this crummy dump.' She held up a hand. 'No, honey, I know you don't have motels in London. No, you don't have to come along. I can handle the *Times* journalist. With one hand tied behind my back.' She had three university degrees, in subjects ranging from English literature to computer science, but she liked to play the Southern belle, lesbian version. She knew that people always paid more attention to your jugs than your certificates. In her case, that meant a lot of attention. Even her ever-so-gay editor couldn't keep his eyes off them.

Blinking, she gave the bath and its clawed feet a cursory inspection. It wouldn't have been the first time she'd brought herself to climax in one when she was touring books, but she really preferred the shower. What was it with the Brits and their baths? How the hell were you supposed to get clean, sitting in water you'd just made dirty? She turned the regulator up as far as it went, and stepped into the torrent. After ten minutes, the last of her jet lag was well on its way to the departure lounge.

She decided she'd hit a club. As she got dressed in her standard evening wear—boot-cut, slim-fitting black Levi's and matching shirt with polished quartz buttons, custom-made for her—she thought about the book she'd read on the plane. She knew she'd met the writer at one of the mystery conventions—was it Madison, Wisconsin?—but she was having trouble recalling what he looked like. Why was it that Brits thought they could write American characters? Then again, there were several American crime writers who imagined they could write Brits. The hero she'd shared her journey with was one hell of an asshole, even by real-life FBI standards—and that was saying something. She got hit on all the time by serving cops and special agents, who thought she should get some first-hand knowledge of their business, even though she made no secret of her sexuality. Anyway, she was at a loss as to how sucking their dicks would provide insight.

She sat at the dressing-table, her thighs crushed against the underside of the drawer. The mirror was in the shape of a large male head with an extravagant quiff that spread halfway up the wall. Anything that covered the pink-and-white stripes was fine by her. She applied her usual light foundation and bright scarlet lipstick, leaving her eyelashes and the surrounding area untouched—if they ain't looking at your titties, they'll be looking at your mouth, one of her few male lovers had told her. Eyes were off-limits for most men, and hair was just a distraction. That was why she kept her blonde locks short and unshowy.

The author made sure there were several copies of her novels on the table in the adjoining sitting room. The journalist in the morning wasn't likely to fall for such blatant product placement, but the photographer would appreciate it. She stood her latest work, *Slim Pickings on the Pecos,* against a pile of the others. The jacket showed a lowering red sky over the river of the title. It was a good job, better than her publishers back home had done. They preferred a busty blonde with a come-and-fuck-me-boys look, even though her heroine, Detective Dusty Jaxone, was average in looks and size. That was why she was popular as hell, especially with women readers who were sick to the front teeth of smart-ass medical examiners and kickass private eyes.

It would soon be midnight. Time for a cocktail before

she went out. With any luck, she'd be several sheets to the wind by the time she hit the dance floor. One thing to be said for Wilde's was that it listed the best lesbian and gay clubs in its information pack. She phoned room service and ordered a pair of margaritas. They ought to keep her axles greased.

A couple of minutes later there was a knock on the door.

'Is that room service?' she said, overemphasising the drawl because she knew the Brits loved it.

'Yes, madam,' came a deep voice.

The best-selling author went to the door and opened it, thinking as she did that it would have been a good idea to look through the spy-hole first. But, hell, it was only room service, and they'd moved faster than a rattlesnake's tail.

When she saw the misshapen face outside, the smile vanished from her lips faster than the Sacramento Mountains sucked down the evening sun.

The e-mail from my mother duly arrived. I read it and realised that she hadn't come up with an answer, though she did point out a couple of things I'd missed. Set with a capital 's' was the ancient Egyptian god of disorder, and in a cryptic crossword, that could suggest that letters or words had been mixed up—fair enough, and that was the reference of 'set' that had been at the tip of my tongue, but it didn't get us much further. More interesting was Fran's reading of 'by the westernmost dunes'—she wondered if the use of 'by' could mean 'next to', and that therefore we shouldn't be looking for the most western beaches such as Cornwall in England, but those in Devon, the only county next to Cornwall. Again, fair enough, but what was I supposed to send Flaminio/Doctor Faustus? I had no choice. It had to be Katya, even though her only connection was the dead critic named Alexander.

Heart thundering like a bass drum, I logged on to my e-mail programme. At exactly 11.59 there was a chime and an e-mail arrived from *nextiswho?*—the sender's new address. I hit Reply and sent the Bulgarian's full name. Then it struck me—what was going to happen *next?* Would Sara, or whoever had set up the clue, answer immediately, or was I going to have to spend the night monitoring the news? In the rush towards the deadline, I hadn't considered the time after it. I stood up and stepped away from the laptop, but kept my eye on the screen. Screw the guy in the room underneath, I needed to walk. I only got halfway towards the discoloured wardrobe when I heard the chime. The bell had tolled. Was someone about to die?

I clicked on the new message, and my heart sank like a stone.

> Who? Never heard of her. Right sex, though.
> "Now hast she but one bare minute to live..."
> Doctor Faustus

Jesus. If the bastard who sent the message was to be believed—and what had been said about the Mary Malone murder showed insider knowledge—there was a woman in London being murdered as I stood in front of the screen. I replied, asking for more time, but there was no response. I recognised the quotation—it was from Marlowe's *Doctor Faustus,* one of the few set-texts that I'd actually paid attention to at university. It should have read

> Now hast thou but one bare hour to live,
> And then thou must be damn'd perpetually.

My mind filled with visions of violence and death. Because I'd arrogantly assumed I could solve the clue and hadn't involved my mother earlier, I had condemned a woman to death. It wasn't just Faustus who'd been damned for eternity. I had been too.

The sound of her mobile woke Karen Oaten instantly. She had got home from the office at eleven and gone straight to bed. Although she had grabbed the phone automatically—she'd had long years of practice—her brain took a few seconds to function and she had to ask Amelia Browning to repeat what she'd said. The alarm clock showed 00.46.

'Dead woman at a hotel in Soho,' the detective sergeant said breathlessly. 'We need to get over there and take it from Homicide Central.'

'Hold on, Amelia,' Karen said, blinking in the bright light she had turned on. 'What's so significant about—'

'Single stab wound to the heart,' Browning interrupted. 'And a message on the body.'

Oaten felt her stomach flip. It sounded very like the White Devil's modus operandi. 'What does it say?' she asked, gripping her phone tightly.

There was a pause. 'It…it says "Ask Matt Wells about this", guv. There was music playing as well.'

'Jesus Christ.' The chief inspector swung her legs out of bed and padded over to the wardrobe. 'Where's Taff?'

'At home, I suppose. But I can—'

'You're on night duty in the office, sergeant, and that's where you have to stay. How did you find out about the murder?'

'I was monitoring the emergency frequencies.'

'Good work.' Most of Oaten's team spent night duty catching up on their paperwork or playing solitaire on their computers. Amelia would have finished her paperwork long ago. 'Have you spoken to anyone in Homicide Central?'

'Yes, guv. I thought it was best if I declared the VCCT's interest.'

'Well done again. But that's enough. I'll take over now.' Oaten cut the connection and started to dress. She could imagine how well a call from a lowly sergeant in her team would have gone down with whichever grizzled senior officer was in charge. After she'd put on a pair of sensible black shoes, she called John Turner.

'Sorry, Taff, but I need you.' She explained the situation, then arranged to meet him at the hotel. It was on Charlotte Street and seemed to be in the colour supplements every weekend.

It wasn't till she was in her car and heading for Soho that Karen thought about the mention of Matt. Why had the killer left a message referring to him? She called his home numbers, both open and ex-directory, and his mobile. Each time she got his answering service and had to leave messages. The fact that he wasn't picking up gave her a bad feeling. He and his mates were up to something, she was sure of that. Surely they hadn't managed to provoke Sara to murder?

She left her car outside the police tape in the Soho street. Uniformed officers were struggling to hold journalists and photographers back. As she bent under the cordon, she heard a familiar voice.

'Is this a case for the VCCT, Chief Inspector?'

Karen Oaten ignored the tall figure in a dark blue Barber jacket. Jeremy Andrewes, crime correspondent of the *Daily Independent,* had been a colleague of Sara Robbins's.

Oaten had little time for the aristocratic newshound, although he was less of a muckraker than most of his breed. She wondered how the pack had heard about the murder. A hotel employee had probably earned a nice little bonus.

Inside the hotel's opulent lobby, she recognised detectives from Homicide Central. They were talking to hotel staff and guests, some of whom looked shell-shocked.

John Turner came up to her, wearing a white coverall, the hood up. 'It's on the third floor, guv,' he said, leading the way.

'Any witnesses?'

'Not so far.'

'Who found the body?'

'A room-service waiter. The door of the suite was a couple of centimetres open.'

'Who's in charge from Central?' Oaten asked, as she pulled on a set of protective clothing and gloves.

'DCI Younger.'

'Could be worse.' When she was ready, she followed the Welshman up the stairs. CSIs had run tape down one half and were examining the floor and banisters for prints.

They came out into the third-floor corridor, black-and-white geometric paintings mounted on the pale pink wallpaper. The victim's suite—the Windermere—was first on the left, a large Japanese fan spread open and mounted on the grey door. As they went in, they met Dr Redrose on his way out.

'Ah, the chief of the elite,' he said, jowls wobbling. 'I was wondering when you'd make an appearance.'

Karen gave him a dispassionate look. 'Going somewhere, Doctor?'

'I'm finished,' Redrose said, one hand on his protruding stomach. 'A simple case. One stab wound to the heart, a smooth, two-edged blade. The murderer is right-handed, probably not as tall as the victim, who is fractionally over six feet, and the time of death was after 11.00 p.m. according to the body temperature, though I gather the poor woman placed a room-service order at 11.53 and the waiter found her at 12.10, so you already have a tight window.'

'Hello, Chief Inspector,' said a grey-haired man with a curiously boyish face.

'Ditto, Colin,' Oaten said, looking around the spacious suite.

There was a pair of cocktail glasses and a tray on the floor near the door, and some damp patches on the puce carpet. Beyond them, the body of a tall woman with short blonde hair, wearing what looked like a black cowboy outfit, lay on the floor. Her arms were at exact right angles to her torso and her legs were straight, the heels of her boots touching. Her shirt was stained with blood. Her eyelids were wide apart and her mouth open, as if in utter astonishment.

'The shape of the cross,' Younger said, in a faint Scottish accent.

Karen Oaten nodded. 'No sign of a pentacle?'

'Like the author who was killed in Fulham?' The chief inspector shook his head. 'No.'

'Maybe this was all the bastard had time to do,' John Turner said.

Oaten nodded. 'What about the message?'

Younger handed her a transparent evidence bag. 'It was lying over her face.'

The words 'Ask Matt Wells about this' were written in capitals, in blue ink. Oaten's expression remained impassive.

'Turn it over,' Younger said.

She did so and saw the words 'FECIT DIABOLUS' in red ink. Whoever had spoken to Amelia Browning had failed to mention that.

'It's the same killer,' Turner said.

'Given that we didn't release the Latin words to the press, I'd say there's a good chance of that, Taff,' Oaten said. She looked at Younger. 'I gather no one saw anything.'

He shrugged. 'Someone must have seen the killer. All the exits are alarmed, so he—or she—must have come in through the main entrance. The problem is, the bar was busy and it would have been easy to slip in unnoticed. We're talking to everyone who was in the building when we arrived. We'll narrow it down and get a description.' He frowned. 'If you don't take the case from us.'

Oaten glanced at Taff. 'We're taking it—it's clearly linked to the Mary Malone case. We'll have to take that too. I'll talk to your super. I'd like your team to stay on the case. Taff here will act as liaison.'

Younger's face flushed. 'So we do the hard graft and you get the glory?'

Oaten shook her head. 'You know I don't work like that, Colin. Give me a break, for Christ's sake. Apart from these murders, we've got the shooting south of the river, plus what looks like the makings of a major gang war in East London. I'm asking for your help. Don't make me show my teeth.'

Younger pursed his lips, and then nodded. 'Fair enough.'

'What's the victim's name?' Oaten asked.

'Obviously we haven't had a formal identification yet,

but the books over there have got her photo on them. We also found her passport. She's Sandra Lee-Anne Devonish, born San Antonio, Texas, on January 15th 1970. According to the back of the books, she's one of the world's highest-selling crime novelists.'

Karen Oaten felt a chill finger stir in her gut. Another crime writer. She was certain Matt knew something about the case. The message that Sara or whoever killed Sandra Devonish had left on the body suggested there had been some kind of communication. Where the hell was Matt when his fellow crime writer was being stabbed with such frightening precision?

'What was the music?' she asked, coming back to herself.

'Sorry?' Younger had also been lost in thought. 'Oh, yes. According to my sergeant, who knows about rock— I only listen to the classics—it's a song called "Friend of the Devil" by the Grateful Dead.'

Karen Oaten grunted. The tabloid papers would love that.

15

I couldn't stay in my hotel room any longer. The thought that someone was being killed because of my failure to crack the clue drove me on to the streets of Bloomsbury. I brushed past a kid who asked for money, provoking justified abuse. I walked around the quiet streets and lost track of time. Eventually, in front of the British Museum, I looked up at the neo-classical facade and tried to get a grip. The shouts of some pissed students brought me back to reality. There were people laughing and enjoying themselves, but I had put myself beyond the boundaries of ordinary humanity. I had tried to take on a killer and someone else had paid for my arrogance.

I found a public phone and called Karen's mobile.

'Matt,' she said in a low voice, 'where are you?'

'Never mind. There's been a murder, hasn't there?'

'How did you know that?' she demanded. 'Where are you? I need you to come in.' Her tone was icy.

'Who was it?' I asked, desperate to know whose name had been concealed in the clue.

'When I see you, I'll tell you,' she replied. 'One thing you might like to know now, though—there was a message on the body. The Devil did it, in Latin, as in Mary Malone's garden.'

'Shit,' I said. Had Sara struck again so quickly?

'That's not all it said.'

Something about her tone made me instantly apprehensive. The White Devil had tried to frame me several times.

'Suddenly you've gone all quiet,' she said ironically. 'The killer also wrote "Ask Matt Wells about this". So, I'm asking.'

'You know I didn't kill anyone.'

'So why should I tell you who the victim was?' She had obviously had it with me.

'Tell me who it was, Karen. Please.'

'Screw you, Matt,' she hissed. 'Who do you think you are? Why should I share information with you when all you do is disappear so you can run your personal campaign?'

I took a deep breath. 'Because I'm the only person who can catch Sara. When it comes to the crisis point, I'll be the bait she can't resist.'

'And how many people have to die before you eventually play that heroic part?'

My stomach somersaulted as I realised she would have seen the number I was calling from on her screen. If she'd got someone to find the phone booth's location, a car full of cops could be on its way as we spoke.

'I'm hanging up, Karen. Last chance to tell me the name. You know I can make good use of it.'

'Do I?' she said, the anger in her voice replaced by what sounded like regret. 'Maybe I did once. But you're flailing about now, Matt. Come in, for God's sake.'

'The name, Karen.'

There was a pause before she spoke again. 'It'll be on the news soon enough. Sandra Devonish.'

I broke the connection and ran for my hotel. I stopped

a couple of times to check that there was no one on my tail. Either I'd got away in time or Karen hadn't traced the number. I wasn't taking any chances about where I spent the rest of the night. I went up to my room, packed up the laptop and the rest of my gear, and went out past the dozing night porter.

Back on the street, I saw a cab and hailed it.

'Where to, squire?' the driver asked.

I told him to drive towards Victoria and thought about it. Getting out of London was tempting, but I needed to be close to the scenes of the crimes. Maybe I'd be able to prevent another. Christ, who was I kidding? I hadn't been able to help Sandra Devonish. I'd met her a couple of times at crime-writing conferences in the States. She played the Southern belle, with the full set of long vowels and perfect manners, then would turn into a wisecracking, in-your-face lesbian. She could drink most men under the bar. I shook my head to dispel the vision of the stunning American. I needed to think about what to do now. I couldn't handle this on my own any longer. It could be risky meeting up with Rog and Pete, but it had to be done. If we were going to catch Sara, we needed to go on the offensive and to do that effectively, we had to be together.

I took out my laptop, booted up and asked the driver to pull in. My wireless card picked up a signal and I logged on to the Internet. I sent a message to Rog's ghost site. I told him and Pete to meet me on the Embankment, under Hungerford Bridge. I sent Andy a text saying the same thing. Then I walked from Victoria to Embankment, checking there was no one on my tail. As I was going under the railway bridge, a low whistle came from my left.

'Over here, Matt,' Pete said in a low voice.

I joined him in a dim alcove. 'God, it's good to see a friendly face,' I said, grabbing his hand.

'Steady on,' he said, trying to look at my face. 'What's up?'

I told him about Sandra Devonish. I could see he was trying to make sense of the clue now that we knew the answer, but that wasn't the priority right now.

'Where do you think we should go, Boney?' I asked.

He thought about it. 'You've got a safe house for yourself, haven't you?'

'Yeah, but it's outside the M25. I don't think we should leave the Smoke.'

He nodded. 'How about my place? The bitch from hell won't be able to get past my alarm system easily.'

'No chance,' I replied. 'Karen knows where you live. She'll check it out.'

'We can hide in the wine cellar.'

'No, I can't take the chance. If we get taken into custody, protective or not, we'll never catch Sara.'

Footsteps approached. Pete whistled again and Rog came across.

'Good to see you,' I said, punching him lightly on the chest. Two of them had made it. Now there was only Andy.

'We need to find a base in London,' I said to Rog. 'Preferably not too far out of the centre.'

'No problem,' he said, fumbling in his pocket. 'These are the keys to my cousin's flat in Camden Town. He's on holiday. I'm supposed to water the plants, but I haven't managed that yet.'

'Em, brilliant,' I said, taken aback by the quick solution to our most pressing problem.

Andy arrived a few minutes later.

'What did you do with the van?' I asked.

'Left it outside the hire place. It's no use to us now.'

'But they've got your credit card.'

'No, they haven't.'

I stared at him. 'What did you do?'

He shrugged. 'I…em, I bought a fake card from a friend of a friend.'

'Bloody hell, you took a chance,' I said.

'It worked all right when they swiped it,' he said. 'What's the problem? I thought I was meant to use my initiative.'

'You did well, big man,' I said, trying to placate him. 'How was Mrs Carlton-Jones?'

'All right,' he said. 'I didn't get the impression that she'd been hiding her daughter.'

'Do you think it was Sara on the motorbike?'

'Could well have been.'

He was right. And she could well have used the bike to get to and from the latest murder scene.

Half an hour later we were all safely inside Rog's cousin's flat. It was a decent-size, two-bedroom place near the tube station. There were even two good-quality computers, which gave us more power in that department. Rog made a pot of coffee and we sat round the dining table.

'So what happened with the clue?' Rog asked.

'I knew the dead woman, Sandra Devonish,' I said.

'I've heard of her,' Andy said. 'I think I read one of her books. Set in Texas?'

I nodded. 'She was quite a woman.'

'Sandra Devonish,' Rog said, taking a large notebook from his bag. '"The sun set by the westernmost dunes of Alexander's womankind." Oh, I get it. Alexander's womankind—Sandra comes from Alexandra, the female version of Alexander.'

'Fuck,' I said, under my breath. I should have spotted that. But it wouldn't necessarily have helped, as I couldn't think of any other Sandras I knew and I wasn't even aware that the dead woman was coming to London.

'The sun set…' Pete said.

'My mother spotted that "set" might be the Egyptian god of that name—among other things, he was the god of disorder, so the words, syllables or letters in the clue would be jumbled up.'

Rog looked up from his notebook. 'Wasn't the Egyptian god of the sun called Ra?'

I groaned. 'You're right. And the dunes are made of sand. So that was another pointer to Sand-ra.' I slapped my forehead. I'd been duped twice. 'And "by the westernmost dunes" means next to the place with the most westerly beaches in this country, which is Devon rather than Cornwall.'

Rog nodded. 'And the "kind" at the end of "woman-kind", if it's taken to mean "kind of"—'

'Comes out as "-ish",' I completed. 'Jesus! I should have got that.'

The three of them demurred.

'Come on, man,' Andy said, 'I'd never have worked that out.'

'Yeah, it was pretty cryptic,' Rog said. 'Pete and I didn't have a clue either. Don't beat yourself up about it.'

'But a woman's dead,' I said. 'I should have guessed the next victim would be another crime writer.'

'Why?' Pete asked. 'The White Devil didn't kill people in the same line of work, did he?'

That was true. But I still blamed myself for not involving my mother sooner. She might well have got the answer in time. Then another thought struck me. Would Sara, or whoever was aping her and the White Devil, have kept her promise and spared Sandra if I had identified her?

I tried to get some sleep on the bed next to Andy. I still felt responsible. Karen was right. I wasn't up to fighting this war, even with my friends on my side. But it was too late to change tactics now. I had to make sure there were no more deaths, and in order to do that, we had to track Sara down.

Sleep climbed all over me like a ravenous bear and I fell into the depths.

Faik Jabar's shoulder had been treated by the Kurdish doctor, whose name was Jemal Dawod, and it no longer hurt him so much. The doctor had a house near the Lea Bridge roundabout in Clapton. Faik heard the roar of traffic and wished he could go back to his parents' house. It was only a mile or so away, but the area would be swarming with Shadows and Jemal wouldn't let him out during the hours of daylight. Late in the evening, after Faik woke from a deep sleep, they had eaten a meal of spicy stewed lamb that the doctor had prepared.

'That was good,' Faik said, emptying his glass of water. 'Now I must go.'

'It is very dangerous for you.'

'And for you. The Shadows know where you live.'

Jemal Dawod nodded. 'But they have been told that I did not kill the Wolfman.'

'What about the guard you took out?'

'His memory will be jumbled up for some time.'

'But you were seen trying to take me away.'

'I already told them that I needed another doctor to look at you. Now I will say that you escaped from here.'

'Will they come?'

The doctor shook his head. 'They only ever contact me by telephone. I think they are very busy trying to find the Wolfman's killer.'

'I cannot risk being caught again.'

Jemal smiled. 'In that case, you must stay off the streets.'

'They will not see me.'

The doctor smiled again. 'You are forgetting something.'

Faik stared at him. 'What?'

'The person who killed Izady—maybe that is the same person who wore the *burqa* this afternoon. He may also be looking for you.'

'He?' Faik sat back. 'You think a *man* was wearing the *burqa?*'

Jemal Dawod raised his shoulders. 'This is London, not the Middle East. People have different ideas about tradition.'

'Who do you think this killer is?'

'At first I assumed he was working for the Shadows. That explained why he killed Izady. I guessed he'd double-crossed them.'

Faik got up from the low table and shook the tingling from his legs. 'But it doesn't explain why he only shot me in the hand and then knocked me out, rather than killing me.'

The doctor lit a cigarette. 'No, it doesn't. I thought perhaps he left a witness to recount what had happened to the Kurds. But then the Wolfman caught you, so the Shadows couldn't have hired the killer.'

'So who's this killer with the false beard working for?'

Jemal Dawod blew out a cloud of smoke. 'I have no

idea. But I don't think you should chance meeting him again.'

Faik looked at his watch. It was well after midnight. 'I must go, Doctor. Thank you for everything.'

'Make sure those wounds in your legs don't get infected. You have my mobile number. Call me in a week and I will remove the stitches from your hand.' Jemal embraced the young man. 'May Allah protect you.'

'And you,' Faik said, turning towards the door.

'You have forgotten something else,' the doctor said.

Faik looked back. 'I have?'

'If you are escaping, you must leave your mark on me.'

'No, Doctor,' the young man said, his mouth slack.

'Otherwise the Shadows will not believe me and I will be killed.'

Faik took a deep breath. Jemal Dawod was right. They couldn't risk it. He went up to the doctor and made him stand in front of the sofa. 'I'm sorry,' he said. Then he drew back his undamaged hand and landed a powerful uppercut on the other man's chin. He crashed back on the cushions, blood flowing from his lower lip, which had been punctured by his teeth. Faik made sure he was comfortable.

Going to the front door, he let himself out. The night air was chill and he suddenly felt very weak. But it was too late to go back. If he kept to the back streets he should be home soon, as long as he didn't meet any Shadows. He tried to establish a steady rhythm, but his injured thighs caught painfully on his jeans and the breath was ragged in his throat. Soon he was very thirsty. He stopped after about ten minutes, bending down behind a car. When he stood up, a figure in black biker leathers was standing on the other side of the bonnet, pointing a silenced pistol at his chest. The visor of the helmet had been raised and Faik saw wisps of beard on the upper cheeks.

'Will you come with me?' the man asked, his voice hoarse. 'I have so much to show you.'

Faik Jabar felt a strange emotion, a kind of attraction to the armed figure. Although he didn't have much choice, he moved round the car, walking willingly to meet his fate.

Jeremy Andrewes was in the basement of the family house in Chelsea. When he had started working for the *Daily Independent,* his father had banished him to what had been the kitchen and servants' quarters on the grounds that, since he was working for a 'socialist rag', he should experience life below the stairs. Over the years, Jeremy had done the place up and he still used it for work, even though his parents were long gone and his own family—a docile wife and three rampant boys—had the run of the whole house as well as the Hampshire estate.

He sat staring at his computer screen, trying to get an original angle on the murder of the American crime writer at Wilde's. It was 5.00 a.m. and he was being pressured by his editor. He had a contact in Homicide Central, a disillusioned old timer who regarded DCI Younger as a jumped-up schoolboy. The detective had told him about the message on the body that said 'Ask Matt Wells about this'. He'd tried to do that, but the writer wasn't answering any of his phones. He'd also pressed Karen Oaten and John Turner about potential leads, but he couldn't give away the fact that he knew about the message. The chief inspector had made a brief statement without mentioning it. She wouldn't confirm that the murder was linked to the Mary

Malone case either, but no one had much doubt about that. So, what to do? Andrewes wasn't a fan of tabloid-style journalism, but he badly needed to put one over his rivals on the other papers—he'd been beaten to several exclusives and his standing was at an all-time low. Since Matt Wells wasn't answering his calls, he was the one to be thrown to the wolves.

Before he did that, he called Josh Hinkley. Perhaps the other crime writer would have some startling insight.

'What?' came a hoarse voice.

'Josh, it's Jeremy.'

There was a pause. 'Do you know what fuckin' time it is?'

'I do. I'm working.'

'Well, have a cigar, public school boy. Normal people are in their beds.' Hinkley laughed coarsely. 'And they aren't on their own. Move over, darling.'

Andrewes shook his head. He was wasting his time, but this was his only chance. 'Another crime writer's been murdered.' He told Hinkley about Sandra Devonish—the victim's name had been confirmed after her British publisher had identified the body.

'Christ!' Hinkley exclaimed. 'It *is* a serial killer, then.'

'Looks like it, though DCI Oaten hasn't confirmed that and there's been nothing said about the black magic stuff.' He paused. 'You do realise that this killer is targeting crime novelists.'

'I'd better make sure my alarm system's working, then. Thanks for the tipoff, Jerry.'

Andrewes nearly laid into Hinkley for addressing him that way, but he managed to control himself. 'I didn't call to warn you, Josh. Your friend Matt Wells is mixed up in this somehow.' He told him about the message on the body.

'Oh, yus!' Hinkley exclaimed. 'That's very juicy! What do you think it means?'

Jeremy Andrewes raised his eyes to the ceiling. 'I was hoping you might be able to cast some light on that.'

'Oh yeah?' There was the sound of a cigarette lighter, followed by deep inhalation. 'Well, it's obvious, isn't it? It's that crazy woman he used to shag.'

'I'd got that far on my own, Josh. But what do you think Wells is up to? He's not answering any of his phones.'

Hinkley drew on his cigarette again. 'If the White Devil case is anything to go by, he and his headbanging rugby mates are trying to track her down.'

'They're not exactly succeeding, are they? Did Wells give you the impression he was going to play the caped crusader?'

'Not really. I told you, he was pretty down in the dumps about his friend Dave Cummings being shot. The fucker chucked me out.'

Andrewes made his mind up. Screw his informer in the Homicide Central and screw Matt Wells—he was going to go for broke on this. 'Josh, I want you to give me the full lowdown on Wells—big-headedness, unreliability, what he was like when he was with Sara Robbins. Basically, anything that makes him look flaky.'

'Yeah, I can do that,' Hinkley said with a laugh. 'How much imagination am I allowed to use?'

'As much as you like, but I'll be quoting you.'

'That's all right, Jerry. I'll do anything for publicity.'

'Oh, and, Josh?'

'What?'

'I need it now.'

'Aw, come on. I'm bloody knackered.'

'Anything for publicity?'

'Fuck you. All right, let me think.'

Andrewes spent the time opening a new file in his word processing system. He titled it 'JoshdumpsonMW'.

'Em, Jerry?' Hinkley's tone was suddenly apprehensive.

'What is it? Getting cold feet about ratting on your so-called friend?'

'Nah, bollocks to that. I was just wondering—do you think Matt might be the killer?'

Andrewes stifled a laugh. 'What, and he left a message incriminating himself on the body?'

'That might be a distraction. I had a killer do that in one of my books.'

'This isn't fiction, Josh. This is the real world, and Sandra Devonish was stabbed in the heart.'

'Yeah, well, serves her right for being a bad-tempered dyke. She kneed me in the balls when I came on to her in Washington. I thought I could convert her.'

Jeremy Andrewes managed to bite his tongue. 'Are you ready to talk now?'

'Yeah. Here I go.'

As Hinkley came out with a character assassination that Carlos the Jackal would have been proud of, the thought that Matt Wells could have been the killer kept nagging away at Jeremy Andrewes. And while he didn't believe for one moment that Wells would murder his fellow crime writers, he knew that suspicion would sell plenty of newspapers.

The Soul Collector woke in her van. She opened the back door a few centimetres and listened. Although she had parked a long way up a track in rural Worcestershire, she couldn't be sure no one had spotted the vehicle. The early dawn light was faint and mist had gathered over the fields. She decided she was safe for another half-hour.

Sara Robbins used the time to go over her plan. She had timed everything carefully and had built in an extra ten minutes. Today was the day that she put the squeeze on the former SAS men. The cottage in Berkshire was waiting to receive guests. She'd bought it with funds that not even a genius hacker would have been able to identify as hers. The other properties were in compound names, including her mother's, that Matt and his friends might well have found. They were welcome to check them out.

She put her papers into a folder and stuck it under the front seat. She had memorised everything and she was ready. This was the biggest test of her abilities yet. Killing people was easy, if you were cold enough about it—and she certainly was. But kidnapping people, keeping them alive, that was more of a challenge. As was luring and out-thinking three former elite soldiers. Not even her brother had managed to pull anything like that off. She loved him, but her ambition was to be even more ruthless, even more invincible. Today would be the making of her. The Soul Collector was the god beneath the ground, the final enemy of mankind—Hades, Persephone, Hecate, Dis, Proserpina, Hel, Lucifer. It was striking how many of those ancient deities were female. Women were usually seen as the source of life, but not Sara Robbins.

The Soul Collector was Death Incarnate.

16

I was woken by a hand shaking my shoulder.

'Matt? You've got to see this.' Pete's expression was a mixture of anger and dismay.

'What is it?' I asked, sitting up and stretching my arms. I looked at my watch and saw it was eight-thirty.

Rog was sitting in front of a computer. He looked over his shoulder. 'Morning, Matt. Take a deep breath.'

I rubbed my eyes and bent over to read the text that was displayed. I immediately recognised the layout of the *Daily Indie*'s website. Then I started to read.

'"American Novelist Murdered—Five Questions for Matt Wells."'

I sat down heavily on the chair that Pete had brought over. 'What is this?'

'That scumbag Jeremy Andrewes seems to think you're behind the killings,' Rog said.

After a description of the event, written in a tone more appropriate to the paper's tabloid rivals, came the questions:

One—why did Matt Wells's name appear on a note left on Sandra Devonish's body?

Two—why is Matt Wells not answering any of his phones?

Three—what is the connection between this murder and the shooting of Matt Wells's close friend David Cummings?

Four—has Matt Wells been in contact with his former lover, Sara Robbins, sister of the notorious White Devil?

And, five—does Matt Wells hate his fellow crime writers so much that he could kill them?

There followed a lengthy list of my supposed transgressions at crime-writing festivals and events, largely based on the testimony of the bullshit-merchant Josh Hinkley. Throwing him out of my apartment had obviously not been such a smart move.

'How much of this is true?' Rog asked.

'A bit,' I admitted. 'But it's all been given the worst possible spin. For instance, I *did* pour a pint of beer over Josh Hinkley in Manchester, but that was because he kept feeling up my publicist. I *did* tell Sandra Devonish to fuck off, but we were both rat-arsed, and she said it to me first. And I suppose, though my memory's a bit hazy about this, I might have called the Crime Writers' Society "the Jurassic Park of literature" during an event in Aberdeen, but that was probably because bleeding Josh had called it something much worse. I could kick that wanker's teeth in.'

'Probably not a good idea at this current juncture,' Pete said.

There was a series of knocks on the door.

Pete walked over, silenced Glock in hand. He looked

through the spy-hole. 'Slash,' he said, taking off the chain and letting the American in.

'Goddamm English weather!' he said, shaking his soaked blonde mop. He was carrying a flagon of milk in one hand and a large bag of shopping in the other.

I scrolled down the rest of the article. There was a section about Sandra Devonish, mentioning her best-known books and the movies that had been made from them—one was pretty good, I remembered. There was also what was obviously a publicity photo of her standing against one of those huge cacti in a red desert. Then there was a sanctimonious wrap-up from Jeremy Andrewes, in which he regretted putting 'this paper's own crime colum-nist on the spot', but that 'the truth and the need for the police to carry out their duties without interference from a misguided crime writer take precedence over personal considerations'. He wouldn't be getting a Christmas card from me again.

'What now?' Pete asked, patting my shoulder.

'I have to make sure that Lucy, my mother and Caroline, let alone everyone else, have checked in okay,' I said.

'Breakfast coming up,' Andy said.

I took out my laptop and logged on to my e-mail server. Everyone had sent confirmation messages. I knew that Caroline would be climbing the walls wherever she and the others were, especially if she'd seen Jeremy Andrewes's article. There wasn't anything I could do about that. I thought about contacting Karen. It would have been easy enough to send her an e-mail or a text, but I didn't want to. The bottom line was that any message from me would compromise her even more in the eyes of her boss and of her team. We were going to have to work out our own solutions to this nightmare. She'd be up to her ears in other business anyway, given Dave's murder and what looked like the start of a serious gang war in the East End.

Andy prepared the usual gargantuan breakfast, but none of us was complaining. We might not get the chance to eat for some time, and sitting round the table gave us the opportunity to work out a plan of action.

'I vote we go and throw those shitheads into the river,' Andy said, dipping a sausage into the yolk of a fried egg.

'You mean Andrewes and Hinkley?' I said. 'I'll get them when this is all over. The question is, what do we do now?'

Pete was fastidiously cutting away the rind from his bacon. 'Are you going to stay underground, so to speak?'

I'd been thinking about that. Although the *Daily Indie* had demanded that I report to New Scotland Yard—having really pushed the boat out by making my relationship with Karen public—there was nothing in the article or in any of the other papers' coverage saying that the police wanted to see me. Obviously Karen did, in order to stop me chasing Sara, but I hadn't done anything illegal—apart from carry a pistol, and no one had any proof of that.

'I can't see the point in breaking cover,' I said. 'The only way we're going to get close to Sara is to use what we know. If we share it with the cops, Sara will respond either with a killing spree or a rapid disappearance.'

'Or both,' Rog said, raising his knife.

'Thanks for that, Dodger.' I looked around the table. 'Where do we start, then?'

'Well, we've got the three properties that Sara bought in the south-east,' Rog said. 'The flat in Hackney, the house in Oxford and the farmhouse in Kent.'

'True enough,' I said, 'not that she's necessarily using them.'

'She's probably got them booby-trapped,' Pete said.

Andy grunted. 'Probably. What about your millionaire friends, Boney? Have they seen her recently?'

Pete shook his head. 'The last actual sighting I have of her is in Zurich nearly a year ago.'

'What do you think she looks like now?' Rog asked, pushing his plate away.

I glanced over at him. 'How do you mean?'

He shrugged. 'Well, she's hardly going to be letting the CCTV cameras of the capital record her as she was two years ago. She's a fugitive, isn't she? Wanted for her part in several murders. At the very least she's going to be using disguises.'

'Good point, Dodger,' Pete said. Then he frowned. 'What do you mean, "at the very least"?'

Rog grinned. 'Ever heard of a thing called cosmetic surgery, Boney?'

'Shit,' I said, dropping my cutlery. 'That would make our job a whole lot harder.'

Andy shook his head. 'I don't see why. We just nail anyone acting suspiciously. She's probably hired people anyway.'

'That would be "nail" as in what you failed to do with the motorbike rider you saw trying to hand something to Sara's birth mother?' I asked, with more sarcasm than he deserved. He shouldn't have called me Oates.

'Steady on, Matt,' Pete said. 'The last thing we should be doing is taking shots at each other.'

'Quite right,' I said, raising my hand. 'Sorry, Slash.'

'Forget it,' he said with a grin. 'I'm not the person on the front page of the newspaper.'

That made us laugh, but not for long. Andy brought over another pot of coffee and we refilled.

'Okay,' I said. 'Plan. For a start, we're not doing anything on our own. We stay in pairs. That way we reduce the chances of being surprised by Sara or her sidekicks.'

'How about checking the properties?' Rog asked. 'For a start, there's the one in Hackney. That shouldn't take long.'

I nodded. 'Okay. Who's going to do that?'

Pete looked around the table. 'We haven't decided on pairs yet.'

'Boney, why don't you do that with Andy?' I suggested. They both agreed.

'What about us?' Rog asked me.

'I need to keep checking my e-mails in case Doctor Faustus or Flaminio sends another clue,' I replied. 'In the meantime, you can start tinkering with those bank accounts of Sara's you've been logging.'

'Tinkering with them?'

'Yes, Dodger,' I said, with a thin smile. 'I want you to transfer as much as you can from them into a new account in my name. That should get her attention pretty quickly.'

'Way to go, Matt!' Andy said.

'Yeah,' said Pete. 'Make her squirm!'

I suddenly felt a wave of emotion. Up till now we had basically been chasing the game, but now we were going on the attack. The question was, how many people were going to end up dead before we flushed Sara out?

Karen Oaten was sitting in front of the Assistant Commissioner's desk, in a low chair that she was sure he had carefully chosen to emphasise his superior position.

'Tell me, Karen,' he said, flicking a speck of dirt from his uniform tunic. 'What are you doing to find Matt Wells?'

She tried not to sigh too obviously. It was clear that her boss had paid more attention to the *Daily Independent* than the other papers. Then again, the Matt Wells angle was sure to be copied across the media as the day progressed.

'I've applied to have his phones tapped and his Internet service provider monitored.' She rubbed her forehead. 'But it's likely that he's using other numbers and sites. He's been preparing for Sara Robbins's return for some time.'

'Is that who you think murdered the two crime writers?'

'There's no evidence of it, though the note mentioning Matt suggests someone with an agenda. Sara Robbins did threaten him in an e-mail after the White Devil's death.'

The AC picked up an expensive-looking pen and held it like a surveyor judging an angle. 'I have to tell you, Karen, that questions are being asked about your team. The outbreak of killings in East London is unlikely to have come to an end. The shooting of the Shadow hard man by someone wearing Muslim women's clothes is going to make things worse. I understand you've kept Ron Paskin in charge.'

'Yes, sir. He has the experience and the manpower to handle it.'

The AC raised an eyebrow. 'Is that a hint that you need more bodies, Chief Inspector?'

'I always need more bodies,' Oaten replied. 'At least, living ones. My monthly report has stressed the need for more detectives and support staff in the VCCT ever since I arrived.'

'Just be thankful you have a team to command at all,' the AC said firmly. 'There are plenty of senior personnel in the divisional homicide units who would be delighted to see the disbandment of what they feel is the interfering VCCT.'

'Yes, sir. I am aware of that.'

The man behind the desk opened a file. 'No fresh leads in the Mary Malone case?'

'No, sir.'

He opened another file. 'The Dave Cummings shooting?'

'No, sir.'

The AC looked down at her. 'And the Eastern Division murders? Are they just tit-for-tat gang idiocy?'

Karen Oaten held his gaze. 'I'm keeping an open mind, sir. Do you know something I don't?'

'I have spoken to Detective Superintendent Paskin, but he assures me he's copied you on all the case notes.' The AC pushed his chair back and stood up. 'Come on, Karen,' he said. 'Don't you think it's a bit of a coincidence? A series of murders starts that we can link, at least in principle, to Sara Robbins, and at the same time someone starts taking out gang members in East London?'

Karen chewed her lip. The thought had occurred to her. She didn't like the feeling, not least because the idea was interesting. She decided to play devil's advocate.

'There's no evidence whatsoever tying the crime-writer murders even to that of Dave Cummings, let alone to the East End killings, sir.'

'Indeed there isn't,' the AC said, looking at the photograph of the Metropolitan Police rugby union team that he had captained. 'But that doesn't mean there isn't some connection.'

If Amelia Browning had come up with an evidence-free idea like that, Karen would have sent her off with a verbal slap. But the AC wasn't prone to flights of fancy and he did have an outstanding record as a detective. She knew that she'd be a fool to ignore his input, even if it was nothing more than a hunch.

'So you want me to take over the cases from Ron Paskin, do you, sir?'

'Not necessarily,' her boss replied. 'Just consider the possibility that there's more to the gangland murders than meets the eye.'

'Right, sir,' Oaten said, standing up.

'By the way, how's that young sergeant coming along?'

'Amelia Browning? She's keen and I think she'll make the grade.'

The AC opened the door of his office. 'Good. I had a feeling she would when we interviewed her.'

As she left, Karen twitched her head. The AC might have given the impression of being the most strait-laced of commanders, but he had the ability to put his finger on things with unerring accuracy. It was about time she did the same, if she wanted to remain in charge of her team.

I watched as Rog's fingers flew over the keyboard like a concert pianist's. He had already managed to transfer a million dollars from an account in Venezuela to the one he'd set up in my name in London. Now he was working on the sum of two million in an Indian bank. I'd asked him before he started if he was happy about breaking the laws of numerous countries.

He just shrugged and said, 'Whatever it takes to get Sara off your back'.

Sometimes my friends made me feel very humble.

Andy and Pete had left, armed and wearing baseball caps with large peaks. I didn't think anyone would be looking for them on the CCTV cameras that were every-where in the city these days, but there was no point in risking it. I had the feeling we were going to have to resort to disguises before the chase was over and I didn't want to use them up prematurely.

After I'd checked our weapons and ammunition clips, I sat in front of my laptop, trying to resist the temptation to check my e-mails obsessively. It wasn't long before I succumbed. There was nothing of importance. While I was on the Internet, I decided to have a look at the Crime Writers' Society website. I got an unpleasant surprise.

Josh Hinkley had posted a call for my immediate ex-pulsion, on the grounds that I had brought the Society into disrepute because of my 'cowardly refusal to help the police'. Fortunately, there were several other members who wrote in to say that Josh was, in varying degrees of politeness, full of shit. What the hell was wrong with him? Obviously he was in bed with Jeremy Andrewes, but that was just a publicity gimmick. I knew Josh was jealous of the fact that *The Death List* had sat at the top of the best-seller list for months. But laying into me on a private site was another story. Then I remem-bered something Andy had said. What if Sara *had* got to Josh? He was sufficiently lacking in morals to work for her, especially if there was money involved. Then I had another, even worse thought. What if Josh had murdered Mary Malone and Sandra Devonish?

I got up and walked over to the window. The street below was full of slow-moving cars and the pavements were busy. Somewhere out there, I was sure, Sara was plotting her next move. Could it really be that Josh Hinkley was doing the same thing? Maybe Sara had killed Dave, but it was Josh who had killed the crime writers, entirely on his own. Jesus, the nightmare was getting even worse. How many vicious bastards were out there? I thought of the gangland killings in the east of the city. The answer to that question was, plenty. But Josh Hinkley a serial killer? He had a nasty side, and he certainly loathed crime writers who sold better than he did—Mary Malone and Sandra Devonish both came into that category, as had I with my book. Plus, he was doing his best to put me in the frame for the American's murder. Was that to keep the spotlight off him?

I went back to my laptop.

'That's it,' Rog said, turning to me. 'You're now three million dollars better off.'

'What's next?'

'A juicy little bank in Costa Rica, with a security system that a child could break. She's got two million in there.' He grinned. 'But not for long.'

'Shouldn't you take a break?' I said. 'I mean, log off so that there's no chance of you being traced.'

'Trust me, Matt, there's never been any chance of me being traced.'

I let him get on with it, wishing I had a skill that would help find Sara. But I didn't, so I checked my e-mails again. Christ. There was a message from a sender called *the-thirdisaman,* and the title was 'Something rotten in the state of Matt Wells'. The killer was back in touch. I opened the message and read:

Did you like it, Matt? The clue, I mean. Actually, there were any number of clues in the sentence I gave you, but you didn't get any of them. So, because I'm a gentle soul at heart, I'm giving you some help this time. Note the sender of this message. That means the next victim, my third, is a…have you got it yet? That's right, a man. Clever crime writer. Why should you trust me? Well, have I lied to you yet? Sandra Devonish—you knew her from those ego-boosting conferences you used to go to in the States, didn't you?—was lying in the shape of the cross. And why was that? Because I am Doctor Faustus and I have made a deal with the devil. If I gather souls for him, I can do anything I like—and, unlike Christopher Marlowe's Faustus, I don't have a time limit. I can continue for as long as I want, or until you catch me. There's been no evidence so far of you pulling that off. Oh, and just to be sure that you know I'm the real deal—I spitted the lovely Sandra with a single thrust to the heart, and I left the Grateful Dead playing "Friend of the Devil". Neat, eh?

I suppose I'd better give you the next clue now. Here we go:

The river shrinks bears
And the ice crows for a wife.
The lean man's imperial heiress
Is the thirsty draw of nothing.

If you don't work that out, there's no hope for you, Matt. Or rather, there's no hope for the person whose name is hidden in that verse. As this clue's so easy, I'm not giving you more time. You've got until midnight

tonight to answer. I'll be e-mailing you at 11.59. Don't
be slow in replying...
     In blood,
     D.F. alone
     (Flaminio's on a break)

'Fucking hell,' I said.

Rog came over and read the message. 'Oh, great,' he
said. 'Now the cow's writing poems.'

'Sara never showed any interest in poetry when I knew
her. Then again, this isn't exactly at Seamus Heaney's
level.'

Rog looked at me as if he wasn't sure who that was, but
he didn't have the nerve to admit it.

'Nobel literature prize winner,' I said. 'From Northern
Ireland.'

'I knew that,' he replied indignantly, hitting Print. In a
few seconds we were both poring over hard copies.

I looked at my watch. It was eleven-thirty. We had just
over twelve hours. I went back online and forwarded the
message to my mother. At least she'd have more time to
work on it this time.

'Can you run it through your decryption programmes,
Dodger?'

He nodded. 'There's something going on here, but I
can't put my finger on it.'

I looked at the clue. 'There's a truckload of things
going on,' I said. 'Water, the cold, crows—the most in-
telligent of birds, but they're also linked with death, since
they eat carrion.'

'Charming,' Rog said.

'"Lean",' I continued. 'That could be a reference to thin or starving, linking up with "thirsty" in the last line. "Imperial" suggests power, colonies—'

'Mints.'

I put my elbow in his ribs. 'Be serious. An heiress is a female child, one who stands to inherit something—a country, an empire?'

'Not if she's hungry and thirsty. She'll be dead—like the next victim.'

'Thanks a bunch, Dodger. Run your programmes, will you?'

I let him get on with that. It didn't matter that he wasn't making any more transfers from Sara's accounts for the time being. He'd done enough to attract her attention. I thought about sending Karen the clue. That way I'd at least protect myself from criticism of the kind Jeremy Andrewes and Josh Hinkley had poured over me. But when it came out that I'd been in contact with the police, Sara or whoever was playing at Doctor Faustus would know I'd broken the rule. That might lead to even more innocent people being murdered, including my family and the guys. No, I had to keep the clue secret. That decision almost crushed me.

I struggled to my feet and went over to the bookcase. Rog's cousin had a decent dictionary and thesaurus, as well as a one-volume encyclopaedia. I took them to the dining table, along with the hard copy of the message. Then I started checking every word for synonyms—I didn't bother with antonyms at this stage as there were no negatives in the poem. I also split up the lines into couplets, since each pair formed a sentence. I was working on the idea that each would give me a name. It was possible that every line did that, making four names, but I reckoned the existence of sentences was significant. If the first clue was anything to go by, there would be more than one definition of each name, and the writer had said that this clue was easier than the previous one. Two names, but they weren't necessarily in the right order.

I sat back in my chair. Was the third victim, supposedly a male, another crime writer? I'd made the mistake of not following up that angle the last time. I hadn't brought the Crime Writers' Society directory with me, but I could access the online version. Then again, that wouldn't have helped me with Sandra Devonish—foreign writers could join as overseas members, but most didn't. I considered going down the list of names, trying to fit each one to the clue, but that would have taken more hours than I had. There was no choice but to split the clue into its constituent parts—sentences, lines, words, syllables, even individual letters. I was sure there were puns and word-play in action. I was useless at spotting those in cryptic crosswords, but my mother wasn't. I would check the ghost site for her input soon.

In the meantime, I looked at the rest of the message. The tone was sardonic, just what I would have expected from Sara. But there were a couple of points that didn't ring true. By the time I knew her, I'd stopped going to crime-writing conferences as I couldn't afford them. How did the writer know that I'd met Sandra Devonish? She was only a passing acquaintance, someone I'd drunk with in a group a couple of times. I was sure I hadn't mentioned her to Sara, who'd never shown much interest in crime novelists anyway. Had she been talking to some other crime writer, who'd witnessed me and Sandra in the bar at the conference hotels? Who could that be? Josh Hinkley was a likely suspect, but hundreds of people attended those events, the majority of them fans and booksellers rather than writers. It would be a serious struggle to identify the source of information, and a waste of precious time.

The other thing that struck me as anomalous was the whole Doctor Faustus angle. Although Sara had been brought up by her foster parents as a Catholic, she'd never shown the slightest interest in religion—in fact, one of the things that I thought kept us together was a mutual impatience with all things divine or paranormal. I forced myself to see the Sara who had betrayed me as a devil-worshipper like Faustus, but that didn't ring true. For one thing, she was too conceited about her own abilities to make any kind of Faustian pact. Besides, she didn't need the devil's help. She'd already had plenty from her brother and she could hire as much as she wanted.

I went on with the lists of alternatives. Somehow it was easier to live with the idea of Sara as the writer of the messages. If there was another ruthless killer out there, my chances of surviving would be halved.

The aristocrat put down his coffee cup and got up from the long table. His ancestors had eaten from it for over two hundred years, and it would cost a small fortune to restore it; a small fortune he didn't have. The first earl had been ennobled by King George II for generously supporting the country's foreign wars. The origins of the family wealth had been in slaves, tobacco and the port wine trade—about as politically incorrect as you could get nowadays. But there was none of that left. The present earl had spent far too much on his private interests, not that he regretted a penny of it.

He strolled out on to the terrace that ran the length of the family seat. It was a fine spring morning, the dew burning off in clouds of steam in the light of the sun. The prize-winning herd of Aberdeen Angus cattle was grazing in the field to the left of the arrow-straight road that bisected the open panorama ahead. The site had been carefully chosen and landscaped to keep the Berkshire countryside below out of sight. On the right were the goats that produced overpriced and foul-tasting organic cheese. The earl never ate any cheese other than Stilton. Loyalty to the traditions of England was paramount.

He stepped briskly across the uneven flagstones, the steel caps of his brogues clicking loudly. The main facade of the castle, with its high, mullioned windows, dated from the 1750s, but at the western end it had been built on to the original medieval stronghold. The grey limestone bastion stood up to receive the sunlight, rooks circling above the red and black family flag—in its centre was the coat of arms, a unicorn rampant on a silver background. The first earl had carried out his own researches into the supernatural.

His heir paused at the bottom of the great fifteenth-century wall of the fortress. It had never been taken in battle or siege. On one occasion, the defenders had been forced to eat the horses and then every other living thing inside. Foot soldiers and archers, who complained that their womenfolk had been slaughtered for meat by their commander, were hung from the walls after the siege had been lifted. Because the country needed strong leaders, he had never been prosecuted. That set an example to his descendents.

A mobile phone rang inside the earl's tweed jacket. He answered it and spoke briefly, then walked round the tower, the bottoms of his cavalry twill trousers absorbing dew from the grass not yet reached by the sun. By the great studded door, he stopped for a moment before taking out a set of keys and opening the three locks that had been set into the black-painted wood.

Inside, the air was dry. The original ceilings were no longer there, only the firing slits remaining. They had never been closed up. It was good to have fresh air in the refurbished bastion. The second earl had no doubt found that necessary. He had been involved in a Hell-fire Club at Oxford that had been notorious for unbridled licentiousness and depravity. The university authorities had eventually reprimanded the unruly students, though only commoners were sent down—the scions of noble families were given a metaphorical clip on the ear and left to find new ways to corrupt themselves. When he was older, the second earl set up his own version of a Hell-fire Club in this very fortification. It was rumoured that defrocked ministers and former monks made merry with willing nuns and local wenches carted in for the ceremonies. It had also been said that few of the latter were ever seen again.

The present earl breathed in the castle's air, then turned on his heel after satisfying himself that the grated window at ground level was immoveable. Pulling the door to, he heard the scream of a peacock, one of several he allowed to wander the grounds.

As he walked back along the front terrace, His Lordship caught sight of himself in one of the windows. He stopped and tightened his regimental tie—he had been a captain in the Queen's Own Horse Guards—then smoothed a hand over his well-disciplined and still jet-black hair. Despite his fifty-five years, he was slim and fit. His uneven face was smoothly shaved by the cutthroat razor he stropped every day. It was a matter for regret that he had produced no son and heir. His wife, Priscilla, had died three years ago, of complications following a supposedly routine breast remodelling procedure. She was past child-bearing age, anyway. There was still time for him to marry again and continue the bloodline. If he could find a suitable bride.

The phone rang again. The earl's expression lightened after he answered it. He went back inside through the main entrance.

Soon there would be another rite for him to preside over.

17

Pete Satterthwaite and Andy Jackson stood outside the flat in East London that Sara had bought in the name Angela Oliver-Merilee. Although the main road looked like it ran through a war zone, with the shop windows covered in heavy wire even during opening hours, the side street was tree lined and quiet. The cars parked on both sides were the standard people-carriers and hatchbacks of the urban bourgeoisie.

'It's the upper flat,' Pete said, as they approached number twelve. Across the street, two young Indian boys were playing with water pistols. They stopped to look at the men.

'Smile, Slash,' Pete said, under his breath.

The American obliged, making one of the boys run inside.

'Nice one.'

'Sorry. I'm no good with kids, Boney.' Andy stepped up to the street door and moved his finger to the higher of the two bells, but he didn't press it. With Pete shrouding him from view, he slid two flat steel rods into the keyhole and manipulated them. Andy hadn't needed tuition from Dave in opening locks because he'd learned in the youth gang he'd run with back in New Jersey. There was a click and the door opened.

'We're in,' Andy said, moving forward. He had his right hand on the butt of his silenced Glock.

Pete closed the door quietly behind him. The house had been divided into two flats, with common access. The sound of a television at high volume came from the ground-floor flat—according to the records search that Rog had carried, it was owned by an eighty-two-year-old man. They moved carefully up the narrow, uncarpeted wooden stairs. There was a smell of damp about the place.

At the first-floor door, which had recently been painted green, Andy stopped, his left hand raised. He put his ear to the door, then looked round at Pete, shaking his head. They both knew that an absence of sound didn't mean the place was unoccupied. According to the local council's database, the owner lived alone and paid full council tax, but Pete and Andy knew there was no such person as Angela Oliver-Merilee. So who was using the flat?

Andy stuck his weapon in his belt and took out the steel rods again. Pete raised his Glock in a two-handed grip, pointing it at the door above the American's blonde mass of hair. They were taking a chance. If the occupant was inside and had put on the chain, Andy would have to shoulder-charge the door quickly.

Again, there was a dull click. Andy put the rods away and opened the door enough for him to slide his fingers round the edge, then moved them upwards.

'No chain,' he mouthed to Pete. Then he stood up, took his Glock from his belt and nodded. The door opened as he pushed it. Andy stepped in quickly, his weapon raised. He moved his arms up and down, covering the angles that a potential assailant could come from. When Pete entered the flat, Andy passed him and went through the living area to the rear. There were two open doors, one to a bathroom and the other to a bedroom.

'Nobody at home,' the American reported, lowering his pistol.

'What a relief,' Pete said. He put his weapon in his jacket pocket and looked around the place. It had been furnished sparely, but with good taste. A burgundy-coloured leather sofa and armchair were facing a medium-size high-definition TV, with a modern standard lamp between them. The walls had been papered in white and there were a couple of framed Cézanne posters. At the back, a breakfast bar separated the living area from a well-equipped kitchen. The windows, front and rear, were covered by Venetian blinds that let in only a small amount of light. In the bedroom, there was an antique wardrobe and a double bed, its pale blue cover neatly in place.

Pete opened the wardrobe. He found three pairs of black jeans, one of which he held against his hip. The flat's occupant was shorter than he was, so around five foot nine, and solidly built—the shirts were size large. There were bundled pairs of socks on the floor of the wardrobe, as well as folded boxer shorts.

'Looks like a *bloke* lives here,' Pete said.

Andy went into the bathroom. It smelled of pine. He touched the wash basin. It was wet, as was the bath behind the shower curtain.

'Someone was in here earlier today, Boney,' he called. He ran his eye over a toothbrush and tube of toothpaste, a razor and can of foam and a plastic comb. There were no hairs on the latter, nor were there any in the bath. The metal bin was empty, suggesting that the occupant was very fastidious—or very careful. Andy looked at himself in the round mirror, wondering whose face had been in it a few hours before.

Pete was in the kitchen, opening drawers. They were filled with cutlery and other utensils. The pedal bin was empty and there were no plates in the sink or on the drying-stand.

'Someone's taking a lot of care not to leave traces,' he said.

Andy checked the cupboards. There was very little food in the place, only a few tins of tuna and mackerel. The fridge contained a tub of butter and a jar of capers, and the freezer seemed to be filled with ice-cube trays.

'Hang on,' he said, dropping to his knees. He took out the trays and stacked them on the floor. 'What have we here?' He removed a clear freezer bag. Inside it was a padded envelope, with no writing on it. He felt the weight. 'There's something heavy in here,' he said. The envelope wasn't sealed. He slid his hand in and pulled out a switchblade knife.

Pete put down his pistol and took the knife from Andy. He opened the blade and ran his latex-covered finger along it. 'Jeez, this baby is sharp enough to skin a cat. It's clean, though, and it's been oiled.'

Pete looked round. 'Look at this lot,' he said, holding out his hand.

'Nine-millimetre rounds,' Andy said. 'Oh shit. Where's the gun?'

They searched the flat again, but found nothing. Another striking feature was the complete lack of anything personal—documents, bills, books, music, photographs.

'Whoever hangs out here is armed,' Pete said, when they'd finished.

'And it looks like he or she doesn't have any interests except weapons.'

'I'm pretty sure that knife is a spare,' Andy said. 'The other one will be in our friend's pocket. Say, isn't it around here that those gang murders have been happening?'

The bald man stared at him and nodded. 'What are you getting at?'

'I don't know….' Andy moved lightly over the bare floorboards. 'Shall we ask the old guy downstairs about his neighbour?'

'And leave a witness that we were here? I don't think so, Slash. Judging by the racket coming through the floor, he's in a world of his own anyway.'

'What are we going to do, then? Wait for Armed and Dangerous to come back?'

Pete looked at his watch. 'Let's give it an hour,' he said, squatting on the floor behind the sofa, his back against the wall.

Andy dropped down behind the breakfast bar. 'Hey, Boney,' he said, after a few minutes.

'What is it, Slash?'

'This could be the piece of shit who killed Dave.'

'Yeah, but we have to be sure of that before it's payback time.'

Andy gave a grim laugh. 'I think I can get a confession.'

'I believe you. But Matt will have to be in on that.'

After about twenty minutes, the sound of the street door closing was just audible above the television. There were footsteps on the stairs.

Pete stood up slowly, gripping his pistol in both hands. Andy was also covering the door.

They heard the footsteps stop on the landing outside. There was a pause, then came an almost inaudible sniff. A key was slotted into the lock and the door was opened quickly. Something flew into the flat, landing with a thud on the floor and rolling towards the sofa. Before Pete or Andy could react, the door was slammed shut.

There was a bright flash as the grenade went off.

I checked the ghost site about half an hour later and opened the new folder that had arrived from my mother and Caroline. They were being very businesslike about the deadline—then I realised that Caroline must have written the text, with Fran dictating parts. They used to call my ex-wife 'Ice-for-Blood' at the first bank she worked for. I was so naive that I didn't get why they thought of her in that way, but later I went in that direction myself: Caroline referred to me as 'glacier-heart' during the divorce. I'd been proud of that for about one minute, and then Lucy walked in.

There was no instant good news, but they had come up with plenty of interesting angles. 'The river shrinks bears' was hard to fathom, but they wondered if there was a diminutive at play—small bears are cubs, though they didn't know what to make of that. Neither did I. Was the next victim a cub reporter? A debut novelist? As for 'The ice crows for a wife', Fran and Caroline thought that was a series of metaphors. 'For a wife' was the easy one. Who would call for a wife? A man—so that was confirmation that the victim was male. Maybe the person who set the clue really had made this one more straightforward. But what about 'the ice crows'? My mother and ex-wife had been playing with partial anagrams—they came up with 'swore' (could that be a reference to Josh Hinkley, the most foul-mouthed person I knew? He was also a crime writer, but it seemed very tenuous); 'worse'; 'screw' (that was probably Caroline's); 'score', 'wise' (Did I know anyone of that name? No. Anyone who was wise? Not many.); and 'woes'. They thought that was a dead end, and I agreed.

Moving on to 'The lean man's imperial heiress', Fran and Caroline pointed out the male reference. Including the mention in the body of the e-mail text and in the sender's name (thethirdisaman), that made four times that masculinity had been stressed. Could it be deliberate overkill? Maybe the target was actually a woman, a married one, as suggested by the use of 'wife' in the previous line. Very helpful. As for 'lean', did I know anyone who was unusually skinny? Not really. Apart from junkies, most people were overweight these days, myself included, thanks to the additional muscles I'd acquired. My mother and ex-wife picked up on the colonial aspect of 'imperial'—did I know anyone from a former colony? A few, and there were millions more I'd never heard of. Again, not much help. As for 'heiress', that suggested 'daughter'—they had immediately thought of Lucy, though they accepted she was safe where they were. But was the intended victim female? The White Devil had told plenty of lies during his persecution of me—and, more to the point, he'd covered up or failed to tell me about even more things. Sara might be following his example.

In the fourth line, 'Is the thirsty draw of nothing', Fran and Caroline spotted the opposition with the first line—'thirsty', in the sense of 'dry', as against the liquid of 'river'. But 'draw of nothing' had them stumped. What kind of draw was meant? One where stalemate ensues, or an attraction? Perhaps there was even a hint of artistic technique—but how could you draw nothing? As for the last word, it could simply mean the letter *O*;

or it could be hinting at a person, as in 'no thing'; or it could just be there to show that the answer of the clue was without substance—i.e. that we were wasting our time trying to find it. Three seriously unhelpful alternatives. I thanked Fran and Caroline, sent my love to Lucy and logged off.

Back at the dining table, I started rearranging the words of the message. There was a disturbing number of permutations, but even more worrying was the fact that I wasn't getting anywhere. It was past three—only nine hours to go. Should I call Karen? I dismissed the thought, but only after long consideration. I asked Rog what he had come up with and was handed a sheaf of printout, none of which left me any the wiser. Could the clue be an acrostic? I wrote down all the first letters—they made no sense in the order they were in. I changed the order, trying to make a name. I found 'Rich'—which applied to several crime writers and a hell of a lot of other people; 'Martin'—I knew several of those, both first names and surnames. Should I tell them all to go into hiding? I needed another name; 'Watt'—I didn't know anyone by that name, nor any Martin Watts. I was clutching at straws and I knew it.

I got up and went to make coffee. As I waited for the kettle to boil, I thought about the first line, 'The river shrinks bears'. What was that supposed to mean? I thought back to the ground rules of cryptic crosswords. Repunctuate. If I put a comma after 'shrinks', the sense, such as it was, became very different. Rather than the ridiculous vision of large furry animals being reduced in size by the river, I now had the river doing two things—becoming smaller itself and 'bearing' something—carrying? I felt the metaphorical ice in my brain crack. A shrunken river meant a smaller one. So a stream, a burn, a rivulet? I was on the brink of a breakthrough, I was sure of it.

Then my phone beeped twice. I'd been sent a text. Apart from Rog, only Pete and Andy had my new number. What had they discovered in the flat? I hit the buttons and read the message.

Josh Hinkley walked into the pub in Soho and went straight to the bar. He didn't care if the person he was meeting was there already. He urgently needed a drink. He ordered a double ten-year-old Macallan and emptied it in one. That immediately put a different complexion on the day.

He'd spent most of it on the phone to members of the Crime Writers' Society, or answering their e-mails. It seemed that Matt Wells had a lot of friends, and they objected to his being pilloried in the press and on the Internet. Some had even accused Josh of shamelessly seeking publicity. Well, that was true enough, not that he could admit it. So he'd given them a load of bollocks about how crime writers had a duty to assist the police. Some of his fellow novelists had refused to accept that Matt had chickened out by going underground. Eventually, Josh had told one of them where he could stick his telephone and put his own in one of the kitchen drawers. That didn't stop it ringing, so he left.

It was only when he was approaching the Goat and Gooseberry that he remembered why he was going there. He'd got a call from another crime writer before the hue and cry had started, asking if they could meet. A year ago, Josh Hinkley wouldn't have bothered to cross the street to talk to Alistair Bing, but now he wanted to pick the diminutive Yorkshireman's brains. Bing had started off about ten years back with a desperately tedious series about a pair of rural coppers, set in the Moors. The fact that one of them was a black man and the other a half-Chinese woman didn't help on the realism front. For some reason, his publishers had continued with the series for six books before finally realising that sales so low couldn't be justified, even with a minimal advance. Everyone—Josh included—had assumed that was the last they'd hear of Alistair Bing, but he turned out to be a persistent bugger. He managed to reinvent himself as a writer, coming out with a hard-as-nails ex-FBI protagonist called Jim Cooler, who basically went around the world beating the shit out of bad people and giving one to every luscious female he encountered. The first book had rocketed to the top of the charts in every significant country, turning Bing into a publishing sensation and a very wealthy man. Now Hollywood producers were his best friends.

'Hello, Josh.'

Hinkley turned and took in the short, bespectacled multi-millionaire. He still dressed like a 1950s schoolmaster, but now the tweed jacket was bespoke and the glasses the best that Milan could provide.

'Alistair, how the hell are you? I'm just getting another. What would you like?'

'It's all right,' Bing said, his voice still the drone of the permanently unhappy Northerner. 'I've got one over at that table.' He moved his arm limply.

'Let's go, then.' Josh Hinkley led him back to his own table. A half-pint glass was sitting there, three-quarters full. 'Sure you don't want a shot to go with that?'

'Oh no, I never drink spirits.' Alistair Bing carefully folded up the newspaper he'd been reading.

'So, what brings you to London?'

'Oh, I live here now. Off Harley Street, actually.'

'Really?' Josh Hinkley had assumed Bing was tied to the north by chains of Sheffield steel. 'We're practically neighbours.'

'Yes, I walked past your place the other day. I imagine it's nicer inside than it looks from the outside.'

Hinkley was unimpressed, both by the slur on his home and the idea of Alistair Bing checking up on him, but he managed not to let that show. 'I like to be close to the people I write about,' he said, aware that he sounded like a bleeding-heart liberal. The reality was, he hated the sleaze-balls who hung around the pubs and strip joints. His double flat was on the top of a building otherwise used as offices; it was an air-conditioned oasis where he could hide away and write.

'So,' he said, forcing himself to be sociable, 'you're a Londoner now.'

'Oh no, never that,' Bing said mildly. 'But I'm on national radio and TV so much that I needed a base down here. I ended up buying the whole house.' He gave a slack smile. 'It's an investment, you know.'

'Right,' Hinkley said. Now he *was* impressed. He was still paying off a mortgage.

Bing took a small sip of beer. 'The first Jim Cooler movie's in pre-production, so I'm flying to L.A. every month.'

Josh Hinkley bit the bullet and asked how that was going, trying to damp down his jealousy. One of his Lenny 'The Gore' Gray novels had been made into a TV series, but it had been miscast and directed by a smart-arse who ballsed up the story in a big way. He was forced to listen to Bing talking about Hollywood stars like they were his best mates. But there was something different about his fellow author. When Josh had first met him, at a bookshop event somewhere in the Midlands, he'd been shy and nervous. Now he acted like he was a master of the universe and nothing seemed to faze him. He appeared on late-night review programmes and took on so-called intellectuals, he wrote columns for the broadsheets that combined analysis of modern life with unexpected wit, and he even turned up on kids' TV as the token person with a brain who didn't mind being asked brainless questions. There must have been something in the water up north. It certainly wasn't in the beer—Bing still hadn't finished his half-pint.

Eventually Josh Hinkley couldn't take any more name-dropping, even though Bing had offered to introduce him to several of the movie executives and television producers he knew. 'This Matt Wells thing, Alistair,' he asked. 'Where do you stand on that?'

'I'm with you, Josh,' Bing said, smiling ingratiatingly. 'I think the way he's behaving is absolutely outrageous. It was bad enough the first time round, with that White Devil killer. He should be co-operating with the police. It isn't as if he has to go out of his way to do that—he's sleeping with a senior detective.'

'So you agree that he should be booted out of the Crime Writers' Society?'

Alistair Bing nodded. 'Certainly. I've sent the directors an e-mail supporting you.'

'Thanks.' Hinkley was pleased, but he was also slightly suspicious. He couldn't see what was in it for Bing. 'Of course, you'll make some enemies.'

The other author shrugged. 'That's life. Sometimes

you have to make difficult decisions.' He leaned over the table. 'I can assure you, that's nowhere near the hardest one I've taken.'

Hinkley wondered what could have been so difficult for Bing. Shall I accept two million pounds for my next four books or not? Shall I sell my character to Hollywood so I can set myself up for life, or stay unknown? Shall I buy a whole house in Harley Street, or just half? There was something about the way the Yorkshireman was looking at him that hinted at hidden depths. The bastard was probably a grand master at chess as well. But there was one area where Josh was sure Alistair Bing would never succeed.

'How's your love life?' he said, wondering if he was ever going to get another drink.

Spots of colour appeared on Bing's cheeks. 'Well, you know, I'm not much of a ladies' man.' He looked at his beer.

'Oh, come on,' Hinkley said, determined to rub his nose in it. 'There must have been dozens of willing young nubiles in Hollywood.'

Alistair Bing nodded, but his eyes stayed down.

'Or do you prefer men?'

That made Bing look up. 'Definitely not!' he exclaimed, spittle flying from his lips.

Hinkley sat back. 'Calm down. I don't care one way or another.'

'I do,' Alistair Bing said firmly. 'I suppose I'd better get you another drink.' He picked up the empty glass and went to the bar.

Josh Hinkley watched the diminutive figure thread his way between the raucous drinkers. He was no nearer to understanding what had turned a minor writer of police procedurals into a massive best-seller. Maybe it was the fact that his books were bland and unchallenging. He almost convinced himself that was the case. As Alistair Bing came back, his forehead lined as he concentrated on not spilling the pint, Hinkley realised that he hated the Yorkshireman's guts.

18

I read the text message from Andy aloud. '"At London Hospital. Bastard threw grenade. Pick us up." What the fuck?'

'It could be a trap,' Rog said.

'He used the right confirmation code.'

He shrugged. 'Maybe Sara or her sidekicks got it out of him.'

I stared at him. 'Why would they send me to the London Hospital? It's hardly the ideal place to stage an ambush.'

'She could be trying to distract you from solving that clue.'

I nodded. 'Which means that you have to keep working on it. Keep in contact with my mother and Caroline via the ghost site.'

'All right,' he said reluctantly. 'But I'd rather come with you.'

'Please, Dodger,' I said, as I checked my Glock and slipped it inside my jacket. 'We can't all be in the same public place.'

'What if the cops are there?' he asked. 'If a grenade went off, someone will have reported it.'

'I'll have to take that chance.'

I heard him say 'Good luck' as I left. I hailed a passing

taxi and told him the destination. The traffic was heavy and
it was nearly an hour before we reached the hospital in
Whitechapel. I worked on the clue during the journey, but
I had little inspiration. 'The river shrinks'—a stream, a
brook, a runnel? 'Bears'—carries, produces, suffers? 'The
ice crows' Ice—cold, hard, opaque? Crows—calls out,
verb, or black carrion birds? Cries or ravens? What were
crows known for? Crow's nests? As the crow flies? And
who was 'the lean man', never mind his 'imperial heiress'?
As for 'the thirsty draw of nothing', the last word said it
all. I only hoped Rog, Fran or Caroline had more ideas.

As we went down Whitechapel Road, I leaned forward
and asked the driver if he would do a U-turn and then wait
for me as near the hospital as possible. The twenty-pound
note I showed him provoked a broad grin. I got out and
crossed the road. The hospital was a large Victorian building with modern additions. There was no sign of any police
personnel, but if Karen or her team were around, I probably
wouldn't see them. There was nothing for it. I walked into
the Accident and Emergency unit and headed for reception.

A pretty nurse asked if she could help.

'I have friends,' I said, in a heavy accent that I hoped
sounded Eastern European. 'They hurt.'

She nodded and smiled, obviously used to dealing with
people whose English was limited. 'What are their
names?'

I looked blank.

'Their names,' the nurse repeated. 'What are they
called?'

I looked around helplessly, checking if there were any
police in the vicinity.

'Ah, na-ames,' I said. 'Yes. Nishani and Pepa.'

She tapped on her keyboard. 'Oh, I remember. Gentlemen who'd been in a fire?'

That must have been how the guys had explained their injuries.

'They okay?' I asked.

'I think they're being treated now,' she replied. 'If you take a seat, I'll see if I can find out.'

I moved away, but not far. I located the CCTV camera nearest reception and turned my back to it casually.

A few minutes later the nurse called me over. 'Your friends have just been discharged,' she said.

I saw two familiar figures. Pete had a bandage round his forehead. Andy seemed unhurt, but as they came closer I realised they both had bloodshot eyes.

'What happened?' I said, as soon as we were out of earshot.

'Whoever the motherfucker was,' Andy said, 'he or she realised we were inside and threw in a grenade. Some kind of special-edition number—it went off with a loud enough bang, but its main effect was to fill the room with tear gas. By the time we got out, the piece of shit was long gone.'

'You all right, Pete?' I asked, as I led them to the taxi.

'Yeah. You should see the sofa.'

'And you didn't see anything of who threw it?'

They both shook their heads.

I told the cabbie to take us to Camden Town. 'What about the flat?'

'Somebody was living there,' Andy said, 'but we couldn't be sure if it was a man or a woman. The boxers made it seem like a man, but if it's a woman, she's bigger than Sara.' He took something out of his pocket. 'Nine-mil Parabellum shells—there were twenty-five like this one.

There was also a seriously sharp switchblade. They were hidden in the deep-freeze.'

'How do you think you were spotted?'

Pete scratched his head beneath the bandage. 'I think he or she smelled the oil from Slash's lock tools.'

I sat back and thought about what they'd found in the flat. The knife could have been used in the Sandra Devonish murder, and it also could have been used to cut the hairs from Mary Malone. But the pistol ammunition was another story. Could it be that the flat that Sara bought had nothing to do with whoever had killed the two authors and was sending me messages? Maybe she'd rented it out without changing the name of the council tax payer. Or maybe it was part of a carefully laid plan to mess with my brain before she struck decisively.

'Sorry I sent you over there,' I said.

'We went willingly,' Pete said, with a wry smile. 'We almost caught the bastard.'

'You almost caught *a* bastard,' I said. I told them about the second message.

'You and Rog will work it out,' Andy said, with a lot more confidence than I was feeling.

'What about the other properties that Sara owns?' Pete asked.

'Haven't you had enough for one day? Anyway, now we've got to try and save someone's life.'

I looked at my watch. It was nearly five. There were seven hours until the deadline.

Faik Jabar was chained to a chair, the television in front of him showing children's programmes at high volume. He knew exactly where he was, but that was no help. He tried to recall anything else that might. After the man had found him in Hackney, he had taken off his helmet and put his pistol in his pocket. They'd walked westwards and then north through back streets. Faik felt the relief grow as they got closer to his parents' house. Maybe the man was going to take him there. He'd asked if he worked for the King, but the man didn't answer. Faik's thighs were burning and he was flagging. They had reached Matthias Road, only a few minutes from Green Lanes, when the bearded man gripped Faik's arm tightly.

'Don't struggle or make any noise,' the man hissed. 'You know the Shadows control this street.'

The truth was that Faik was too exhausted to offer resistance. He'd allowed himself to be helped up the stairs to the top-floor flat and remembered being guided to a chair, where he passed out. When he woke up, he found himself in chains.

'What's going on?' he asked. 'Help!' Then he realised that the TV wasn't on for his benefit. He would have to shout very loudly to be heard above the sounds of pop music and cheering children.

Faik tried to make sense of what was going on. The bearded man had said he had so much to show him, but he didn't even seem to be there. Why had he chained Faik up? The pain in his full bladder was making it hard for the Kurd to concentrate, but he forced himself to admit that he had gone willingly with the man. He'd found himself drawn to him. That disturbed Faik. He wasn't gay. What was it about the bearded man? Faik remembered what he'd seen beneath the false beard in the Shadow basement after Aro Izady was shot. The man was a monster, literally—he had killed a fellow Kurd, but still Faik felt attracted to him. What was going on?

Eventually the pressure in his bladder was too much for him and he let go. For a short time, the warmth was comforting—it reminded him of when he was a little boy. But soon the urine cooled and he felt shame. What would his captor think when he saw the evidence of Faik's unmanliness?

The children's programmes were replaced by one of the stupid game shows that were so popular. Faik tried to reassure himself with the thought that his people, the King's family, would be looking for him by now. The doctor would have told them. But maybe the doctor was no longer alive. The Shadows might not have believed him, they might have killed him. So maybe no one was looking for him. The thought cast Faik into a pit of darkness and he scarcely heard the door when it opened.

'Asleep, my friend?' came the familiar voice.

Before Faik could answer, a man was thrown between him and the television. He was balding and his face was pocked by smallpox scars. Blinking hard, Faik saw that he was wearing a gold Rolex and a coat that must have cost many pounds.

'Who is he?' he asked, turning his head.

The bearded man turned his prisoner's head forcibly. 'Watch and learn,' he said to Faik. 'Afterwards I might even unchain you.' He sniffed the air. 'Oh, I'm sorry, my friend. I should have left you a bottle.' He gave a soft laugh. 'Never mind. You aren't the only one who'll have pissed his pants by the end of the evening.'

The man on the floor whimpered and tried to get to his feet. Izady's killer was round in a flash to whip the legs from beneath him. Then he kneeled on his captive's back, a knife at the man's throat.

'If you try that again, I'll cut open your belly and tie you up with your own guts.' He leaned closer. 'Do you hear me?'

The man on the floor nodded his head rapidly.

'Who is he?' Faik asked, licking his dry lips.

The bearded man looked round at him. 'I'm sorry, my friend. I would give you something to drink, but I don't think you'd keep it down.'

There was a high-pitched sound from the man with the Rolex.

'This piece of excrement works for the Albanian mafia. He's Safet Shkrelli's chief accountant.'

Faik's eyes opened wide.

'I see you know the name.'

Faik nodded.

'The Albanians have a lot in common with the Kurds and the Turks,' the bearded man said.

Faik nodded. 'They…they keep as much business as they can in the family.'

'Very good, my friend. This fucker of children is Safet Shkrelli's first cousin.'

A feeling of deep foreboding overwhelmed Faik. 'What are you going to do to him?' he asked.

'What are *we* going to do to him?' the bearded man corrected. 'Don't worry, we aren't going to kill him.'

Faik breathed out. 'Good.'

The bearded man smiled. 'We're just going to hurt him till he tells us everything he knows about the Albanian mafia's business in London.'

'You are insane!' the man on the floor said.

'And then we're going to give him back to Safet Shkrelli, for a price.' The man with the beard looked back at the Albanian. 'Me? Insane?' He plunged the combat knife into the man's thigh, ramming a handkerchief into his mouth before the scream could be heard. 'Oh, no, I'm not insane.' He looked round at Faik. 'I'm the sanest person you'll ever meet.' He laughed. 'I just enjoy hurting people.'

Then the worst experience of Faik's short but horror-filled life began.

When we got back at Rog's cousin's flat, I immediately checked for messages. There were two files from my mother and Caroline. I asked Rog if he'd got anywhere.

'Your mother and Caroline think that the first two lines refer to the name Brooks.'

I looked at the screen. As they'd thought, 'The river shrinks' was a diminutive. One of the words for a small river was 'brook'—and an archaic synonym for 'bears', in the sense of allowing something, was 'brooks'. The second line clinched it. 'Crows' were 'rooks' and ice, or cold, made people say (or 'crow') 'brr', although 'br' with one 'r' would produce the same sound. They hadn't got anywhere with 'for a wife', and were assuming it meant the Brooks person was male, as the message said.

'Brooks,' I said aloud, hoping that would give the name familiarity, but it didn't. 'I don't know anyone called Brooks.'

'Me neither. I'm assuming it's a surname. I ran a search on the Internet and came up with a list.' He handed me several pages of printout. 'No crime writers, though.'

'No, I didn't think so.' I ran my eye down the list. There was an admiral, a senior civil servant in the Home Office, a professor of palaeontology and another of veterinary medicine, an actress and a load of less illustrious people. But why would Sara choose any of them?

'Brooks,' I said again. 'I suppose it could be a first name. American, maybe?'

Rog nodded. 'I thought that too. Here's a list of them.'

This printout was shorter. There were a couple of academics, a dancer, a businessman in Idaho, a fireman, and so on. Again, not very likely targets for Sara, and they were all a long way from London.

'Shit,' I said. 'We need more.' I looked at the material from Fran and Caroline. They said they were working on the second couplet, but that they hadn't come up with anything yet. My mother was thinking about the 'imperial heiress'—heiress and wife were both female, and that had made her wonder about the target's gender again.

I went over to the window. It was dark already, and there would soon be only five hours to go. We had one name—surely we weren't going to fail because we couldn't work out the other? I looked at the second sentence again. 'The lean man's imperial heiress/Is the thirsty draw of nothing.' I told myself to ignore the second part—if the pattern was repeated, it would be an alternative clue to the first part. 'The lean man's'—it was harder to take these words separately because of the apostrophe-s. The lean man's what? Who was the lean man?

I sat down and rubbed my eyes, then looked over at the bookcase. On the top shelf was a movie guide I'd always meant to buy. I was about to get up and have a look at it when I had a flash of insight. The words could be taken separately, and 'lean' didn't need a synonym or any other substitute word. It was a name in its own right, that of Britain's most revered film director, David Lean—the definite article might have been used to put us off. But who was David Lean's 'imperial heiress'?

'Yes!' I yelled, punching the air.

'What?' Rog said, pushing his chair back and coming over. Andy and Pete were watching with interest.

'We've been made fools of,' I said, 'but not any more.' I underlined the second, third, fourth and fifth letters of 'heiress'.

'Eire?' Rog said. 'As in Ireland.'

'Correct. And what was the David Lean movie made in Ireland?'

'I know that,' Andy said. 'It had Robert Mitchum in it, and that woman who always gets her jugs out.'

'Kate Winslet?' Pete asked.

'Sarah Miles, you moron,' I said. 'And the movie's name is?'

'Ryan's Daughter,' Andy said, raising his arm in triumph.

Rog looked at me. 'So what have we got? Ryan Brooks?'

I shook my head. 'We're not finished yet. What about 'imperial'?'

'Something to do with the British Empire?' Rog asked.

'There's stuff about the I.R.A. in *Ryan's Daughter,'* Pete said. 'They were fighting against the empire, weren't they?'

He was right, but I couldn't see where that got us. 'What about other empires?'

'The Roman,' Slash said.

'That is the biggie, isn't it?' I said, nodding. 'Wait a minute. Emperors.' My mind was working on some dimension that I couldn't control. The list of emperors that I'd learned in history at school flashed before me—Augustus, Tiberius, Nero... Then it hit me like a lightning bolt and I groaned. 'Of course. It's Hadrian.'

Rog looked at me. 'How do you work that out?'

'Rian,' I said, pronouncing the last four letters of the word like "ryan".

'Bugger!' Rog said, glancing at Pete. 'Sorry, Boney.'

I had moved on to the last line. Hadrian. Obviously there weren't many people called that these days. 'Thirsty,' I said. 'Dry. The third, fourth and fifth letters of Hadrian are *d, r* and *i*—sounds like "dry".'

'So?' Rog said.

'What draws people?' I asked, myself as much as the others.

'A painter,' Andy said. 'A brush.'

I shook my head. 'Another sense of "draw". As in "attract".'

'A poster,' said Pete.

'An advert.' Rog and I spoke simultaneously.

'Also known as an ad,' I said. Now I saw it all. 'And "nothing" in a well-known foreign language is?'

'Nada,' said Andy.

'Oh, Christ,' Rog said, his eyes wide. 'The French for "nothing" is "rien". Ad-rien. Is that Adrienne, female, or Adrian, male?'

'Good question,' I said. 'Run a search on both Adrian and Adrienne Brooks.'

He went over to his computer.

I was frantically trying to think if I knew anyone called Adrian Brooks. It seemed familiar, but I couldn't put my finger on it. Adrienne Brooks? That seemed less likely, for some reason.

'I've got another professor,' Rog shouted, 'with the female name. But she's in Alaska.'

I shook my head. We were casting the net too wide. The first two victims had been crime writers. That was where the answer lay. I went over to my laptop and logged on, then called up the Crime Writers' Society website. On the home page, I clicked Directory. I scrolled down the list of real names, their pseudonyms alongside. And there it was.

'Adrian Brooks,' I yelled. 'It's the real name of Alistair Bing!'

That didn't mean much to the others, but it did to me. I went back to the site's home page and clicked on Members' Details, then clicked on the letter *B* and found a phone number and an address in central London.

I picked up the phone, called the number and waited for the next victim to pick up.

19

The Soul Collector stood in the outhouse next to her cottage at the edge of Oldbury village in southern Berkshire. Although it was only twenty miles from Heathrow Airport, she felt like she was in a safe and isolated place. She looked at the earth floor. She had raked and then brushed it, so there was no obvious sign that it had been disturbed recently. It had been good exercise, digging the metre-deep hole for the three coffins. Now her hostages lay bound and gagged in their last homes. When the effect of the gas she had used to knock them out wore off, they would wake up in the darkness and they would be terrified. The Soul Collector smiled.

Her plan had gone perfectly. First she had picked up Geronimo's wife, Alison. That had been very easy. A knock at the door, having checked there was no one in the vicinity, a blast of the same gas she had used when she had been working with her brother, and into the van. Then she had driven to the school a few miles away. From her surveillance she knew that Rommel's son, Josh, walked the short distance home with the Slovenian au pair Maria. She picked him and the girl up, saying that she was a friend and the mother had been taken to hospital. She sprayed them both on the country road and dumped the au pair in a ditch. Given the disguise she was wearing and the van's false plates, she'd never be traced. Then she'd driven as fast as she could to Wolfe's house in Warwickshire. There was no time for subtlety now—Rommel's wife could be in touch any moment. She knocked out Wolfe's wife with a truncheon blow when she answered the door, cracked the son's head when he came out of the kitchen and gassed Amanda Mary. Then she had disappeared into the twilight.

Back in the cottage, having closed the three padlocks on the outhouse, the Soul Collector assumed the lotus position. As ever, she thought of her brother. He had called himself the White Devil, but to her he would always be Leslie, the name he'd been given by his adoptive mother. Although she'd since discovered that their birth mother had dubbed him Oliver in the days before she handed them over, that name seemed as unreal as Angela, the one she'd been given. Leslie had made her life. Before he had accosted her outside the *Daily Independent* offices, she had been a typical soulless journalist, with her eyes only on the next story. She didn't even have a steady boyfriend, just a string of drunken one-night stands that hadn't even provided good sex. Leslie had given her that. She'd been able to abandon herself to him precisely because he was her brother—breaking the taboo of incest had been incredibly exhilarating. When he'd told her they were twins, she hadn't believed him. There was little facial resemblance between them, though once they were in contact she was able to commune with him in the strange way many twins experience. That had made working with him in his great revenge plot so much easier.

Leslie had made only one mistake. His desire for his

name to go down in history had driven him to involve the writer Matt Wells. The worm who thought he had turned, the useless fuck who was now crying for his friend Dave. Although he hadn't brought about her brother's death—the SAS men who had executed Leslie would soon be paying for that—Matt's resistance had meant that not all the people her brother had planned to kill became victims. She would harvest their souls soon. Her plan had been two years in the making and Leslie would have applauded its subtlety.

Vengeance is mine, the woman thought. Was there anything purer and more life-enhancing than revenge? The Jacobean tragedians knew its worth, despite the fact that ultimately they had to kill their revengers to end their works in ways acceptable to the establishment of the time. John Webster, in particular, had more than passing sympathy for his tragic characters, not least the incestuous siblings Vittoria and Flaminio in *The White Devil.* Although the revengers were punished, their lives and deeds were portrayed as tragic, and therefore noble, while the supposedly virtuous characters were no less corrupt and hypocritical, but much less interesting.

Her brother had shown her that revenge was meaningless without killing. The deceived wives who put laxatives in their husbands' coffee or poured sugar into the petrol tanks of their expensive cars weren't serious revenge-takers. To earn the title of revenger, it was necessary that the people who had injured you died, preferably in as much agony as possible. When Leslie had first given her the opportunity to kill, she had flinched, but only for a few seconds. After that, she'd never had any problem.

The Soul Collector opened her eyes. It was time to

make contact with Wolfe and his men. They were her first targets, even though Matt and his friends were trying to trace her. No doubt the computer expert Roger van Zandt had been responsible for transferring the money out of her accounts. She didn't care about that. She had her own hacker who would respond, but the money didn't matter. All she cared about was taking her revenge, slowly and with exquisite pain. She would deal with the fool Matt and his friends when she was ready.

She laughed. So far Matt had reacted exactly as she had expected. He had gone into hiding, and sent his mother, ex-wife and daughter to a secret location. By doing that, he thought he was minimising the risk to them. He couldn't have been more wrong.

There was no answer from Alistair Bing's land line, but I got through on his mobile.

'Hey,' I said, 'it's Matt Wells.' I'd met Bing at a couple of crime-writing festivals, before he became a best-seller. He'd struck me as a seriously dull person. He wasn't one of those authors who allowed themselves to be addressed both by their real name and their pseudonym, as I did. He seemed to prefer the latter. Maybe he got a kick out of hiding behind an invented identity.

There was a pause. 'Hello, Matt. I'm sorry about your friend.'

'Thanks. Listen, this might sound strange, but you're in a lot of danger.'

'Am I?' Suddenly, there was tension in his voice.

'I think the person who killed Mary Malone and Sandra Devonish is planning to murder you.'

'What? Oh my God!'

'Calm down and listen carefully. It's essential you don't give away to the killer that you know. The deadline is midnight.'

'Deadline?' he asked, his apprehension replaced by curiosity. 'What do you mean? I assumed that stuff in the papers about you being in touch with the murderer was speculation.'

'I'm afraid not.'

'Can you help me, then?'

'Cool it, Alistair. Where are you?'

'In Harley Street, near my house.'

'All right, I'm sending a couple of my friends round to look after you. Do what they say and you'll be all right.'

'Okay.' There was another pause. 'Hold on, Matt. Maybe the killer's watching me. If your friends show up, he might get even more pissed off.'

He wasn't stupid. It was possible that Sara or some sidekick had him under surveillance. 'What do you propose, Alistair?'

'Let me think,' he said, sounding strangely confident. He was probably having an adrenaline overdose. Being targeted by a serial killer was what every crime writer secretly wanted. I'd felt more alive than ever before when the White Devil was toying with me. 'I'll go home, stay in for a couple of hours, then casually walk out and disappear into the West End. I'll go and stay—'

'Don't tell me!' I yelled. 'Don't tell anyone.' It struck me that I had no idea whether Alistair Bing was married, or what his sexual orientation was. Josh Hinkley would no doubt have told me if he was either gay or a serial shagger. 'Does anyone else live with you?'

'Only my mother.'

So the author of the ultra-hard Jim Cooler books, who must have been in his early forties like I was, lived with his mum. His publishers didn't put that in their press releases. 'Is she mobile?'

'What do you mean?' Bing sounded like I'd insulted his family honour. 'She can walk. She's only seventy.'

'Calm down, Alistair. It's important that she doesn't panic.'

He laughed humourlessly. 'Panic? My mother? She's hard as nails.'

I wondered if he'd based Jim Cooler on her. 'Fair enough. Get her out of London, if you can. Yourself as well. But don't go together. Otherwise you might put her in danger.'

'Mother can look after herself,' Bing said, almost fatalistically. 'I'm not sure if *I'm* up to all that.'

'Of course you are, Alistair. Just keep a clear head. Don't tell anyone about this and drop out of circulation.'

'How long for?'

'A few days, I suppose.'

'Should I call you, then? At this number?'

Shit. I'd forgotten to block the caller ID function. 'No,' I said firmly. 'I'll send a text to your mobile, okay?'

'Okay,' he repeated. 'What about the police? Why aren't you talking to that woman in Scotland Yard? The one you're involved with… What's her name again?'

'Karen Oaten.' I sighed, tired of the accusatory tone accompanying the mention of Karen. 'Look, Alistair, I know Josh has been stirring things up in the Crime Writers' Society. I don't give a fuck about that. I've got my reasons for staying out of touch with the police. If you want to talk to Karen, I can't stop you. But the cops have their ways of doing things and they might antagonise the killer, putting you—and your mother—in even greater danger.'

He thought about that. 'All right, Matt. I'll do as you say. Make sure you text me, though. I can't spend too many days out of the link. People from Hollywood call me all the time, you know.'

Tosser, I thought. 'Look, buy a new mobile phone, but use it as sparingly as possible. Have you read my book, *The Death List?*'

'I can't say I have. Why?'

I wasn't sure I believed him. Every crime writer I knew had read the book out of curiosity. 'In it I describe the sophisticated surveillance the White Devil used. Don't log on to your e-mail provider. Set up a new account with a false name at an Internet café.'

'All right.' He gave a weak laugh. 'You're not having me on, are you, Matt?'

Jesus. 'You know what happened to Mary Malone and Sandra Devonish, Alistair? They had something in common with you.'

'What's that?'

'They were both international best-sellers. It may be that they were killed by a jealous crime novelist.'

He wasn't laughing now. 'You mean it isn't her?' he asked. 'The White Devil's sister?'

So much for him not having read my book. 'I don't know,' I said, then realised how feeble that sounded. 'It could be. Now, get yourself organised.'

'Right. 'Bye, Matt. And thanks.' The connection was broken.

I told the others that Brooks was going to duck out of sight.

'So what now?' Andy asked.

I looked at him and Pete. 'If you're up for it, you two can check the house in Oxford that Sara bought.'

'Oh great,' Pete said, with a marked lack of enthusiasm. 'You want to put us in the firing line again. Besides, that city is full of smart-arse students.'

'Fifty per cent of them being female,' I said, to Andy.

'I rest my case,' Pete said.

'What's your problem, Boney?' I asked. 'What do you think the other fifty per cent are?'

'Toffee-nosed gits,' he said.

Half an hour later, Pete and Andy left. I looked at my watch. It was coming up to eight-thirty. Three and a half hours to go before I sent the correct answer. How would the killer react?

20

Karen Oaten was sitting at the head of the table in the conference room on the eighth floor of New Scotland Yard. She was flanked by John Turner and Amelia Browning. Also present were Detective Superintendent Ron Paskin and Detective Inspector Ozal from Homicide East, Detective Chief Inspector Colin Younger from Homicide Central and DI Luke Neville from Homicide West. Just as Oaten was reaching for the phone, Doctor Redrose came in. He offered no apology or explanation for his late arrival.

'Right, let's get started,' Karen Oaten said. 'I've asked you all to this meeting because we need to share insights and ideas. For your information, the Assistant Commissioner was very keen that we assemble. We have a total of seven murders at different locations across the city and we've got either to establish or rule out a common thread. Yes, DI Neville?'

'Excuse me for asking, but what do gangland killings in the east have to do with my crime-writer murder in Fulham?' He gave Oaten a tight smile. 'Which you've taken over, in any case, so what am I doing here?'

Karen gave him an icy look. 'You can't have it both ways, Inspector. The VCCT may have taken the case, as is our right, but we want to keep Homicide West involved. Are you in or out?'

Neville chewed his lip. 'In.'

'Good,' the chief inspector said. 'Let's see if we can find a connection. Your crime-writer murder, as you call it, came first. Give us your thoughts.'

The pale-faced inspector shrugged. 'Not much to say, really. We've been up and down the street, looking for witnesses. No one apart from the teenager saw anything. It was a filthy night, so they were all keeping warm with their curtains closed. We've checked the CCTV recordings at Fulham Broadway station and the traffic cameras there. Your man's also had a look. We didn't spot any familiar faces, or anyone who looked suspicious. If there hadn't been the murder of the second crime novelist, I'd have put the Mary Malone killing down to Satanists. The pentacle and the Latin words, the removal of nail-clippings and hairs, and the decapitation of the black cat are all pointers to devil worship, as is the Rolling Stones song.'

'The Satanist angle is bollocks,' John Turner said, glaring at Neville. 'For a start, how many people have devil worshippers killed in London in the last year?' There was silence. 'Correct. A big fat zero. Even more to the point, Satanists usually leave fingerprints all over the place. They also like to empty their bowels and bladders at scenes.'

'Doesn't mean there can't be a careful one,' DI Neville said.

'There were footprints in the garden and in the house, weren't there?' Amelia Browning asked.

Neville nodded. 'Size nines. We checked the sole. It's from a workman's boot that you can buy on any high street.'

'The CSIs managed to lift some prints from the carpet in Wilde's,' DCI Younger put in. 'They reckon it's the same pair as were used in Fulham.'

Oaten nodded. 'Okay, let's move on to the murder of Dave Cummings,' Oaten said. 'Taff, you've got this one.'

The Welshman glanced at the file in front of him. 'We found a witness two streets away from the scene who saw a motorbike being driven fast at around a quarter to eleven, which squares with the time of death. Unfortunately, the witness, who's an elderly lady, couldn't say anything about the bike or the registration number. All she remembers is a figure dressed in black, crouching low.'

'Sounds like a professional hit man,' DCI Younger said.

Turner nodded. 'The main issue with this killing, which certainly bears the marks of a professional, is its links with the White Devil case. Dave Cummings was injured in the legs by the Devil's sister, Sara Robbins. Those wounds were replicated, and the shots to the head mirror those which killed her brother. CSIs have found various traces including mud and wool fibres, but Matt Wells, who found the body, and his friends were in the house not long after the murder. The likelihood is most of the traces came from them.'

Doctor Redrose looked at Karen. 'I take it Matt Wells's friends are also—how shall I put it?—out of circulation?'

Oaten caught his eye and nodded. 'And just to be clear, I have had no contact with Matt Wells since we took him to the Yard after his friend's death, apart from a phone call when I urged him to come in.' She looked around, challenging them all with her eyes, but no one spoke. 'Go on, Taff.'

'It appears Dave Cummings opened the door to his

killer—there's no sign of a break-in. It's impossible to be sure, but the likelihood is that the killer was in some sort of disguise, maybe as a postman.'

DI Neville swallowed a laugh. 'What? He—or rather, she—was wearing a postie's uniform under the leathers?'

'Have you got a better idea?' Turner demanded.

DCI Younger raised a hand. 'It strikes me that there's no evidence to connect the killer of Mary Malone—and Sandra Devonish, for that matter—with the person who shot Dave Cummings. The modus operandi is different, there was none of the devil-worship paraphernalia, no music playing and no message, in Latin or any other language.' He ran a hand over his grey hair. 'Just a thought.'

'Thanks, Colin,' Karen Oaten said. 'You're quite right. Despite the absence of evidence, I'm sure that Sara Robbins was behind the shooting of Dave Cummings, even if she contracted it out. Apart from the Latin reference to the Devil, there is indeed no direct evidence that Sara Robbins murdered the two crime writers.'

DI Ozal looked at her. 'But you think she did.'

Oaten remained impassive. 'She's definitely a suspect, Inspector. I don't think Matt would…Matt Wells would have gone underground with his friends if there hadn't been a direct threat of some kind.'

Superintendent Paskin nodded. 'I know what the newspapers are saying, stirred up by another crime writer as far as I can see. But do you really think Wells has been in touch with Sara Robbins?'

All eyes were on Karen Oaten. 'Vice-versa, I'd say.'

'Why would she do that?' Paskin asked.

'Because she's emulating her brother—you'll remember he sent Matt texts to work on. I think Sara Robbins is doing something similar, her aim ultimately being to kill Matt in revenge for what happened to her brother.'

'As far as I recall,' Paskin said, 'three unknown men killed the White Devil. Wasn't there a hint they were Special Forces?'

Oaten nodded. 'Matt had to be careful about that in his book.'

'What if Sara Robbins is after them too?' Amelia Browning asked.

Neville laughed. 'I'd like to see a woman try to take out three SAS types.'

Oaten ignored that and continued to look thoughtfully at Amelia. She twitched her head. 'Superintendent Paskin,' she said. 'Maybe you could tell us how you're getting on with the four murders in your area.'

The superintendent gave her an avuncular smile. 'We've arrested another Turk for the murder of Mehmet Saka, the first victim. There was a family feud and the killing doesn't appear to have any connection with the subsequent ones. The second, the Kurd Nedim Zinar, was an enforcer of sorts for the King.'

'Of sorts?' asked Doctor Redrose.

'Well, he was a big softy really, wasn't he, Mustafa?'

DI Ozal gave a solemn nod. 'Even some of the ethnic Turks liked him. He used to help people out.' He glanced at his boss. 'We used him as an informer occasionally.'

'Could that have been a motive for his murder?' Turner asked.

'I doubt it, Taff,' Ron Paskin said. 'I'd say he was chosen because he was an easy target.'

'Easy?' Amelia Browning said, screwing her eyes up.

'He was over six feet and sixteen stone. Whoever stabbed him must have had some nerve, let alone strength.'

'True enough,' the superintendent said. 'What I meant was that it would have been easy to establish his routine. He parked his car in a conveniently quiet alley.'

'It was one of your lot, wasn't it?' DI Neville said to DI Ozal. 'The Turks hate the Kurds. They told me that when I was on my holidays there.'

Paskin put a heavy hand on Ozal's arm. 'You're over-simplifying, Inspector,' he said, his eyes cold. 'Mustafa here has his ear to the ground. He'd have heard if this was a gang killing.'

'You're saying it wasn't?' Neville asked. 'What about the other bodies you've got? They're all gang-related.'

'Thank you, DI Neville,' Oaten said. 'Go on, guv.'

Paskin took a deep breath. 'Right, Karen. To finish on Nedim Zabar, the presence of ammunition in his vehicle suggests he was carrying a weapon, probably a pistol. It wasn't found at the scene. The CSIs weren't able to identify any prints from the time of the murder. And, surprise, surprise, there were no witnesses.'

'The killer gets a handgun,' Neville said. 'And, guess what? Two people are shot dead.'

Ozal glared across the table at the Homicide West man. 'There's no proof that the weapon taken from Zabar was used in the killings of Aro Izady and the Wolfman.'

'All right, calm down,' Oaten said. 'Guv?'

The superintendent gave her a long-suffering look. 'The body of Aro Izady, a cousin of the King and one of his numbers men, was found in a basement used by the Turkish Shadow gang. He'd been shot in the head at close range.'

'We think two other men were present,' Inspector Ozal said, taking up the story. 'One was Faik Jabar, also linked to the King—a witness saw him getting into Izady's car. The other, we haven't been able to identify beyond the fact that he had a beard.'

'There was blood from another person at the scene,' the pathologist put in. 'It seems this Jabar was also shot, though not fatally.'

Ozal nodded. 'Quite so, Doctor. There were bloodstains in the room and on the stairs outside, as well as two nine-millimetre cartridges. Faik Jabar has not been seen since. One of our informers said that he had been picked up by the Shadows and was being, as he put it, cross-examined.'

'You mean tortured,' Neville said.

'Well done, Inspector,' Paskin said, without audible irony. 'We have a witness who saw a young man with a bandage on his hand and blood on his legs come out of a house in Stoke Newington with a moustachioed man. Tests on blood found there show the same group as that found in the Shadow store, and the DNA will confirm that, I'm sure. As they were getting into a green Opel Astra, the well-known Shadow enforcer known as the Wolfman—we don't know his real name—came running down the street to stop them. A woman—or possibly not—in a *burqa* shot him three times. No one realised straightaway what had happened, which means a silencer was used. By the time people had got to the Wolfman he was dead—three shots to the chest—and his killer had vanished. I'm guessing she—or he—had a car round the corner. The young man and the other man with the moustache drove off in the Astra.'

'What do you think about the use of the *burqa* by the killer, DI Ozal?' Karen Oaten asked.

'It's a first, at least in this country,' the inspector replied. 'As to the shooter's gender, you wouldn't find many Muslim men who would willingly put it on.'

'How about non-Muslims?' Younger asked. 'Could one of the other gangs be involved? White villains or Yardies?'

'It's possible,' Paskin said, 'but there's no evidence for it.'

'Seems a dead cert to me,' Luke Neville said. 'The Wolfman—crazy name—kills the Kurd Nedim Zinar. Next up, he puts on a false beard and coerces Izady into driving up Green Lanes, collecting the young guy on the way. There's obviously something said in the basement and the young guy kills the older guy. Then the Wolfman shoots him dead and the other young guy in the hand, and takes him prisoner. Then the King's men get on Wolfie's tail and set up the *burqa* hit.' He looked around. 'Bingo. Cases closed.'

Ozal laughed. 'Very clever. The problem is, we haven't heard a whisper from any of our snouts to back that up.'

Neville grinned. 'Well, maybe you need to check out the quality of your snouts.'

Oaten looked at Paskin, who shook his head once. 'Thank you, gentlemen,' she said. 'Let's move on to what is hopefully the last murder. DCI Younger?'

'Sandra Devonish, best-selling American crime novelist, found dead in her suite at Wilde's hotel yesterday evening.'

'Single stab wound to the heart,' said Redrose, 'suggesting a fair degree of skill.'

Younger looked at him. 'Or luck.'

The pathologist gave a snort of disdain.

'We've got conflicting witness statements,' DCI Younger continued, unperturbed. 'Unfortunately the ground-floor bar was very busy with a group of advertising executives. One woman said she saw a tall man in a grey suit walk towards the stairs. The receptionist saw a woman in a red coat walk into the lobby and then out again a few minutes later. And a man who was drinking at the bar said that a bearded man in motorbike leathers went past, holding his helmet under his arm.'

'That sounds suggestive,' Amelia Browning said.

'Yes, it does,' agreed Younger. 'Unfortunately, no one has corroborated the sighting and no one saw a motorbike rider leave the hotel. We're still checking the CCTV recordings.'

'We've already mentioned the modus and the scene,' Oaten said. 'What else?'

The pathologist raised a pudgy hand. 'Nails had been recently cut from both toes and fingers, as well as hairs from the back of the head and the pubic area.'

'As per Mary Malone,' DI Neville put in.

Karen Oaten nodded. 'What else?'

Younger looked at her. 'I'd say the killer took a hell of a risk. He—or she—went into a crowded hotel and managed to stab the victim, arrange the body and set the music playing a couple of minutes before the room-service waiter went to the suite. We're looking at a very assured and cold-blooded killer.'

John Turner frowned. 'You mentioned luck before. That doesn't sit with your picture of a well-organised killer.'

'No, it doesn't,' Younger admitted.

'The fact is,' the Welshman continued, 'if the room-service guy had knocked earlier, when he—or she—was inside, the killer could have put on an American accent and asked him to leave the order outside.'

'You're meant to sign for it,' Neville said, tugging his lower lip.

Turner fixed him with a steely eye. 'Do you think they insist in a place like Wilde's?'

'There's something else,' Amelia Browning said. 'How did the killer find out that Sandra Devonish was staying at Wilde's?'

There was silence.

'I mean, hotels like that don't give out that sort of information. Who knew that the writer was going to be in London?'

Younger was nodding. 'That's a good point, Sergeant. We've spoken to her publishers. They told us that they always put their important authors in Wilde's.'

'So who would know that?' Browning persisted. 'People in the publishers.'

'We've established alibis,' Younger said.

'In the hotel?'

'As you said, they don't give guest information out. They fired a receptionist last week for inadvertently confirming a footballer's presence to a tabloid, so I think we can be pretty sure that the staff were on their toes.'

'Where does that leave us?' Redrose said, glancing pointedly at his watch.

Amelia Browning stared over at him. 'With a killer who knows the world of crime writing, Doctor.'

'How about a crime writer, then?' Luke Neville said. 'Such as Matt Wells.'

Karen Oaten didn't raise her head from her notes. 'Tell him, Taff.'

'Matt Wells has a solid alibi for the Mary Malone murder.'

'And the other one?' Neville asked.

Turner glared at him, then shook his head.

Neville looked around the table. 'DCI Oaten said at the beginning that she wanted to establish a common thread in these killings. At the very least, she needs to find Matt Wells. His friend was shot, two fellow crime writers have been killed, one wearing leathers like the biker seen near Dave Cummings's place. And...' His voice trailed away.

'And what?' Turner demanded. 'He dressed up in a *burqa* to kill a Turkish hard man?'

Neville looked down. 'He could have,' he said, though even he didn't sound convinced.

'What about ballistics?' Oaten asked.

'We've got a match between a bullet found in the wall of the Shadow basement and the three in the Wolfman's body,' Ron Paskin said.

'But no match with the bullets taken from Dave Cummings,' added John Turner.

'So,' Oaten said, looking round the table. 'Two different shooters, or just the one using different weapons?'

There was no reply.

'And what about the person who's murdering crime writers? He or she isn't using firearms at all. Does that mean we've got three different killers loose in London?'

Again, there was silence. The meeting broke up shortly afterwards.

The earl was in his London club. He didn't like to be away from his country estate—there had been so much going on there recently—but he couldn't avoid this trip. And the business had been concluded satisfactorily. Not that he'd had much to do with that. He had no knowledge of the illicit drugs trade, despite having had a healthy appetite for cocaine in his student days. Fortunately his companion had been able to extract a reasonable price. Then it had been straight to his bank to make the deposit that would have calmed his account manager down substantially. If they went on like this, the family would soon regain much of its lost standing; because money was all that counted, for aristocrats even more than for the common hordes. Inheriting property was the norm for his class. Keeping the banks happy was much less common.

He sipped the distinctly average tawny port and nodded at the old idiot across the table. Inbreeding had done the aristocracy no favours. At least the earl didn't have to worry on that score. He had inherited his family's devotion to the black arts, as well as the considerable talents required to treat with the order's acolytes.

He got up and went up to the room he always took. It was on the top floor, in what would originally have been the servants' quarters, but he liked it because it reminded him of his house at school. When he had been a fag, the head prefect had demanded the use of his mouth and backside. He had prayed for salvation—not to the feeble god the school worshipped in chapel every morning, but to the Lord Beneath the Earth. His father had given him the order's archives to study before he went to senior school. His prayers, or rather the replies to them, had worked. The prefect slipped outside his room and fell down the stairs, breaking his neck. The fact that the earl had rubbed soap on the floorboards was not noticed, the police being admitted to the school only on sufferance.

That had been his first death dedicated to the Lord Beneath. There had been countless others since, and it wouldn't be long until the next one.

The earl picked up his mobile phone and made a call to one of the order's most devoted supplicants.

21

'**B**ugger,' Rog said, his fingers tapping rapidly on the keyboard.

I went over. 'What is it?'

'Hang on.' His eyes were locked on the screen, as he scrolled down rows of numbers and letters. 'That was close. You almost lost everything in your new account.'

'What?'

'Sara's hired someone red-hot. I got there in time, but only because I'd programmed an alert code. All the money I transferred from Sara's accounts was about to go out again.'

I slapped him on the shoulder. 'Well done, Dodger. Sara knows we're on to her.'

He nodded. 'That's what you wanted, isn't it? But are Pete and Andy safe at her place in Oxford?'

'I'll send a text warning them to be even more careful.' After I'd done that, I looked back at Rog. 'So is that account secure now?'

'I've built a massive firewall and I've also alerted the bank's security department—anonymously, of course. I don't think Sara's hacker will get in again.'

'She's not going to be happy that I've got her money,' I said, wondering what that might drive her to.

'Matt?' Rog said. 'Why did you warn that Alistair Bing guy? You solved the clue. When you send the answer at midnight, he should be off the hook.'

'You're right,' I replied. 'He should be—if you're prepared to trust a murderer who sends puzzles.'

'Got you,' he said, looking round at me. 'That tosser Hinkley's got to you, hasn't he?'

'Yes. Jeremy Andrewes, too. When this is finished, I'm going to have a serious conversation with that pair.'

'What about Karen?'

I stepped away, unwilling to discuss that—not because I wanted to keep Rog out of the loop, but because I wasn't sure how to handle her. If I contacted her by phone or e-mail, she'd have to respond officially, which would get me nowhere. But trying to see her would be risky, as well as putting her in a difficult position. She'd probably try to arrest me for my own protection.

'All right, don't tell me,' Rog said. 'I only thought you might want my help since I'm such a stellar performer with women.'

I laughed. Rog wasn't unattractive, but he'd never been able to hold a woman's attention, never mind affections, for more than a few weeks—that was, if he managed to pull in the first place. He and Andy were at opposite ends of that spectrum.

'How are we going to nail Sara, Matt?' he asked, his tone serious. 'Pete and Andy aren't going to find her in Oxford. If she's there, who's doing the murders in London?'

'It's only an hour by car or train.'

'Or motorbike,' he said.

'What?'

'Remember the biker that Andy saw outside her mother's place?'

'Shit,' I said, shaking my head in disgust. How could I have forgotten Doris Carlton-Jones?

'He said the biker was trying to give the old woman something.'

'That's right. I wonder what it was.'

'Do you think she's been in contact with Sara? Or vice-versa?'

I considered that. Sara could have found out who her birth mother was. She had that right, though she'd have had to find a way into the adoption agency's database rather than present herself in person—that would have been dangerous, given her status as a wanted woman. If she'd hired a geek who could empty bank accounts, the same specimen could easily have traced her birth mother. The question was, had Doris Carlton-Jones met her daughter? I'd mentioned that Sara and the White Devil had been adopted in *The Death List,* and found out the identity of her mother by the judicious application of sweet talk and bribery. But I hadn't told the woman who her daughter was.

'There's only one way to find out,' I said, looking at my watch. It was coming up to ten. 'But it's too late for a visit tonight. The deadline's coming up.'

'It's probably a long shot, anyway. Do you think the cops know about her?'

He had me there. I hadn't told Karen the woman's name, but she might have followed the trail from the newspapers without telling me. Given that the motorbike rider had shot out Andy's windscreen, I didn't think there were any police personnel watching the house in Sydenham— they'd have shown themselves. Maybe Mrs Carlton-Jones had been in touch with the real police about the shooting. It was possible that Andy and I had made her suspicious.

'And the answer is?' Rog said, cupping his hand round his ear.

'Sorry, mate, I was just thinking it through. Frankly, I don't know. We'll go and talk to her tomorrow.'

I sat down in front of my laptop and tried to think of all the possible consequences of sending the name Adrian Brooks at midnight.

Faik Jabar looked at the man on the floor. His head was a bloody pulp and his bare chest was covered in long knife cuts. He was still breathing, but there was a rattle in his throat and he was mumbling incoherently.

'Do it,' the bearded man said, pointing the silenced pistol at Faik's groin. He smiled crookedly.

Faik looked at the knife he was holding. It was dripping blood. The Albanian had gabbled information about his family's business after the bearded man set up a camcorder on a tripod. Then he had been beaten with a hammer and slashed with a combat knife. Faik's captor had taken off his chains. His wounded thighs were in agony because of the wounds and the urine that had soaked into his trousers. Now his captor had given him the knife and told him to cut off the Albanian's nose. When Faik objected, saying he thought the man was to be ransomed, the bearded man gave a sharp laugh and pointed to the camera. Then he turned it off.

'I will send them the disk and they will prepare payment. He will be alive when I set him free, but that doesn't mean he has to be a complete man.'

Faik swallowed. He felt like a small boy who had

strayed into adult business. The muzzle of the gun was pointed at his crotch and it didn't waver.

'I'll shoot you there and leave you to die,' the bearded man said. 'You know I'm capable of it. Think how much nicer things will be when you've done what I want. I can make things very…enjoyable for you.'

The sexual tone turned Faik's stomach. He'd been forced to watch his captor maim the victim. The idea of performing sexual acts with him was horrible. Faik knew he had to fight back. He took a deep breath and looked past the gun.

'All right,' he said, blinking hard as he got to his feet and stepped closer to the Albanian. He had the knife in his right hand and he knew he would only get one chance. He had calculated the distance. The man with the beard was about two metres away—too far to charge him. He'd considered throwing the knife—he'd been taught how by one of the King's bodyguards—but he knew he'd be shot before he even let the blade go. He had only one option. Bending over the gasping Albanian, he brought the knife close to his face. Then, with a sharp cry, he fell to the floor like a stone, narrowly missing the blood-drenched body.

Faik lay there, waiting for the bullet. It didn't come. He had made sure that the knife clattered away out of his reach, reckoning that would put the killer off guard.

'Get up!' the man with the gun screamed, his voice suddenly high. 'Get up!'

Faik heard rapid footsteps moving to the dresser, and then towards him. A cork was unplugged and a liquid drenched his head. The smell made him gag. It was some spirit, whisky or rum. Faik didn't drink alcohol—his mother would have disowned him.

A hand sheathed in latex grabbed the back of his collar and he was heaved round. Now he was facing the man. He rolled his eyes, showing the whites. That should convince the bastard that he was out. The problem was, Faik couldn't see while his eyes were like that. He waited a few seconds, then felt the cold metal of the silencer on his forehead. It was time.

Faik lashed sideways with his right arm, making contact with the gun. It flew out of the bearded man's hand. Then he got hold of the bloodstained sports shirt and pulled the fucker down, jerking his body to the side. There was a squelching sound as the man's face landed on the Albanian's lacerated chest. Faik forced himself to his feet, ignoring the pain from his thighs. He swung one foot back and smashed it against the side of his opponent's head. He was only wearing training shoes, but the blow was solid enough. The bearded man fell back on to the Albanian's body further down.

'Fuck you!' Faik yelled, giving him another kick. Then he reached for the gun and pointed it at the man's head.

Slowly, the face turned towards him. The beard was drenched in blood. 'You don't want to shoot me,' the killer said, his voice soft and enticing. 'We can be friends.'

Faik felt a mixture of repulsion and excitement. He held the gun on him. 'Take it off,' he said, breathing hard. 'Take off the beard.'

The man stared at him and then smiled. 'All right,' he said, struggling to his feet and standing up. He gripped the hairs at the side of his face and gently pulled. The thick covering came away.

'Ah-yeeh!' Faik said, stepping back. What he had seen when the beard had slipped before was only a hint of the full horror. The man's upper lip was in two parts, revealing the pink of the gum beneath. There were livid, raised scars across the cheeks and the chin was irregular and swollen, the skin discoloured as if it had been repeatedly punched. 'What happened to you?'

The man touched the flaps of his upper lip with his tongue. Faik could now see that there were small scabs on it, as if the skin had been punctured.

'This?' He laughed softly, the sound incongruous. 'Don't you fancy me now?'

Faik gagged on the bitter liquid that had rushed up his throat. 'Is that…is that why you're doing this?' he asked, inclining his head towards the Albanian. 'To make him uglier than you?'

The laugh was repeated. 'You're clever as well as beautiful. Come on, we can have a wonderful time together.' The man raised his hands slowly and began to open the buttons of his shirt, then latched his fingers on to the collar of the T-shirt beneath and ripped it apart.

Faik watched in astonishment as the material was parted. He saw a pair of dark nipples and soft, heavy breasts.

'Don't worry, I'm not a transsexual.' Without the beard, the woman's smile was pitiful. 'I'm yours.'

Faik Jabar let out a cry of anguish and repulsion, then staggered to the door of the flat. In a few seconds he was on the pavement, breathing in the cold night air. He jammed the pistol into the waistband of his still damp trousers. Before he started to move forward, he looked up to the top floor. The curtain was half-open and the face of the monster looked down at him. Now there was no trace of a smile. He remembered something from school about hell, fury and a scorned woman.

* * *

Pete and Andy took the train to Oxford and walked to the house. It was over a mile from the station, in what was obviously a well-heeled area. Apart from a pissed student lurching home, the place was deserted. The building was detached and about twenty metres back from the road. There was a thick and high privet hedge all round the front garden.

'Good cover,' Andy said as they approached. 'And no lights. Let's hope that means no one's at home.'

The street was quiet, cars parked on both sides. A narrow path ran up the left side of the property to a tennis club.

'Not even lunatic Oxford professors will be playing at this time of night in March,' Pete said. 'How convenient. There's a side door.'

Andy pulled on latex gloves and took his lock-picking rods from his pocket.

'How long do you give me, Boney?' he asked.

Pete shone his torch around the door. 'I can't see an alarm. How about one minute, Slash?'

Andy succeeded, just. They went in, closing the door behind them. There was cast-iron garden furniture on a wide wooden veranda. Pete was shining his torch around the rear door.

'Yup, there it is,' he said, pointing to a small plastic box at the top of the black-painted door. 'Circuit breaker.' He took out the electronic device with a pointed end that Rog had given him. 'Let's see if this thing works.' He held it towards the top of the door for five seconds. 'Okay. See what you can do with the lock.'

Andy worked his rods again and there was a click. 'Dammit,' he said in a loud whisper. 'There's a mortice lock as well.'

Pete moved the electronic device round the window. 'You'll have to cut the glass.'

'Sara or her sidekicks will know we've been here.'

'Tough,' Pete said. 'You heard Matt. Any pressure on the bitch is good news.'

Andy took a glass-knife and two rubber suckers from his backpack. After he'd attached them, Pete held them while he did the cutting. The pane was soon removed and they climbed in.

'Motion sensors,' Pete said, holding Andy back as he moved across the kitchen. He held up the device again. 'Okay.'

They moved forward and made it to the hall, opening the door carefully.

'Jesus, did something die in here?' Andy said, as a wave of rank air hit them.

'Very likely,' Pete said, on his knees by the alarm box. Rog had given him another device that was supposed to scramble the unit's brains for up to half an hour.

'What is that stink?' Andy said, shining his torch around the spacious area.

'Whatever it is, it isn't far away,' Pete said, close behind him. They came round the bottom of the wide staircase.

'You have got to be kidding,' Andy said, putting a hand over his nose and mouth.

Pete shone his torch on the swollen figure that was lying facedown inside the front door. 'I'm glad we came in the back,' he said, breathing only through his mouth.

'Is it a guy?' Andy asked, peering at the head.

'Those look like suit trousers. Pinstripe. Hold on.' Pete took out his digital camera and shot a series of photographs. 'That'll keep Matt happy.'

Andy looked up at him. 'We're going to have to turn the poor bastard over.'

They took hold of the bloated shoulders and managed to get the body on to its back. Pete stepped back and took more photos. The face would scarcely have been recognised by the corpse's best friend.

'Look at that,' Andy said, pointing. 'Throat's been cut.'

Pete nodded. 'Check his pockets. Maybe there's some ID on him.'

Andy blinked hard and then slid a hand into the trouser pocket nearest to him. He shook his head. 'Zilch.'

Pete tried the pocket on the other side. 'Something in here.' He brought out a rectangular card. 'James Maclehose,' he said, 'and a load of letters after his name. Consultant plastic surgeon. There's an address in Harley Street.'

'He must have really got someone pissed,' Andy said, leaning over the dead man's face. 'His nose has been cut off. Christ. And his lips.'

Pete had put the stained card in a plastic bag. 'You know what, Slash?'

'Tell me,' Andy said, raising an eyebrow.

'We'll have to turn him over again.'

'What, so the cops don't realise he's been moved?'

'No. So we can check his back pockets.'

They manoeuvred the body again.

'Nothing in here,' Pete said.

'But I've got this.' Andy held up a piece of folded paper. 'I think there's some writing, but it's run.' He held the paper up to Pete's torch beam. '"Sorry, but…".' He squinted in the torchlight. 'Nope, can't make it out. Why's someone saying sorry? For killing him?'

'Fuck knows. Let's get out of here before I puke my guts up.'

Pete walked to the kitchen.

'Hey, Boney,' Andy said, 'you need to reactivate the alarm system.'

'No, I don't. The place is going to be swarming with cops as soon as we're clear of it.' He went through the window-space.

When they were back on the street, Pete took out his mobile and started texting. By the time they reached the main road, he'd had a reply.

'Good,' he said. 'Matt agrees. I'll call the cops from the city centre.'

As they walked between medieval college buildings, Andy nudged his friend.

'What do you think about Oxford now, Boney?'

Pete raised his arm and sniffed his jacket. 'I still stink of that poor bastard.' He glanced at the American. 'What do I think about Oxford?' He shivered. 'I still bloody hate it.'

Andy nodded. 'Me too. But you get a better class of corpse here.'

Pete stared at him and shook his head. 'Sometimes I despair of you, Slash.'

'Me too, man,' Andy replied, watching a blonde young woman in a short skirt get off her bicycle. 'But I can get over it.'

'Aw right, mate,' said Josh Hinkley, his feet in their black pointed cowboy boots on the kitchen table. 'But tell Spider he's dead if he doesn't show up for poker on Friday. See ya.' He dropped the phone on to the book he'd been reading—*Offshore Investments Made Simple*. His broker had told him it was worth its weight in platinum, which had made Josh laugh. He still thought the guy was a champion arse-licker.

'Time for a drink, I reckon, Josh, old man,' he said aloud, getting up and heading for the fridge. He took out a bottle of Urquel lager and flipped the cap. 'Oh yes, my beauty,' he said, after a series of gulps. Since his wife, Lou, had up and left, he'd taken to talking to himself. It wasn't as if anyone could hear him. Or his music. From the stereo came the sound of The Kinks playing 'All Day and All of the Night'. He'd always liked Ray Davies and his mates. A genuine London band with genuine London style.

Not that he was a Londoner himself. According to his website, he'd been born within the sound of the Bow Bells, but it would have needed a clear day and a massive sound system to have carried the ding-dongs to the hospital in Harlow. Still, at least his ma had been a real Cockney, even though she wasn't too clear about who his old man was. It was a toss-up between an Irish labourer and a Glaswegian layabout. Josh's money was on the former—he had a hell of a work ethic. For the last ten years he'd spent as much time as he could reading the competition. He had transposed American characters to the U.K. and altered the dialogue appropriately. So far as plot was concerned, there was nothing new under the sun, as he liked to say at book signings. Some arsehole critics had clocked what he was up to, but his readers didn't care. And then, out of the bleeding blue, along comes that little squit Alistair Bing with his Jim Cooler books and outsells him all over the world.

The phone rang.

''Allo, darling,' Hinkley said with a wide grin. 'Yeah,

you're bloody right I'm waiting for you. Get that pretty little Chinese ass of yours over here right now, you hear?' He dropped the phone and dug around in his pocket for the bag of coke he'd scored earlier. He chopped some lines on the antique farmhouse table that Lou had made such a fuss about polishing and got to work with a rolled-up fifty-pound note.

'Yeehah!' he shouted, as he made his way unsteadily to his top-of-the-range Bang & Olufsen stereo system. A few seconds later, The Jam were crashing their way through his favourite track, 'Private Hell'—another set of genuine London sons; well, Surrey sons. And with Chop Suzy on her way, what more could a man ask?

Josh Hinkley slid slowly to the parquet floor. His head was spinning, but he still couldn't get Matt Wells out of his mind. The fucker. He was knobbing that blonde bint from the VCCT, so he got the heads-up on every big case in the city. She probably knew exactly where he was and what he was doing. The rozzers were letting Matt break as many laws as he liked. But he was going to get the tosser; he'd already set the wheels in motion. Mr I Know More About Crime Than Any Other Novelist was going to come a very big cropper.

The buzzer went. Hinkley went to the door and pressed the entry button. Suzy and her honey-pot would be on their way up in the lift. He spat on his fingers and smoothed them over his hair.

'All right, darling,' he said, pulling open the door, 'let's be having you!'

Before Josh Hinkley's lights went out, he registered that something very bizarre had happened to his visitor's face.

22

The half hour before midnight had passed more slowly than a penguin marathon. I looked at my watch so often that Rog asked if I'd discovered a new way of jerking off. I couldn't make sense of what Pete and Andy had found in Sara's Oxford house. The apologetic note on the dead man suggested that someone else may have dumped the body. I'd be thinking about that later, though there was no chance of checking the house again—Pete's call to the cops would have turned the street into CSI Oxford. London cops would soon be swarming all over the clinic in Harley Street, too.

At last the deadline was close. I logged on to my e-mail server. There was a message from a different address, *answerplease3*. I wrote, Your target is Adrian Brooks, the crime writer Alistair Bing. I expect you to keep your word about not killing him.

At exactly midnight, I hit Send. The message moved to the Sent Items folder without any problems. I felt like a footballer who'd just won the Cup final. I'd taken on Sara, or whoever she'd hired to kill the crime writers, and I'd won. How would she like that?

There was a chime as an instant reply came through. My heart dropped like a stone.

Well done, Matt. Though I did say it was an easy one. The thing is, I made the rules and I can break them. You know where Josh Hinkley lives, don't you? Maybe you should get round there. Then again, given how nasty he's been about you in print recently, maybe you shouldn't. The delightful Karen might put you in the frame as the killer.

Doctor Faustus

'Fuck!' I yelled.

Rog pushed me aside and keyed out a string of abuse. I managed to stop him before he sent the reply.

'Forget it,' I said. 'There's nothing we can do.' I turned away.

'Maybe it's just a bluff,' Rog said. 'Why don't you ring this Hinkley guy from a public phone?'

It wasn't a bad idea. There was a phone across the road. I pressed out the number, my heart thundering. It rang ten times before it was picked up.

'Hello,' came a neutral male voice.

'Is that Josh?' I asked, in a Cockney accent.

'Who's calling, please?'

This time I recognised the voice. It was DI John Turner, his Welsh vowels not completely obscured.

I broke the connection. If Taff Turner was there, something terminal had happened to Josh Hinkley. It would be on the TV and radio stations soon enough.

'What now?' Rog asked.

'I've got a visit to make. You should get some sleep.'

'I won't be sleeping much tonight. I want to get Sara even more now.'

'Get back to nailing her funds,' I said, squeezing his arm. 'I don't care where you put them, but I want her running on empty. Then we'll see how clever she is.'

'She probably has accounts we don't know about.'

'Find them, Dodger. I'm depending on you.'

'Right,' he said. 'Don't worry, Matt. We'll get her.'

I got my gear together and left the flat. I had to do this on my own and I couldn't tell the others where I was going. The chips were down now and anything might happen. I had to be sure I didn't land my friends in even more danger. The death of Dave still haunted me like a witch's curse.

I looked at my watch, all traces of the naive optimism I'd felt before I sent the answer vanished. I resisted the temptation to make a surreptitious visit to the crime scene at Josh Hinkley's house, and started walking south-west.

'Who was that?' Karen Oaten asked.

'Some wide boy,' John Turner replied. 'He hung up rather than give a name.'

The chief inspector glanced at him. They were wearing white coveralls, the hoods up. They had arrived at eleven-thirty, called to the scene by DCI Younger. The narrow street in Soho had been blocked at both ends by patrol cars, their roof lights flashing. Uniformed personnel, some of them armed, were present and a striped barrier tape had already been set up around the street door to keep curious local residents, passersby and journalists at bay. The CSI vans were parked haphazardly and personnel in blue coveralls were already heading into the building. The ground and first two floors were used as offices. Josh Hinkley occupied the top two.

Younger brought them up to speed. 'One of the neighbours called about the noise at 10.43,' he said. 'Uniformed
officers got here at 10.57. There was no answer to their
buzzing and knocking. They got the phone number and
tried it. Nothing. The music was seriously loud and—'

'Loud music's a matter for the council, Colin,' Oaten
said. 'We wouldn't usually intervene, never mind kick the
door down.'

'No, but that wasn't all. There was blood on the outside
of the street door. And the uniforms found that—' Younger
pointed to a clear plastic evidence bag on the hall table
'—in the lift.'

Oaten picked it up. Inside was a long-bladed combat
knife with a serrated edge. There was a streak of blood
down the centre of the blade.

'The body's upstairs,' Younger said.

'All right,' said Oaten. 'We should get up there. Was
anything else reported?'

Colin Younger nodded. 'The officers said there was a
strong smell of perfume.'

Oaten looked at him. 'It couldn't have been aftershave?'

'I asked. They were pretty sure. So there had recently
been a woman in the flat.'

'Did they see any women on the street?' Turner asked.

Younger shook his head. 'People only started to gather
when the sirens started.'

There was a bustle at the door.

'Here we all are again,' said Redrose, the pathologist.
'When did you last eat, Inspector Turner?'

Taff muttered something that no one else caught. It
could have been Welsh for 'Delighted to see you, Doctor',
but Oaten thought it unlikely.

'Come along, then,' said the potbellied doctor. 'Let's see what our killer's left us this time.'

Younger led the way. Three CSIs were examining different parts of the spacious flat. There was a long living area filled with high-quality furniture, including an Eames chair. An expensive-looking stereo system was on a mahogany table. There was a CD in a plastic evidence bag next to it.

'Do we know what music was playing?' Oaten asked the nearest technician.

'Not yet,' replied the woman. 'I've checked the disk. The same song's repeated all the way through.'

'I presume there's a timer on that machine,' the chief inspector said. 'Was it activated?'

The CSI nodded. 'It was set for 10.30 p.m. And the volume was at maximum.'

'I've finished with the stairs,' another white-suited technician said. 'Just keep clear of the areas I've flagged up.'

Oaten stepped ahead and started up the wooden staircase. It looked like it had been newly built.

'This would originally have been attic space,' the medic said. 'A friend of mine lives in a similar place round the corner. He hasn't been able to get planning permission for a conversion.'

'I wonder how the dead man managed that,' Turner said.

His boss rubbed her thumb and forefinger together.

'Surely not,' Redrose said, feigning shock. 'Corruption in the City of Westminster? Never.'

Oaten reached the top step and found herself in a wide hallway. There were five doors, all of them open. Flashes from the police photographer suggested which room was occupied by the body.

'Look at this, Taff,' Oaten said over her shoulder.

'Jesus.' The Welshman's eyes were fixed on the far wall. 'Is that blood?'

Redrose pushed past them. 'I think the odds are very high.' He went over to the bed, on which the naked body of a middle-aged man was sprawled.

Oaten and Turner moved into the thickly carpeted bedroom. On the wall above the king-size bed, there was a pentacle. The circle enclosing the five-pointed star was about a metre across. The red liquid that had been used had dripped in places, but the words within the lines were legible.

'"FECIT DIABOLUS",' Turner read. 'The Devil's done it yet again.'

Oaten took in the scene and moved forwards.

When they got to the bed, the Welshman's hand went to his mouth.

This time even Oaten had to blink hard. The victim's abdomen looked like a grenade had gone off over it.

Shortly afterwards the female CSI advised them about the music that had been playing. One of the uniformed policemen had identified it as 'Devil Woman' by Cliff Richard.

'No wonder the neighbours called us,' Colin Younger quipped.

Oaten looked at him thoughtfully. 'The reference to "woman" is interesting, isn't it?'

'Oh, you mean Sara Robbins.'

'Maybe.' Karen Oaten saw Doctor Redrose wave.

'Look what I've found,' he said, brandishing a blood-stained object in a pair of forceps.

'It's paper,' Turner said. 'Where was it?'

'Under the body,' the pathologist replied. 'In case anybody's interested, the cause of death was a stab wound to the throat, which was then cut from ear to ear. The abdomen has been slashed open numerous times. There was no shortage of blood for the killer to use as ink.'

'Can you read it?' Karen Oaten asked, straining to make out the words that had been laser-printed on the paper.

Colin Younger nodded. 'It says "Ask Matt Wells about this".'

There was a sudden silence in the dead writer's bedroom.

I tried not to, but eventually I'd dropped off in the armchair. I hadn't turned any lights on in the house and I'd reactivated the alarm system, so I had to keep still. Obviously I managed that, although my sleep had been anything but peaceful. Dave's body flashed before me, and then I was chasing a woman who I thought was Sara, but showed herself to be a hideous devil when she turned on me, snarling.

I woke up when the key was turned in the lock and the alarm started to beep. I listened to the footsteps on the polished wood hall floor. Fortunately, only one person had come in. I stood up slowly and took the silenced Glock from my pocket. I heard a bag being dropped on the floor and then a long sigh. I padded to the door, and then showed myself.

'Matt!' Karen said, her hand flying to her chest. 'Jesus, you almost gave me a heart attack.' She was sitting at the bottom of the stairs, one boot removed.

I checked that she'd put the chain on the front door.

'What the hell are you doing here?' she demanded. 'And why are you holding a gun?'

'Are you going to behave?' I asked, trying for a winning smile but giving up. 'I'm serious, Karen. I need to talk to you. After that, I'm going to walk out of here and you aren't going to follow me.'

She stood up and glared at me. 'Who do you think you are? You disappear, leaving all sorts of questions unanswered, and then you come back and order me about. Screw you!'

I glanced at my watch. It was four-thirty in the morning and we were in danger of waking the neighbours. 'Calm down, will you? I'll answer any question you ask.'

That seemed to mollify her slightly, though she stepped out of the way when I tried to embrace her. She went to the kitchen and filled the kettle.

'You know that Josh Hinkley's been murdered?' she said over her shoulder.

I had decided I was going to come clean. 'Yes.'

Karen told me the details, watching me cringe. 'There was a message under the body, saying "Ask Matt Wells about this", like there was with Sandra Devonish.' She caught my eye. 'I'm asking.'

I sat down at the minuscule kitchen table and started to talk. A mug of coffee was thumped down in front of me and Karen sat opposite. Our knees touched. She tried to move back, but there wasn't room.

After I'd gone through the clues I'd tried to answer and the sender's responses, she slumped in her chair.

'Why didn't you tell me about all that earlier?' she asked, her tone acid.

I shrugged. 'Because I was specifically told not to involve the police—other people could have been murdered.'

'What, more than Sara Robbins has killed so far?' She looked at me in disbelief. 'And you've had a hot line to her. Anybody else would have run screaming to us, but Matt Wells? No, he's smarter than the Met's finest, he can

handle serial killers on his own.' She laughed bitterly. 'I'll
be sure to mention that to Sandra Devonish's family when
they arrive to collect her body.'

I was finding it hard to look at her. 'I did what I could,'
I said, in a low voice. I caught her eye. 'Look, there's
something else you don't know.' I told her about what Pete
and Andy had found in Sara's house in Oxford.

She looked at me with slightly less ferocity. 'And the
note says "Sorry"? What about?'

I shrugged. 'I wonder if there's someone else involved.
There have been those gangland killings too. Do you know
who's behind them?'

Karen shook her head. 'Could be a straightforward war
between the Turks and the Kurds.'

I didn't think she was convinced by what she'd said,
but I let it go. 'We don't actually know that Sara's responsible for the crime-writer murders. The messages I got
were signed Doctor Faustus and, at the start, Flaminio.'
She looked blank. 'The revenger in Webster's play *The
White Devil*.'

'You don't seriously believe that someone else sent
them?' Karen asked, her eyes wide.

'I'm not sure. There are some anomalies. For a start,
Doctor Faustus and Flaminio are male characters.'

'Big deal. Maybe she thinks she's her brother reincar-
nated.'

That wasn't beyond the realms of possibility. 'Then
there's the fact that the last message header was *thethirdisaman.*'

She squinted at me. 'So?'

'Think about it. The first victim was Mary Malone, the
second Sandra Devonish—'

'And the third, despite your cleverness, was indeed a man, Josh Hinkley. I still don't see what you're getting at.'

'Well, the overwhelming likelihood is that Sara murdered Dave.'

She nodded slowly. 'Making Hinkley her fourth victim. Yes, but maybe she sees Dave's killing as separate.'

'So she has two death lists?'

Karen frowned. 'The second one consisting of?'

'Me, my family and my friends. Probably including you.' The last sentence slipped out before I could stop myself.

'In fact,' she said, with a tight smile, 'your name will be on both lists.'

'On the other hand,' I continued, eager to move on, 'maybe Sara's only interested in me and my people.'

'But if it isn't her, who is it going after the crime writers? The officers who found Josh Hinkley's body said they smelled perfume in the air. Could it be another woman?'

I looked at her. I should have asked more about Josh. Whatever he'd said about me, he didn't deserve to die the way he had. 'Maybe the Satanism angle isn't so weird after all. Maybe some devil-worshipping female psycho has it in for crime writers.'

'I don't suppose you could suggest a name,' she said drily.

'You've got me there. But I'm working on it.'

'Spit it out, Matt. What are you planning?'

I shook my head. 'Need-to-know basis only, Karen. Remember how tight a rein her brother kept on me. She could nail me at any moment. That's why I'm armed. You might want to think about getting armed protection yourself.'

'Why don't we apply for it together?' she said bitterly.

'You're not going anywhere after what you've put me through these past days. I thought you loved me, Jesus, I thought I loved you. But at the first sign of danger, you run away and leave me in a shit storm.'

I couldn't blame her for feeling that way, even though I hadn't felt able to act any differently. 'I do love you, Karen,' I said, trying to get her to look at me. 'Part of the reason I went underground was that I didn't want you close if Sara got to me.'

She glanced at me, then turned her head away. 'You have no idea how much crap's been dumped over me because of our relationship. For Christ's sake, there are people in the Met who think *you* murdered the crime writers.'

'Because of the notes fingering me? They smack of the White Devil—remember how he tried to frame me. That could mean Sara is behind the crime-writer murders, even if she isn't actually carrying them out herself.'

She sat up. 'You're the one who slept with her for a year, Matt. You must have some idea how her mind works. How are we going to catch her?'

I told her about Rog's campaign against Sara's wealth, and about the other properties my ex-lover had bought.

'We'll check them, but how likely is it she'll be there?'

'Someone was living in the Hackney flat and someone left that body in the Oxford house.'

'It isn't very likely they'll go back to those places. Though, if you'd bothered to contact me earlier, we could have run surveillance operations. Tosser.'

I deserved that for not keeping in touch. I could have texted her, but that would have done her no good if anyone in the Met had found out we were communicating.

I stood up.

'Where are you going?' she said, getting up and trying to block the door.

'Don't, Karen. You have to let me go. There are things you can't do. Ultimately, I'm the one Sara wants. You asked how we can catch her. I'm the answer to that. When she runs out of money, she'll come after me pronto. All I have to do is let her know where I'll be.'

'Are you out of your mind?' she said, pounding her hands on my chest. 'Can't you understand? I don't want anything to happen to you.'

I put my arms around her. She resisted at first, but eventually she acquiesced. 'I didn't say anything about letting Sara hurt me,' I said. 'What do you think I am? Some kind of hero?'

She laughed softly. 'No. *Some* kind of man.' She pulled away and looked at me. 'A brave but headstrong one. If you get yourself killed, I'll…' She let out a frustrated moan. 'I'll move into your flat and throw all your CDs into the river.'

'That's it then,' I said, kissing her on the lips. 'It's been nice knowing you.' I turned away and headed for the front door.

She caught up with me as I was unfastening the chain. She held me close and kissed me. 'Don't do anything that makes me cut you loose,' she said softly. It was still a definite order.

I nodded, but didn't make a verbal commitment. Nailing Sara and the people she probably had working for her couldn't be done by observing the law. That way lay death, which wasn't in my diary for this or any other year soon.

I returned her kisses, then slipped into the early morning gloom.

* * *

The man in the white mask breathed in the smoke from the paltry offering. He patted the mandrill's head and then turned to the kneeling supplicant.

'Faustus, what else did you take from your victim that we can dedicate to the Lord Beneath the Earth?'

The naked man smiled. 'Before I killed him, I made him transfer a million pounds to the account in Venezuela. The money will soon be at your disposal, Mephistopheles.'

'Untraceable?'

'You can be sure of that.'

'Very good, Faustus.' The masked man leaned closer. 'You are doing well. We must consider who will be the next sacrifice.'

The supplicant extended a hand towards Mephistopheles' robes, but withdrew it when Beelzebub bared his fangs then snapped them shut.

'Be careful, my Faustus. You know how protective my familiar is.'

'My apologies,' the naked man said, lowering his head. 'I wished to ask if you would permit me to decide on the identity of the next victim.'

The man in the mask stepped back and looked around the large subterranean chamber. 'Do you have someone in mind?' He raised his hand. 'Don't tell me. Only make sure that the tribute to the Lord Beneath is substantial, Faustus.'

It was cold, but the supplicant did not shiver. He was possessed by a fire that burned through his veins and made him more powerful than any man.

23

The Soul Collector was in position near the rendezvous point. She had been in the hide for four hours. She assumed the former SAS men had returned to their homes from Aberdeen as soon as they had been told about their missing family members. The details did not concern her. She had watched the television news the night before and in the morning. There had been no mention of the story. She knew that was because the men were intending to act themselves. She kept them on tenterhooks till midday.

At that time, the woman had called the man known as Wolfe—the lawyer she'd used to employ the trio had given her the number. She'd disguised herself on the only occasion she met the solicitor and the only address he had for her was in Madagascar, so the targets had no means of tracking her. But now there was no longer any need for self-effacement.

'This is Sara Robbins,' she said, when he answered breathlessly. 'The White Devil's sister.'

'You have the three of them?' Wolfe said, after a pause.

'I do.'

'Where are they?'

'This is not going to be a conversation. Don't speak

until I tell you to. Listen and do exactly what I say or Amanda Mary and the others will experience agonising deaths.' She stopped to test him. The former Special Forces man knew the meaning of discipline; he did not speak. 'Good. Amanda Mary, Josh and Alison are perfectly well. I have no interest in harming them. That does not apply to you and your men. I'm going to give you a map reference. The three of you will go there together at exactly six o'clock this evening. Don't worry, I'll give you a chance to defend yourselves. Bring all the weapons you want, but the three of you must stay close together and you must be unaccompanied. If anyone else comes, you can be sure you'll never find your loved ones. Do you understand?'

'Yes.'

'I'm now terminating this call. I'll text you the map reference and send you some photographs to keep you honest, as the saying goes.'

The Soul Collector broke the connection, then sent the location and three photographs. There was one of each of the hostages, bound and gagged, in their coffins. She was sure they'd get the message about how serious she was.

The woman looked around the clearing in the New Forest, near the south coast. It was half an hour's fast walk from the nearest road and even during daylight hours, there had been few people around. Certainly none had seen her setting up her equipment and constructing her hide. She was equipped with night-vision gear, as well as black combat fatigues and helmet. By her side on the ground-sheet were her laptop and auxiliary weapons—silenced Ruger Standard pistol, sheathed combat knife and six fragmentation grenades. A modified Walther WA2000 sniper's rifle, the short stock against her right shoulder, was her main weapon, and her H and K pistol was in her belt.

The fact that she didn't hear or see them coming didn't surprise her. She knew they would come well-equipped, and not just with weapons. They didn't have night-vision gear, but they made it to the centre of the clearing by crawling from three different points. When it was exactly six o'clock, one of the men stood up.

The Soul Collector had rigged up a speaker on the opposite side of the clearing. She spoke into the microphone on her cheek.

'Stand up, all three of you,' she ordered. 'If you want to see your loved ones alive.'

The other two men slowly rose from the grass.

Now she needed all the marksmanship skills she had learned. She had to take the three of them out in rapid succession. She could see their shapes clearly enough, she had practised the shots hundreds of time. She aimed at the back of the man on the left's thigh—she was sure they would be wearing upper-body armour.

She fired once; twice; and thrice. The men grabbed their legs, their gasps audible, then they crashed to the ground. The specially made compound in the darts was both fast-acting tranquilliser and muscle relaxant. The beauty of it—a very expensive beauty—was that the victims would remain conscious and able to feel pain, but unable to speak or move.

The woman collected her auxiliary weapons and walked slowly to the three men. She removed the men's Uzi machine-pistols, semi-automatics and knives. Then she turned them all on their backs and looked into their glazed eyes.

'It's time for you to pay for what you did to my brother,' she said. Bending forward, she spat in each of their faces. 'Yes, I know I said you'd get a chance to defend yourselves and to save your people.' She laughed. 'I lied. They'll take days to die.' She squatted next to one of them and stripped off his balaclava. 'Wolfe. Also known as Sergeant Norman Lashton. You were the man in charge. I'm going to execute your men in the same way you killed my brother.'

The Soul Collector stood up quickly and fired three shots into the heads of Rommel and Geronimo from point-blank range. Then she lowered her face over Wolfe's.

'But you aren't getting anything as quick and easy, you murdering scum. I'm going to cut everything I can off you and leave you to bleed out. You'll still be alive when the crows are eating you for breakfast.'

It took her half an hour to finish with him. Then she went back to the hide, stripped off the mask, coverall and shoe protectors she'd put on before starting the knife work, and packed up. She was still smiling when she got back to the hedge where she'd stashed her motorbike.

Roger van Zandt finished the pot of coffee he'd made and went back to his laptop. Matt had sent a text a few minutes earlier, asking him to hack into the website of the Harley Street clinic where the dead man in Oxford had worked. The idea was to access patient records. That could have been a motive for murder.

Rog hammered away at the keys and was soon working on the site's firewall. He had spent the night transferring as much as he could from Sara's various accounts. He'd come up against two banks that had security systems he'd need more time to crack, but they were in the Virgin Islands and Manila, and he didn't think Sara would be able to withdraw cash from them in the U.K. Unless she was travelling with a suitcase full of cash—which couldn't be ruled out—she was about to become as poor as a church rat.

There was a triple knock on the door. He got up, heart accelerating despite the prearranged signal, taking the silenced pistol from the desk.

'Are you decent, ducky?' came a familiar voice.

Rog exhaled in relief and opened the door to Pete.

'Jesus, Boney, what do you smell like?' He closed the door and undid the chain, then opened it again.

'Sorry, I got too up close and personal with the deceased.' Pete Satterthwaite headed for the bathroom.

'Where's Slash?'

'He's meeting Matt. They're off to check on Sara's mother. What have you been up to?'

'Draining the deadly Sara's deposits. I'm going to hack into the database of the Harley Street clinic where your Oxford corpse worked. You can help me go through the files when I'm in.'

'*If* you get in,' Pete corrected.

Rog gave him a long-suffering look. 'Have you ever known me to fail?'

'I remember you missing a couple of tackles against the Essex Elephants once.'

Pete had stripped to his boxers, his discarded clothes in a garbage bag at his feet. 'What do you reckon, Rog? Has Matt got the nerve to pull this off? Without Dave and Karen to help, he's got a lot on his shoulders.'

Rog stopped typing. 'Yeah.' He looked round again. 'He'd better. Otherwise we're up to our necks in dung.'

'Delicately put, Dodger. I've never been keen on co-prophagy.'

'What?'

'The eating of ordure,' explained Pete. 'Shit-gobbling. Crap-chewing. Excret—'

'I get the picture!' Rog yelled. 'Now go and clean yourself up.'

Pete looked at himself in the mirror, a smile on his lips. Then he thought of the ruthless Sara Robbins and got serious at speed.

I'd texted Andy after I left Karen's place. We were both in baseball caps, with me wearing a false moustache as well.

'Where are we going, boss?' Andy asked in a low voice.

I looked at him, but he wasn't being ironic. When I told him our destination, he nodded. It seemed that he had no problem with me running the operation. I was the one who had doubts, but there was no time for them now. I got us each a ticket to Sydenham Hill from a machine. The early train wasn't full.

'Where did you and Pete go after you got back from Oxford?' I asked, as we pulled out.

'Needed a drink. Problem was, we stank. Eventually we found a twenty-four-hour pub next to the meat market at Smithfield. Everyone stinks there.'

I took a sniff. 'But you don't any more.'

'Good nose, Sherlock. I went back to my place to clean up and change.'

'You what?' I said, raising glances from other travellers. I lowered my voice. 'Are you out of your mind? Sara or Karen might have the place under surveillance.'

'Well, they didn't. Anyway, I took precautions on the way up here. Trust me, nobody was on my tail.'

So much for me being in charge of things.

'Let me see that note you found on the body in Oxford,' I said, my mouth close to his ear.

He opened his bag and handed me an old newspaper. Inside was a plastic bag. I examined the writing, making sure no one else could see what I was looking at. *Sorry* was the only clearly legible word. The script looked like it could have been Sara's. But why would she have left a note, never mind a body, in the house she herself had bought? Was she so confident that no one could touch her?

'We're going to see Mrs Carlton-Jones, I guess,' Andy said.

'Correct, Watson.'

'Ha. How do you want to handle it?' He was asking me to play general, after all. I wasn't sure I wanted to do that any more. The idea that my decisions could lead to my friends being injured, or worse, was getting hard to handle.

He nudged me gently in the ribs. 'I trust you, Wellsy. Dave once told me that he was certain you'd nail Sara, even if something happened to him.'

I felt my eyes dampen. Dave had said something similar to me, but I'd laughed it off. I never imagined anything would happen to him. He was our strong man, he'd been through SAS service in Northern Ireland and the first Gulf War, he'd won medals. He was our own local hero and now he was gone. I blinked and looked out into the drizzle that was blurring the shapes of the houses and car breakers' yards.

I managed to order my thoughts. Leaning close to the

American, I told him what I wanted him to do. He showed no surprise and nodded his assent.

When we came out of the station, we separated. I took a detour to Northumberland Crescent to allow Andy to get into position. Then I walked up the quiet road to number 47. There was a small Toyota in the driveway. As I'd expected, Sara's birth mother was still at home at this early hour. I put my hand under my jacket and grasped the butt of my silenced Glock. There was no sign of a motorbike, though. I was still puzzled about what the rider—presumably my former lover—had been trying to hand Mrs Carlton-Jones.

Taking off my cap and putting it in a pocket, I looked at the upstairs windows. All the curtains were open. Unless her bedroom was at the back, the occupier was up and about. I went up the paved path, looking into the front room as I approached the door.

I took a deep breath, one hand still on my weapon and the other holding my Crime Writers' Society ID card. It had been designed in the form of a warrant card. I wondered if any of my fellow novelists had used the card for nefarious purposes. Josh Hinkley, the poor sod, would have been a likely candidate, perhaps to get complimentary services from the knocking-shops near his flat.

I rang the bell. After about a minute, a grey-haired woman appeared behind the small diamond-shaped window in the door. She didn't seem to have changed much since I'd tried to interview her for my book. I hoped the moustache would prevent her from recognising me.

'Who is it?' she said, keeping the door closed.

'Detective Chief Inspector Mark Oates,' I replied, holding up my card. 'We spoke on the phone a few days ago.'

There was a pause. 'I remember, Chief Inspector.' The chain rattled and the door opened.

With my thumb obscuring the Crime Writers' Society logo, most of the photo, and my name, I kept my card visible long enough for her to register that it was official, but not long enough for her to see the details. She didn't complain when I put it back in my pocket. People had a worrying tendency to believe that strangers were who they said they were. Then again, Doris Carlton-Jones might know exactly who I was and was luring me into a trap. What if the motorbike rider had been trying to hand her a weapon, and had been back since I pulled Andy off the surveillance? Then again, I could just be getting paranoid after everything that's happened.

The woman was dressed in a dark blue trouser suit. She led me into the sitting room. 'Sit down, Chief Inspector,' she said. 'How is Inspector Jansen?'

'He's well,' I said with a smile. 'Hard at work.'

'Undercover,' she said, looking at me seriously. 'Which you, presumably, are not, since you carry identification.'

'Just plain clothes,' I said. Mrs Carlton-Jones didn't miss much. 'I won't beat about the bush,' I said. 'It's come to our attention that your daughter has returned to London.'

'My daughter?' she said, her eyes wide. 'I... My husband and I didn't have children.'

'I'm aware of that,' I said. 'But *you* did, before you met Mr Carlton-Jones.'

Now she looked upset. There were beads of sweat on her brow and she started rubbing her hands together. 'I... Yes, I did,' she said, looking down.

'Contrary to what you told Inspector Jansen,' I said harshly. 'Let's stop these games, Mrs Carlton-Jones. It's in the public domain. We've made the connection to Leslie Dunn, the White Devil. His twin sister, your daughter Sara Robbins, is wanted for murder, conspiracy to murder, kidnapping and malicious wounding, as well as fleeing a crime scene. I have a simple question for you.'

'I know what it is,' the elderly woman said, her voice querulous, 'and the answer is no, I haven't seen her.'

I was watching her carefully. She was pretty convincing, but I needed more, and needed to seem authoritative. 'Then you'll have no objection if I search the house.'

She met my gaze. 'Shouldn't you have a warrant for that?'

'I should, and I will get one if necessary, though failure to co-operate won't do you any favours. If you allow me to check the house, I can be out of here in a matter of minutes and it'll be the last you hear of it.' I gave her what I hoped was an encouraging smile.

'Oh, very well,' she said. 'Go where you like.'

I stood up. 'Thank you, Mrs Carlton-Jones,' I said, raising a hand. 'Please don't get up. I'd prefer to do this on my own.' I looked around the room, then moved to the rear, where a door led into the kitchen. I opened cupboard doors and ran my eye over the fridge door for any sign of messages from Sara. There was nothing. I checked the drawers too, in case there was a concealed weapon. There were kitchen knives, but that was all.

I went out of the door that opened on to the hall. There was a cupboard under the stairs—it was full of boxes and a vacuum cleaner. Moving upstairs, I glanced out of the window on the side of the house. I couldn't see Andy. There were four doors on the first floor, two of them open. The front room must have been the main bedroom, a double bed with an embroidered cover neatly spread over it. There was a photo of Doris Carlton-Jones with a smiling bald man, presumably her dead husband. She looked reserved. I wondered if there had ever been a time when she wasn't troubled by the children she gave away in the first days of their lives. The woman looked at least ten years younger in the shot, so it had been taken long before the White Devil and Sara became the focus of frenzied tabloid attention. I tried to imagine what it must have felt like, to know that your children were vicious killers. I shivered as Lucy's face flashed before me. My beautiful daughter was in hiding because of the woman downstairs's child. Strangely, I didn't feel anger, but sorrow. I told myself to get a grip. Sara might be waiting for me down the hall.

I took out my pistol and walked to the first door. I touched the handle, then opened the door quickly. Inside, both hands gripping my weapon, I pointed it at the corners, one by one, as Dave had taught us. Nobody. The room was a study, a computer on a desk and rows of books on the shelves. It didn't take me long to find *The Death List*. The spine showed it had been opened frequently. My photo was on the back cover. That put me on my toes. I went towards the next door, glancing into the bathroom to be sure it was empty. I breathed in and followed the procedure again when I flung the door open. This room too was unoccupied. The duvet on the single bed was plumped and perfectly aligned. I slid a hand underneath. It was stone cold. Back on the landing, I looked up at the ceiling. There was a panel in a wooden frame. I took the chair from the study and stood on it. I was in an awkward position, because I couldn't cover more than one angle with my pistol. There was nothing for it. I pushed the panel up and aside, then looked around. Apart from the water tank and a lot of insulating material, the space was empty.

I put the panel and chair back, and went downstairs, pistol back in my jacket. Mrs Carlton-Jones was waiting for me.

'Satisfied?' she asked brusquely. Clearly she was no longer shaken. 'Chief Inspector, I can assure you that if I saw Sara Robbins, I would tell the police immediately. I know what she looks like, thanks to the photographs that were all over the newspapers and TV channels.' She shook her head. 'And that awful book her lover wrote.'

I tried not to look embarrassed and was glad she hadn't recognised me. It was suddenly obvious how much pain *The Death List* had caused. I remembered what Karen had said, about the book being a Faustian pact. I'd arrogantly signed up to write it, oblivious to the feelings of others—not just of Sara's birth mother, but of the families whose members the White Devil had slaughtered. Maybe some stories were better left untold.

I thanked Mrs Carlton-Jones.

As she closed the door, she said, 'I hope we won't meet again.'

I walked away, feeling like a leper. Then I saw Andy appear from behind the garage. His expression was grim and he was carrying what looked very much like a human skull.

Faik Jabar had found a heap of old clothes outside a charity shop in Stoke Newington. They didn't smell too good, but neither did he. In a dank alleyway, he stripped off his trousers, gasping as the fabric came away from the wounds on his legs. The trousers were an old man's, the bottoms flapping above his trainers, and the ancient tan duffel coat was tight across his shoulders. At least the pistol he'd taken from his tormentor fitted into one of the inside pockets. Head down, Faik walked out on to the pavement and headed west. He had no money, so he couldn't use public transport. Walking was the only option. It took him three hours to get to Soho.

The strip joints and massage parlours were open, but there wasn't much activity. At the first one he tried, a thick-set muscle-man told him to go fuck himself, there were no Albanians there. But he struck lucky at the next one. He went upstairs, following the signs to !Sexy Susie's Sauna EtSEXera!. When he asked for Safet Shkrelli, the bottle blonde, who must have been older than his mother, told him to wait.

A thin man with a pencil moustache, wearing a grubby suit, came out to meet him. 'What does a piece of crap like you want with Mr Shkrelli?' he demanded, eyeing the young man and wrinkling his nose. 'What are you? A Turk?'

'Kurd,' replied Faik. 'Tell him I know where his missing numbers man is.'

The man raised an eyebrow, then took out his mobile. He spoke rapidly in a language like no other Faik had ever heard. When he'd finished, he smiled insincerely. 'Mr Shkrelli would like to see you. Come downstairs when I call.' He headed for the street.

A few minutes later, Faik heard his voice again. When he reached the main door, he saw a black Mercedes at the kerb, its engine idling and the nearside rear door open. His weapon was taken by a gorilla. Faik thought of what had happened the last time he'd got into a gang member's car, but he didn't hesitate. Someone had to stop the bitch with the devil's face who had set the gangs at each others' throats, and Safet Shkrelli was the best bet, probably the only bet.

Neither the man from the sauna nor the heavily-built driver spoke to him. They went north, but after King's Cross he was told to put his head between his knees. He felt the point of a knife in his side, so he obeyed. He preferred not to know where Shkrelli lived.

After what Faik thought was about twenty minutes, the car drove over gravel and stopped. He was told to stay as he was, then a door opened and a black hood was pulled over his head. He was led inside, tripping on steps. It seemed they walked for a long time before he was pushed into a seat and the hood tugged off.

Faik blinked and took in a large, young-looking man with close-cropped black hair. He was sitting behind an enormous desk.

'I'm Safet Shkrelli,' the man said, picking up a silver revolver with pearl handles. 'Tell me why I shouldn't shoot you right now.'

'You know why,' Faik replied. His voice was steady; he had nothing to lose. 'I can take you to your numbers man.'

'Where is he?'

Faik shook his head slowly. 'I take you there,' he repeated. 'Then you protect me.'

Shkrelli thought about that. 'Is he alive?' he asked.

'He was when I last saw him—just.'

'What happened to him?'

'I'll tell you when we get there.'

The muzzle of the weapon was suddenly pointing at Faik's face. 'Are you setting me up, boy?' the Albanian asked. 'Are your people planning on ambushing me? I use dum-dum bullets. Do you know how much damage one of them can do? Your own mother won't recognise you.'

Faik held his gaze. 'This is no set-up, Mr Shkrelli. There is no ambush. All I want is for you to protect me until you find the…the person who took your man.'

Safet Shkrelli drank from a bottle of water. 'So take me, boy. Tell me the district.'

'Stoke Newington.'

The hood came back down over Faik's head. He was taken through the process in reverse and heard someone else join the driver in the front of the car. After they had driven for about a quarter of an hour, the hood was removed. Faik looked around, recognising the streets around Finsbury Park station. Ahead, he could see two more black Mercedes and behind was a black Land Cruiser. All the vehicles were full.

'Tell us the address,' the driver said.

Faik did so and the driver relayed it via his hands-free device. The column drove down Green Lanes. People stared and some of them raised mobile phones to their ears. The local gangs—the Shadows, the King's men— wouldn't be slow to gather. Faik's armpits were drenched in sweat, but his breathing was regular. The lead car turned into the street and stopped, blocking the road. Men got out, their hands in their jackets. The man with the thin moustache got out and beckoned to Faik to follow. He did so, then headed for the door he had come out of that morning—it seemed like days had passed.

When he pushed the door open, not particularly surprised that it hadn't been shut by the last person to leave, he turned his head and saw Safet Shkrelli get out of the second Mercedes. Bodyguards quickly gathered around him and walked him to the house. Suddenly it struck Faik that if his captor had managed to remove the body, Shkrelli would dispose of him in seconds. He went up the stair quickly, nervous for the first time.

He needn't have been. The Albanian numbers man was still in the second-floor flat. His body was on the living room floor, as it was when Faik had escaped. But his head was on top of the television, his hands in the bathroom and his feet in the bedroom.

After looking around, the man with the moustache threw up on Safet Shkrelli's shoes.

24

I walked towards Andy, signalling to him to stay where he was to avoid scaring the neighbours. I joined him at the rear of the garage.

'It was in a trunk in the garage,' he said. 'I forced the door at the back because I got curious.'

I pulled on latex gloves like the ones he was wearing and took the skull from him. I had no idea how old it was, but it was very clean and so white that I wondered if it was plastic. But the feel of it was definitely bone. The question was, who did it belong to? And also, where was the rest of the body?

There was the rasping roar of a motorbike engine.

'Shit!' Andy said, running past me to the front of the garage.

I followed him, trying to shield the skull under my jacket. I was in time to see a figure in black leathers and helmet crouching over a powerful bike, as Doris Carlton-Jones climbed on behind. Jesus, was it Sara?

Before I could put the skull down and draw my weapon, the metallic red motorbike rocketed down the street. Not long afterwards I heard a less deafening engine noise to my left.

'Get in, Matt!' Andy said, from the driver's seat of Mrs Carlton-Jones's hatchback.

Somehow I managed to do that without dropping the skull. Andy reversed at speed, spun the wheel and set off down the street.

'Hot-wired,' I said. 'Nice one, Slash.'

'Being in a teen gang had its uses,' he said, swerving out of the driveway and accelerating after the motorbike. 'So the old woman was in on it all along. I've seen that machine before.'

I grabbed my door handle as he braked hard and then turned out of the crescent. The motorbike was still in sight, but there were several cars between it and us.

'Looks like Sara and she have had a family reunion,' I said. 'Bloody hell, what are you doing?'

Andy had veered into the opposite lane, provoking loud horn blasts.

'That's an idea,' he said, hitting his horn. In under a minute, we were only one car behind the bike. 'It's a Transalp, a powerful beast. This piece of crap has got no chance of catching it on an open road.'

'Cool it, big man,' I said, my heart still pounding. 'The rider's bound to have seen us.'

'Good,' the American said, slamming the gas pedal to the floor and overtaking the car ahead. 'Maybe she'll make a mistake.'

There was no sign of that. The motorbike had clear space in front of it and we struggled to stay in touch. The lights ahead were green, but by the time we approached, they were changing.

'Brace, brace!' Andy yelled, following the bike to the

right and narrowly missing a pair of boys who had started to cross the road.

'Will you slow down, Slash?'

The bike had sped away again, towards Dulwich.

'Where do you think they're heading? Maybe they're going to murder someone else,' he said, running another light, just as it was clear the motorbike was gone for good.

'Fuck!' Andy roared, slamming his hands on the wheel. 'Did you see which way it went?'

'No. That supermarket rig got in the way.'

'Forget it,' I said. 'Pull in over there. I need to see if Doctor Faustus has sent another message.'

I pulled out my laptop. It took a few minutes for the wi-fi card to latch on to a signal. I opened my e-mail programme and watched the new messages stack up. Most were from family and friends, reporting in. Caroline said Fran and Lucy were fine, but I could tell she was going spare in the safe house. I assumed the last message was porn spam—the sender was *mynameishelen*—but I checked before deleting and saw I'd nearly screwed up in a big way. It was from the killer. I read it aloud:

Well, Matt, here I am again. I bet the sender name's got you wondering. Call yourself an English graduate? Who did Faustus lust after? That's right, Helen of Troy. Why am I using her name? That's for you to work out. Hey, guess what. It's deadline time again. Since you identified Adrian Brooks correctly—even though I couldn't resist dealing with your treacherous friend Hinkley instead—I'm giving you even less time. Answer this by twelve midday, and I mean today, clever boy:

I have enslaved Scotsmen
As well as bestial Ozzies.
Tiny Goethe polishes us sadly,
Building cheaply for blind Cain.
(Not to mention Abel.)
See you in hell!
Helen.
(And Doctor Faustus, of course)

'What's that all about?' Andy said with a groan.

I was writing the clue down in my notebook. When I'd finished, I sent it to Caroline and my mother, then logged off and closed the laptop.

'What does it mean?' I repeated. 'We've got just over three hours to work that out.' I looked at the title again. 'Helen. Is that Sara finally hinting that she's been sending the messages and doing the murders?'

'What, because she's used a woman's name?'

I nodded, still examining the words. 'Goethe wrote a version of *Faust,* so Helen fits with that as well as Marlowe's *Doctor Faustus.*'

'Who's Goethe?'

'Eighteenth-century German writer,' I replied. 'Bestial Ozzies? Is that a reference to the ex–Black Sabbath singer?'

'What? Ozzie Osbourne?' The American grinned. 'I saw him live when I was a kid. Sick, but a gas.'

'Yeah, bestial would go with him,' I said, trying to concentrate. 'Bestial means "beastly" or "brutish".'

'There was that story about Ozzie biting the head off a bat on stage. That was pretty brutish.' Andy looked around. 'Are we staying here?'

'What? No.'

'Shall I take this heap back to the Carlton-Jones pad?'

I stared at him. 'No chance. I don't want her to have a set of wheels.'

'We could stake the place out.'

I shook my head. 'She probably won't be going back there in a hurry.'

'You don't reckon she'll report her car stolen?'

I thought about that. 'She might, I suppose. Give me a few minutes with this bloody clue.'

Andy grunted. 'Shit, we'd better cover that thing up, man.'

I looked round. The skull was sitting on the back seat, its teeth set in an uneven smile. Whose body had it come from? Andy got out and took off his jacket. He put it over the skull and got back into the driver's seat.

'Let's go,' he said.

'Okay. Park near my old flat in Herne Hill. We can get the train to the centre from there.'

As Andy drove, I ran my eyes back and forwards over the lines, scribbling down ideas. 'I have enslaved'—I have captured, I have taken prisoner, I have sold into slavery? Why Scotsmen? I didn't know many, though that probably wasn't significant. Scotsmen could be Celts. Therefore, Celtic Football Club supporters? Meaning Glaswegians? There were a couple of Glasgow crime writers who got completely pissed at festivals. Could one of them be the target? Scotsmen: Highlanders, Lowlanders, islanders, Gaelic-speakers, Picts?

I moved on to the second line. 'As well as bestial Ozzies.' I didn't buy the Ozzie Osbourne connection. Who else were Ozzies? Was it a reference to Aussies, Australians? Or something to do with the Wizard of Oz? There were beasts in that. Flying monkeys, as far as I could remember. 'Tiny Goethe polishes us.' Goethe as the author of *Faust,* who made use of Helen as a character? I racked my brain. What else did Goethe write? He was a polymath, but my knowledge of German literature didn't go much further. I had a vague idea about a work called *The Sorrows of Young Werther.* Could that link up with the word 'sadly'? But I definitely didn't know anyone called Werther. I'd have to do a search on the Internet for Goethe's life and works. Was he a 'tiny' man? And why was he polishing? Was he into buffing things up? Buffing people up, as in 'us'?

I shook my head. I was getting nowhere with that line, so I moved on. 'Building cheaply for blind Cain.' As far as I could remember from the Old Testament, Cain wasn't blind. He was a murderer, though, which was suggestive. The first of that kind, and his victim was his own brother, the Abel of the fifth line. But Sara didn't kill her brother, the White Devil. She worshipped him. Someone else's brother, then, but whose? And why was the German poet 'building cheaply'? Was he a cowboy builder in his spare time? Could the target be one of those? No, that didn't work. There were thousands of cowboy builders in London alone. How could I find the right one? As for the last line, why was Abel not to be mentioned, even though his name was the clue's last word? Was that significant, mentioning something even though it was said not to be? Hell's teeth, my mind was about to experience meltdown.

We left Doris Carlton-Jones's car, taking the skull wrapped in Andy's jacket. She wouldn't find her wheels—unless Sara had put a bug on the hatchback.

Of course, as the latest impenetrable riddle showed, anything was possible.

Jeremy Andrewes had eaten a stodgy breakfast at an old-fashioned gentleman's club, but the indigestion he now felt was worth it. He had got his hands on a seriously juicy story. A gangland informer he sometimes used had rung him and told him that one of the journalist's lot—i.e. the aristocracy, or 'nobs', as the snout called them—had moved into cocaine dealing. A photo of the said nob arrived on his phone. The man in question was standing behind a table. On it were clear bags filled with a white powder and piles of banknotes. Even better, Jeremy recognised the man's unmistakable face immediately—he was a longstanding friend of his father's. It was easy to arrange a supposedly social breakfast.

After they had exchanged gossip about who was marrying whom, who was two-timing whom and with whom, and who had the best chance of getting fox-hunting made legal again, the journalist cut to the chase.

'Tell me,' he said, with a sly smile, 'how's the Colombian marching powder trade?'

The earl blanched. 'What?' he said, in a faint voice, his unprepossessing features twitching.

'Don't worry, I'm not going to write a story about you,' Andrewes lied. 'I'm only interested in the people you do business with. I know you wouldn't be foolish enough to set yourself up against them.' He was pretty sure he'd been provided with the information to ensure the earl's good behaviour—whether Jeremy exposed him or just hinted that he might do so in the future, the effect would be the same.

'What were you doing?' the journalist continued. 'Buying or selling?'

'Selling, of course,' the earl said, glancing around the wood-panelled room. 'I…I happened to, em…come across a quantity of the drug and I wanted to get rid of it as soon as possible.'

'For what would appear to be a substantial amount of money.' Andrewes grinned. 'That should help with the maintenance of the castle. As well as with your other pursuits.'

The older man's expression was grim, but he didn't speak.

'All right, tell me who you sold to,' the journalist said.

There was a long pause. 'You promise you won't refer to me? These people were pretty…unpleasant.'

You must have felt right at home, Andrewes thought. 'My word is my bond. I'm working on a big exposé of the drugs trade in London. This will only be a small piece in the jigsaw.'

The earl dabbed a napkin to his damp lips. 'Very well. It would be a good thing if the people I sold to were cleared out of this country.'

The journalist made no comment, even though that was hardly the *Daily Independent*'s line on immigration. 'Let me guess,' he said, trying to make things easier for the other man. 'Kurds? Turks? There's been some messy stuff between them recently in East London.'

'Has there?' the earl said indifferently. 'No, no, these people were Albanians.'

'Really?' Jeremy Andrewes was impressed by the older man's nerve. The Albanians were the up-and-coming force and they were even more ruthless than the Turkish Shadows. 'I don't suppose you got any names?'

'Nobody introduced themselves, if that's what you mean.'

The journalist tried to disguise his disappointment.

The earl gave a twisted smile. 'But I'm not a complete idiot. I did do my homework. They're a family called Shkrelli.' He struggled to pronounce the name and spittle flew from his mouth.

Andrewes felt like a runner who'd just broken the hundred metres world record. A member of the peerage selling coke to the most violent gang in the country—his editor would kiss his feet. He managed to end the conversation and get out of the club, without, he hoped, making the earl suspicious. He thought about going back to his flat to write the piece, but he wanted to be in the office when he submitted it.

He hailed a taxi, took out his BlackBerry and started on a first draft. He was so engrossed that he didn't notice the figure in black leathers to the rear, weaving through the traffic on a powerful motorbike. It was still there, fifty metres behind, when he got out and went into the *Daily Indie* building.

Pete was squinting at the computer screen as he scrolled down the plastic surgery clinic's records. Rog had got into them, but he needed a break from his laptop so Pete had taken over. There were drops of sweat on his bald head. The only problem with Rog's cousin's flat was that the central heating control was jammed at twenty-five degrees

Celsius. Even though the window was open, the room was like an oven.

'Gotcha!' Pete said. 'Get a load of this, Dodger.' He pointed to the screen.

'Are you sure?' Rog said. 'You've only been looking for a few minutes.'

'Oh, I never take long,' Bonehead said archly.

Rog went over and leaned towards the screen. 'Lauren May Cuthbertson, date of birth 23/5/1972, address Flat 15, Gannett House, Ambledon Street, Stoke Newington.' He turned to Pete. 'What's the big deal?'

Bonehead clicked on the link titled Pre-Treatment Photo. 'What do you reckon?'

'Jesus.' Rog stared in horror at the face that appeared before him. The nose was bent and flattened. There were also large and pendulous tumours on both sides of the mouth. 'It's the Elephant Woman.'

'Near enough.' Pete clicked on the Post-Treatment Photo.

They watched intently as the image recomposed itself.

'What happened to her?' Rog said.

The tumours had gone, but the skin around and below the mouth was swollen, heavily bruised and scarred. But that wasn't the worst feature. Although the patient's nose had been straightened and reconstructed, something terrible had happened to her upper lip. It was split open, the pink gum and front teeth visible. Lauren Cuthbertson was staring straight at the camera, her expression dull-eyed.

'Scary woman,' Pete said. He clicked off the photo and on to her patient file. He moved through it slowly so they could both get the gist. It seemed that the tumours, though not malignant, had grown substantially in the year before the operation. The nose had been damaged in a fight when Lauren Cuthbertson was a teenager. The surgeon, James Maclehose, the man whose body had been found by Pete and Andy in the house in Oxford, had been successful in removing the tumours and in fixing the nose. However, the upper lip had been damaged during surgery. Furthermore, skin grafts placed over the wounds left by the removal of the tumours had not been successful. The patient had been advised to undergo further surgery, but she had refused, claiming that Maclehose was incompetent. The surgeon's notes stated that she had been abusive, and had threatened him and his staff. The last time she was in the clinic, the police had been called after she smashed an antique vase over Mr Maclehose's computer.

'What do you think?' Pete asked.

'What was the date of the operation?'

'January 21st. And she was last in the clinic on February 29th.'

'Under a month ago.' Rog ran his hands through his hair. 'You think she killed Maclehose?'

Pete nodded. 'She's five foot ten and twelve stone three. If she works out—and the notes say that her level of physical fitness was high—she could have overpowered him easily. You saw the most recent photo. She didn't exactly look friendly.'

'Mm.' Rog moved closer and hit the keys until he found the payment records. 'I tell you what puzzles me. She lives in Stoke Newington, in what doesn't sound like high-end housing. How did she afford a Harley Street surgeon?'

'Good point.'

Rog brought up a statement of account. 'Look,' he said, pointing. 'She paid by cheque. Twelve thousand, four hundred and thirty-seven pounds.'

'And seventy-three pence,' Pete added. He shrugged. 'Maybe she inherited the dosh.'

'Or she's protected.'

Pete looked at him. 'What do you mean?'

'All those murders in East London—she lives in the vicinity.'

'You mean she's in one of the gangs?'

Rog nodded. 'Could be. They're not all from abroad, you know. And, as far as I can remember, no one in the home-grown gangs has been murdered.'

'Bloody hell, Dodger, you're using your imagination a lot there. Anyway, why was the body of the surgeon left in a house owned by Sara Robbins?'

'That I don't know.' Rog smiled. 'Yet. I'm going to get into this Lauren's bank account and find out where the money came from.'

'If she's in a gang, it could have all been cash deposits,' Pete pointed out. 'We should tell Matt.'

'Tell him what? Wait till I've checked the source of her funds. My money's on it being dirty.'

Pete shook his head. 'I'm not taking that bet. What I don't like is the idea that the cow's running around scot-free. If she really did kill the surgeon, you'd better hope she doesn't realise you've been snooping on her bank account. Otherwise you might be her next victim.'

'We, Boney,' Rog corrected.

Pete looked nervously at the door, and drummed his fingers on the butt of his pistol.

* * *

After Andy and I had got back to Victoria, we exited the station and headed for a cyber-café. I needed to see if Caroline and Fran had come up with anything on the clue. My own thoughts were still random and chaotic, and there were only two hours left till the next deadline. Even though Doctor Faustus had killed Josh Hinkley instead of Adrian Brooks, I had to believe that I could save the target.

While Andy went to the counter to buy coffee and a Danish, I logged on to my e-mail programme. My heart skipped a beat. There was nothing from Caroline or Fran. Jesus, could Sara have got to them via the signals? Surely that was impossible. I'd been moving around and the likelihood of her picking up my wi-fi signal in the huge city was minimal. So why hadn't they replied? Maybe the message hadn't got through. I sent it again, then looked at my watch. I couldn't afford to wait. Someone's life was hanging by a thread. I had to find the solution.

Andy came back with a mound of pastries and two mugs of coffee.

'On a diet?' I asked, taking out my notebook.

'Yeah, boss,' he said, grinning. 'Whatever you say, boss.'

I looked at the clue. 'Bestial Ozzies.' Could that mean animals from Australia? Possums? Crocodiles? Wallabies? Tasmanian Devils? Koalas? None of them seemed to get me any further. I reread the last two lines. There was some game being played with Cain and Abel. Why was 'Cain' 'blind'? I tried to remember the conventions of cryptic crosswords—this may not have been a crossword, but it was definitely full of hidden secrets. Repunctuate. I did that, removing all the full stops, commas and brackets.

Zilch. I removed all the capitals. Ditto. What else? Anagrams. Bugger that—too time-consuming. Word order. I fiddled with that for a couple of minutes, but, again, decided it would take hours. Homophones. The only one that struck me was 'Abel'—it sounded like 'able'. Words with two or more meanings. I'd already played around with 'bestial', meaning 'animal', and got nowhere. It also meant 'brutish'—brutish Australians? The only Aussie crime writer I knew was clever, witty and re-markably well-behaved. How about part for whole? Could 'Ozzies' mean a specific Australian rather than Austra-lians, plural? And the same for 'Scotsmen'?

Andy put a sticky finger on the first line of the clue. 'The English enslaved the Scots, didn't they?'

'That's one way of looking at it,' I said, raising an eyebrow at him. And then I got it. 'Shit!' I said, making the pretty girl at the till laugh. 'You're in this, Andy. Or should I say Andrew?'

He stared at me. I looked back down at the clue. '"I have enslaved Scotsmen". They're Andrews, plural.' I brought my hand down on my knee. 'That's it. Jeremy Andrewes.'

'The shithead journalist who's been busting your balls?'

I nodded. 'Like the other clues, this is a series of alter-natives for the different syllables. "I have enslaved Scots-men" means that the Scotsmen, the Andrews, are mine—so "my Andrews". "My" is made up of the last two syllables of "Jeremy".'

The American was chewing slowly, his eyes on the clue.

'"As well as" is another way of saying "and", as in "Andrews".'

Finally, I understood the 'bestial Ozzies'. I'd been close.

'It *is* an Australian animal—the kangaroo, also referred to as "roo".'

'He was in *Winnie the Pooh*,' Andy said. 'I used to like that cartoon.'

'I'm very happy for you, Slash. "Roos" sounds like "r-u-e-s", meaning "repents" or, I suppose, "feels sad", as in "sadly" in line three.'

Andy was struggling to keep up. 'What about "Tiny Goethe polishes", then?'

I thought about that. Sara or her sidekick had no doubt chosen Goethe to distract me because of the Faust connection. 'Goethe was a German. We would have called him a "gerry" if he'd turned up in the Second World War.'

'You mean, like the first bit of "Jeremy"?'

'Well done, big man.'

'Yeah, but why "tiny"?' Then Andy laughed. 'Maybe it's the mouse in *Tom and Jerry*. He was pretty small.'

I thought it was probably just that Jerry was a diminutive of Jeremy, but I let him have it. '"Building cheaply" is "jerry-building" and "blind Cain"…what is that? Blind. Yes! To make someone blind, you take out their eyes. "Eye" sounds like the letter "i"—take it from "Cain" and you get "can", which means "able", as in sounds like "Abel", the Biblical character. Voila.'

'Jeez, Wellsy, it's a hell of a lot just for two names.' He peered at the clue again. 'What about "polishes"?'

I looked at the letters that made up Andrewes. 'It's an anagram. You can get "sand" or "sander" out of the surname. Sanding is a form of polishing.'

Andy looked at his watch. 'We've still got an hour and a half. Are you going to tell this Andrewes guy to watch out?'

I shook my head. 'No, I'm not. I'm not going to send the right answer at noon, either.'

Andy switched into John MacEnroe–mode. 'You cannot be serious. Sara might take him down.'

'Not if we're looking after him.'

He smiled. 'I get it. You're going to use Jeremy Andrewes as bait.'

I nodded. 'I think he deserves that, after all the bollocks he's written about me recently.'

'Neat, my man, very neat.' The smile vanished from his lips. 'There's only one problem. To draw her out, we're going to have put Andrewes where he makes a good target. That means we'll be targets too.'

'Correct,' I said, catching his eye. 'But I'm prepared to risk it, for Dave. You?'

'Count me in,' Andy said, without a second's hesitation.

25

Karen Oaten and Amelia Browning were standing outside the house in Stoke Newington with Ron Paskin. CSIs in dark blue coveralls were going up the steps to the front door. There was a crowd of rubberneckers behind the barrier tape. Inspector Ozal and other Homicide East detectives were moving through it, asking people if they had seen anything suspicious.

John Turner brought a painfully thin, elderly woman forward. She was dressed in a faded blue coat and tattered slippers. 'This is Mrs Maisie Jones,' the inspector said. 'She lives across the street.'

'I saw them,' the woman said, gripping Karen Oaten's arm with a clawlike hand. 'There were a lot of them. In big, black cars.' She leaned closer. 'They looked *foreign.*' She spoke the last word with a grimace.

'When was this, Mrs Jones?' Paskin asked, with an encouraging smile.

'Only about an hour ago,' she replied. 'Some of them went inside. They were all dressed in suits—looked expensive— except for one man. He was young, but he was wearing the sort of clothes that old men who live on the streets have. Dirty. I bet he smelled. He looked frightened an' all.'

'And then what happened?' The superintendent asked patiently.

'The men at the cars got spoken to by the locals.' Maisie Jones looked up at Paskin. 'They're mostly Turkish, you know. Criminals, the lot of them. They were telling the others to sling their 'ook, weren't they? Well, they didn't like that one little bit. I saw them take out their guns and the shooting started.'

When Oaten and her subordinates had arrived, an ambulance was taking away the third and last body. Even though uniformed personnel had arrived very quickly, the shooters had dispersed and none of the 'big, black cars' had been found.

'Did you see the men come back out of the house, Mrs Jones?' Amelia Browning asked.

'Ooh, call me Maisie, love,' the old woman said, with a loose smile that revealed ill-fitting dentures. 'Yes, I did. The young bloke was marched to the second car and another man got in the back with him. I think he was the boss, because three or four others were standing round him to make sure he didn't get hit. Quite a few of the men in suits were hit, but only the one got left behind. They tried to grab his body, but they were outnumbered by then, so they had to drive off.'

They waited for more, but Mrs Jones seemed to have said her piece.

'Would you like Sergeant Browning here to help you home?' Oaten asked. 'See if she saw anything else,' she added, in a low voice to Amelia.

'Wonderful,' Paskin said. 'Gunfight at the O.K. Corral. When we got here, the kids were picking up the cartridge cases and throwing them at each other. Thank Christ no actual weapons were left behind.'

'The local gang members would have grabbed them,' Turner said. 'This is Shadow territory, isn't it?'

The superintendent nodded.

'What about the intruders?' Oaten asked.

'Albanians, we think,' said Paskin. 'The dead guy had a letter in his pocket. One of my team has been learning the language.'

'Do you think this was an attempt to move into the area, guv?' the Welshman asked.

'No, Taff. They don't work that way, do they? At least, not in broad daylight.'

Karen Oaten nodded. 'You're right. The Albanian families tend to buy their way in using middlemen. When they've got a foothold, they either kill or kidnap the local leaders and their families. They don't go for all-out war in the streets.'

'So what were they doing here?' Turner asked.

Paskin looked up at the second-floor windows. A uniformed officer had seen the open door and gone to investigate. He was in shock and the pathologist was still trying, literally, to piece together what had happened upstairs.

'I'd say the young guy led them to the flat. The guy whose body was dismembered was probably an Albanian.'

'Sounds reasonable,' Oaten said. 'They'd have been hoping to find him alive. Otherwise they wouldn't have come in such numbers.'

Turner looked at his boss thoughtfully. 'Do you reckon the young man's still alive?'

'Not if he had anything to do with what happened to the victim, Taff,' Ron Paskin said, his expression grim.

'The Albanians are usually all related,' Oaten said. 'Like the original Sicilian mafia.' She turned to the superintendent. 'I'd like to attach one of my people to your team till the situation out here is resolved.'

Her former boss nodded. 'No problem, Karen. I could do with an extra pair of hands.' He looked down the street ruefully. 'An extra hundred pairs of hands.'

Oaten and Turner glanced at each other. They both knew that feeling. They walked to the chief inspector's car, the Welshman asking bystanders to move aside.

'What do you think, guv?' he asked.

'That the killer's losing his grip. Dismembering a body is a big step from the earlier killings.' She got in and started the engine.

'We don't know that the person who chopped up the Albanian also killed the Kurds and the Turks,' Turner said.

Oaten looked over her shoulder and reversed down the street. 'Not for certain, no. The CSIs have got plenty of fingerprints in the flat here, but nothing to compare them with from the other scenes. But you know the murders are connected, even if the same person didn't actually carry them out. Personally, I think it is the same killer.'

'Could it be Sara Robbins?'

'If it is, Matt had better keep his head down because she's really lost it now.'

Turner pushed himself back in his seat as she accelerated. 'Steady, guv. It's a busy road.'

Karen Oaten braked hard behind a bus. 'Remember something else,' she said. 'The body in the house in Oxford. It looks like she owns that property—the name on the deeds is a composite of her mother's maiden name and the names given to Sara and her twin before they were adopted. What kind of person keeps a rotting corpse in their hall?'

John Turner didn't answer. He remembered all too well the last person he knew who had done something similar.

Oaten's phone rang. She fitted the earpiece and answered.

'Yes, Doctor Redrose,' she said, shaking her head at the Welshman. 'How can I help you?' She listened, her jaw dropping. 'Are you sure?' She listened again, and then thanked him and signed off.

'Jesus,' she said. 'The old ghoul has his uses.'

'What's happened?'

'After the case conference, his curiosity was piqued. He didn't do the autopsies on the gang victims. He went to the morgue and checked the finger and toenails of the two Kurds. Guess what he found?'

'Don't tell me they'd been clipped.'

'Yup. But only one toe in each case, as if the killer was being careful not to draw attention.' She gave a hollow laugh. 'That's how Redrose spotted it, of course. Nobody cuts only one nail themselves, at least not usually. He's pretty sure that a small number of hairs have been taken from the head and groin of each dead man too. Not enough to make a conclusive link.'

'But the toenails do that,' Turner said. 'The likelihood of both victims having cut one nail recently must be minimal.'

Karen Oaten nodded. 'So there's a good chance that the same killer is behind the crime-writer and the gangland murders. Or the same killers.'

The inspector swallowed hard. 'And that devil worship played a part in them all.'

Neither of them needed to say it aloud, but the White Devil was even more in the frame—and, apparently, even more dangerous than ever.

* * *

I found out from a friend at the *Daily Indie* that Jeremy Andrewes was in the office. Andy and I were outside in Clerkenwell Road—he was twenty metres left of the entrance to the paper's building, and I was about the same distance to the right, both of us on the opposite side of the road. If the journalist stayed inside, I didn't see how Sara could get to him, unless she was already in the office. I didn't think that was too likely. You needed an electronic pass to get past the security door in reception. I could have got in using mine, but it would take me a long time to check the whole place. Besides, I was in the news. As soon as anyone recognised me, I'd have difficulty getting out again and that would screw up my plan completely. I'd removed the fake moustache. I didn't think it would fool people who knew me well.

Ten minutes before twelve, I nodded to Andy and then retired to a café down the road that supported wi-fi access. I booted up my laptop. On the ghost site I found a message from my mother. That was a major relief. She'd cracked the 'Andrews' part of the clue, but hadn't got Jeremy. Then again, she didn't know the journalist, so she hadn't been able to make the leap that I had.

I clicked on the message that appeared at exactly 11.59. It was from *wotacarveup*. I wrote my reply—Karen Oaten—and sent it. Two minutes later, an answer arrived.

Karen Oaten? You really have lost your grip, Matt. And to think that I'd have kept my word if you'd got the right answer...
Soon it'll be your turn.
Doom and disaster!
Helen

I smiled and logged off. Then I picked up my mobile and speed-dialled Jeremy Andrewes's number.

'Crime,' he answered.

'A very good description of your articles, recently.'

'Hello, Matt.' He didn't sound even slightly embarrassed. 'All's fair in etc., etc. Where are you?'

'Never mind that. I've got an exclusive for you.'

'Really?' As I'd expected, he was suspicious. 'Why don't you write it yourself?'

'Because I'm too busy trying to stay alive.'

He thought about that for a while. 'All right,' he said, at last. 'What are you going to do? Dictate your story to me over the phone?'

'No chance. My mobile frequency might be being scanned. I need you to meet me.'

'Fair enough. Where?'

'In front of the British Museum. You've got fifteen minutes.' I cut the connection, put the laptop in my bag and went out on the street. Andy had moved nearer the paper's entrance. He was looking out for me and watched carefully as I hailed a cab. I made sure I raised my right arm. If I'd have used the left, he'd have known something was wrong.

I was at the museum in five minutes. That gave me a bit of time to check out the courtyard in front of the wide steps that led to the entrance. It was filled with the usual crowds of tourists and school groups. That was why I'd chosen it. It was busy enough not only to tempt Sara or her sidekicks into thinking that they could have a go at Andrewes, but also to give me cover. There were also security personnel all around. They might come in handy when it came to preventing Sara's getaway, as well as protecting innocent bystanders. I felt queasy about inciting her to violence in such a public place, but I had no option. If I'd invited the journalist to my flat, she'd have smelled a rat, and I'd also have run the risk of the cops finding out where I was, assuming they had the building under surveillance.

I went up the steps and looked at my watch. I reckoned we had five minutes or less. Andy would follow Jeremy Andrewes—he knew what he looked like from the photo above the article he'd written in today's paper. But if he couldn't find a taxi immediately, the journalist would get away from him. If Sara arrived on her motorbike, which I was almost certain she would do even though the only bikers we'd seen in Clerkenwell had been couriers, I needed to position myself as far from the gate as possible. I walked along inside the row of columns and sat halfway down the steps at the far left facing the courtyard. There was a snack vendor in a trailer about ten yards away. Japanese visitors were queuing in an orderly line to sample his wares.

A minute to go. I looked around as casually as I could. I saw a taxi stop on Great Russell Street. Jeremy Andrewes got out and walked towards the gate. Other taxis passed in both directions, but none stopped. Andy had been delayed. My heart was beating faster than normal. When I saw the helmeted head of a motorbike rider through the railings, it started to pound. The biker, clad in black leathers, entered the courtyard about five yards behind Andrewes. I stood up, trying to see any sign of a weapon, particularly a silenced pistol. Sara might get a shot off before the journalist reached me. But there was a crowd of screaming primary school kids between the pair and me, and Jeremy Andrewes had to weave through them. Those movements made him less of a target, though Sara would probably have no qualms about hitting the children. Then he saw me and waved.

I was watching the biker. The leathers disguised the shape of the body beneath, but it definitely could have been a woman's. The helmet was still on, the visor down. That was enough to make me positive that the biker was up to no good. The bike was red and looked like the one we'd been chasing earlier.

Kids were swarming around as I went down the steps.

'Matt,' Jeremy Andrewes said, with a smile on his lips that I knew was untrustworthy. He was wearing the tweed jacket and corduroy trousers that had resulted in people on the *Daily Indie* calling him 'Squire'.

I manoeuvred myself so that I was between him and the motorbike rider. 'Hello, Jeremy.' I turned towards the courtyard. The biker had stopped by the snack trailer. The tinted visor gave the impression of a robot. I immediately thought of the Terminator, a relentless machine in human form. The only difference was that Sara was much more dangerous than Arnold Schwarzenegger ever was.

'What is it?' Andrewes said, turning in the same direction as I had.

'Nothing,' I said. 'Bloody kids. You can never visit a museum nowadays without thousands of them getting in the way.'

'We can't talk here,' he said, frowning.

'Why not? It isn't raining, for a change.'

He peered at me through thick lenses. 'Oh, I get it. You've got people watching us.'

I shook my head, wondering where Andy had got to. My stomach tightened. Could Sara have caught up with him?

Andrewes took out a gadget and fiddled with the buttons. 'All right if I record you?'

'Sure.' I sat down on the steps. After he'd inspected the surface, he joined me.

'Jeremy Andrewes, interviewing Matt Wells, date—'

'Never mind that,' I said, keeping an eye on the figure in leathers. 'Here's the story. I know the identity of the person responsible for the murders of Mary Malone, Sandra Devonish—' I broke off as the biker began to walk across the courtyard in front of us.

'Yes?' prompted the journalist.

'Em, Sandra Devonish, Josh Hinkley, Dave Cummings and several gang members in East London.'

'What?' Andrewes said, his eyes wide. 'One person is responsible?'

I watched the helmeted figure out of the corner of my eye as it moved up the steps towards the museum entrance. The biker could now approach us behind the columns without me seeing. But it was imperative that I didn't turn my head to avoid putting her off, assuming it was Sara. I took a deep breath and tried to get my heart rate under control.

'Are you all right?' Andrewes asked. I was pretty sure he was worried he might not get his exclusive rather than genuinely concerned.

'Sure,' I said, my voice hoarse.

'You're saying the same person killed all those people?'

I nodded. The temptation to look round was enormous, but I fixed my eyes on the short Japanese woman who was buying several cans of lemonade.

'I suppose you're going to tell me that's Sara Robbins,' Andrewes said, determined to steal my thunder.

Somehow I resisted the urge to tell him that she was creeping up on us with murder in her heart. Where the hell was Andy? I'd been hung out to dry. Unless—

'Sara Robbins?' said a female voice behind us.

We both turned our heads. The motorbike rider had sat down two steps above us. She had raised her visor only a few centimetres, so I couldn't make out her face. She pulled off one glove and unzipped her jacket, then slipped her hand inside. When it came back out, she was holding an object that I couldn't immediately identify. She leaned forward and gripped Jeremy Andrewes's shoulder with her other hand and pulled him back, so that the hand holding the object was near his neck.

'This is a spring-loaded stiletto,' the woman said. 'I can have it in his jugular before you move, Matt.'

'What?' Andrewes said, his voice rising several tones. 'Who are you?'

It was a good question. The voice had a similar timbre to Sara's, but there was a lot of East London in it. Then again, Sara was quite capable of picking up accents. She used to do a very convincing Margaret Thatcher.

'I'm your death,' the figure in leathers said. Then she gave a laugh that was as depraved as the White Devil's. 'Don't move, Jeremy, and don't even think about calling out.'

Thinking about it, I realised there was a lot of similarity between the two voices. Sara had obviously been turning herself into a female version of her brother.

'Let him go,' I said, looking into my own eyes, reflected in the visor. 'It's me you really want, Sara.'

The laugh was repeated and I felt revulsion, but something else as well—a strange mixture of fear and fascination. I didn't know where Andy was and I was looking my nemesis in the face. But there was something more…

'I don't want you, Matt,' the figure in leathers said. 'At

least, not yet. Andrewes is the one I'm after today.' She leaned closer, the knife with its invisible blade only centimetres from the journalist's jugular. In the courtyard below, people were chattering and children yelling. Nobody was paying the slightest attention to the three of us.

My mind was in freefall, thoughts and ideas flying around like bullets on the ricochet. Why was Andrewes the one she was after? What had he done to deserve death?

'Sara?' I said. 'Why do you want to kill an innocent man?'

The laugh that came from the helmeted figure in leather was grotesque. 'Innocent?' she said. 'How many journalists are innocent?' I'd been about to shove Andrewes aside, but suddenly there was a blur of movement behind the motorbike rider and she was driven into the journalist, who toppled forwards. The woman sprawled over him, and then slid rapidly down the steps before her helmet made contact with a paving-stone. The person who had piled into her went down the steps on hands and knees and sat on her back, then twisted her arm behind her.

I got up and joined them. 'Jesus, Rog, you took your time. I didn't see you when I got here.'

'I was just inside the main doors. That way no one saw me, including this specimen.' He bounced on the woman's back to stop her struggling. 'Sara Robbins, I presume?'

Two security guards were pushing their way through the crowd of kids and tourists.

'Yes, I think…' Before I finished the sentence, the biker managed to throw Rog off her back with a heave to the side. She launched herself at Jeremy Andrewes, who was sitting rubbing his head. I raced up the steps and hit her in

the belly with a tackle that Dave would have been proud
of. But I wasn't quick enough. The stiletto had already
caught the journalist in the throat. He started to gasp, blood
pumping out between his fingers. The woman had got
back on her feet and was now moving quickly towards me,
clutching the knife. There was no time to think. I dropped
the upper half of my body, let her torso crash on to my
back, and then powered my shoulders up as fast as I could.
I felt the weight fly off me and looked round to see her hit
the bottom step headfirst. A loud crack rang out.

*...images flashing...columns turning, blurred faces,
stone steps. Then darkness. I can't see, I can't move, can't
speak. I'm going... NO! No, I can't die. I've got everything...money, the power of the Lord Beneath the Earth,
Mephistopheles...why aren't they helping me? I can't die.
I'm a predator, not prey. The flat in Hackney...the enemy
was inside, and the grenade I tossed should have taught
them a lesson. They never caught me, they never caught
on I was a woman. The beard was a good one, though I let
the beautiful Kurdish boy see past it. I was never in love
before...sex meant my so-called father sticking it in me
when his bitch wife was drunk. I never wanted that again.
Until I saw Faik. Instead of submitting to the urge to kill,
I just shot him in the hand. And rescued him. I'm sure they
thought it was a man disguised as a woman. No one could
imagine it was a woman disguised as a man disguised as
a woman...not even Sara would have thought of that. They
never caught on I was a woman. She must have been
impressed, she must have...*

*Followed my gorgeous Faik but...but I couldn't express
my desires...only my violence. I thought Faik would*

respond to that, but he was a strange kind of gang member, he didn't want to hurt the Albanian, he looked at me with horror... My face, my ruined face...and Sara so beautiful, with her good surgeon...and me far too ugly to fix. Though I was sorry as soon as I'd done him, I wrote her that. Violence. She knew that I need it as she does. She encouraged me to start killing...the animals, making sure I threw what was left of the cats and dogs into the canal. But Sara was impatient...she said I couldn't just kill anyone, the victims had to be strong, dangerous, otherwise there was no point. Hard men, beasts of the street, I decided. Stabbing the fat Kurd was my first. Nervous before, but in the end it was easy. Power exploded inside me like Sara said. Killing for myself, killing for Sara, killing for Mephistopheles and the Lord Beneath the Earth. Where did one begin and the other end? It was all the same to me. Mephistopheles wanted funds for the order so I took drugs from the Shadows and set up the sale to the Albanians. I would have ransomed their man if Faik hadn't run away in disgust.

Oh, Faik, where are you now?

If only you could see how beautiful I am inside, so perfect...my ability to destroy...dedicating that to the Lord Beneath the Earth seemed to make sense. But now I think... Sara, Sara, my... NO! I can't be dying, I can't, oh, Faik, why did you reject me?

Jeremy Andrewes was sprawled on his back across the steps, his legs jerking out of control. His clothes were soaked in blood and his eyelids were fluttering. I kneeled down beside him and put pressure on the wound. I knew it was far too little, far too late.

'Matt,' he croaked.

I leaned closer.

He was panting for breath, his windpipe partially severed.

'Coke…deal,' he said, tongue loose over grey lips. 'Sh… Shkrelli family and Earl…Earl Sternwood. That…bastard did…this…'

The journalist's body tensed, then his eyes rolled and he slumped back on the stone steps.

Before I could take in what he'd said, a security guard got me in a neck-lock. 'VCCT,' I gasped. The pressure was relaxed. He must have thought I was a member of the elite squad. I gave him Karen's mobile number.

'This will get you Detective Chief Inspector Karen Oaten,' I said, rubbing my throat. 'Tell her Matt Wells has made a citizen's arrest and that there's been a murder here.' The guard looked at me dubiously and then did as he was told.

'Good tackle, Matt,' Pete Satterthwaite said, coming down the steps and grinning. 'You all right?'

'All the better for seeing you, Boney. I wasn't sure you guys had made it.'

'I was covering the far side of the yard.'

Rog looked up at us and shook his head. Jesus, had I killed Sara? I ran down the steps and looked at the figure in leather. She wasn't moving.

Her left hand was flung out in front of her, but the right was hidden beneath her body.

I dropped to my knees beside the motionless figure. I wasn't going to wait for Karen before I confirmed who the woman was. Rog and I rolled her over gently. I could hear sirens approaching. I put my hand under the bottom of the helmet and eased it off, pushing my hand under the head of the woman I'd once loved to stop it banging on to the paving-stone. It was as loose as a flower with a broken stalk. I took a deep breath and looked at the face that was revealed.

It made me wince. Disfigured and split, the skin was discoloured and with an unnatural sheen, crisscrossed by scars. As for the upper lip, its halves had parted like the stumps of an octopus's tentacles.

'She's Lauren May Cuthbertson,' Pete said. 'Rog and I reckon she killed the guy in Oxford. He was her surgeon.'

I rocked back on my heels, as uniformed police shouldered their way through the crowd. The fact that the dead woman wasn't Sara had been a shock, but Pete and Rog seemed to have made sense of who she was. The problem was, my adversary was still at liberty. I'd just killed one of her sidekicks, admittedly by accident, and I wondered what the cost of that would be. I doubted that Sara would see any mitigating circumstances.

Then, as I stood up and looked around the crowd, the blood tingling in my legs, I had another unpleasant thought. I still didn't have the faintest idea where Andy was.

26

'Pull in over there, please,' Andy Jackson said, as the taxi approached the British Museum.

He'd been unlucky outside the newspaper offices. Just as Jeremy Andrewes had hailed a cab, a woman wearing stiletto heels stepped off the pavement and collapsed into the road as her ankle gave way with a horrible crack. Andy stepped in front of a white van, forcing it to brake hard. He then picked the woman up carefully and took her into the *Daily Independent* building, telling the receptionist to call an ambulance.

By the time he got back outside, Andrewes was long gone. That wasn't a problem in itself, as the American knew where Matt had sent him, but the point of him tailing the journalist was to see if anyone else was. He was so far behind that he didn't see anyone suspicious on the short journey. That state of affairs changed when his taxi went along Great Russell Street. He saw a stationary red motorbike, a Transalp he'd seen before, on the same side of the road as the museum. Near it was the helmeted figure in black leathers he was sure had picked up Doris Carlton-Jones earlier. Not only that, but there was another identical motorbike parked about twenty yards further on. Andy tried to make sense of the fact that there were two bikers, but couldn't reach a conclusion. He knew that Rog and Pete were covering Matt's back. It seemed to him that the best thing he could do was to keep an eye on the rider who was watching through the railings. He wanted to check that Matt was all right, but decided it would be better if he stayed in the taxi, ready to give pursuit.

Ten minutes later, that decision paid off. The figure in black leather outside the railings suddenly turned away and mounted the nearer of the two bikes. It was started and moved off quickly, cutting in front of a people-carrier to join the left-hand lane, before heading west.

'Follow that bike,' Andy said to the cabby.

'You're 'avin' a laugh,' the middle-aged driver said, looking round.

'There's a twenty in it for you, on top of what the meter shows,' Andy said, watching the red metallic machine slow down behind a bus.

'Fair enough,' the cabby said, pulling out. 'Follow that bike…that's a good one!'

To Andy's surprise, the rider made no attempt to overtake the bus until it pulled in at a stop near Tottenham Court Road station. Then the bike's right indicator flashed and the rider headed north, towards Euston Road. The pattern of careful riding was maintained through Camden Town and Highgate, until the bike finally came to a halt in front of a block of flats in Hornsey. Andy told the driver to stop and waited till the rider had gone inside. He saw a key flash in the afternoon sun. Then he paid the cabbie off, bonus included, and got out.

At the glass door, he examined the names on the panel of buttons. He didn't recognise any of them, but that wasn't a surprise. If this was Sara, she'd hardly have written S. Robbins on the entry-phone. He considered using his lock-breaking rods, but decided against it. Sure enough, a young black woman came out and let him pass without a second glance. The entrance hall smelled of mildew and worse. There was nothing for it but to go up to each floor and snoop around. Maybe he could find a talkative old woman who knew everyone in the block. He tried texting Matt, but the signal was weak and he gave up, not wanting to lose his target. But if that had been her, who was the other rider? Andy scratched his head and then headed for the stairs.

Opening the door, he looked up. The stink in the stairwell was much worse: piss, pot, stale beer—the calling cards of teenage boys. There didn't seem to be anyone around. He set off up the stairs, hoping he didn't have to go all the way to the top. The display panel above the lift went as high as fourteen. His knees weren't what they used to be—too many games of gridiron and rugby league.

He reached the first floor, his breathing hardly affected. He peered through the small safety-glass window in the door. There was no one visible. He put his shoulder to the door, wincing when it gave out a loud creak. After he'd gone through, he grabbed the handle to stop it slamming. Then he turned to the front and saw a red object swinging fast towards his head.

Andy Jackson went down in a constellation of shooting stars.

'Clear the way, please,' shouted a male voice over the sirens that were still blaring on Great Russell Street.

I stood up, looking at Rog and Pete. I mouthed to them

to go. They got the message and slipped away through the crowd, taking my bag with them. They headed towards the museum—there was an exit at the rear of the building. I had no choice but to face the music. Fortunately, Karen arrived not long afterwards, the morose Welshman in tow. She favoured me with a neutral stare, and then turned her attention to the bodies.

'Is that Jeremy Andrewes of the *Daily Indie?*' she asked.

I nodded.

'And the woman?'

'Lauren May Cuthbertson,' I said, parroting the name that Pete had said. I watched as uniformed officers urged the crowd to disperse. CSIs were soon on the scene, and police tape sealed off half of the courtyard and steps. Taff Turner called for witnesses and got his subordinates taking preliminary statements.

Karen came closer. 'What happened here?'

I told her, skating over my use of Jeremy Andrewes as target-man.

'So you're saying the woman stabbed Andrewes to death and then you killed her by accident?'

'Yes.'

She glared at me. 'Were you on your own? Where are your friends?'

I played dumb, but that didn't get me anywhere.

'Right, that's it. I'm taking you in.'

'You can't,' I said. 'The dead woman has some connection with Sara. We'll only catch her if I can set a trap.'

'You arrogant tosser,' she hissed. 'You still think you know better than the professionals, don't you?'

I shook my head. 'I can do different things, that's all.'

'Put your hands out,' Karen ordered. She signalled to a

CSI, who came over and put transparent evidence bags over my hands, attaching them with tape.

I bit my lip. Being caught up in police procedure was the last thing I needed right now. The fact that I had an illegal and silenced handgun in my jacket made things even more critical.

The potbellied pathologist arrived and cast a cold eye over the corpse, and an even colder one over me. 'I wondered if you'd turn up again,' he said, as he put down a foam pad and kneeled on it.

'Ditto, Doctor,' I said.

He started examining the dead woman. I heard him say the words 'severely damaged upper lip' and 'recent surgery' to his assistant.

Taff Turner came up to Karen, led her away and spoke to her at length. Their eyes were on me most of the time. Then Karen came back over.

'It seems that your story is broadly corroborated by witnesses,' she said, pursing her lips. 'I'm still livid with you, Matt. Why didn't you call me before you came here?'

I shrugged. 'There wasn't time.'

Her eyes flared. 'That's pathetic. You thought it was Sara, didn't you? You wanted all the glory of catching her for yourself.'

I felt my cheeks redden. Maybe she was right. I wasn't too clear about my motives any more. I'd never killed anyone before. Even though Lauren May Cuthbertson was a murderess and even though it was an accident, I felt guilty and tainted. Finally I understood the difference between writing about death and causing it. The only good thing was that I obviously had nothing in common with Sara and her brother. They enjoyed dispensing death; I just felt sick. Then again, I'd lured Jeremy Andrewes to what seemed to be his predestined end.

'Get me out of here, Karen,' I said. 'I need to catch up with the guys. I don't know where Andy is. He should have got here a few seconds after her.' I inclined my head towards the body.

'You're staying with me,' she said, stepping towards the pathologist.

I looked over my shoulder as casually as I could. There were armed police on the museum steps, and more in the courtyard. Running for it wasn't an option.

Karen was holding up an evidence bag and examining the contents, a mobile phone. I walked over to her quickly.

'Maybe Sara's number is in the memory,' I said.

She moved it out of my reach. 'Maybe it is. We'll check that.'

'Give it to me,' I said, dropping my voice. 'I'll keep you in the loop.'

'Like hell you will,' she said, shaking her head. 'It's over, Matt. Be thankful that I haven't cuffed you.'

'Why?' I demanded. 'Because I nailed a murderer? Maybe she's the one who was running rings round you, not Sara.'

'That's really going to help your situation,' she said, her eyes on my chest. 'You'd better not have a weapon on your person, Matt.'

'Then I guess you'd better not look.' I flapped my hands in the evidence bags. 'Come on, Karen. Let me go.'

'No chance.' She went over to John Turner and spoke to him, then came back to me. 'I'm taking you to the Yard. You owe me an extremely detailed statement.' She took my wrist and led me away, telling a young uniformed police-man to come with us.

After we'd ducked under the barrier tape, the constable led us through the crowd. Karen's BMW was on the pavement outside the museum gates. She opened the front passenger door, signalling to me and the PC to get in the back. Karen started the engine, did a three-point turn and drove west.

She looked at me in the mirror. 'You're saying that the dead woman's face was messed up by the surgeon James Maclehose, whose body was found in Oxford.'

I nodded. 'The likelihood is that she killed him, as well as the crime writers.'

'She may have been behind the gangland killings too,' Karen said.

'You found a connection?'

She nodded. 'Nail clippings were taken from all but one of the victims.'

'Satanism?' I asked. 'Were there pentacles and so on?'

She shook her head. 'Do you even realise how much shit you're in, Matt?' she asked, turning southwards.

I tried to ignore that.

'Maybe Sara isn't even in the country any more,' Karen said. 'Have you thought of that, Mr Smart-arse? Maybe she hightailed it after she murdered Dave. There were no hair or nail clippings taken from him, by the way.'

'I don't think it's very likely. I still think Sara set this whole thing up to hurt me and to see me pilloried. She'll want to finish me off now, especially when she finds out I did to her sidekick.'

'She's probably got others,' Karen said.

'Quite possibly.' I wasn't going to give her the name of the earl that I'd got from Jeremy Andrewes. 'But the heat's on now. It won't be long before she strikes again.' I needed

to check my phone. 'Sorry about this,' I said, ripping the
bags from my hands before the constable could intervene.
Karen couldn't do anything except look unimpressed. She
managed that very well.

I looked for text messages. There weren't any. Where
the hell was Andy?

'Nothing from your darling Sara?' Karen asked scath-
ingly.

I shook my head. I needed to check my e-mails. Maybe
Sara had sent another one.

'Karen, you have to let me go. I've already lost Dave.
If I'm responsible for another of my friends' deaths, I
won't be able to live with myself.'

She snorted. 'No chance.'

I wanted to tell her how much I needed her, but I was
deterred by her tone more than the presence of the constable.

As Karen stopped at the traffic lights by Leicester
Square Tube Station, her mobile rang. She spoke into the
hands-free mike and then listened.

'In the name of God!' she said, breaking the connection.

'What is it?'

'I shouldn't be telling you this, but you do have a valid
interest. A hiker found three male bodies in the New Forest
this morning. Two of them had been shot in the head and
the other cut to pieces. The local Serious Crime Squad has
just identified them.'

'The SAS guys who killed the White Devil,' I said, my
stomach contracting like an oyster drenched in lemon
juice.

Karen pulled into the kerb. 'How did you know that?'

'It's obvious. Three men, two shot in the head. Sara

went for her brother's killers after she got their ex–brother in arms, Dave.'

'Yes, well, that's only the half of it. A family member of each is missing. An eleven-year-old girl, a six-year-old boy and one of the wives.'

I put my hand to my forehead. This was it. Sara had upped her game. I had no choice but to do the same.

'Let me go,' I said, pleading one last time. 'You have to trust me, Karen.'

She shook her head slowly. 'You have to be charged and processed, even if it was manslaughter. You also witnessed the Andrewes murder.'

That did it. Before the constable next to me could move, I pulled out my Glock and jammed the muzzle of the silencer into his side. His loud gasp made Karen turn round.

'Are you out of your mind?' she demanded. 'Threatening a police officer with an illegal firearm?'

'At least no one can say you let me go voluntarily,' I said, giving her a slack smile. 'You can do whatever you like to me when this is over, but for now I need my freedom.'

Looking around, I opened the door and stepped into the crowd on the pavement. I held the pistol under my jacket and kept my head low. I was lucky. There was a taxi at the next corner. I told the driver to head north and got out near King's Cross. Then I took another cab towards Highgate. The man I wanted to see lived somewhere in the northern suburbs: that man being the most dangerous gangster in south-east England.

When Andy Jackson came round, he blinked and then gasped in pain. He could only see out of one eye. He could

also only breathe through his nose, as there was something round his mouth. He tried to stand up, but discovered that his arms were tied behind his back and that he
couldn't move his legs. Looking around, he saw he was
in a van that seemed to be stationary. There was some
light from the rear windows, though makeshift curtains
covered them. There was thick gauze between him and
the driver's compartment. He tried to jerk his body
towards it, but there was only a slight movement. He
lowered his gaze and realized then that he was in a
wheelchair.

His throat was parched and he had a splitting headache,
but Andy was still able to think. His jacket and boots had
been removed, but not his trousers. In a specially sewn
addition to the left rear pocket, a few centimetres from his
pinioned right hand, was an extra-slim pocket knife—he'd
learned always to carry a concealed blade. He could feel
its outline against his buttock. If he could get his fingers
into the narrow space at the side of the pocket and open
the blade, he'd be back in business.

If only he could move his fingers...

I swore beneath my breath when I realised I hadn't
forced Karen to give me the dead woman's mobile. I'd lost
a potential link to Sara. I texted Rog and asked him to send
Karen the addresses of all the properties Sara had bought.
I also told him to see if he could trace any more, probably
under a different name. If he did, he wasn't to supply
Karen with that information. We would need to act on it
ourselves. I asked if he or Pete had heard from Andy. They
hadn't. Where the hell had he got to? He wasn't answering his phone. I left him texts and messages, aware that

Sara or some other antagonist might pick them up. I didn't care, it was worth a try. But no answer came.

Then I called Safet Shkrelli. He didn't sound at all pleased to hear my voice.

'You've been having dealings with Earl Sternwood,' I said, before he hung up.

'His Lordship?' the Albanian said sarcastically. 'I've got more important things on my mind right now.'

'How about we trade information, Safet? You tell me about Sternwood and I'll tell you about the person who's been doing the gangland murders in East London.'

'What?' he said, failing to disguise his surprise. 'You must know I've just lost a relative over there. What do you know?'

'I killed her,' I said, trying to sound swollen with pride. I wasn't, but the only way to impress gang bosses was to commit murder. I hadn't known any Albanians had been killed out east, but I didn't admit that.

'You?' Shkrelli said, in disbelief. 'You're a fucking writer.'

'Turn on one of the rolling news channels.'

There was a pause. 'All right. Go to Highgate Station. One of my people will pick you up.'

'I'll be there in two minutes. How will I know your man?'

He gave a hollow laugh. 'Don't worry. After what you did to Mustafa, everyone knows what you look like, Matt Wells.'

Shit. I hoped that the knocking-shop muscle-man hadn't been transferred to driving for Shkrelli.

As it happened, I'd never seen the driver of the black Mercedes and the accompanying hard man before. They were both big, wearing black suits, and their faces were covered in heavy stubble. One of them directed me to the back seat, removed my weapon and phone, and then forced my head between my knees. When we stopped about a quarter of an hour later, I had no idea where I was. A hood was slipped over my head before I was allowed out of the car.

When the hood was removed, I found myself standing in front of Safet Shkrelli. He looked more like a businessman than a gangster, in his white shirt and red silk tie. Then he stared at me and I saw the emptiness in his dark eyes.

'Sit down, Matt Wells,' he said, pointing to an empty chair. There was a young man sitting next to it, wearing an ill-fitting track suit. His face was cut and bruised and one hand was bandaged, while his feet were bare. I wondered if that was to stop him from running.

'Tell me about this woman you killed,' the Albanian ordered.

I gave him a partial version of events. After I'd described her face, Shkrelli asked the young man if that was what he'd seen.

He nodded rapidly, his eyes wide and bloodshot. 'The lips,' he said, 'like a rabbit's. But the eyes, they were a demon's…' His head dropped.

The gang boss turned back to me and slid a folder across his desk. 'This is what she did to Lefter Omari, my cousin, who was my chief accountant. According to Faik here, she was going to ransom him. Obviously there was a change of plan.'

I took in the photos of a severed head, hands and feet, as well as a torso that looked like a pride of lions had feasted on it.

'Why did she do this?' Shkrelli asked. 'Was she mad?'

I shrugged. 'Probably.'

'They said on the TV that the police are looking for you.'

'Tough,' I said, as nonchalantly as I could.

'Don't play games, Matt Wells. You called me some days ago, telling me the woman Katya was in danger. I succeed in protecting her, still. But I read in the newspapers about the woman you loved, this Sara…'

'Robbins,' I said. That wasn't the way I wanted the conversation to head. 'Never mind her. One of my friends has gone missing and I think this Sternwood scumbag might have him. What can you tell me about the earl?'

'Why should I tell you anything, Matt Wells?' Shkrelli said.

'Because Sternwood is a risk to you.'

'I fix my own risks,' the gang boss said bluntly.

'I can fix this one more effectively and no one will be able to trace it back to you.' I'd played all my cards. Either he'd bite or I'd be turned over to Mustafa.

'You have capable men?'

I nodded.

'And no police will be involved?' He gave a crooked smile. 'I know you are screwing the VCCT woman. Maybe I should get *my* men to find out everything you know about her.'

'No police,' I said, holding his gaze despite the thundering in my chest.

Finally Shkrelli looked away. 'Very well. If you guarantee you can silence Sternwood, I will let you prove that to me.' He raised a thick finger. 'But if you fail, I will silence *you* permanently, writer.'

I tried to look laid-back.

The Albanian took another folder out of a drawer and pushed it towards me. 'I always do my homework before I enter into business deals. You're in luck. I have an English investigator working for me. This is his report. Go now.'

I remained sitting. 'Let me talk to our friend here,' I said, leaning towards the young man. 'Faik, right?'

He kept his eyes to the ground. 'Right,' he said. I picked up an East London accent.

'What are you? A Turk?'

He looked up quickly and said something in a language I didn't recognise but it was obvious he'd sworn at me.

'I am a Kurd,' he said, glancing at Shkrelli. 'I work for the King.'

I'd heard of that gang.

'Let him come with me,' I said to the gang boss. 'He's seen enough.'

Safet Shkrelli thought about it and then nodded. He stood up and took a roll of bank notes from his pocket. 'I thank you for helping me, Kurd. It was not your fault that my cousin was killed.' He nodded to the heavy at the door.

A few minutes later we were back in the car, hoods on our heads.

'Where you want to go?' the driver asked.

'Kentish Town Station,' I said. 'How about you, Faik?'

'That's okay,' he replied.

When we got there, the hoods were removed and we found ourselves on a rain-dashed street corner. The young Kurd watched the car accelerate away, his face slack. I could see that he'd been through hell. He also knew things that I didn't.

'Faik, come with me. I have clothes you can wear.'

He looked at me with sad eyes. 'I want to go home.'

I put my hand on his arm. 'Later. I need to talk to you.'

He considered that, and then nodded. 'I need a bath,' he said. 'And maybe a doctor.' His legs suddenly gave way and I caught him in my arms. I helped him into a taxi for the journey to Rog's cousin's flat. I didn't think there was anyone on our tail. I almost had to drag Faik up the stairs. Pete opened the door on the chain.

'Who's that?' he asked.

'Just let us in,' I said. When he did so, I took the Kurd straight to the bathroom and left him to it.

'Any news from Andy?' I asked the others.

They both shook their heads.

'Any more properties bought by Sara, Rog?'

'Maybe. I'm working on a name that I think she used only once.'

I filled them in about Shkrelli and Faik. Then I split the investigator's report on the ninth Earl Sternwood into three parts and handed them out.

Pete sat back in his chair. 'Very thorough,' he said. 'But what makes you think this guy's got anything to do with the murders, Matt?'

The photo of the aristocrat had been in the section I'd kept. I showed it to them.

'Bloody hell,' Rog said. 'What happened to his face?'

'Which is not dissimilar to Lauren May Cuthbertson's,' Pete said.

I nodded. 'I doubt that's a coincidence, particularly since the crime-writer murders and the gangland ones seem to be linked.' I told them about the nail and hair clippings. 'And there's more. The first Earl Sternwood was notorious for the Hell-fire Club he ran.'

'The what?' Rog asked, looking round from his computer.

I repeated the phrase. 'It involved black-magic rituals, sexual depravity and heavy drinking. The meetings were attended by members of high society, bishops and university professors. Oh, and local wenches and nuns were brought in—most disappeared after the parties.'

'Black magic,' Pete said. 'The pentacles and so on. But why would a peer of the realm kill crime writers, let alone gangbangers?'

I raised my shoulders. 'I think we should ask him that question, don't you?'

'Gotcha!' Rog said. 'Another of Sara's house buys. Nine months ago. This one's in a village called Oldbury. In Berkshire.'

I felt an icy finger jab into my gut. 'Shit. Earl Sternwood's castle is in the very same county.'

A moment later Faik let out a shriek of agony.

27

Andy Jackson's face was drenched in sweat. He'd been heaving and twisting against his bonds and had finally got hold of the penknife. But opening it was proving a step too far. He had splintered his thumbnail against the narrow groove in the blade, and he couldn't get it to move. The light from the rear doors had almost gone.

Then he heard footsteps. He relaxed, making sure his expression didn't give him away. A key was inserted into the lock in the rear door, then it opened—at first by only a few centimetres, and then enough for a torch to be shone on to him. He tried to make out a face, but the light made him blink.

'There's no escape, Inspector Jansen,' said a female voice. 'Or should I say Andrew Jackson.' There was a bitter laugh. 'Save your strength. You're going to need it.' The light went out and the door was closed again.

Doris Carlton-Jones. When had Sara Robbins's birth mother discovered his true identity? Surely not the first time he'd met her, when the biker shot out his windscreen. Perhaps she'd known all along, and Sara had just been toying with them.

The front door opened and someone—presumably

Mrs Carlton-Jones—got in. The engine was started and the
van moved off. Andy expected the wheelchair to shift, but
it had been well-secured.

He started fumbling with the knife again. His fingers
had benefited from the short rest, and he felt the blade
move under his thumb, then slip back into position.

Andy told himself to keep calm, taking deep breaths. He
could take the old woman even with his hands tied. As soon
as she released the wheelchair, he'd heave it into motion.
Someone would see him, someone would call the cops…

Then he heard the roar of a high-powered motorbike
behind the van. It hadn't been the old woman who had
poleaxed him. It must have been Sara Robbins.

That made him concentrate even harder on the knife.

Dave had taught us basic first aid. After I'd dressed the
wounds on Faik's thighs and checked there was no infec-
tion in his hand, I helped him get dressed. Rog had found
some clothes.

I checked my e-mails again. Still nothing. No text messages, either. I sat by my computer, hitting Send and Receive
every minute or so. While I did that, Faik ate his way through
two pizzas Pete had heated up for him. In between bites, he
told me about the treacherous Kurd who'd been shot, as well
as the doctor who had rescued him from the Wolfman. There
was no way of knowing the identity of the person wearing
the *burqa* and *chador* who had shot the Turk, but I was
pretty sure it was Lauren Cuthbertson. Faik was almost
more appalled that a non-Muslim might have worn the
garment than he was by the deaths he had witnessed.

The young man came from a London community that
I knew nothing about, one based on violence and coercion,

but also a strange kind of honour. They killed only to protect their business, which was bad enough—but why had Lauren Cuthbertson been murdering gang members? And why had she dismembered the body of the Albanian accountant? Because Sara had told her? There had to be more to it than that. At least killing the surgeon who had disfigured her made some kind of sense—she'd taken revenge, just as the White Devil had done with his first victims. She'd left no traces except that stained and almost illegible note of apology—could that have been for Sara? There had been very little evidence at the crime scenes in East London too. That smacked of the extreme care that Sara learned from her brother. Had she trained the disfigured young woman from Stoke Newington?

Were there others like her on Sara's payroll?

But I suddenly found myself thinking about Doris Carlton-Jones. Maybe *she* was the one behind the murders. Could the elderly woman be a cold-blooded killer like her daughter? She'd certainly kept very calm when I was searching her house. She must have called the motorbike rider, presumably Lauren, when I went upstairs. When Andy appeared with the skull (and whose was that?), she took the opportunity, while I was distracted, to dash to the road. The rider wore black leathers and helmet, as Lauren had. Maybe Karen was right when she suggested that Sara had nothing to do with the crime-writer and gangland murders. Maybe she had killed Dave and the former SAS guys, and left the rest to her mother and Lauren. But how would Doris Carlton-Jones have found a stone killer with a ruined face on her own? There wasn't a section for those in the Yellow pages.

There was a chime from my computer. I leaned forward

and saw the name of the new message's sender: *dc-j/urgent*.
It looked like Sara's mother was indeed calling the shots.
I read what she'd written:

There's been enough killing. And enough pretence. I
don't know what you did to poor Lauren, but at least she's
at peace now. I'm sorry for everything she did. I tried to
stop her, but she was a different person after the operations. Mr Wells, I have to tell you that my daughter Sara
has contacted me. Apparently someone has been
removing large sums of money from her bank accounts.
She is sure you are behind that so I have arranged for your
friend Andrew Jackson to be taken prisoner. Unless the
money is returned to Sara's accounts, I will have no option
but to leave him where he is. It will be a cold, slow and
thirsty death, with no chance of him ever being found.
When you have returned the money, I will e-mail you from
a different address and tell you where your friend is.
Doris Carlton-Jones
P.S. I was very glad to find my husband's skull in Mr
Jackson's pack. I obtained it at some expense from the
undertaker before the cremation, but I grew tired of
having it on my dressing-table. It was fitting that I put
it in the garage. He spent hours in there every weekend,
carving wooden animals for the local children.

The hairs on the back of my neck stood to attention. The
woman was clearly demented. She seemed to be suggesting that Lauren was responsible for all the murders.
Perhaps she didn't know what Sara had done to Dave and
the other SAS men. Multiple killers were still at work,

including, I was sure, Earl Sternwood. Could Sara be manipulating everyone, including her birth mother? I wouldn't have put it past her. But what was I to do about Andy?

I told Rog to start returning the money to Sara's accounts. He wasn't happy.

'Em, what is happening?' Faik asked from close behind me.

I tried to block the screen. 'You don't want to read that, my friend.'

He looked at me dubiously. 'Are there more like her? Is the killing to go on?'

I shook my head. 'It's finished,' I said, with more conviction than I felt.

The young Kurd nodded. 'I don't want anyone else to die like the Albanian did.' He headed for the door. 'I will send you money for the clothes.'

'Forget it,' Rog said.

I gave him my card. 'Call me if you need help, okay?'

He looked at me solemnly. 'I'm finished with life on the streets. I'm going to study.'

'Good for you. What do you want to do?'

'Teach. I want to make sure kids don't screw up like me.'

'Good luck,' I said, extending my hand.

He nodded solemnly.

I closed the door behind him. At least one person had come through the cycle of violence to the good. Then I thought of Andy. Was saving him going to be simply a matter of giving back Sara's money? Every relevant synapse in my brain was pulsing, 'No!'

* * *

The Soul Collector was driving the van skilfully, gripped by cold fury. Her motorbike was now in the back, beside the bound American. The woman next to her was silent. They had talked about the death of Lauren May Cuthbertson after her death was confirmed on the radio and decided who would pay for it.

As they approached the London orbital motorway, Doris Carlton-Jones looked at her daughter.

'Will he go there?' she asked. 'Will he understand?'

Sara Robbins shook her head. 'Matt Wells isn't smart enough.'

'Is he smart enough to find Lauren's people?'

'Probably.'

'That may be good for us.'

The Soul Collector glanced at her passenger. 'What do you care? Your part in this is almost over.'

The older woman looked away. 'You're right,' she said casually. 'I don't care what happens to any of them. What about your money?'

'Do you seriously imagine that's important to me? Even if I didn't have plenty in places no one can find, I'm only interested in one thing—the complete destruction of Matt Wells and everyone he cares for. You're the one who wants the money back.'

Doris Carlton-Jones pursed her lips, but didn't reply.

Her surviving child drove on to the M25 and headed eastwards as fast as the van's engine would tolerate.

Woe betide the police officer who stopped her for speeding.

* * *

The more I thought about it, the less I was convinced by Doris Carlton-Jones's message. It started off sounding reasonable and then talked about Sara as if she was a normal, if rich, person, rather than a calculating killer. And as for the bit about her husband's skull—how many widows hit the undertakers with a request to remove the deceased's head? The woman was demented. The question was, how much of her children's propensity for murder had been inherited? I had an idea why the skull was so shiny. She would have boiled it for days. Bottom line—how much could I trust the woman? Answer—not at all. But that didn't change the situation with Andy. Even though Sara was getting her money back, he was obviously in serious danger. You wouldn't want someone like Doris Carlton-Jones to decide whether a friend lived or died.

Rog confirmed that two of the transfers had been reversed. I looked at my watch. Eleven o'clock. At least we hadn't been given a deadline this time. I wondered about that. The implication was that Lauren Cuthbertson had written the puzzles containing the crime writers' names before she killed them. Was she capable or educated enough to come up with such complex riddles? Since I had nothing better to do while Rog was at work, I noted down the details of the dead woman from the ghost site. I might as well see what else I could find out about her.

When I'd been researching *The Death List,* Rog had shown me how to access the databases of several government agencies. By good fortune, they covered East London, the area where the White Devil had grown up. I started snooping. I fully expected the security on the websites to have been improved over the past couple of years, but it seemed that the agencies hadn't bothered. In less than five minutes, I was reading Lauren Cuthbertson's school reports. She'd been to primary and secondary school in Stoke Newington. She had four O-Levels, all in maths and science, but she'd failed English and French. Her teachers said she was an average pupil, whose homework was often poor. There was no mention of her having been disruptive—perhaps she'd stored it all up. She left school at sixteen and was on benefits for two years. When she signed off, it was to work in a supermarket in Hackney. Not exactly master-criminal material.

I hacked into the G.P. surgery where she was registered. The computerised records only went back five years. She had been prescribed drugs for the swellings on her face, but there was no referral to the Harley Street clinic. Who had arranged and paid for that?

I sat back in my chair and looked out into the night. The streets lights were dulled by rain that was hitting the windows. I checked my e-mails. Nothing; and no texts from Andy. I went back to the dead woman's past. The magistrates' courts: maybe she had a criminal record. I followed the instructions and found myself in a well-maintained archive. Unlike the surgery, the paper records dating back twenty-five years had been scanned and classified. I typed Lauren Cuthbertson's name in and found a single entry, referring to a shoplifting charge in 1986, her last year at school. I opened the case file. It seemed she had been caught leaving a Woolworths with three music cassettes, a book and a chocolate bar. Because she'd been stopped numerous times before, the store decided to make an example of her. I scrolled down the record. Lauren had been warned as to her future conduct by the magistrates and ordered to do a week's community service during her next holidays. A fine was not considered appropriate because of her 'troubled family situation'. That made me sit up. What family situation? I got into the local Social Services database and searched for her name. She'd been through six different sets of foster parents since she was six, as well as being in care several times. The root of the problem was that her father had murdered her mother when Lauren was in her first year in primary school. I scrolled down further. Wrong. Her adoptive father had murdered her adoptive—Jesus, she'd been adopted.

I felt the blood rush through my veins. The White Devil and his twin, Sara, had also been given up for adoption. That Lauren had too was a hell of a coincidence. I got into the Adoption Register. That was tricky because there was a better firewall, but Rog had left me a program to get past it. I typed in Lauren's full name and waited for the details of her birth parents to come up. It took nearly a minute, but I'd already guessed who her mother was. The archive showed her to be Doris Merilee, now known by her married name, Doris Carlton-Jones. Christ, Sara and the White Devil had a half sister. The records were incomplete, the mother having declared that she'd given birth in France and had lost the certificate. She'd also given a different man's name as father. That had been enough for me to miss the fact that Sara's mother had given birth to three rather than two children when I researched my book. All three children had turned out to be murderers. What did that make their mother?

I told Pete and Rog what I'd discovered.

'But where does that leave us, Matt?' Boney asked. 'Lauren Cuthbertson's dead. How do we find Sara?'

'How we find Andy is more urgent,' I said. 'Though he and Sara might well be in the same place.'

'Where are you thinking?' Rog asked.

'Where's that cottage you found again?'

'Oldbury, Berkshire.'

'Right, we'll hit it first. If it's no good, we'll move on to Earl Sternwood's castle.'

We started gathering up our weapons.

Andy Jackson couldn't be sure how long the van had been moving, but he guessed it was about two hours when it stopped and the engine turned off. He'd spent the time persevering with the blade, but the movement of the vehicle and the fact that all the nails on his right hand were now broken meant that he hadn't succeeded. He listened as the front doors were opened. The wind was blowing through trees and he could hear cars in the distance. The curtains didn't permit any helpful visuals. After stopping and starting frequently in the first half hour of the journey—standard city driving he figured—the van had stopped and a helmeted figure in black leathers had manoeuvred the motorbike up a plank into the cargo space. He tried to see where they were out the rear doors and was rewarded with a heavy punch to his jaw.

After that the van moved more quickly. He reckoned they'd been on a motorway. Then it was driven more slowly again. Now it was stationary, he wondered if he'd reached the end of his road. He struggled desperately, but still couldn't get the knife open.

The rear doors opened and a torch was shone in his face. He tried to make out the person holding it, but saw only a helmet with the visor down. Was it Sara Robbins? Why was she still hiding her face? Was there some hope, if she didn't want him to be able to identify her later? Then he saw she was carrying something, a motionless bundle wrapped in blankets. Jesus, was it a person? The face and head were covered, though loosely enough to suggest it would be possible to breathe. As he was sizing up the bundle, which had been laid on the floor on the other side of the bike, the torch was switched off. He'd seen enough to realize it wasn't large enough to be an adult.

Andy Jackson was in the dark in the back of the van, but he wasn't alone any more. He had to see if the new arrival was alive. He slid his fingers back into his back pocket and started trying the knife again. The van's engine was started again and it moved off. Soon it was being driven at speed, presumably back on a motorway. But where were they heading? Andy realised that Matt and the others could have no idea of his location. He had to save himself and the person who had been wrapped in the blankets, if that person was still breathing.

Fortunately Rog's cousin had a half-decent set of wheels, a Suzuki 4x4, and Rog knew where the spare keys were.

'You drive, Dodger,' I said. 'West for the M4.'

When we were under way, I took out my mobile and called Karen.

'Where are you, Matt?' she demanded. 'You do realise you're looking at prison now?'

'Never mind that,' I said. 'Remember I told you about Sara's birth mother?' She got the name right. 'Yeah, that's her. Can you notify the authorities at ports and airports, especially in the south-east?' I gave a description. 'She might have altered her appearance.'

'What's she done?' Karen asked.

'For a start, she's Lauren Cuthbertson's mother too.'

There was a pause. 'You mean Lauren Cuthbertson was Sara Robbins's sister?' Karen said.

'Half sister. You'd better advise them that Sara might be trying to go through as well.'

'They were issued with her details and description after the White Devil case.'

'Yeah, but she might well look different now and you can be sure they'll both have different identities.'

'All right. Matt, please tell me where you are and what you're doing.'

'I'm trying to save Andy's life,' I said bluntly.

'I can send backup.'

'Uh-uh. I have to do this on my own.' I felt Pete's eyes on me again. 'I'm not losing another of my friends. I'll be in touch.' I cut the connection.

'You have to do it on *your own?*' Boney said ironically.

I caught his gaze. 'If this gets messy, which it could well if Sara's around, you two are in the clear as far as the authorities are concerned.'

'If we don't get wounded,' Rog pointed out.

'Or killed,' Pete added.

'Matt,' Rog said, turning his head. 'Something's been bothering me about the properties Sara bought. Why did she put them in her mother's maiden name? Surely she'd know we might spot that.'

I thought about that. 'I'm not sure she would. I didn't mention her mother's maiden name in *The Death List*. It's true that the tabloids dug it up, but I think Sara was probably cocking a snook at everyone looking for her. You know, giving us a pretty obvious clue and seeing if we noticed it. Besides, the name on the deeds was Angela

Oliver-Merilee, remember? She also used the names she and her brother had been given by Doris. Not many people are aware of them.'

'Why didn't she use Lauren Cuthbertson's original first name as well?' Pete asked.

'There wasn't one in the files,' I replied. 'For some reason, Doris Carlton-Jones didn't give her a name. Maybe Sara doesn't know about her.'

'I doubt that,' Rog said.

'So do I.'

'Sara will know we went to the flat in Hackney,' Pete said. 'Was Lauren staying there, do you think?'

'Probably,' I said. 'There's no current address for her in Stoke Newington. I doubt it was Sara. She'll be staying in the Ritz or such like.'

'Bit of a risk,' Rog said with a grin.

'I've had enough word-play, thanks. She's changed her appearance, I'm sure of that,' I said.

'Maybe she used the surgeon who botched Lauren's operation,' Pete said.

That struck me as unlikely. It would have been much safer for her to have surgery abroad. But she'd probably given her half sister the money to pay for the op.

'There is a chance she's waiting for us to show up at the cottage,' Rog said, his face sallow in the headlights of the cars coming towards us.

I nodded. 'We'll just have to take that chance, won't we? For Andy.'

'Yes, we will,' Pete said forcefully.

I kept my laptop on as we sped down the M4. The wi-fi signal was patchy, but as we passed Slough, it picked up and I saw there were no further messages from Doris Carlton-Jones or from Doctor Faustus

When we approached Oldbury, I got Rog to pull in to a lay-by. There was a large house beyond and I picked up a signal. I found a mapping site and downloaded a plan of the village.

'That must be the cottage,' Rog said, checking the description of the property on his laptop. 'There are about a hundred metres between it and the next house.'

'Let's have a look at the cottage's layout, Dodger,' I said.

It appeared on his screen.

'Single-story, but long—the two original cottages have been knocked together.'

'What's that?' Pete asked, pointing to a rectangular shape on the end of the building away from the village.

'Outhouse, according to the spec,' Rog replied.

'How do we do this?' Boney asked.

I had been thinking about the training we'd got from Dave. 'Pete, you've picked up some of Andy's lock-picking skills, so you go for the front door. I'll be right behind you. Dodger, you cover the rear in case someone makes a run for it.'

'What if you guys come under fire?' Rog asked.

'Blow the back door in with a grenade and take the shooter from behind,' I said.

'And if the place is booby-trapped?'

'Jesus, Dodger,' Pete said. 'Improvise. Or run away.'

'Screw you, Boney. Dave told us to take every possibility into account.'

'You're right,' I said, trying to calm them down. 'But

we haven't much time. Who knows what kind of state Andy's in by now?'

They nodded, and Rog drove on. He stopped on the verge about a quarter of a mile before the cottage and doused the headlights.

'Right, guys,' I said, 'let's get geared up. Keep the noise and lights down.' I opened my door carefully and got out.

Pete swung open the rear door, and he and Rog started rummaging in their bags. I was wearing jeans and a donkey jacket. I fitted on the head-set of my walkie-talkie and pulled a balaclava over the strap. I slipped off my belt and slid through the straps of my combat knife's sheath. I stuck my second Glock 19 into my belt above my backside. The pistol with the silencer would be staying in hand.

'Grenade?' Pete said in a low voice, holding out a bag.

'Don't mind if I do,' I replied, taking three. I shone my torch on them. One was a smoke grenade and the other two were fragmentation. I hoped I didn't have to pull the pins on any of them.

We moved apart and checked that our communication units were working. Then Rog set off across a field, heading for the back of the cottage. Pete and I found a gap in the hedge and went into the large field that went all the way to Sara's place on the other side of the road. We had good cover and were able to get right in front of the buildings. Parting the branches, I saw the property clearly. There were no lights on in the cottage or outhouse. The nearest streetlight was about fifty metres down the road towards the village, so we would be well obscured from passing cars.

'Let's go,' I whispered to Pete.

He nodded and moved ahead to the gate. When he'd crossed the road and was on the short path to the door, I followed. By the time I got there, he already had the lock-breaking rods out. He fiddled with them for several minutes, but didn't make any progress.

'Looks like there are mortice locks near the top and bottom,' he said in a low voice. 'Sara really doesn't want uninvited guests.'

'Any sign of an alarm system?'

'Strangely, no.'

'Rog?' I said.

'Receiving. I'm in position. No lights or movement at the back.'

'I'm sending Pete round to try the locks there.'

'Okay.'

I nodded to Boney, and he set off round the house in a crouch. I felt exposed at the front door, so I headed away to the right, thinking I'd check the outhouse. But when I got there, I found three heavy-duty padlocks on the bolts. Short of blowing my way in with grenades, I was stuck. Unless there was a door at the back. I pushed my way through the vegetation at the side of the wooden structure. There wasn't a door, but a window had been boarded over.

'Matt?' came Pete's voice in my ear. 'This door's got mortices too. We'll have to cut the glass.'

'Okay. Run your deactivation unit around it first.'

'I was actually intending to do that,' Bonehead said snidely.

I smiled, then took out my combat knife and started to lever away the boards. When I'd got one off, I looked in. Complete darkness. I listened carefully. Nothing. I decided to risk my torch, briefly at first. It was soon clear that the building was empty. It didn't look like Sara was hiding there, but I had my Glock at the ready when I'd made a space big enough to clamber through. I dropped on to the floor on my hands, feeling hard earth on my fingertips.

'We're in,' Rog said through my earpiece. 'No one around so far.'

I shone the torch again. There were tools hanging from a row of hooks on the wall, but apart from that there was a strange absence of the gear you'd expect to find in an outbuilding—no logs, lawn-mower, old boxes or other junk. I walked towards the front doors, then stopped. The earth beneath my boots was less firm. I looked down and made out an area several yards long and wide, with a slightly different texture. I hadn't noticed the three low posts that came out of the floor until then. They each stood about fifteen centimetres from the surface. I went over to the nearest one and kneeled down by it. In the torchlight I could see that they were circular plastic pipes, about five centimetres across. I shone my light down, but could make nothing out. Then I heard a sound that made my flesh creep—a kind of muffled screech. I knew without a shadow of a doubt that it came from a human being.

'Rog! Pete!' I said, forgetting to keep my voice low. 'If there's nothing in the cottage, get over to the outhouse. There's a window I've cleared on the far side.'

'What have you got?' Pete asked.

'Someone who's been buried alive. Out.'

I shone the torch on the wall and took down a couple of spades and a snow shovel. One of the former had traces of earth on the head. Going back to the tube through which the sound had come, I hacked away at the earth around it. The surface had been smoothed down, but when I broke through the crust, I found that the earth shifted easily. By the time Pete and Rog arrived, I had already piled a heap by the wall.

'I think there are three people down here,' I said, pointing at the pipes. 'We'll take one each.'

It was hard work, but when I got about a metre down, my spade hit wood with a resounding thud.

'Give me a hand here,' I said.

Soon we'd cleared the earth from a roughly made rectangular box. We all climbed out of the hole and I inserted the spade beneath the lid. There was a loud creaking as nails came away from the wood, then the cover shifted.

'Bloody hell!' Rog said, as we took in the diminutive figure.

It was a young girl, her hands bound and resting on her abdomen. Her eyes were wide in terror. There was another piece of rope round her ankles, and her knees were raw from the countless times she had banged them against the coffin lid.

I got hold of her shoulders and pulled her up as gently as I could, then handed her to Pete. When she was on the floor, Rog started cutting her bonds. That was difficult, because she was jerking around like a dying fish, croaking something that we couldn't understand. Eventually I understood. She was desperate for water. Pete went back to the cottage to get some.

'What's your name?' I said, taking her in my arms.

She continued to shudder violently, but she managed to speak again.

'Am...Ama...Amanda Ma...Mary.'

I smiled at her. 'Hello, Amanda Mary. I'm Matt and this is Roger.'

She stared us as if we were aliens. When Boney came back with water and some bread that he'd found, she drank desperately, spilling much of it over her pink blouse. I reckoned she was eleven or twelve. I also had a pretty good idea who she was. To have got the former SAS men to ignore their training and allow themselves to be taken out, Sara had used their family members as leverage. The only question was, whose daughter was she? I couldn't face telling her what had happened to her father now. I kept her in a tight embrace while Rog and Pete dug down to the next coffin. This time it was a boy, who didn't look more than six. He couldn't speak at all—just drank and then stuffed bread into his mouth. Finally, Pete and I got a middle-aged woman out.

As I'd suspected from the moment I saw Amanda Mary, there was no trace at all of Andy.

28

Karen Oaten was driving down the fast lane of the M4, blue lights flashing and siren blasting.

'Jesus, guv,' John Turner said, hands clutching his seat. 'Can we get there in one piece, please?'

'Come on, Taff,' she said, swerving inside an ambulance that was also in full emergency mode. 'When have I ever put as much as a scratch on a car?' She sounded in high spirits, but it was only for show. Matt's call, saying that he'd found three people buried alive in a property owned by Sara Robbins, had almost made her scream—not because he'd saved three people's lives, but because he'd told her that he'd already left the cottage. She was sure he was in pursuit of Sara, but he hadn't bothered to tell her where he was going.

'What did the AC say about Matt pulling a gun on you?' The Welshman was still outraged by the writer's performance.

Oaten kept her eyes on the road. 'He doesn't know.'

'What?'

'Calm down, Taff. I decided against publicising that and I managed to get the PC to keep it to himself, at least for the time being.'

'But why?'

The chief inspector glanced at him. 'Would you rat on your wife?'

Turner sighed. 'She's hardly likely to wave a gun at me or anyone else.'

'Matt left because I was taking him to the Yard.' Oaten's hands were tight on the wheel. 'What did you expect me to do? I love the stupid bugger. It's not as if he's a master criminal. And remember, his best friend was killed.'

'The law's the law, whoever you are,' the inspector muttered.

'Oh, come on, Taff, how many times have you over-looked things team members have done?'

He glared at her. 'Involving firearms and murderers, none.'

Karen Oaten took a deep breath. 'Look, I didn't say Matt was off the hook. At the end of these cases, I'll review the situation.'

'You'd better,' the Welshman said, 'or the AC will tear your head off.'

Oaten thought back to the scene in the house in Stoke Newington—blood everywhere, but no body. It was obvious it had been in parts, though. 'Nice metaphor, Taff.'

Inspector John Turner raised an eyebrow. 'What? Oh, I see what you mean. Sorry.'

They proceeded to the cottage at Oldbury, a truce of sorts established.

It took us only half an hour to get to the railings that marked the limit of Earl Sternwood's domain. The moon was casting a fitful light across the acres of parkland and forest. I got out of the Suzuki and listened. Apart from the faint noise of traffic in the distance, there was no sound. We checked our gear.

'Oh shit, I just remembered this,' Pete said, holding up a brick-size block wrapped in clear film.

It was plastic explosive. Dave had trained us how to use it, but this would be the first time for real.

'Yeah, take it,' I said. 'We're trying to get into a castle, after all.' I looked at the satellite photo I'd found of the estate. A faint line wound through the dark patch of forest in front of us. 'This looks like a path. If we follow it, we come out right in front of the main buildings.'

'Fair enough,' Rog said. 'As long as His Lordship hasn't had mines laid.'

'We'll just have to take that chance,' I said. 'For Andy.'

The others nodded and we set off. It was quiet in the woods, apart from the scurrying of small animals and the faint flap of owls' wings. I was glad I had company. I wouldn't have fancied walking through the ancient forest on my own—there were too many obscure places for enemies to conceal themselves. After about ten minutes, I made out the lights on the main house. There weren't many of them. Either Earl Sternwood was strapped for cash—which seemed unlikely, given the drugs deal he'd done with the Albanians—or there wasn't much going on. The area that the map showed as taken up by the castle was completely unlit. If I'd located it correctly, it was a brooding, shadowless presence.

We reached the tree line. Now the mass of the old stronghold was visible, its vertical walls blocking out the stars and satellites that stood low in the northern sky. We squatted down behind a tree and looked at the photos that Safet Shkrelli's investigator had obtained. They gave us an idea of the tower's size, but didn't tell us anything about the interior structure. On the other hand, the meetings of the notorious Sternwood Hell-fire Club had taken place in a subterranean cavern. I reckoned that the present earl kept his secrets down there and that Sara wouldn't have been able to resist stashing Andy there.

'The door's at the back,' Pete said.

'Right,' I said. 'I'll go first. If a motion-sensor turns on lights, I'll see if I can spot it. We'll need to shoot it out.' I racked the slide on my Glock, then nodded at the others.

'Three, two, one, go,' I said under my breath, running across the gravel as fast as I could. I made it to the castle wall without anything happening—at least, anything obvious. I had no idea how good the earl's security system was. I might already have been spotted.

'One at a time,' I said via my cheek-mike.

Pete came first, then Rog. I led them round the side of the tower, pointing to the two cars that were drawn up to the rear. It didn't look like many people were around, though there was plenty of parking space on the far side of the house.

We reached the door. It was a great wooden thing with metal studs all over it, but it didn't look old. The locks were also modern and solid. I wouldn't have fancied trying to pick them. Pete moved past me, heading for a square ventilation panel. It was about a metre above ground level, with each side measuring about three-quarters of a metre. It would be a tight fit, but I reckoned we could make it— if we managed to separate the louvred panel from its metal frame. Boney set about it with a chisel, cursing under his breath. After five minutes, he had to admit defeat. I had a go, but the join was tighter than a banker's lips.

'Only one way to go now,' Rog said.

'Don't tell me,' Pete whispered. 'The plastic.'

I nodded. 'Who wants to lay it?'

Rog was already rummaging in Boney's pack.

'Not too much,' I said. 'Maybe the explosion will be muffled by the stone walls. In any case, we'll have to get inside very quickly after it blows.'

Pete and I watched as Rog rolled out four strips of the explosive, and then moulded them round the frame till they joined up. He pushed a detonator in and set the radio-controlled fuse. He ran back and we retreated behind the cars, an old Land Rover and a Citröen people-carrier. That made me wonder how many were in the opposition team.

'Ready?' Rog asked.

Boney and I nodded, then put our fingers in our ears. Rog pressed the button on the control unit. There was an explosion that wasn't as loud as I'd expected—the walls must have absorbed a lot of the noise. When I looked up, I saw the remains of the panel hanging down.

'Nice one, Dodger,' I said, getting up and running towards the hole. Dust and smoke were still rising when I reached it. I pulled myself over the rough edge and dropped into the tower. It was dark as the devil's armpit, but I couldn't hear any of the sounds people usually make after explosions, such as loud screaming or shouted orders. I moved aside as the others came through.

'What now?' Pete asked. He shone his torch around the square area. There was no furniture or anything else in it, just bare stone walls and a few arrow slits. Stone projections showed where the castle's upper floors would have once been. The only direction to go was down.

'There,' Pete said, pointing to a large flagstone that had initially looked the same as the others. There was a small indentation on the right side, and in it had been fixed a well-disguised steel ring.

I went over and got two fingers under the ring. Then I looked at the others. 'Ready?'

'Let's roll,' Pete said, brandishing his pistol.

Rog shook his head in disbelief. 'Just do it, Matt.'

I nodded. 'Lights out.'

We switched the torches off. In the darkness, I braced my back and heaved.

The stone panel came up with surprising ease.

Now came the difficult part.

Andy had been using the vibration of the van, which was being driven at high speed again, to help him edge his fingers round the small knife. Finally he managed to grip it and slide it out of his pocket. Now he had to be seriously careful—if he dropped it, he'd lost the game. After a struggle with his damaged nails, at last he succeeded in levering the blade out. He stopped to rest his quivering fingers, then started to saw through the ropes that had been looped tight around his wrists. He felt the point jab into his skin several times and blood began to run, but he was glad he always kept the knife sharp—that meant he got his hands free quickly. He removed the gag and breathed deeply through his mouth. Then he cut through the bonds on his ankles and then stretched his legs without standing up—he wasn't sure if his shape might be visible in the rear-view mirror. Besides, his only chance was to play possum until Sara or the old woman got close. He flexed his fingers and toes, feeling the pain of his blood circulation returning to normal. It was a good pain.

He was about to lean over the motorbike and see who was wrapped in the blankets when the van decelerated and took a left turn. Only a few seconds later, it pulled into the side and the engine was killed. Andy heard the driver's door open, followed soon after by the rear doors. The interior lights came on in the cargo space. He was leaning forward, feigning unconsciousness and waiting until his captor came close. When he heard movement on the other side of the bike, he opened one eye slightly and saw the back of a figure wearing black leathers. He took a deep breath and decided to go for it, in case the person he assumed was Sara was about to harm the other captive.

Andy launched himself over the motorbike, one arm whipping round the biker's neck. It was then that he realised he might have screwed up. Sara was still wearing her helmet. She was also in good shape, pushing back hard and almost loosening his grip. But he wasn't standing for that. With his free hand, he raised the knife and jammed it into her upper arm. That brought a yell of pain, then an elbow in his chest. He concentrated on moving the knife as much as the leather would allow and forgot about the helmet for a few moments, during which his captor crashed it into his face. He felt his nose shatter, not for the first time in his life. That made him change tactics. He let go of the neck and dragged the woman over the bike. Then he picked her up by scruff and groin, and rammed her head repeatedly against the side of the van. When he judged her brain would be suitably scrambled, he dropped her, moved round the motorbike and picked up the shrouded figure.

As Andy leapt from the van, he was aware of another person standing nearby. He couldn't understand why Doris Carlton-Jones was dressed so weirdly, but he wasn't sticking around to ask as she was holding a silenced pistol. He shoved her backwards with his spare hand and took the low hedge in a running jump. He heard the cough of the pistol a couple of times, but didn't feel any hits. Then he was sprinting downhill, heading for a substantial wood beyond the field that was visible in the moonlight. His knees were creaking, but they didn't give out.

When Andy got to the tree line, he burrowed into a heap of leaves, blowing like a walrus. There was no way Sara or her mother would find him now. Sure enough, the van started up and moved off a few minutes later. Then it struck him. He'd seen Doris Carlton-Jones's face, but he hadn't seen Sara's. Maybe it hadn't been her in the helmet after all.

There was a faint groan from the cocooned figure he had laid on the leaves. Andy tugged the blankets away and sat back in amazement as the silvery light fell on a dirty, tear-stained face; one that he knew very well indeed.

I shone my torch down the dark stairway. It turned back on itself after ten steps. I stopped at the corner, one arm raised to restrain the others.

Rog sniffed. 'What's that smell?'

The air was filled with the unmistakable odour of burning flesh. I immediately thought of Andy. What were the lunatics doing to him?

I moved my head round the stone wall. The next flight of steps, about twenty, was clear. Light showed at the bottom. I beckoned the others forward and we went down as quietly as our boots allowed. An ornate doorway had been cut into the stone. It was covered in strange symbols.

When we reached the bottom, I became aware of a monotonous chanting. It sounded like there were dozens of people in the cavern ahead. I struggled to understand what was being said and then I realised it was in Latin. The only word I could make out was 'diabolus'.

'Oh great,' Pete whispered. 'How many of them?'

I looked cautiously round the doorpost. I could hardly believe my eyes. The place was as ornate as the most baroque Catholic church, the walls covered in frescoes and light coming from gold chandeliers. Then I saw what the paintings depicted—demons tormenting the damned, monstrous beasts as foul as those spawned by the imagination of Hieronymus Bosch, and, in the centre, a huge, black, bat-winged Lucifer rising out of the earth.

Then I heard a terrible scream. Over to the right stood two people in what looked like monks' robes, the cowls raised. They had their backs to us and were watching the smoke billow from a raised altar. I tried to locate the people who were singing. There was no sign of anybody else and I realised that the chant was coming from speakers set in the rock walls. It was a recording, unless there was some choir loft nearby.

I pulled my head back. 'Action, guys. Looks like they're in the middle of a sacrifice.'

'Andy?' Pete asked, his eyes wide.

'I can't see, but we have to go in now. There only seem to be two of them. My guess is that one is Sara.

'We'll start with a couple of smoke grenades to mix things up,' I said. 'Then, Rog, you go right, you, left, Pete. I'll head straight towards the bastards. Only fire if you're sure you're in danger. Okay, let's do it.'

We clasped hands, then Rog took the grenades from Pete's pack.

'One left, one right, Dodger. Try to leave some visibility for me in the middle.'

'Check.' Rog pulled the pins and released the catches. Then he tossed the grenades where I wanted. They went off with more of a thump than a bang.

I sprinted forward, Glock in my right hand. I'd removed the silencer as I wanted to scare the shit out of the targets. As the smoke began to billow up, the pair in robes turned towards me. My stomach somersaulted when I saw their faces. Both were white—one with a sick smile and a devil's goatee and the other misshapen and pustular. Then I heard a crazed shrieking and some kind of ape came scurrying towards me, its red eyes crazed and its bared fangs yellow. I pointed the Glock at the roof and fired. The sound of the shot boomed around the cavern and the creature turned tail. I heard someone yelling the name Beelzebub.

I kept running, but the two figures had separated and disappeared into the smoke. Maybe the grenades hadn't been such a good idea.

Then I heard shots and yelling from the left. Pete was in action. I made it to the altar and peered at the motionless object that was burning on a heap of wood. It was a sheep. So where was Andy?

High-pitched screams to my right distracted me. Moving closer, I saw the ape on top of one of the masked people, its coloured rump wriggling as it tried to bite. Then there was a spitting sound and the creature crashed down on its victim, its back feet quivering briefly before it expired. I ran close and held the muzzle of my Glock to the side of the robed figure's head.

'Let go of the gun and pull your hands out,' I said. 'Slowly!'

Rog appeared and dragged the animal off the man. I grabbed the pistol that was on the pseudo-monk's abdomen.

'Mission accomplished, Matt.' I looked over my shoulder and saw Pete arriving with company. He'd looped the other monk's belt round his neck and was covering him with his Glock.

I pulled the person on the floor up. The pair of them stood with their heads hanging, like two masked kids on Hallowe'en who'd been overzealous with the tricks. Except these two were killers, and one of them was Sara Robbins. Before I could confirm that, Pete's prisoner started shrieking and trying to pull away.

'You killed Beelzebub!' came a high-pitched voice. 'You killed my mandrill, my familiar…'

'Not us,' Rog said, pointing at the other prisoner. 'This asshole did.'

Pete's prisoner tried to leap forwards, hands clawing the air. Boney elbowed the figure with the devil mask in the ribs. That stopped the movement, but the abuse and threats to the other mask-wearer continued.

I nodded to Pete and he pulled off the mask.

'Earl Sternwood,' I said, taking in the face disfigured by a prominent harelip.

I turned to the other prisoner and moved closer, my heart pounding and a worm of doubt wriggling hard. 'Is it you, Sara? Did you really give up so easily?'

Manic laughter came from behind the disfigured mask. I wrenched it off and saw…someone who definitely wasn't my ex-lover, no matter how much plastic surgery she might have undergone. I knew who it was, though.

'Alistair Bing!' I said, failing to conceal my surprise.

The laughter continued. Tears were wetting the cheeks of the diminutive man.

'Aka crime writer Adrian Brooks,' I said to Rog and Pete.

'Obviously you expected to see your former beloved,' Bing said. His Yorkshire accent was strong. 'It never occurred to you that someone else could be behind the murders.'

I stared at him. 'You killed the crime writers? You sent me those puzzles?'

He nodded beatifically, like the Pope acknowledging his worshippers—the Pope of Hell.

'But why?'

He laughed. 'Always the rationalist, Matt. Didn't your experience of the White Devil teach you anything? Some people exist in a dimension incomprehensible to common humanity.'

'That'll be right,' I said, not stinting on the irony. 'Don't tell me. You needed the experience of killing to become a true crime writer.'

Alistair Bing looked like I'd slapped him in the face. 'You're oh-so-clever now, aren't you, Matt? It's a pity you couldn't save Sandra Devonish. Or Josh Hinkley.'

'You broke your word with Josh, you piece of shit.'

He gave me an icy stare. 'You have no idea who you've been up against. I am Doctor Faustus, I've made a deal with the devil and—'

'Yeah, yeah, spare me the bullshit. Just tell me why you slaughtered defenceless novelists.'

'The great Matt Wells, global best-seller and crime columnist, clueless. How the mighty are fallen.'

The way he said the word 'best-seller' gave me an insight into his sad mind.

'That's what this is all about, isn't it?' I said. 'You were jealous of us, weren't you?'

His eyes narrowed. 'The books at the top of the best-seller lists were no better than my early books.'

'Oh yes they bloody were,' I said. 'Besides, you're a best-seller yourself now. What was the point of killing Mary, Sandra and Josh?'

He looked at me with arctic eyes. 'I made my Faustian pact and killed three crime writers who sold better than I did in the past. You were to be next. *The Death List* knocked me off the top of the best-seller list in seven countries.'

'But first you decided to make a fool of me with your smart-ass clues.'

Alistair Bing nodded. 'And I succeeded.'

'Just like in an Agatha Christie novel, eh?' I said. 'Haven't you noticed that real life is more like heavy-duty noir than Golden Age word-play?' I turned to Earl Stern-wood. 'What was your role in all this?'

The earl was still staring at the dead mandrill. 'Mine?' he said weakly. 'Alistair had the benefit of my teachings. I led him to understand that only by experiencing killing would he become a successful writer.'

'And he believed that?' I said, glancing at the snigger-ing Yorkshireman.

'He did. The fact is, he did become a best-selling author after his first murders.'

'His first murders?' I repeated. 'Who were the victims?'

'Oh, just scum,' the earl said carelessly. 'Prostitutes, their customers, drunks—the detritus of humanity that disfigures London.' He seemed unaware of the irony in his words.

'It was your idea to write "The Devil did it" in Latin, was it?'

The earl nodded. 'Latin was, of course, the main language of the Christian Church, and of its opponents.'

I looked at Bing again. 'Why the music playing at each murder scene?'

'To add to the feeling of devilry,' he said, giving me a thin-lipped smile.

It was my turn to laugh. 'What? Cliff Richard?'

'My mother loves Cliff,' he replied, looking affronted.

I went up to him. 'You sick fuck. You couldn't just kill them, could you? You had to get up close, and throttle them, cut them, stab them. And then cut their nails and hair.' I remembered what he'd done to poor Mary Malone. 'You abused a dead woman.'

He shrugged. 'Killing that way is like sex. In fact it's better than sex. There's no need for consent.'

I turned away, shaking my head. 'You must have fitted in well here,' I said, glancing at the horrific artwork.

Bing sniggered and it was all I could do to stop myself flooring him.

'What about the gangland murders in East London?' I said to Sternwood. 'We know that Lauren Cuthbertson was responsible for them. She was part of your pathetic cult, wasn't she?'

'How do you know that?' he demanded, confirming my suspicions.

'It was her face,' I said. 'You couldn't resist corrupting a disfigured person.'

The earl looked past me to the mandrill he'd called Beelzebub. 'Lauren was a great help to me. We knew her as Asmodeus.' He touched his split upper lip with his tongue. 'But there was no question of anyone corrupting her. She took to murder with pleasure and ease.'

'You needed the money from the drugs she stole,' Bing sneered. 'You even got me to extort money from Josh Hinkley.'

I stared at the earl. 'The killings were all about money?'

'Not exactly,' he said, avoiding my eyes. 'Lauren and Faustus here chose their victims. But she was happy to donate the funds she acquired to the Order of the Lord Beneath the Earth.' He glared at me. 'Until you killed her today. The sheep was sacrificed to speed her soul on its journey to our master.'

Pete and Rog exchanged glances that showed exactly what they thought of the cult and its worshippers.

I looked at Sternwood and Bing. 'Did you know that Lauren Cuthbertson was Sara Robbins's and the White Devil's half sister?'

They both looked taken aback in a big way. Apparently not.

'I assume Lauren was Helen in the last message,' I said to Alistair Bing, then turned to the earl. 'You sent her after Jeremy Andrewes because he'd found out about your drug deal with the Albanians.'

'You can't prove any of this,' His Lordship replied dully.

Alistair laughed. 'Yes, he can. I hereby swear that I had nothing to do with the Andrewes murder. I only wrote the clue.'

'Which I cracked, asshole.' I looked at Sternwood. 'That means you'll be spending the rest of your life in jail.'

'What did you do with the nail clippings and hair from the bodies?' Pete asked.

The earl gave him a solemn look. 'We burned them, to the greater glory of Satan.'

I stared at him, but he didn't turn away. It seemed that the paragon of the aristocracy meant it.

'You killed Beelzebub, Faustus!' Sternwood screamed. He made a grab for Pete's pistol and managed, after a brief struggle, to loose off a shot.

Alistair Bing, known to his mother as Adrian Brooks, international best-selling crime writer, collapsed backwards, a crimson flower blossoming on his chest.

Pete pulled hard on the rope round the earl's neck, while I tried to get his hand from the Glock. His eyes bulged and his face reddened. Then there was another shot and the struggle ceased immediately.

Earl Sternwood, last of his line, lay dead by his own hand, blood welling from his doubly disfigured mouth.

I looked round the painted cavern with its clawed demons and gaping maws. The sound of the underground river could be heard now, running away yet further beneath the earth.

The killer of the crime writers and his spiritual adviser had departed this life, but still we had found no sign of Sara.

Or Andy.

29

Caroline came round to find herself tied by the hands and ankles to the double bed in the safe house. She tried to clear her mouth, but realised she'd been gagged. As her mind cleared, she tried to remember what had happened. Someone at the door…someone had knocked, said they were with the police. A woman's voice. Why had she opened the door? A reflex action, you didn't expect the police to attack you…to spray something in your face that makes you crash to the floor and lose consciousness almost immediately.

Oh Christ, she thought. Lucy! Where was she? Turning her head, Caroline managed to see down the hall. The door to the room her daughter had been using was open, the bed-clothes strewn across the floor. Lucy had been studying in there. Where was she?

Moaning through the gag, Caroline had another thought. What about Fran? Matt's mother had been in the sitting-room. She'd said 'Don't—', as Caroline had opened the door. Had she been sprayed too?

The woman. There was something about her. Caroline hadn't seen the face before, but…she seemed familiar. This wasn't her first experience of knock-out gas. Two years ago, when the White Devil had been killing people across London, the woman who'd been Matt's lover had leaned out of a car window near Caroline's bank in the City and asked her something, then suddenly she had fallen into darkness. She had woken up in hospital, to find Lucy in the bed beside her and Matt revelling in having put a stop to the White Devil. The idiot. Sara had got away…and now she was back… Oh, Lucy…

Then Caroline looked down. A belt had been strapped round her abdomen, and a red light was flashing on top of a square box that had been attached by black tape.

She knew instantly that it was a bomb. What she didn't know, and the tension was almost unbearable, was when it would go off.

Amelia Browning was standing at the entrance to the foot passengers' waiting area at Dover Eastern Docks ferry terminal. She had already checked three groups that had boarded ships, comparing faces with the images that Chief Inspector Oaten had sent to her mobile phone. Three times she had returned empty-handed to the waiting room. It was beginning to look like she'd drawn the short straw. Other VCCT officers were checking vehicles for Sara Robbins or her mother, since this was the nearest port to the house the woman had bought in rural Kent—where DCI Oaten had organised surveillance with the local force. But there had been no sign of the suspects anywhere. Maybe they were lying low or had decided to risk air travel. Amelia was tired and hungry, but the terminal's idea of catering was even more criminal than the Met's.

People started coming through passport control. A young couple in blue denim from head to toe, including caps and trainers in the material, were arguing in a language that Detective Sergeant Browning couldn't identify. She took out her copy of the *Daily Indie* and pretended to read it, all the time casting surreptitious glances at the people who had just arrived. None of them was over fifty, never mind as old as Doris Carlton-Jones, and none of them bore any resemblance to Sara Robbins—though, if she'd had major plastic surgery, Amelia wasn't sure she'd recognise her.

The departure of the next ferry to Calais was announced. People started gathering up their luggage and heading for the ramps that led up to the passenger bridge. Amelia folded her paper. She was about to follow the others when an elderly Indian woman in a *sari* came out of the toilets. Her hair was an unnatural shade of black and she was carrying a large cuddly toy. There was something about the way she walked that caught the detective's eye. She didn't glide, like most Indian women in the full-length garment; her gait made the fabric bulge at the knees.

Amelia Browning stopped at the bottom of the ramp and turned away from the woman, her face towards the ship's high stern. When she heard the soft sound of the *sari* passing, she looked round.

'Mrs Carlton-Jones?' she said, her voice as natural as she could make it.

The woman turned her head, then realised her mistake. The handcuffs were on her before she could take another step.

I called Karen when we got back to the car.

'Are they all right?' I asked, meaning the woman and the two kids we'd disinterred.

'They're in hospital. The paramedics were more concerned about their psychological than their physical state, particularly the woman's. They thought the kids would get over it quicker.'

'Not when they find out they're fatherless.'

'I didn't tell them that. Anyway, where the hell are you?'

'Sternwood Castle. At least, I was.'

'Don't you bloody run away again, Matt.'

'Andy's still missing. Sara must have him. We're going to check her other properties.'

'If you mean the ones in Hackney, Oxford, Kent and Scotland, don't bother. I've arranged search—there was nobody there—and surveillance. We've also just picked up Doris Carlton-Jones in Dover.'

'No sign of Sara?'

'No. Maybe her disguise was more convincing.'

'And her face more changed.'

'What were you doing at Sternwood Castle?'

I gave her a quick run-through.

She let out a long sigh when I'd finished. 'Jesus, Matt. When will the killing stop?'

'*We* didn't kill anyone tonight.'

'So you say.'

'Don't worry, I taped the whole thing. And thanks for the vote of confidence.'

She laughed bitterly. 'You're a long way from getting one of those.'

'End of conversation then,' I said, and broke the connection.

Rog and Pete were pretending not to have overheard.

My phone rang. I didn't recognise the number.

'Matt, it's me.'

'Andy! Thank Christ! Are you okay? Where are you?'

'Yes to the first question. Where are we?' I heard someone else speak. 'Blidbean in Kent. But, listen, you're not going to…'

'Blidbean?' I said. 'Never heard of it. What's the nearest—'

'Shut the fuck up, Matt!' he yelled. 'I've got Lucy with me. Sara and her mother grabbed her.'

My veins had filled with ice. 'Lucy? Is she all right?' I asked hoarsely.

'Yes, in a minute you can speak to her, but there's something you have to sort first. Tell Karen that your mother and Caroline need help.' I listened, then told Pete to call Karen, repeating the address of the safe house in East Grinstead that Lucy had remembered. Then I spoke to my daughter.

'What happened, darling?'

'I don't know who it was,' she said, the words spilling out in a babble. I caught 'motorbike helmet', 'sprayed in the face' and 'woke up with Andy staring at me'.

I didn't scare her by asking anything about Sara. How had she found them? Lucy actually sounded over the worst. I knew Andy would have helped on that count, and she told me that the farmer's wife had given her clean clothes and something nice to eat. Apparently there were some very sweet kittens too, could she have one? I said that her mother would have to rule on that.

As I was talking, Rog was driving towards the motorway at full pelt. Boney had briefed Karen and not long after we'd reached the M4, she called me back.

'We were lucky,' she said. 'There was a bomb squad unit only a few minutes away from East Grinstead.'

I felt my stomach cartwheel. 'A bomb squad unit?'

'Someone—you can guess who—had fitted bomb-belts to them both. The timers had been set for midnight.'

I looked at my watch. It was half-past eleven. 'Shit,' I said. 'Close one. Are Fran and Caroline all right?'

'They've been taken to hospital, but I gather they were conscious, just drowsy. They'd been sprayed with some kind of knock-out gas. Rings a bell, eh?'

'Yup. Thanks, Karen.'

'I take it you've turned back and are waiting for me at the castle.'

'Em, no. We're going to pick up Lucy and Andy.'

There was silence for a while.

'All right, Matt. But I'll be expecting you and your friends in my office at nine tomorrow.'

'Do I need a lawyer?'

'I'd have thought you'd already have instructed one.' She hung up.

I'd completely forgotten about my impending man-slaughter charge.

30

The night continued to be a busy one. We picked up Andy and Lucy in a deserted part of Kent and drove to the hospital in East Grinstead. Caroline was out of bed. She wasn't talking to me, though she did behave in an appropriately maternal way to Lucy.

I sat next to my mother, who was still lying down, her face pale. 'I'm sorry about all this,' I said. 'How do you feel?'

'I'm all right, dear. It's the gas. I still feel a bit dizzy.' She looked at me. 'It was her, wasn't it?'

'Probably.'

'And she hasn't been caught?'

I shook my head. 'They may still get her.'

'You don't really believe that, do you, Matt?'

I shrugged. 'Sara isn't omnipotent. Andy could have caught her tonight, but he concentrated on getting Lucy out of her clutches.'

'Good for him,' she murmured, her eyelids fluttering as she dropped off again. I hadn't managed to tell her that Slash rescued Lucy without knowing who she was. That made him even more of a hero in my eyes.

Lucy appeared on the other side of the bed, having

been passed fit by the doctors. She bent over and gave her grandmother a kiss.

'Are you okay, then?' I asked.

'They want me to stay the night in case I have a reaction to the gas.' She looked at me apologetically. 'Mum wants to talk to you now.'

On the way to the private room that my ex-wife had got for herself, I prepared for my hearing to be assaulted. Instead, Caroline was calm and collected.

'If you ever allow anything like that to happen to Lucy or me again,' she said, 'I will personally detach your scrotum and its contents from your supposedly he-man body.'

There was more but, when Caroline showed no sign of stopping, I went to make sure that Andy was okay. He'd been given several stitches to his forehead, but his skull hadn't been fractured.

'Bloody hell, Slash,' I said. 'How did you manage to stay conscious, never mind open that mini-knife and cut through the rope?'

'No sweat,' he said. 'They breed us tough in New Jersey.'

Karen chose that moment to step through the cubicle curtains.

'Hi, doll,' Andy said with a grin. 'How's it hanging?'

I managed to swallow my laughter. The American really was a hero for talking to her like that. We left him and went outside.

'Any sign of Sara?' I asked.

Karen shook her head. 'We're still checking, but…' Her words trailed away and she ran her eyes over me. 'Where are your weapons?'

I feigned innocence.

'And where are Rog and Pete?'

'I'm not sure.' That was partly true. Pete had gone off in a taxi to pick up his Cherokee, taking all our gear with him. He was somewhere between East Grinstead and Bromley. Rog, however, was out in the car park. I didn't mention that.

She laughed. 'Honestly, Matt, what do you take me for? Someone blasted their way into Sternwood Castle and several shots were fired in that awful cave. I suppose you're going to tell me the earl and Alistair Bing did all that.'

I remembered the tape. 'Em, no. But I promise we had no choice.'

'The AC will be the judge of that, and you'll need to convince the local force too.'

I raised my shoulders. 'Piece of cake. Are you okay?'

She shook her head at me. 'I'm at the end of my tether.'

'You took the words right out of my mouth,' I said, putting my arm round her.

'Isn't that a song by Meat Loaf?' she asked, shaking free of me but managing to smile wanly.

'It is,' I said. 'You always did have a worrying taste in music.'

She stopped and faced me.

'Don't think you're in the clear, Matt. There are things ordinary citizens can't do.'

'Like murder and mutilate innocent crime writers, spray knock-out gas into people's faces, attach bombs to them and bury people alive?' I asked.

'And you believe that's a valid justification for taking the law into your hands?'

'No,' I said, taking hold of both her hands. 'But this is.' I kissed her on the lips, and eventually she responded. By raising her leg to my groin.

'Don't take advantage of me when I'm on duty,' she said, her voice softer than her knee.

I stepped back and watched her walk away. It hadn't been necessary that she came to meet me. The fact that she had suggested that we weren't completely washed up.

I said goodnight to Lucy before Rog and I went back to London.

For the rest of the night, Meat Loaf had no chance. There was only one song playing repeatedly in my head. It was by Bob Dylan and it bore the name of my former lover and perhaps future nemesis, Sara.

31

Andy, Pete and Rog showed up at New Scotland Yard the next morning to give statements, as did I. The VCCT threw the kitchen sink at us. We were questioned on our own by Taff Turner and a young sergeant called Amelia Browning. She was smart and almost got me to contradict myself several times. Then the Assistant Commissioner stepped in and interrogated me himself, but I still didn't change my story. I was charged with the manslaughter of Lauren Cuthbertson, but my lawyer didn't think it would go to trial. There were plenty of people who had seen the dead woman murder Jeremy Andrewes and attack me.

Doris Carlton-Jones refused to say a word, presumably forewarned by Sara. That left her at the mercy of the detectives and prosecutors, but I wasn't complaining—she could have made life difficult for me and Andy if she'd accused us of impersonating police officers. Then again, she had a lot of explaining to do herself, not least about her husband's skull. Then came the funerals. Karen warned me not to attend, but I felt it was my duty. She felt it was hers too, so we went to four of them together. Two of the dead passed without ceremony. Lauren Cuthbertson had no family willing or able to arrange a service—so much for

Sara and her birth mother's feelings for her. Sandra
Devonish's mother and father collected her body from the
morgue. Her funeral would take place in Texas. Karen
said they seemed bewildered rather than grief-stricken.
Not for long, I suspected. I decided to steer clear of Earl
Sternwood's service; according to one of the newspapers,
it was 'pagan in the extreme', whatever that meant. And I
left Alistair Bing/Adrian Brooks to his mother to bury—I
hoped without any memorial stone.

The first funeral we attended was Mary Malone's. It
took place in a churchyard in Wiltshire, where her parents
were buried. It was a cold, wet day and the rooks were
screaming at each other from the tops of the bare trees.
There was only a handful of people. In death, as in life,
Alistair Bing's first victim passed almost unnoticed. An
elderly woman wept continuously throughout the service.
I found out from the vicar that she was a devoted fan, who
had travelled from the south of France. That made my eyes
damp.

The second service was for Josh Hinkley. To my surprise,
he'd asked for a humanist service before cremation. The
readings were from his own books (which was less of a
surprise), interspersed with songs by Ian Dury, The Kinks
and The Jam. There was a booze-up in a pub in Soho afterwards. I only stayed for one drink, but that was long enough
for me to be cut dead by the chairman of the Crime Writers'
Society and by a tiny Chinese woman with a large chest. Apparently she was Chop Suzy, the tart the dead man had been
expecting the night he was murdered. Karen told me that a
woman with a posh voice had told Suzy to stay away from
'her husband'. Female impersonation was obviously another
of Alistair Bing's skills, unless he'd got his mother to do it.

Then there was Jeremy Andrewes's funeral. It took place in a pretty churchyard in Hampshire, near the family seat. No one spoke to Karen and me until we were leaving.

'You're Wells, aren't you?' said an elderly, red-faced man. 'How dare you show your face here? You're responsible for Jeremy's death. If you make money from it, I shall surely seek you out.'

Keeping quiet seemed the best option, even though I'd already decided not to write about the case in my column or make a book out of it. I'd learned my lesson after *The Death List.*

Then came the worst of all—Dave's funeral. This time it was a beautiful day. The church in Dulwich was packed. There was an honour guard of soldiers from the Parachute Regiment and the SAS, in full dress uniform but without weapons, and the service was traditional, on the wishes of his wife, Ginny, and his parents. I stood with Karen, Pete, Rog and Andy, who'd been released from hospital with a warning, already disregarded, not to drink for a month. We sang hymns that I knew meant nothing to Dave. Unlike many soldiers, he was completely without faith and I was sure he would have laughed at the idea of 'Onward, Christian Soldiers' and 'Jerusalem' being heard at his funeral. I hoped it made the family feel better, but they certainly didn't look comforted. On the way out of the church Ginny hugged Andy, Rog and Pete, but kept her hands by her sides when it was my turn. She didn't let me finish the first word of my condolences.

'Bastard,' she said, her eyes wide. '*You* killed him, not that bitch you used to fuck.'

Her kids started crying and an elderly man tried ineffectually to lead her away.

'You killed him,' she wailed, trying to pull her hand away to hit me. 'You killed my Dave…'

As Karen took my arm and walked me to the gate, I caught sight of Lucy and Caroline. My daughter looked horrified, while my ex-wife's expression was inscrutable. She certainly wasn't displaying anything akin to sympathy, but there was no reason she should have.

Karen drove my car towards Brixton, and then pulled in to the side of the road. She turned to me and took my hands.

'Look at me, Matt,' she said, waiting for me to do so. 'It's not true. You didn't kill Dave. You did everything you could to save him, with your alert codes and reporting systems. It isn't your fault that he opened the door to Sara. Do you hear me? It isn't your fault.'

My breathing was rapid and the blood was rushing through my veins and arteries in a hot flood.

'I love you,' Karen said. 'Do you hear me, Matt? I— love—you. I want to spend the rest of my life with you. No one could have done more to find Dave's killer. You should be proud of that.'

But I wasn't. I knew I never would be. After a time, the weight of what Karen had said finally hit me.

'You…you want to spend the rest of your life with me?' I repeated, turning to her.

She nodded and smiled.

And suddenly it struck me that I wanted that too. More than anything, even catching Sara.

'All right,' I said. 'Let's spend our lives together.'

Karen laughed. 'That's another bloody song, isn't it?'

'Sort of. The Stones.'

'Ha!' she said, started the engine. 'Jagger and Richards. Old rockers never die.'

'Well, that's reassuring, isn't it?' I said, rummaging in the glove compartment and coming out with a CD.

It was only as the first tom-tom beats of 'Sympathy for the Devil' came from the speakers that I remembered it had played at full volume, over and over, in Mary Malone's house after her murder.

Alistair Bing and his demented Faustian pact had successfully ruined one of my favourite pieces of music.

Gradually, things got back to normal. I changed the alarm codes in my apartment and had a new security system installed in the Saab. Lucy went back to school, though the teachers said she was hard to reach for some weeks. Caroline told me our daughter needed to see a psychiatrist because of what I'd got them into, which made me call her a fool for failing to check her car for bugs—one was found by the police, obviously put there by Sara. Strangely, that seemed to clear the air and we managed to spend a day with Lucy and talk her through what she'd been through. She started to feel better almost immediately.

My mother was more shaken than any of us, and I had to go over her house changing the security locks and upgrading the alarm. She had difficulty getting back to writing stories. I'd been struggling with exactly that since the White Devil had first got his claws into me, but at least I had plenty of years to get back into things. Fran seemed to have aged enormously in the course of a few days.

As for my friends, they seemed to have taken most of what had happened in their stride. Andy, Rog, Pete and I met for dinner every week, but we didn't go to the pub. It wouldn't have been the same without Dave.

I found myself waking up in the middle of the night, even on the few occasions when I wasn't plagued by violent dreams. For a few seconds I would feel all was well with the world, then I'd remember that Dave wasn't in it any longer—and that Sara was, even though she'd lost a large part of her funds and her five properties in the U.K. had been sequestered. When the CSIs were going over the cottage, the flat and the houses, in each one they found the words 'The Soul Collector' carved in a hidden place. Sara had collected Dave's soul, as well as those of the three SAS men who had killed her brother. It was only a question of time before she made another attempt to take mine. In the meantime, I planned to make the most of life with Karen.

And then one morning, six weeks after Sara had disappeared, she called me. The number was withheld and it was impossible to tell where she was. I pressed the Record button on my phone.

'Matt,' she said, her voice curiously soft. 'I bet you've just been dying to hear from me.'

'No,' I said, determined not to show her how I felt about Dave's murder.

She laughed. 'Come on, I know there are things you want to ask me.'

'No.'

'Well, I'll tell you all the same.' Her tone grew sharper. 'It's important you know that you've made things even worse for yourself and everyone you care for.'

I couldn't restrain myself any longer. 'Because I killed your murdering bitch of a sister?'

'Nicely put, Matt, but true enough. Let me ask you, when did you discover that we were related?'

'Not long after I sent her to hell.'

'I know you don't believe in the rubbish that Earl Sternwood and the others did. Don't you want to know how my
sister got involved with him?'

I did, but I wasn't giving her the satisfaction. 'No.'

'Apparently she'd always been interested in the occult.
She found out that the order behind the old Hell-fire
Club still existed and she went to a meeting—a conclave,
they called it. As soon as the earl saw her face, she was in.
Apparently he felt she was a kindred spirit.' She laughed.
'Did you know that he considered the Sternwood lip an
honour and would never consent to plastic surgery?'

'Fascinating,' I said, with plenty of irony.

Either she didn't hear that or she ignored it. Maybe she
thought I'd be writing her sister's story, in which case she
had a shock coming.

'My mother told me about Lauren over a year ago. At
first I was angry that she'd kept silent for so long, but then
I felt the joy of having a sibling again.'

I managed to resist telling her exactly what I thought of
Doris Carlton-Jones and what she'd done with her husband's
head, as well as Lauren's rampages in East London.

'After I met Lauren, I was even more delighted. I could
see she had similar qualities to my brother and me. I
bought her an identical motorbike to mine to muddy the
waters. No doubt you already guessed that. As well as
that, when I told her about the wonderful surgery I had to
my face, she insisted I pay for her operations. They were
much more necessary, of course. She wasn't exactly one
of nature's beauties. After that idiot of a surgeon ruined the
good work he'd done, there was so much anger in her. I
know my darling brother would have loved that.'

No doubt, I thought—given that he was a twisted piece
of shit too.

'In case you're wondering, Matt, I made contact with my mother a few months after your book was published. I thought she'd be sickened by it and I was right. What I didn't expect was that she'd be so keen on helping me and, more recently, Lauren. Of course, my sister had already made her own arrangements with the late earl. Her putting the plastic surgeon's body in my Oxford house was a surprise to me. It seems she was jealous that I have the looks I do.'

I didn't tell her that Lauren had left a note saying 'Sorry'.

'Then I realised that killing Dave had fired you up. I heard from my mother that a large man with a slight American accent had driven at Lauren when she was handing over a weapon. When I showed my mother a picture of your friend Andy, she recognised him immediately. She knew who you were when you impersonated a detective at her house, but you had no idea, did you?' She laughed. 'That ridiculous moustache.'

I wasn't going to dwell on that. 'How did you get into Dave's house?' I demanded.

She laughed again, and the sound made me shiver. 'I had a Salvation Army uniform on. Strange that no one noticed me. I swapped my helmet for the bonnet before I walked up to his door. The idiot fell for it and took the chains off. I changed back into my leathers afterwards.'

I pressed my fingernails into the palms of my hands. She talked about wanting revenge for her sister. I wanted it for Dave.

'Actually, I do want to ask you something,' I said.

'At last.'

440   *Paul Johnston*

'Or rather, I want to tell you that I understand exactly how your mind works. Those people you buried alive, the two kids and the woman.'

'What about them?' she asked, as unconcerned as if they had been insects.

'You were never going to tell anyone about them, were you? The idea that they'd take days to die, screaming themselves hoarse through their gags, made you moist, didn't it?'

There was a gratifying silence. Then she tried to have the last word.

'You know exactly how to do that, Matt.'

'Yeah,' I said. 'By running a knife through your shrivelled heart.' I hung up.

I should have felt good after that fleeting victory, but I couldn't. Even though I hadn't meant to kill Sara's sister, I'd become a member of the putrid club that they, their brother, Earl Sternwood and Alistair Bing belonged to—the club of those who have brought death to their fellow human beings. What made me feel worse was that, although I'd never forgive myself for Jeremy Andrewes's death, I now had no regrets at all about my part in Lauren May Cuthbertson's demise.

When Karen came in that evening, she immediately saw that something had happened.

'What is it?' she asked, after she'd kissed me.

I'd been considering all day whether to tell her. I was inclined not to, but I'd been guilty of too many lies and omissions.

'Screw her,' Karen said, after I'd told her about the call.

'It isn't just her,' I said. 'It's me. I want to kill her.'

To my surprise, she didn't seem to be particularly shocked. She kissed me on the lips and handed me a bottle of gin. 'Just make sure you do it in another country,' she said with a smile.

That wasn't a bad idea.